# HEART FOR A HERO

## ED DITTO
### &
## LAURA D. PATRICK

American Quilter's Society
P. O. Box 3290 • Paducah, KY 42002-3290
www.AmericanQuilter.com

Executive Editor: Andi Reynolds
Editor: Nicole C. Chambers-Kaya
Graphic Design: Barry Buchanan
Cover Design: Michael Buckingham
Photography: Charles R. Lynch
Ed Ditto photo: Tom Tohill
Laura D. Patrick photo by Bryan Bacon. Copyright 2008 The Huntsville Times.
All rights reserved. Reprinted with permission of The Huntsville Times.

Text © 2009, Author, Ed Ditto and Laura D. Patrick
Artwork © 2009, American Quilter's Society
Library of Congress Cataloging-in-Publication Data

Library of Congress Cataloging-in-Publication Data

Ditto, Ed.
  Heart for a hero / by Ed Ditto & Laura D. Patrick.
     p. cm.
  ISBN 978-1-57432-976-6
  1. Loss (Psychology)--Fiction. 2. Quilts--Fiction. 3. Quilting--Psychological
aspects--Fiction. 4. Domestic fiction. I. Patrick, Laura D. II. Title.

PS3604.I89H43 2009
813'.6--dc22
                                        2008053110

**Cover quilt:** HEART FOR A HERO—designed by Laura D. Patrick & Ed Ditto. Made by Judy Daniel, Lin Hayden,
Laura D. Patrick, Carla Sewall, Carol Trice, and Carole Worsham. Machine quilted by Lisa Marshall. Fabric
is from the "Oasis" line by Benartex, Inc.

To Flossie

**Part One: Baby Blues**

*Grant me, oh Lord,*
*For the coming events,*
*Enough knowledge to cope*
*And some plain common sense.*

—from "A Hospital Corpsman's Prayer"

## ▶▶▶◆◀◀◀
## Chapter One

Piper Jo Hathaway pulled a pillow over her head.
As if being bombarded by the telephone wasn't
enough, next door in the TV room one of the twins was
waging psychological warfare on her with the remote.
Goosing the volume so Cinderella's sobbing cycled higher
and higher.

She figured the phone was most likely Ellen calling for
the seventh time that afternoon. PJ loved Ellen like a sister,
but lacked the energy for one of her signature braniac crises
just then. And as for the TV terrorist, that had to be Baker.
He was her special little guy, of course, but he'd mastered
the remote control long before he'd mastered the potty.

*I just got done telling him!* PJ thought. *Like I've
told him a gazillion times already: don't mess with the
remote!*

*Because Momma's going for a nap! I'm exhausted,
I was up half the night, so just sit here and watch the
movie and eat your snacky and give Momma some peace
and quiet, OK?*

*Please?*

She'd felt guilty as soon as she'd spoken, but Lizzie and
Baker had dutifully nodded their small blonde heads, faces
smeared with graham crackers, and PJ, in her pajamas at

1

three in the afternoon, had fled the confusion in their eyes and burrowed into the quilts on the guest bed. Horizontal at last, thank God. But still she couldn't sleep.

Hadn't done it in three years, really, not since she and Ross brought the twins home. At least not what you'd call sleeping.

Right now she was doing the same thing she always did while other people slept: suffering through a vague dismal trance, with one eye on the clock and the other turned inward, feeling...*cold.* With the world greyed out, like she was floating on her belly staring down into an endless depth of dirty icewater.

She tossed on the couch, feeling no air-hunger in her chest, no suffocation or sadness or resolution—just a terrifying chill, like she was missing out on the warmth of life and it was all her fault. And this was how she'd felt since she lay watching Ross cry in the delivery room.

Ross had eventually stopped.

But these days anyone could make Cinderella cry at the push of a button.

~

Button-pushers. Earlier, when PJ had seen the caller ID light up—*USPS*—she'd groaned. It was Ellen calling from the post office. And if anyone could see through the façade PJ was struggling to keep propped up, it'd be Ellen Sanders, button-pusher *par excellence.*

So she dealt with Ellen by pushing a button of her own.

The answering machine clicked on, and she heard Ross's voice, friendly and upbeat. "Sorry we're not here," he said, and his words struck to her heart.

*I sure wish you were,* she thought. *Stupid business trips, keeping you on the road.*

The machine beeped and Ellen exclaimed "PJ!" loud enough to make the speaker crackle. "Haven't seen you in a while! Listen, *Homo sapiens* is a social-type animal, OK? Call me. Bye."

She'd tried again a few minutes later. "PJ? Ellen here. I should've said I'm not just calling you to catch up—we've got some business to take care of. Can you get back to me chop-chop? Thanks."

Her third message was a touch more ominous. "PJ, I'm still at work, still at the post office. There's ah...a package here that...well, I need to talk to you about it."

Followed by: "PJ, look. This package is pretty creepy. I'm going to check the regs, but either you come down and see me or I'm gonna have to—well, call me, OK? I think it'll save us both some trouble."

And then, of all things, Ellen had called and asked, "By the way, what's Lizzie now? Four? Five?"

Finally, and inevitably, she'd gone off the deep end. "PJ, how long has your grandmother been dead?"

That was Ellen for you. Loved her, loved her...but when PJ was around Ellen she was forever wishing she could shove her fingers in her ears. If not to block out the things Ellen said, at least to block out the volume at which she said them.

~

And the volume was very loud now. PJ could see the TV without being there; every frame of the movie might as well have been etched inside her skull.

It was the scene where Cinderella was trapped in her room while the Duke sat in the parlor fitting the wicked stepsisters with the glass slipper. The life of Cinderella's dreams was one locked door away, but her stepmother was patting the key in her pocket with a sly contented smile.

Her smile promised a lifetime of domestic slavery for a certain wanna-be princess: bed-making, floor-scrubbing, runny-nose-wiping, peanut-butter-sandwich-fixing. Middle age looming ahead, with her good yoga-body now blown all out of shape despite all the exercise she did, never getting anything quite right, career abandoned, no time for herself. Wondering if this was all there was. How she'd gotten locked in. Where the key was.

And afraid—so desperately afraid—that when she got old and used-up, her prince would run off with a mermaid.

Ross, PJ's prince, had a little comedy routine he always

did when the family watched this movie. He meant it to be funny, PJ supposed.

He'd grab Lizzie and tickle her ferociously. "Fight back, Cinderella," he'd tease as she shrieked in delight. "Scream for help! Break the door down, lay the wicked old bag out with a mop-handle! Get a life! Do something!"

That was Ross's advice to Cinderella: do something.

So PJ resolved to do something. She'd extricate herself from the quilts, get up, send the kids to time-out for not minding her about the remote. She'd hug them when time-out was over and march them out back into the fine spring air to play on the swing set.

She'd take a shower, do her hair, put on clothes and makeup. After she'd gotten herself together she'd perch on the deck where she could keep an eye on the twins, warming herself in the sun, and she'd work on those Broken Sugar Bowl quilt blocks she hadn't picked up in…how long had it been, anyway?

And tomorrow she'd go down to the post office and see what had gotten Ellen all bollixed up. PJ's grandmother was probably still showing up on some junk-mail list, so they'd get that straightened out.

Then she'd pick up a couple of steaks. And when Ross got home from his trip she'd have them waiting on him, medium rare, with asparagus and hollandaise, a baked potato, and Miles Davis on the stereo.

And wouldn't he be surprised? Standing there all handsome in his suit with his jaw hanging?

"You look great," he'd say. Then he'd kiss her while the bells rang.

This was how the script was supposed to be written. And she knew she could make the scene play out that way, if she could only—

But no, that ringing was the phone. PJ sat up, suddenly aware of the throbbing in her chest. Ellen calling for the eighth time, she was sure of it. She really should get up and see what Ellen thought was so urgent.

But…

*Let's say I get motivated and do everything that needs doing in the whole entire world,* she thought. *Then*

4

*what? It's just going to get messed up again. The yard'll need mowing again, the house'll get dirty again, or the laundry'll need washing again. So what's the use?*

She slumped over and wriggled back into the quilts. Deeper this time, trying to escape the happy pealing of wedding bells from the next room. Not Cinderella after all.

Just a cold, frightened woman in a cold, frightening place.

~

It took until the next afternoon for PJ to warm up. When she herded the twins into the post office she found Ellen behind the counter wearing her best postmaster's uniform and an expression of utmost bewilderment. Beside her stood an equally befuddled clerk clutching a bouquet of wrenches.

The counter was engulfed in a mad tangle of sticky labels and wax paper ribbon and coagulating ink. The machine that had regurgitated this mayhem—and was still unraveling tentacles of ribbon into it—lay disassembled in the gears and springs of its own bowels.

*That thing looks like I feel,* PJ thought. *Laid open and spewing nonsense.*

Ellen scratched her neck with a screwdriver and shrugged. "Bert, if this was my Husky we'd just cut the thread and call it good. But this thing can smell fear. I think it's actually warping the space-time continuum."

"Your husky?" said Bert, his confusion obviously growing. "Your dog?"

"Husky," repeated Ellen. "Husqvarna. You might've seen their chainsaws? They also make sewing machines."

She studied Bert's blank face. "Oh, never mind," she sighed. "A genius is always misunderstood."

Then she saw PJ. "Hey, girl!"

"So what's the deal on this package—" PJ tried to ask.

"Keep after it, Bert," said Ellen, thrusting the screwdriver at him, and she crooked her finger at PJ. "You three come with me."

She ushered PJ and the kids into a side office and sat them all down.

"A lolly for the gentleman?" she asked Baker, unwrapping it.

Baker lunged off his chair. "Yeah-yeah-yeah!"

"Yes ma'am," PJ mommy-whispered.

"Yes ma'am," Baker repeated. He stuck out his hand.

"Charmed," Ellen said, shaking it. She handed a second one to Lizzie. "And here's yours, precious. How old are you now?"

"Three-point-five," Lizzie piped, kicking her legs. "Lollypops are made from fruck-toes."

Ellen's laugh shook the walls.

"Fructose, ma'am," PJ hissed again, her neck flushing. "And say thank you."

"Thank you, ma'am," Lizzie repeated.

Ellen was still chuckling. "Three and a half and so bright! Like her mom. Are you quilting yet, sweetie?"

"Lizzie takes gymnastics," PJ said.

"Hmm," frowned Ellen. "Well, look here, Lizzie." She pointed to the far wall, where two posters hung over two picture frames.

"Aren't those pretty? They're pictures of stamps, like you put on letters, and they have quilts on them. That left one is the Nappanee Amish series, the thirty-four centers—see the one that looks like a star? The other one's from Gee's Bend in Alabama. It was a little nowhere town, and each generation of women taught the next one how to quilt with very little input from the outside world. So they developed their own style. Aren't they wonderful?"

"All the colors," Lizzie said.

"So many! And what you see in the frames are the blocks I sewed to match them. I made 'em myself, isn't that cool? I even appliquéd on the prices and the words. So every one of those blocks I made is just like a stamp! Takes a lot of smarts to do that. You think you're smart enough?"

Lizzie's eyes grew wide. "Yeah!"

"Say yes ma'am, Lizzie," PJ said.

But Ellen waved her off. "Oh, PJ, let kids be kids. Lord knows we make 'em grow up too fast. Shame on you, though, for not starting her already. Him too, for that matter."

6

"I don't think she's old enough..." PJ began, already knowing it was hopeless. There was no winning this conversation; next they'd be talking about where PJ had been and why she hadn't been attending the meetings of their quilt guild.

~

And why *wasn't* she going to those meetings? Lack of time, sure, though it went a lot deeper than just...

PJ gripped the arms of her chair, put the thought away from her, and tried to concentrate on what she was saying to Ellen.

~

But Ellen was already interrupting. "Pish-posh. Three-point-five is plenty old. We used to teach our three- year-olds to quilt. Now we teach them cheerleading. Never let the old folks tell you they had it rougher than us."

"Excuse me?"

"Don't screw up your face like that, honey, you'll get wrinkles. Look, quilting is about togetherness. Cooperation. Cheerleading is, what, competition? Individuality?"

Ellen thumped her desk. "Somebody's gotta fail. The kids in gymnastics class know that, that's why they're all on Prozac. Back in our grandparents' day kids quilted with grownups and everybody talked their problems out instead of medicating them. Now we ignore our kids and they take shotguns to school."

*This gets worse and worse,* thought PJ. "So..." she said slowly, "your theory is that if everybody quilted everybody'd be happy?"

Ellen threw back her head and bellowed with laughter. "Sure. Why not?"

"Well...good luck with that. Now—the messages—you have a package you wanted to talk about?"

Ellen clucked. "Honey, what's wrong with you? That was the cleverest thing I've said since—ah, forget it. A genius is always misunderstood. Don't go anywhere, I'll be right back."

Lizzie stared mesmerized at the quilt posters and Ellen patted her head on the way by. "Dynamite's on the top shelf, Bert," PJ heard her exclaim as she swept past the counter.

~

The box Ellen put down was the standard red-white-and-blue one available at any post office. But it wasn't the box that caught PJ's eye.

"Oh my God," she said when she saw the address.

Ellen nodded. "I know. I said it was creepy, didn't I? How long has it been since she passed?"

Creepy didn't do it justice. The label said "Bebe Warner." Bebe was PJ's grandmother, PJ's *sainted* grandmother, who had practically raised PJ at the very house, long since sold, that someone had addressed this package to.

And it was only postmarked a week ago.

"Bebe's been dead for eight years," PJ sputtered. "What is this? Where's it from? *Who's* it from?"

"You're babbling," said Ellen. "Look at the postmark: 'Bluff, Utah.' But obviously there's no return address. So… since the recipient's deceased, the regs say I've gotta mark it 'return to sender.' But seeing as how there's no sender, I guess I could be persuaded to hand it to you as the nearest living relative."

*Persuaded?* PJ didn't like where this was headed. "What's it gonna cost me?"

"I think you can figure that out for yourself," said Ellen, her eyes twinkling as she looked past PJ at Lizzie. But then Ellen's face grew hard and she leaned across the desk.

"Now listen. This is big-girl talk."

PJ swallowed.

"There are bad people out there," Ellen continued. "People with information they shouldn't have, and they don't care what the ill effects of using that information might be…for the surviving family members, say."

"You're talking about identity theft," PJ said, surprised by the relief washing through her. Ellen wasn't calling her out! But then PJ felt ashamed of her reaction; instead of feeling relieved she should have been outraged that some scumbag might be sullying Bebe's name by stealing it.

"Good!" said Ellen. "Identity theft! But a long list of other stuff, too. In the Postal Service we get a bunch of training in how to recognize it—drugs, contraband, syringes, live snakes, even explosives, sometimes. You'd be amazed what people drop in mailboxes.

"And this package has all the warning signs. What I'm saying is, be careful how you open it. You probably want to do it in front of a witness."

Suddenly Ellen grinned. "Like me. I miss Bebe, almost as much as you do, I bet. And I'm dying to see what somebody might have sent her after all these years. Whaddaya say? You want to open it?"

▶▶▶◆◀◀◀
## Chapter Two

At a quarter past six PJ leaned into the shower, goosebump-naked, and waved her hand impatiently under the tap for the hot water.

*Come on, washing machine; I don't have time for this.* The laundry was going and the kids were eating mac and cheese, but she hadn't started dinner for Ross yet, and he was due back—

"Hey, Cupcake," his voice boomed.

She shrieked and spun around, then clapped a hand over her mouth and started trembling.

He was wearing the grey suit that squared his shoulders so nicely. He set a paper bag on the vanity and came to her and took her in his arms. "Sorry, sorry," he said, stroking her hair. "I didn't mean to scare you."

"Don't do that," PJ said when she could breathe again. "Wow."

"You OK?"

"Yeah, I'm fine." But her heart was still hammering.

He smiled and slid a hand down the curve of her back. "This is fine, too," he said.

PJ wriggled free. "Give me a minute and I'll be right down. I was just getting cleaned up." But her brain was racing.

*Fine? My rear end is fine? Was he kidding? Was he blind?*

She'd gotten a tattoo back there, once upon a time, and now it embarrassed her. A cupcake, with pink frosting and a cherry on top. During her pregnancy it had swelled to the size of a whole bakery. She was still working on shrinking it back to size.

Ross was bad to call attention to it in naughty moments—one of which looked imminent if she didn't duck into the shower soon. He was examining the walls, the ceiling, the soapdish—doing his best to stare at everything and anything but her chest.

Which was sagging, anyhow. And though the hot water was soothing, she lathered in a frenzy while he told her about the trip. Something about a product development holdup.

She didn't get the half of it. She was an electrical engineer, not an MBA. But then again, she wasn't a double-E anymore, was she? She was a housewife, and a lousy one at that.

"So, did you have dinner plans?" he called above the noise of the water.

"Um, no, I haven't done anything yet." *Should've. Didn't.*

"I could cook."

"No, I'll do it."

"PJ, really, I'll cook. What do you want?"

PJ squeezed her hair out and grimaced, glad for the curtain between them. "Ross, no. I can handle it. I'm capable of cooking dinner." It came out a little sharper than she intended.

"OK, OK," he said contritely. "I never said you weren't."

She shut off the water. When she pushed the curtain aside he was gone. She could hear him downstairs monster-roaring at the twins, and them giggling.

On the vanity was the paper bag he'd left behind. PJ opened it to find a bottle of wine. Chianti.

Her favorite.

**11**

*Poor Ross.* He'd lost before he'd even stepped through the door. When was she going to get it right?

~

Bebe's package sat unopened on the kitchen island, surrounded by the groceries PJ was still putting away. Ross munched a handful of chips, the kids dancing all around him yelling "Daddy-Daddy-Daddy!" while she stacked cans in the cabinets. Finally, he noticed the box.

"What's *this?*" he asked, peering at the label.

"Tarantulas."

"Tarantulas?"

"Or a baboon, or a bomb, or something. I don't know."

He closed his eyes tight, shook his head as if to clear it. "*What?*"

She told him about the package, leaving out how disappointed Ellen had been in her reluctance to open it. Ross lifted the box, and slowly turned it over and over in his hands.

"It doesn't feel heavy," he said, shaking it. "Or like there's anything alive in it. Are you going to open it?"

She closed a cabinet door. "I'm not sure."

"You're not sure? Why? Don't you care?"

PJ took a long breath. *What difference does it make if I care, Ross?*

But it was hard to put that feeling into words. "Um… it's like…right now, that box could be anything. A message of some sort. A bunch of old love letters. Some of Bebe's drawings. Photographs. Who knows?

"But what if I open it and it's something less than that? Less than what I'd hoped for? I'm really afraid of that. You don't know how much it hurts when that happens, Ross."

She blinked tears and pressed her fist to her mouth. "I miss Bebe so much," she choked. "She always knew what to do. What if Ellen's right, and it's some kind of scam? Or what if it's nothing at all?"

He put the package down and started over but she waved him away.

"No, I'm sorry," she said. "I'm being silly. You're right,

we should open it. Maybe it's perishable or there's some kind of time limit to it or something."

"Well," he said, "if that's what you want to do. But let me get the camera, eh? Just in case it's what you want it to be." He frowned. "Or what you don't, I guess."

~

PJ's hand shook as she pinched the tab and pulled it. The string sliced the cardboard as cleanly as the present severing the past from the future. There. She'd done it. There was no taking it back.

Baker and Lizzie wiggled in excitement. She'd shown them Bebe in pictures and explained how important Bebe was in their family, and that Bebe had gone to be with God, but she wasn't sure how much of it had taken. Ross, on the other hand, who'd known Bebe and loved her too, was unreadable.

She looked down into the box. Paperwads hid whatever might be inside. She drew one out, uncrumpled it.

"It's a newspaper from Utah," she said. "A couple of weeks old." She dug some more. And there it was. A plastic shopping bag with something in it that felt soft and yielding.

Like fabric.

Her ears pounded. Her head grew light and fireflies swarmed in her vision. She swayed.

Ross put the camera down and took her shoulder. "Easy, easy. Take a deep breath."

"I think it's a quilt," she said, her voice unsteady. She'd hardly dared to hope.

But when she unfolded it a sickly cloud bloomed into her face. Mustiness, a hint of mildew, and old sweat. Enough to turn her stomach.

It felt gritty, too, and she realized that in spreading it out she'd scattered sand all over the clean countertop.

"This is…" she said, her face falling. "Oh, no."

*This is the ugliest quilt I've ever seen,* she thought.

It was faded and tattered and threadbare. No rhyme or reason to it, either—a crazy patchwork of mismatched fabrics and clashing colors on both sides. And much of the stitching was horrible. Great uneven loops of dull thread here, tiny crabbed seams there. But then again, some of the needlework was as neat as any out there.

Unfathomable. And the stains. Dark brown, faded yellow-orange, crusts of black.

*I don't even want to think about what those are.*

"What's *that*, Momma?" Baker asked in the same grossed-out tone he used to announce he'd just stepped in a dogpile.

"Don't touch it, Baker," she said.

"It's a quilt, Baker," said Ross. "A quilt somebody made and sent to Bebe. Somebody spent a lot of time on this. That's nice, huh?"

"It's not a quilt," PJ snapped. "It's a bad joke. Bebe never worked on this thing."

Abruptly she jerked it off the island, scattering dirt, and she rolled it and stuffed it back into the bag and hurled the bag onto the counter. *No taking it back, no taking it back, no taking it—*

"PJ," Ross said, "come on, now. We still don't know what the story is."

"I know the story," she muttered. "And the punchline, too."

Ross sighed. He tapped his chin and then tugged some more paperwads out of the box.

"Well-well," he said a moment later.

PJ glanced up. Ross held a folded sheet of newspaper with the word "Bebe" written across it in black magic marker. He offered it to her, his gaze steady. "Maybe this is the key."

She unfolded it.

"Dear…" and she had to clear her throat.

"Dear Bebe, I don't need this anymore. But I'll be waiting for you. Love, Silver." PJ looked at Ross. "That's all it says."

Ross bit his lip. "Silver? Who's Silver?" He paused. "And where's he going to be waiting?"

~

Bedtime. Again.

They'd moved Baker and Lizzie into separate rooms a couple of months ago. There was square footage to spare in this awful mini-mansion, so why not use some of it? Half the rooms were still standing empty, three years after they'd moved in.

*It was like a machine came squatting along and pooping these houses out one by one,* PJ thought as she walked down the hall. *I wish we had a different place. Maybe one of those cute Frank Lloyd Wright knock-offs over in North Chattanooga. Something with character, where I could push the kids through the Riverpark for exercise. They'd love that. And a smaller house would have been easier to keep clean.*

But then she frowned. *What are you whining about?* she scolded herself. *Four walls and a roof are a lot more than some people have. You've gotta quit this—you're driving yourself crazy!*

She sat down on the edge of Baker's race-car bed. He had "the rubbies," his main drowsy signal, slowly working his soft fists around in his eyes. It melted her, as always, and she opened his favorite storybook.

"And they all went to heaven in a little rowboat," she finished, and she replaced the book on his nightstand. "Kiss-kiss."

Baker squirmed around to see her, his bright blue eyes so like Ross's. "Big boys shake hands," he said solemnly. "For a business deal, like when we bought the soccer van."

"Bedtime is serious business," PJ agreed. "OK, we'll shake hands, then. Put it there, podner."

He did. They pumped, one-two-three.

"It's a deal," he said.

"It's a deal," she echoed, meaning it. Then she leaned over and kissed him anyway.

It was Ross's night with Lizzie. As PJ walked by Lizzie's room she could hear him in there, still. PJ smiled; Ross loved reading to the kids. They were free to interrupt him anytime as long as they brought a book. So she stopped by the kitchen.

When he came down she had two glasses of Chianti

waiting on the coffee table and she was clicking through the channels for the Braves game.

"That's what I'm talking about," he said. He hurdled the couch, threw himself into it, and scooped up his glass.

"Veddy nice," he said, smacking his lips.

They sipped their wine and watched the game. PJ tried not to think about the package or the quilt it had contained, tried to stay in the moment, tried to focus on Ross.

But he kept drumming his fingers on his thigh, so it was small wonder when, during a commercial, he put his arm around her and pulled her closer. PJ regretted she'd encouraged him, but forced herself to relax. He kissed her, pinched her nose and winked, and thumbed the mute button as the game resumed. She exhaled.

~

A half-inning later she was still nestled against his shoulder—warmer now, enjoying the peace and starting to doze off—and suddenly he was reaching down, sliding her glasses from her face, and kissing her softly. She pulled back, startled.

"What?" he said. "Man, you're jumpy tonight."

"Ross, I really don't feel like it." She retrieved her glasses from him and put them back on. "Could we just—I don't know—sit here? Watch the game? Finish the wine?"

He started drumming his fingers on his thigh again. Tap-tap-tap.

"Sure," he said, his voice a bit too cheerful.

~

The conversation petered out and PJ went upstairs at the seventh-inning stretch. She was awake when Ross came to bed, though. She held still in the darkness, pretending she was asleep.

"Hey," he said presently, "is there anything you want to talk about?"

"Like what?"

"I don't know. That quilt. Or anything."

"Not really," PJ said. "Why?"

"Well...do you know what Lizzie asked me tonight? Something...well. I was reading to her about the goats and the bridge and the troll under it, and she asked if Momma was the troll that lived under the house. I just wanted to make sure everything went OK today."

*Great,* she thought. *I can't even fool my own daughter. Why was he even reading her that dumb story? She's a little girl; I can't believe I never told him not to read her monster stories! I should go see if she's OK!*

But she kept her voice cool. "Everything's all right, Ross. I'm all right. No worries."

"It's not me, then? Not something I've said? Or done?"

"Ross," she started, and then she sighed. "I'm just tired. I've been working really hard lately—" *uh-oh, now you're lying to him,* she thought, "—and I'm ready to get some sleep."

"OK, if you say so," he said. He leaned across as if to kiss her on the forehead, and then stopped, apparently thinking better of it. "Sleep good, PJ," he told her. And he switched off his light.

What he'd said crept over her in a slow chill: *Sleep good, PJ.*

*Right. Well, I got what I wanted, didn't I? And who is this PJ you speak of? I don't know anymore. Maybe Lizzie's right, maybe I'm the troll under the house. And now Ross tells me to sleep good.*

*But I know this much about myself: I am going to be awake until the day I die.*

### ▶▶▶◆◀◀◀
## Chapter Three

Who was Silver, indeed?

A midnight thunderstorm was moving across the Tennessee Valley. The rain roared on the roof and in PJ's ears. She lay on her side watching the lightning shiver in the windowpanes, her mind gyrating like the storm clouds above as she mourned her grandmother Bebe for the millionth time.

Elizabeth "Bebe" Warner. A woman who'd been so large in love that her absence still left holes in hearts everywhere. Perhaps the largest one right here, in PJ. A sucking chest wound, soldiers called it.

Bebe Reynolds had been nineteen when she married David Warner on Christmas Day, 1949. He was a few years older than her—they hadn't been high school sweethearts or anything—but Chattanooga was a small town and marrying a popular boy with bright prospects was what good folks did.

David's father and uncle sold life insurance together and David was in the Marine Corps Reserve. Bebe's mother and aunts and cousins approved, and her sisters were jealous. He was a fine catch.

Bebe threw herself into her marriage. They bought a sunny little house near David's father's office. She filled it with rocking chairs. It was a rare evening when they didn't host friends, and though their elders frowned on such things, every Saturday night they'd clear the sitting room floor and play dance records.

But the neighbors never complained—they were doing the Collegiate Foxtrot right there along with Bebe and David and everyone else. Some mornings Bebe and David would have to run everyone out to go upstairs and get dressed in time to make Sunday morning worship, bleary-eyed but still full of laughter.

They'd been married for six months when the North Korean Army crossed the 38th parallel and started massacring South Korean civilians.

"The pictures broke my heart," Bebe remembered to PJ many years later when they were sitting by the television watching the Iraqis invade Kuwait. "A little Korean boy crying half-naked in the road, with his leg tangled in barbed wire."

Truman activated the reserves and David knew what was coming. Serving your country when called on was what good folks did. Bebe kissed him goodbye at the bus station downtown.

After he boarded the bus he pulled down the window and waved at her and the others who had come to see him off. Bebe would always remember his strong arm, how the wedding ring gleamed on his finger. His face, shining with confidence.

The bus pulled away in a cloud of black smoke. He wrote her regularly from Camp Pendleton. And then David Warner disappeared into the Korean War.

~

When PJ was five she skipped through the gate to where Grandpa David was shuffling through the garden, hoeing weeds.

He smiled slightly at her and went on with his work. She followed him in silence. She watched his arms, old cords of muscle flexing as he swung the hoe, and she noticed the thing on his arm for the first time.

"What's that, Grandpa?" she asked. "On your elbow?"

He worked on as if he hadn't heard her. Then he stopped.

"Whatsay, Cupcake?" he said.

"That."

He extended his left arm and turned it so he could examine its back. From under his sleeve, down the back of his arm across his elbow, and for the length of his forearm to his wrist ran a furrow of ruined tissue outlined by dozens of white pinholes.

"It's a scar," he said.

"A scar. How did it get there? Did you fall off your bike?"

He hesitated, his eyes distant. "I'm not sure," he said. "God must have put it there." Then he turned his back on her and he went on chopping weeds.

PJ fled crying at once. Crying in terror of the distance in his eyes, and crying in terror of a God who would put something so ugly on her Grandpa's arm.

Inside, she sniffled in Bebe's lap and rested her forehead on Bebe's soft shoulder. She'd interrupted Bebe's sewing and now Bebe soothed her, rocking and humming softly.

"I don't understand," PJ said. "Why was God so mean to Grandpa?"

"Oh, PJ," Bebe cooed. "God wasn't mean to Grandpa David. Now listen. God loves him. A lot. But sometimes when God loves somebody He tests them. And since He loves Grandpa David so much, He gave him a big test.

"Your Grandpa David is very special. He did some very brave things a long time ago. He passed God's test. But remember how I told you nothing that's really worth doing is easy? It wasn't easy for Grandpa David to do these things. He's still doing them, right now, even. So you need to be patient with him. Remember how I asked you to be patient with your Mommy?"

PJ thought about that for a long time. "Is that where Mommy is, then? Being tested by God?"

Bebe laughed. "You could say that, Cupcake. God loves your Mommy too, but maybe your Mommy doesn't love herself so much."

"But I love her.

# GREAT GIFT IDEA!

## GIVE A GIFT SUBSCRIPTION AND SAVE 33%

☑ **YES!** I'd like to order a gift subscription to *McCall's Quick Quilts*. Bill me for only $19.98 for a full year (6 issues) — 33% off the cover price. Plus, I'll receive a FREE gift card.

**GREAT GIFTS FROM THE HEART**

McCall's **Quick Quilts**

**16 fun fast HOLIDAY projects**

EASY
NEW
SKILLS
• in a block
• colorful piecing
• binding
• FAST flying geese

4 SIMPLE
STAR
QUILTS

cozy & cute
SNOWMEN

**SAVE 33% OFF**
Cover price

### GIFT FOR:

NAME

ADDRESS

CITY/STATE/ZIP

### BILL ME:

NAME

ADDRESS

CITY/STATE/ZIP

E-MAIL ADDRESS - TO CONTACT YOU ABOUT YOUR SUBSCRIPTION, EVENTS, AND PROMOTIONS.

☐ Payment enclosed

☐ Bill me later (U.S. only)    ☐ Enter my own subscription

McCall's **QuickQuilts**

79ANB1 QKQ

MᴄCALL'S

QuickQuilts

PO BOX 420239
PALM COAST FL 32142-7348

# BUSINESS REPLY MAIL
FIRST-CLASS MAIL    PERMIT NO. 88    FLAGLER BEACH FL

POSTAGE WILL BE PAID BY ADDRESSEE

NO POSTAGE
NECESSARY
IF MAILED IN THE
UNITED STATES

"Your Mommy loves you too," said Bebe. "And so do I, and so does your Grandpa David."

"But what about God? Is he gonna do something to me like he did to Grandpa?"

Bebe's eyes glinted. "Oh, PJ," she said. "Maybe not like that. But you'll be tested in life—everyone is. The one thing you can always count on, though, is God's love."

~

But where was God to be found in the small hours of the night in a thunderstorm?

*Silver,* PJ thought. *Hi-Yo, Silver.*

Silver couldn't be a nickname for her grandfather David. It was obvious. She'd never heard anybody refer to Grandpa as "Silver," the note in the box wasn't in his handwriting, and besides, he'd been dead for twenty-two years. So he couldn't have written a note on a newspaper that was only two weeks old.

No, Silver had to be a stranger.

But who?

She checked the clock. One a.m. Two hours she'd been obsessing over this, yet she was no closer to an answer.

What could the note possibly mean?

*I'll be waiting for you.*

It implied that Silver felt a strong connection between himself and Bebe. Strong enough, PJ realized, that he'd want to be there waiting for her when she died. On the other side, wherever that was. So that Silver and Bebe could face the light—or the darkness—together.

*So was Silver a family member?* PJ wondered. *A long-lost brother, or an adopted cousin? Something like that?*

No, that wasn't right. Bebe would never have lost track of a family member. Such relationships were sacred to her. The family tree Bebe had drawn in the flyleaf of her Bible overflowed halfway into Genesis. On birthdays and Christmas the mailbox was stuffed with cards from distant relatives.

But to say that Bebe would never lose track of a family

member wasn't exactly true, was it? She'd certainly lost track of her own daughter, hadn't she?

PJ lay in the dark, rubbing her temples.

~

"It happened in his sleep," Bebe told Anne, PJ's mother. Bebe spoke through an embroidered handkerchief she clutched to her face.

Aunt Carol stood with PJ, listening intently, her hand cool on the back of PJ's neck. PJ was "on bereavement," which she took to mean that since a family member had died, you got to stay home from seventh grade. Aunt Margaret sat a little way off from them, whispering to Pastor Ingram, and from elsewhere in the house came the sad murmuring of other people that PJ supposed were also "on bereavement."

"Yes," said Bebe. "In three days. Yes. Oh, good." Bebe glanced at Aunt Carol and nodded.

Aunt Carol gave an exasperated little sigh. "She's his daughter! Why is it even in question whether she's coming?"

Bebe covered the mouthpiece and held a finger to her lips. "No, don't worry about it," she said into the phone. "I'll wire you some."

~

Three mornings after Grandpa David died, PJ waited at the front of the church, dry-eyed, her back pressed to Bebe, feeling Bebe's warm arms around her as friends and strangers filed by to offer their condolences. Everyone was dressed in their Sunday best, their somber clothing muting the bright flower arrangements that surrounded the casket.

"So sad, after suffering so much," they said.

Doctor Kendrick's opinion was that Captain David Francis Warner had died of a massive heart attack. Fifty-nine was young, Doc had told them, but malnutrition, malaria, and a dozen other wartime afflictions had weakened Grandpa's heart to the point where it just couldn't go anymore.

When PJ was able to muster the courage she'd steal

glances at Grandpa where he lay in his coffin. "His *body*, not him," Bebe had said. "You have a body; you *are* a soul. This is just something he left us to remember him by."

Grandpa looked thin. Still and tired. His eyes were closed and his grey hair was combed over in a way she'd never seen Bebe do it.

But he was sleeping now. So PJ prayed that God would help Grandpa sleep well in heaven. She prayed that Jesus would visit with Grandpa on the front porch of his mansion—that they'd sit in the sun, drinking coffee; that they'd play Chinese checkers together. She prayed that Jesus would occasionally let Grandpa win.

She asked God to ask Grandpa to forgive her for lying about who'd torn the back door screen. She prayed that God would—

There was a disturbance in the back. PJ opened her eyes, craned her neck to see. She felt something swell within her.

There, at the door to the sanctuary, Anne Warner was making her entrance.

Bebe gave her a little push. "Go to your mother, Cupcake!" she smiled.

Anne stirred through the mourners, and they made room so Anne and PJ could meet. Anne was wearing a cowboy hat, round black plastic sunglasses, a green scarf, a short skirt. Her honey-blonde hair was gathered into a long ponytail, tied back with a strap as nut-brown as the tan on her legs.

"Oh, baby," she gasped, throwing her arms around PJ. The beads on the leather fringe on Anne's buckskin jacket dug into PJ's ears. People were staring at them.

"I've missed you like you wouldn't believe," Anne said, a little too loudly. "It's such a drag, living without my PJ. Go on, you can cry on your momma. Don't worry about the suede."

So PJ clung to this strange woman she hadn't seen in three years, this woman she'd so longed for, and she cried until she was empty.

~

23

PJ had never seen Marines before. She sat between Bebe and Anne beside the flag-covered casket and watched seven men clad in blue and gold snap their rifles aloft. Each volley of shots made her jump in her seat.

"David would be so proud," Bebe whispered.

A bugle began warbling softly. Men put their arms about their wives' shoulders; old men squinted at the sky; boys looked down and shuffled their feet. Women dabbed their eyes, young and old. Bebe held her chin high, keeping time with a finger. Anne squeezed PJ's arm very hard and shuddered.

Two Marines stepped forward in slow fluid unison and lifted the flag from the casket. In silence they folded it lengthwise, stripes over stars, doubled it to reveal the stars again, and rolled it end-over-end into a tight triangle of white on blue.

The Marine with the most stripes and medals bore it reverently to Bebe. He paused before presenting it to her with great dignity.

"On behalf of the President of the United States," he said, "the Commandant of the Marine Corps, and a grateful nation, please accept this flag as a symbol of our appreciation for your loved one's service to country and corps."

He straightened and saluted—appearing, to PJ, to be cut from the same blue steel as the barrels of the rifles.

Bebe nodded to him. The Marine lowered his white-gloved hand, turned on his heels, and marched away. Bebe leaned to PJ and pressed the flag into her hands, and PJ looked down at it, trying to understand.

From across the open grave PJ heard her Aunt Margaret stifle a sob. Then came a shriek. PJ looked up from the stars and stripes as Anne threw herself across the casket in a faint.

~

That afternoon PJ carried a tray of dirty cups and plates through the hallway, trying to stay invisible.

"Scarlett O'Hara meets Farrah Fawcett-Majors…"

someone was muttering to Aunt Margaret in the living room corner.

"Hush, now," Aunt Margaret whispered.

PJ set the tray on the kitchen counter and started unloading it into the sink.

"I'm sorry, I'm just so wiped out," Anne explained to the room at large. "I drove nonstop for two days to get here. Never even stopped to pee. I can't believe I...I..."

She sloshed her glass of wine down onto the table and sagged into Brody Martin's arms, shoulders shaking. PJ knew Brody from the neighborhood; he was a college boy at UTC. He glanced around the kitchen uncomfortably before raising a hesitant hand to Anne's head.

"It'll be OK," he mumbled, patting her awkwardly.

Aunt Carol shot Pastor Ingram a look PJ recognized and Pastor Ingram cleared his throat. "Anne? Come on outside, I think you could use some fresh air. There's pie, and maybe you could lie down in the hammock for an hour or two."

"It's so hard," Anne moaned. "So hard." She allowed Pastor Ingram to lead her away.

"I think," said Aunt Carol, "that the rest of us ought to pray for Bebe and Anne and PJ." She looked around the kitchen and everyone joined hands to make a circle.

"Brody, would you lead us?" Aunt Carol said.

~

But PJ was all prayed out, and she crept away from the circle after the others closed their eyes.

She went into the bathroom behind the stairs and closed the door, put the toilet lid down, and sat on it. Through the corner of the open window she could see and hear Pastor Ingram with her mother. The old man was sitting on a folding chair from the back porch, and PJ's mother sprawled in the hammock with her face buried in the crook of her elbow.

Pastor Ingram was singing to PJ's mother. "Rock of Ages," in his gentle tenor.

*I shouldn't be eavesdropping on them,* PJ thought. *But what's wrong with Mom?*

Presently Pastor Ingram finished singing. "I'd surely enjoy it if you'd tell me something you remember about your father, Anne," he said.

Her voice was muffled. "I'm too wrecked for any of that."

"You seem fine to me," he said. "Besides, my voice is tired—all the yapping I've done today."

Her laugh was short and sharp. "What do you want to hear? 'Bless me, Father, for I have sinned,' and all that jazz?"

Pastor Ingram chuckled. "Not hardly, that's the store up the road."

"At least you admit to it being a store."

"Well," he said, "let's see if my voice'll hold out, then. I always admired David, you know, for how he tried to take care of you and Bebe and PJ."

"Right," she said, her tone heavy with sarcasm. "Some care."

"He did what he could, I think," Pastor Ingram said. "I still carry the life insurance he sold me, as a matter of fact."

PJ's mother rolled over to lean on one elbow. Dark trails leaked from under her sunglasses.

"All right," she said. "Let me tell you something I remember about Daddy and life insurance. Sure, he set up with Uncle Pete for a while. And he sold policies. So what? He never made ten bucks at it his whole life."

"It was a good thing. You were a beautiful little girl—I remember like it was yesterday!—and he was trying to provide for you."

"Mmm-hmm. Well, why'd you buy it?"

Pastor Ingram shrugged. "You need life insurance."

Anne spat another bitter laugh. "That's a lie. Christians aren't supposed to need life insurance because Christians aren't supposed to be afraid to die."

Pastor Ingram nodded. "You might have a good point, there."

PJ's mother fell back in the hammock. "This is ridiculous."

"Go on," he said.

She grunted. "People—like you—bought life insurance

26

from Daddy because they were ashamed not to. Why else would they? Here he was, the crippled war hero, dragging himself up the sidewalk to ask if they'd give him a little money. And they would. Or at least they did for a while. You did it yourself—you tell me I'm wrong."

"It was a better day and age," Pastor Ingram said. "People helped one another back then."

"Yeah. But then Vietnam came along, and suddenly handing out charity to a disabled veteran got to be too ugly for people around here to stomach."

"Well, people around here, as you put it, weren't ready for that kind of cultural change," he said.

"People around here, as I put it, can go —"

PJ's eyes widened. She'd never heard anyone swear at a clergyman before.

But Pastor Ingram apparently failed to notice. He leaned forward and rested his forearms on his knees and tapped the tips of his fingers together.

When he spoke again he wore a trace of a smile but his voice was hoarse. "Then bless me, Anne, for I have sinned."

Her mother started shaking her head. "What does *that* mean? Are you making fun of me now?"

"No, no. My sin—our sin, really—was failing to take into account how our pity might've hurt a young girl who loved her Daddy." He lowered his head.

Anne's chest heaved.

"So maybe," he continued, "it's our fault a little girl grew up to be a woman who feels guilty for being ashamed of her father. And maybe she's a little angry with him, even, for not being able to pay her the attention a healthy father would've. And maybe she feels guilty about that too."

He paused for a moment. "Anne, I wish we'd have loved you and your family better," he finished. "I hope you can forgive us for it."

PJ's mother covered her face with her hand. Fresh mascara ran down her cheeks. "Did Carol send you out here to feed me this garbage?"

Pastor Ingram looked up at her. "Listen to me, Anne. Look at me. It's not garbage. You're still looking for that kind of attention, aren't you? The kind you wanted from your father. And since you can't have it, you settle for whatever comes your way. Well, there's a better kind of attention waiting on you."

"I'll tell you what," she said. "When I'm ready to trade real men for an imaginary one, you'll be the first to know, OK?"

"Anne, Anne, Anne," sighed Pastor Ingram, "you'll never hear me say this from the pulpit, but Jesus can only take us so far in this life. No, I was thinking about someone else, someone who's in that house right now."

*If not Jesus, then who?* wondered PJ. *Does he mean me? Because I'm right here, Mom. Right here.*

~

She kept watching them through the corner of the window. Pastor Ingram sang again, Sunday morning songs PJ knew every word and note of. Her mother nodded and then slept, and PJ leaned against the vanity and fell asleep herself, lulled by the breeze and by Pastor Ingram's kindly voice.

PJ awoke abruptly, not knowing where she was. The room was dark and her neck was stiff.

*I'm in bed,* she thought. *But I'm still wearing my dress. How did I get up here?*

She looked at her clock on the nightstand and saw it was after eleven. She'd slept the evening away. And then she realized what had wakened her.

There was noise in the house. A thumping from Anne's room—footsteps, drawers being hauled open, knick-knacks rattling. And from down the hall in the other direction, the sound of Bebe weeping.

PJ got up and swung her door open silently and looked out. She could see Bebe sitting at the foot of the stairs, head bowed, wiping her nose. PJ went to her and put her arms around her neck, and Bebe looked down and patted them.

"Go back to bed, Cupcake," Bebe said. Her hair was coming undone and she had dark circles under her eyes.

"What's going on?" PJ asked.

Bebe sniffed and wiped at her cheek with a thumb. "Oh,

28

PJ. Your mother and I have been talking and now she's upset. But you should go sleep. I hate for you to see—"

Behind them, Anne stalked down the stairs, swinging the suitcase she'd only just unpacked that afternoon. Her face was wooden, tight-lipped, her eyes glowing.

"Get out of my way, Mother," she snapped.

Bebe rose. "Anne, please, don't do this. I'm begging you, please."

"Where are you going, Mom?" PJ asked.

Anne stopped. "I'm outta here. I can't stand the smell any longer."

PJ ran to her mother and wrapped herself around her. "It's me, isn't it? I'm sorry! I shouldn't have watched, but I wanted to see you!"

"Watched what?" Bebe said, her eyes traveling back and forth between them.

"Don't give me that look, Mother," Anne said. "I have no idea what she's talking about."

"What did you see, PJ?" Bebe insisted.

"I—I was listening to Pastor Ingram sing to Mom," she stammered.

"Uh-huh, you see, Mother?" said Anne. "A perfectly innocent explanation. You're raising a fine little girl, there. Good luck with it." She disentangled herself from PJ and shoved past Bebe and continued down the hallway with them trailing her.

At the door, Bebe seized the handle of the suitcase and tried to wrest it away from her. "You can't leave like this!"

"Let go!" Anne yelled.

"Look at your daughter," Bebe said. "Look how much she needs you. Don't make the same mistake I did, Anne."

"Mom—" PJ gasped. "What did I do? I'm sorry!"

Anne hung her head. She released the suitcase to Bebe and knelt and rested her hands on PJ's shoulders. Her breath was sour with wine.

"This isn't about you, PJ," she said. "It's about me. I love you, I do, but I can't take this place any longer. Maybe you can come see me in San Diego…if this—woman—will let you."

"Anne, please," Bebe said. "This is so wrong!"

Anne chopped the air with a hand. "Enough." She stood and pulled the suitcase from Bebe's hands, forcing Bebe to lurch towards her. "You, of all people, have got no right passing judgment on me! Who do you think found her asleep and carried her up the stairs, while you were gossiping about me with those spinster sisters of yours?"

"That's a terrible thing to say!"

"Oh? Now I'm the one saying terrible things. That's great, Mother."

"Piper Jo needs you! You've barely spent a moment with her!"

"Piper Jo," Anne said slowly. "Piper Jo. Like I'll ever be able to forget her name. You don't even hear yourself, do you? She doesn't need me one bit. Never has. She's got you, the perfect grandmother. Hah! The martyr, nursing her poor husband all these years since he got back from the war, and raising her granddaughter while her daughter whores around in California. You know what? You're nothing but a hypocrite."

Then Bebe did the most terrible thing PJ had ever seen. She raised her strong hand and dealt Anne a dreadful slap. Anne's head cracked back; she yelped and her cheek bloomed into flame. Bebe's brow was fierce, her eyes righteous, her jaw set.

PJ burst into tears and backed away.

And Anne started screaming at Bebe, screaming words so horrible that PJ turned her back and clapped her hands over her ears.

Anne's screaming went on and on. Then PJ felt the house shudder, heard the front door crash on its hinges.

~

The crashing of the door was the crashing of thunder. PJ startled awake and felt the echoes of the dream fading in her mind. Had she been sleeping? Ross breathed deeply beside her, but she could still hear the crisp slap, still see the crimson mark on Anne's cheek, still feel the tremor in the house.

*My God. I haven't thought about that in years.*

**30**

She touched her cheek. It was wet, as if the tears from that long-ago night had never dried.

She'd never mentioned the fight to anyone, not even Ross. When her mother had slammed the door she'd fled upstairs and locked herself in her room, ignoring Bebe's pleas for entry. The next morning all Bebe did was send her back to school with an extra cupcake. The aunts acted like Anne had never even been there. Like she'd never even existed.

And it wasn't like PJ had ever been able to ask Anne intimate personal questions, either. They'd barely spoken since the twins were born. Of course Anne had spent a day or two with PJ and Ross after the birth, and she'd feigned happiness and hogged the spotlight, but then she'd gotten on the plane back to San Diego. They traded cards these days, with decreasing frequency. PJ might as well have been an orphan.

It was almost funny. An orphan with two mothers, but how different they'd been. Though Bebe had never said anything against Anne to PJ—badmouthing parents to their kids' faces wasn't something good folks did—she'd been devastated by Anne's "loose morals" and had frequently sought comfort from her sisters and friends.

And every time Bebe looked at PJ she would have been reminded of that pain. PJ's father had been a guy named Dewayne that Anne had hooked up with at a weekend rock festival. They'd had their weekend of fun, and now PJ had this whole life to deal with—without either of them. PJ barely knew Nash; he'd had his fling with Anne and moved on, and by the time PJ was three he'd settled in Seattle and started a family and life of his own.

PJ felt she had no claim on him. He'd been polite the few times she'd approached him, but he'd as much as told her that he was embarrassed by her very existence. He'd only been a playful moment for Anne, a lark, free love.

Free love. How Bebe had hated that phrase.

"Love isn't free," she said. "True love costs you everything you have, and then some."

So she'd always disapproved of Anne and Dewayne for not marrying. Though she'd never have held that against

PJ, either. You never made the kids pay for the parents' shortcomings.

And PJ realized she might have finally stumbled onto the true story of Silver. Was there a man in Bebe's life before David? That Bebe had never mentioned?

Or—and her breathing quickened when she considered it—had Bebe taken a lover at some point? Bebe was a healthy woman, after all, presumably with healthy appetites. Grandpa had his good days and his bad days, but on average he was little better than a shell.

No. That couldn't be it. Bebe would never do such a thing. She was a devout Christian, and how could she have hidden it? She was always in the thick of things, always surrounded by people. An affair would have caused talk. And no matter what Anne might say, Bebe *was* the perfect grandmother. Considerate. Wise. Loving.

Loyal.

But then, Silver's note: *I'll be waiting for you.*

What about PJ's grandpa? Bebe's husband? It was more than a little insulting for this Silver to exclude Grandpa from his plans for Bebe in the afterlife. It smacked of something she'd never have suspected Bebe of. And the suspicion, faint though it was, made her furious with herself for being doubtful.

But she couldn't shake the thought. Everyone had at least one flaw. God knew PJ had plenty of her own.

So how could you reconcile it? What if Silver had been Bebe's lover?

It couldn't be. PJ's whole being rebelled at the notion. *Slow down,* she ordered herself. *You're assuming Silver is a man.*

What if Silver was a woman, not a lover at all, but a dear friend? That could explain a lot.

Though not everything. A man had made that quilt. PJ knew that for a certainty. A man had made that misbegotten *thing* that was down there polluting her kitchen.

But if Silver was Bebe's lover, why would he send her such a horrible present?

PJ groaned silently. You could play ping-pong with this until your arms fell off.

*I hate that quilt,* she thought. *Look at what it's putting me through! It's three-thirty in the morning and I'm half-crazy with it!*

Suddenly she decided. She leaped from the bed, bounded down the stairs into the kitchen, snatched the bag and the note off the counter.

She erupted into the night in her t-shirt and panties, not noticing the rain. The trash cans sat under the dripping overhang at the front of the garage. She hauled one open and jammed the horrid quilt deep into the heart of the garbage. Then she slammed the lid down and stood panting.

A strange sense of déjà vu rose up in her. She rubbed her arms, feeling the goosebumps on her skin.

"You will never," PJ admonished herself as the rain soaked her through and through, "question Bebe's integrity again."

When she returned to the bedroom Ross sat up. "Huzzup?" he slurred.

She stalked into the bathroom for a towel, still breathing hard. "I had to put the trash out."

He rubbed his face. "Uh...the garbage doesn't run until Thursday, right?"

▶▶▶◆◀◀◀
## Chapter Four

PJ rolled over to find Ross missing. Then she looked at the clock.

*Sleeping in when you should already have coffee and breakfast made,* she thought. *Nice.*

She hurried into a t-shirt and shorts. When she got to the kitchen Ross was already at the table with his laptop, sipping coffee and studying the screen with his eyebrows lowered. He glanced up when she entered and smoothly palmed the lid closed.

"OK," he said, his expression neutral. "I want you to tell me why you put that quilt in the trash."

She looked through the window into the dim morning. "Um," she began, her mind fuzzy and her stomach churning, "don't you think this can wait a few minutes? I mean, I slept like crap and I need some caffeine."

Then she did a double-take. "You looked in there?"

"That I did. I woke up and put two and two together. And I took it back out. Here it is, right here." He scooped the bag off the floor beside him and placed it on the table.

"Take that off there, I'm gonna have to clean it now," she said.

"OK, OK. But look, I'm not convinced..."

Like she was supposed to be? She hadn't even resolved this for herself, and now he wanted her to resolve it for him? The day was already circling the drain.

She held up a weary hand. "Ross, please, it's really too early for this."

"Just—look." He hung his head. "Just sit down, OK?"

She waited while he went to the coffeemaker and built her a cup, just so. No cream, two sugars, a little cinnamon. He offered it to her, retreated. She inhaled the steam, the warmth of it, and she felt the first sip all the way down to her toes.

*He is such a nice guy,* she thought. *And I'm so close to running him off.*

"I threw that quilt away," she confessed, "because I started thinking Silver might have been Bebe's lover."

Ross's face froze. Then he exploded with laughter.

PJ was deeply hurt, and she must have let it show, for Ross abruptly turned serious. He leaned across the table and took her hands in his.

"Oh, no, no," he said. "No, I wasn't laughing at you for being afraid of that. God, no, I'm sorry. What I meant was—well, come on—Bebe, having an affair? *The* Bebe? It's insane. She ranks up there with Mother Teresa. PJ, there's gotta be another explanation."

She exhaled, long and shaky. "I am so glad to hear you say that. Boy. I was lying there all night thinking I was nuts. But it was all I could come up with."

"So you threw the quilt out. OK, I get it now. But—tell me the truth. You're still worried about it, aren't you? Because I can't imagine PJ Hathaway, the pride of the Blockheads, throwing a quilt in the garbage."

PJ hesitated, then gave a short nod.

Ross shrugged. "So why don't you check it out, then? Ask a few questions; maybe somebody'll know something. There's gotta be an innocent explanation, it'll set your mind at ease, and...ah...it'll give you an excuse to connect up with some of the girls again."

She considered the idea until an evil notion struck her and forced her to chuckle.

"What?" he asked.

"You're good, Ross. You are good. I've gotta hand it to you."

"Hey, I'm just trying to help a sister out." His hands in the air, protesting.

She waved a finger at him, half-smiling. "Don't push it, sister."

~

On Tuesdays and Thursdays the YMCA on Hixson Pike did a mommy-time thing where you could drop your kids off between one and four and go out and take care of business. PJ lived for it.

She signed Lizzie and Baker in, blew a zerbert on each of their bellies, and waved bye-bye as they wandered off into the playroom—Lizzie to poke at the toys on the shelves, Baker to poke at the other kids.

Ordinarily she'd work out in the gym the whole time—treadmill and free weights and yoga, still trying to shrink that cupcake—but today she returned to the van instead.

The weather had cleared, the sun was gleaming in the puddles, and as she drove, she rolled down the windows and cranked up the radio. Old hits, the kind Bebe had raised her on—Dinah Shore and Perry Como and Les Brown.

The day was looking up, if just a bit. It was Ross's doing. Though it was hard to care about much of anything, he was something worth caring about. She was so grateful for him, and to him, despite the faint resentment she felt that he was trying to pressure her back into quilting. But Ross wasn't stupid, and she was stupid to think she could fool him about how tired she got sometimes.

*And that's all it is!* she thought. *OK, so maybe I had a touch of the baby blues for a while. But that was years ago—the kids are almost four! It's just that they're precocious and take a lot of energy to manage. They keep me worn out!*

Would Ross buy that? What would he really think, for instance, if she'd confessed to him how tired she'd been the other night when he'd brought the wine home? How she'd spent most of the day in bed, and was still exhausted? Would he try to make it more than it was? The way he'd slammed the laptop lid when she came down the stairs—yeah. She'd caught that.

Little signs, adding up in his mind. Soon, now, he was going to start asking questions. She'd tell him she just wasn't sleeping well, but he'd start marking data points, drawing connections between them. Trying to identify an overall pattern, see if it looked like a map.

And she thought she knew where that map led. Everyone, it seemed, was trying to cure what you didn't even know you had, to sell you happiness in a capsule. You couldn't open a magazine or a mailbox or turn on your TV without being inundated by it.

PJ remembered a scene from one of their follow-up visits to the obstetrician shortly after the twins had been born. There'd been these two trophy wives in the waiting room. Catwalk-quality maternity clothes and way too much jewelry. Bellies out to here. They were friends, evidently, for they were kicked back in the comfy chairs, comparing notes and having a good scratch.

"You have your prescription already?" the one asked.

"Absolutely," said the other. "The bottle's in my suitcase by the front door. I'll start taking 'em the minute," she patted her belly, "Chaz pops out."

"Which one did you go with?"

"Aventyl."

"Really." Not a question. "That's an older one. Why not Celexa or Zoloft?"

"Well, Jeff wants us to breast-feed, and the tricyclics don't get passed through."

"He wants *who* to breast-feed?"

"Us. Well, me, but he said my new girls got us into this and they might as well do us some good while we're here." The woman grinned wickedly and shifted her shoulders to wiggle her improbable cleavage.

"The Golden Rule," agreed the first. "'He Who Has—'"

Then Ross had stood up. "I've gotta go get a drink of water," he said to PJ. And they'd vented back and forth about it all the way home afterwards.

For two expectant mothers, however trashy, to be joking

about taking antidepressants before even being diagnosed—weeks before giving birth, and without experiencing so much as a single symptom—no wonder the medical journals said antidepressants were over-prescribed. It was like the pill bottle was just another fashion accessory for the modern mommy.

On that kind of thinking she and Ross had always agreed. For instance, Ross hated drunks; he'd seen enough of them when he was a bartender in college, but he also had an older cousin who was a severe alcoholic.

Ross had told her his cousin served nine months in Brushy Mountain State Penitentiary after his fifth DUI. It was hard time, sober time, and while he was sweating it out he confessed to a counselor that he mainly drank to keep from hitting his kids. When the counselor asked him why he wanted to hit his kids, he admitted it was because his father had beaten him up when *he* was drinking.

Which was tragic, Ross said, but in his view the whole thing could have been prevented by a whole lot more talk and a whole lot less alcohol.

And that attitude pretty much put him in the Ellen camp, PJ realized. But she was there too, because she and Ross were already girding themselves for the first parent-teacher conference after the twins went to school.

*Lizzie and Baker have ADHD*, they expected to hear. The twins were too smart and energetic for their own good, and their curiosity lit, burned, and fizzled like a kitchen match. But Ross and PJ had sworn—sworn!—that tranquilizers were too high a price for tranquility.

The very notion made PJ angry. And she could only imagine what Bebe would have said about drugging kids.

Or parents, for that matter. PJ knew that if Bebe had popped a pill every time she felt the weight of her cares—tending Grandpa, raising PJ, being estranged from her only daughter, stretching Grandpa's disability check to feed three people—she would have been chugging a gallon of Valium a week. And doubtless she'd have been featured on the cover of the annual shareholders' report of every pharmaceutical company in the United States.

No, Bebe was stronger than that. When she was tired

she fell back on her quilting, her friends, her family, and her faith. That was enough for anyone.

Or ought to be.

*Maybe treatment's right for some people,* PJ reflected as she neared downtown. *And I'd never condemn them for it, but I don't want any part of it for myself. None of it. The counseling, the drugs, the weight gain, the loss of libido. I just don't have time for it, and I've got that libido thing in spades as it is. The pills would just worsen it. Ross tries to be patient, but it'd be the straw on the camel's back.*

If he saw her working on Silver's quilt, it might distract him. For a while. It might give her a little more time.

*Because there's nothing wrong with me that I can't handle myself. So what's a little insomnia? It's not like I'm drowning my kids in the bathtub.*

She sighed, remembering how she'd cried when she'd first heard about the woman who'd done that. But these days that was the category people put you in. They thought you were psychotic, or else just a crybaby. No middle ground.

And "what would the neighbors think?" was only the first reason of many why opening the door to the treatment routine was like inviting a vampire into your home. You had good intentions, but it got horrible in a hurry. There was so much more than just the depression to be afraid of. Libido and weight trouble and negative stereotyping weren't one percent of it.

What if, for instance, it dulled her creativity? She'd heard that antidepressant medication could do that. Writers couldn't write, painters couldn't paint—so she assumed a quilter wouldn't be able to quilt, either.

*Some choice,* she thought. *Take meds and give up quilting, or go on feeling terrible and try to salvage whatever of it I can.*

And then there was this. When Baker and Lizzie were old enough for school, PJ intended to go back to work. What if she found a job that required a security clearance? If she started some sort of treatment she feared she'd never qualify, never be able to look an investigator in the face and deny receiving psychiatric care.

*They might even want to hospitalize me,* she thought. *And checking "yes" next to the question about whether I've ever been confined to a mental hospital would be about as career-enhancing as dyeing my hair plaid and wearing a curtain rod through my nose.*

*But it's not just the job, either. If I go down that road and some quack decides I belong in a hospital, what'll happen to Lizzie and Baker? At the very least, they'll be hearing about "Momma the Crazy Woman." And at worst? The Children's Services bunch might decide to take them away! Put them in a foster home!*

*When you tell the doctor you're feeling bad, that's what you're signing up for. You totally relinquish control. You might as well be saying "Lock me up and take my kids." And I'm not going there. I. Am. Not.*

PJ shook her head angrily. "It's a moot point anyway!" she told herself. "Get over it! You're OK, you've got a great husband, beautiful healthy kids, a gorgeous house, plenty of food, friends, money, all your arms and legs—so give it a rest! Nobody wants to hear it. Nobody! And especially not Ross."

She brought her fist down on the turn signal hard enough to hurt her hand, and wondered what Ellen, with her quilting equals happiness theory, would've said about the trophy-wife scene at the doctor's office. Some quip like: "A genius is always misunderstood, but you can spot an idiot from outer space."

*I just hope I'm not the one being an idiot,* PJ thought. That made her punch the turn signal again.

~

PJ pushed through the door of the old converted warehouse, tinkling the bell, and the smells hit her immediately. Chemical smells; dyes and fabric treatments and linseed oil from the old pine floor. The bolts stood in racks stretching for a hundred feet in each direction, and even at this hour women and stray men milled in the aisles and lingered over the cutting tables. It was all so familiar, all so evocative.

*I feel better already,* she thought.

A Chattanooga socialite named Kelly Green had opened "Kelly Green Drygoods" in 1921. PJ and Kelly Green Shaw, the current owner, had known each other since they'd met in a quilting class together as teenagers in the back room of this very place.

"Hey, Gwynn," she called to a middle-aged woman wearing a lei's worth of measuring tape around her neck. "You seen Kelly?"

Gwynn pointed. "In the back. Hey, how's it going, PJ? Got something new there?" Meaning the shopping bag.

"Fine, fine," PJ said, breezing by. "Look, I'll catch up with you later."

The bolts of cloth were ranked in neat rows, and passing through them reminded her oddly of passing through the rows of white headstones with Bebe, at the Chattanooga National Cemetery, where the Marines had fired a final volley for Grandpa.

Something wrenched in her at the comparison; at how in the weeks following Grandpa's death Bebe had thrown herself into her quilting like she'd once thrown herself into her marriage. It had been a wonderful time for PJ and Bebe, a time of renewal, a time of growing closer. Not a time of mourning at all.

And how they had prowled these floors! "You can handle anything you want, Cupcake," Bebe had told PJ. "You can take it down, unroll it, feel it, smell it..."

For here there was everything. There were fabrics, rough and soft, that you could rub against your face to savor the texture of; imagining the cold winter nights kept at bay not only by the quilt that warmed you, but by the love it was made with, and held. Colors daring and subtle. Solids and patterns and prints, each vivid, each a distinct personality, each with something important to say.

There were whole kaleidoscopes of thread, precisely-organized, sorted in racks by shade as if cast there by a prism in a sunny window. The spools blurred across your vision, a vibrant palette awaiting the needle rather than the brush, hinting of the day the individual colors would assume their function as the binder of all possibilities together into a single magnificent creation.

The shelves held books, not only for reading, but for smelling and feeling. For trailing your fingertips across the smooth pages, your eyes and your mind alive with the knowledge they contained.

And the quilts on the walls. Wow.

PJ and Bebe had found solace here. And bliss.

~

She discovered Kelly at her desk in one corner. Kelly's reading glasses were blue oblongs reflecting the computer she stared at. She chewed a pencil, scribbled something on a notepad, and frowned.

"Hi, Kelly," PJ said shyly. "How's business?"

"Bad," Kelly said, not looking up.

"Sounds familiar."

"Well," said Kelly, "I could start griping about big-box stores, but that doesn't get my tax return done." She set down the pencil. "So what's up? I haven't seen you in a while. We were wondering if you'd dropped off the face of the earth. The twins keeping you busy?"

"I can't even tell you." *Thank God,* PJ thought. *Once again, the twins save me from having to start in with the excuses.*

"Yeah, I'm sure," said Kelly, who was childless by choice. They were of an age together, and PJ remembered Kelly's lectures on the senselessness of PJ abandoning her career just to add to the planet's population load.

But even as an engineer, and despite her current problems, PJ had never understood why anyone would reduce the idea of motherhood to cold arithmetic. When it came to emotion PJ was an artist. Kelly remained a businesswoman, an accountant. And that was the difference between them.

You could see it in their quilting styles. PJ's was visionary and Kelly's was calculated. It explained why there had always been a slight coolness between them, a faint tension. Not enough to divide them, but enough to signal Kelly that PJ's presence at her desk meant something unusual was going on.

Kelly was clicking her keyboard. "You see the new sign? On the back room?"

"No," PJ said, turning.

Down the way, on the steel door PJ had pushed open uncountable times, hung a quilted sign in a frame:

BLOCKHEADS ONLY
EVERYONE WELCOME

"That's a hoot," she said. "When did you guys put that up?"

Kelly's eyes were still fixed on the screen. "Last spring. My idea."

"Nice. Has it been a whole year?" PJ asked, mentally kicking herself for falling into it again.

"Yup." Kelly hit the return button, sighed, and looked up at last. "OK. What's in the bag, dude?"

~

They stood at one of the cutting tables and spread out the old quilt.

PJ glanced around nervously. She knew full well that there were no strangers in a quilt shop. To unroll your work on a table was to invite people to inspect it. To ask for praise, and criticism. She didn't want to go there.

"Um, I want you to know that I didn't make this," she said.

"I already figured that," Kelly said dryly. "The seams— what is this?"

PJ told the story. "I don't understand this thing," she concluded. "What is it? Where's it from? You know fabric better than anyone I've ever met. So I thought—"

She broke off. Kelly was staring into PJ's eyes with a strange intensity.

"Thank you," Kelly said. "Really. Thank you." She held PJ's gaze for a long moment and then returned her attention to the quilt.

"OK, here's what I see. First of all, this is handmade. My guess is by—"

"A man," PJ finished.

"Well, two men, maybe," Kelly chuckled. "Some good stitching, some bad. But it's a type of stitch I'm not used to—seems way overdone for simple seams."

Kelly took a white glove from her pocket and slipped it on and rolled the quilt between her fingers. "The batting is lumped up like natural cotton. Hard to tell what kind without opening it up, which I hesitate to do. The stitching is silk thread—a heavier gauge than I'm used to seeing in quilts, though. More like something you'd see in a performance fabric, but then why wouldn't the maker use a synthetic? What it tells me is that this was made of what was available, not what might have been, I don't know, desired?"

"Interesting," said PJ. She hadn't made that connection.

"Moving on to the fabric," said Kelly. "It's like, every scrap in the basket. And then some. Naturals and synthetics and every blend in between. There's no order to it—color or pattern or anything. It's chaotic. Maybe that was the point, I don't know. That'd be more your department."

PJ kept silent.

"Oh. Here's some polyester. So this is 1940s or later, or at least it was put together after then. And a lot of these colors look military. Olive drab and grey; stuff I'm not that familiar with. Maybe it was sold before my time. And some of it's starting to rot. It's old; keep it away from sunlight and make sure you store it in acid-free paper. Think about rolling it instead of folding it. And I wouldn't handle it without gloves on. Especially with these stains on it."

"But the piece that jumps out at me," Kelly continued, "is this one." She set the pencil down, leaned closer to the piece she'd indicated, and reached into her shirt pocket and took out a magnifying glass and peered through it.

"See for yourself," she said, handing PJ the glass.

PJ did so while Kelly explained. "That's hand-woven silk, probably from China. Very old, I'd say. See that faded pink? Probably a vegetable dye, it would have been bright red when it was made. It's also hand-embroidered, by the way, in what I'm guessing was bright yellow. I don't recognize the—whaddaya call 'em—ideograms, because I don't read Chinese, but I'm sure you could get someone to translate them. Good luck, or something. Moo Goo Gai Pan. But that's not what's weird."

"What's weird, then?" asked PJ.

"What's weird is why it's in this quilt at all. That square of silk is worth several hundred dollars, even in the sorry condition it's in. It's a highly collectible piece of folk art."

PJ was shocked. She'd never have imagined it, not even if she'd recognized the piece as different from all the others. They were *all* different, that was the problem. "Are you serious?" she asked.

"Yup. So here's the question," Kelly said, tapping the pencil on the table. "Why would someone with hundreds of dollars to spend on a nice piece of antique handmade silk turn around and trash it by sewing it to all this other stuff? Why wouldn't they just buy some nice new fabric off the shelf, and use that?"

"It's a mystery, isn't it?" said PJ.

Kelly folded her arms. "PJ, I look at quilts every day. Dozens of them. And this is easily, easily, the most unusual one I've ever seen. You have to figure this out—there's a heck of a story in here somewhere."

"I know," PJ said, feeling, for the first time, a true sense of intrigue. "I know. But I can't get a handle on it."

"Well," sighed Kelly, "some us are getting together on Thursday to baste a quilt for Sondra—maybe what you ought to do is bring this by. The military-looking stuff might be familiar to some of the girls. Flo, maybe, her husband was in World War II, I think."

PJ lifted an eyebrow. "You haven't been talking to Ross, have you?"

Kelly appeared puzzled. "Your husband? No. Why?"

▶▶▶◆◀◀◀
## Chapter Five

Early Thursday afternoon PJ was futzing around in the kitchen, absent-mindedly worrying how she'd explain her long absence to the Blockheads that night, when Baker meandered in.

He was glazed toe-to-crown with what might have been white icing, except it had a vaguely plastic sheen. He'd left a footpath of it on the hardwood floor, and even now he was reaching a gooey hand towards—

"Baker, stop!" she cried.

His eyes sprang full of tears. She raced over. "What have you gotten into this time? You're supposed to be in the back yard with Lizzie!"

"Toothpaste," he said. He spread his sticky hands in the universal the-fish-was-this-big gesture.

"Toothpaste?" she repeated, thinking: *Great. If Ross thinks a little mystery is what I need to spice up my life, he oughtta see what Detective Hathaway has to deal with around here every day.*

She knelt and thumbed a smudge of the stuff off Baker's cheek. It smelled somehow familiar. Chemical, maybe. Then it hit her.

"Have you been playing in the garage? Around Daddy's workbench? Is that where you found the toothpaste? In a little gun contraption, about this big?" She spread her hands in the same gesture Baker had made.

"Uh-huh," Baker nodded. "The talking gun."

"CAULKing gun, Baker," she snapped. "Oh, Lord. Did you eat any?"

"No, Momma!"

"But Baker, why were you even in there? You know you're not supposed to…"

His lip trembled. "I was just tryinta help."

PJ lowered her head and cursed herself.

"OK, OK," she said. "We'll handle that later. For now let's get you out of these clothes, little man."

~

She stripped him, dumped him in the bathroom, threatened him with five kinds of kiddie-horror if he touched so much as a single thing, and corralled Lizzie in the TV room.

*Just when I think I'm getting my act together, something like this happens.*

And then—as she sat fuming for minute after minute on the edge of the tub gripping Baker in place with one hand and impatiently checking the water with the other—she realized she might as well shut the hot water faucet off. She could sit here the rest of the month and she wouldn't get any. The hot water heater had apparently chosen this very day to give up the ghost. She'd been running the washing machine since morning and she must have run the last of the hot water out of it.

*This is gonna cost somebody a foot rub,* she thought bravely. She felt like screaming.

"All right, Baker," she said. "No time-out, this time. You're getting the cold bath treatment instead. I'll try to make it quick, but I don't want to hear any complaining."

~

When was it she'd noticed the water was getting slow to heat up? *Weeks ago,* she realized. She should have said something to Ross; they could have fixed it already. Dumb mistake. She really didn't need another thing to cope with this afternoon, when she was already so wound up.

She'd been counting on mommy-time at the Y today, too, so she could run for a few miles and work the tension out. But now she had to stay home and play handy woman.

*Well,* PJ thought, *for once I get to put my degree to work on one of these everyday train wrecks.*

She thought through the problem and decided it was probably a burned-out heating element. She fetched the tool tray from the garage, went to the utility room, and jimmied the cover plates off the water heater to reveal the heating elements and the wiring. She guessed that all she had to do was test the electrical resistance of each element with a multimeter. If one or both of them gave a bad reading, she could pop down to the home center for a replacement.

Otherwise, they might have to get a whole new unit, to the tune of several hundred bucks. Which would make Ross fret; he always fretted about unexpected expenses.

*Before I check the elements, though, I ought to make sure the heater itself is getting enough power. Should be two-twenty.*

It was a live circuit, so she inspected everything thrice like she'd been taught in school. The multimeter was set correctly, the circuit breaker was functional, the wires were connected, nothing looked burnt or shorted—all was good.

*Here we go,* PJ thought. She reached out with the probes to test the first pair of wires.

There was a blinding silver flash, a flat impersonal WAP!—and at the same instant everything went black. She lay on her back, stunned, confused, the multimeter hot in her hand. The utility room was stone-dark. From elsewhere in the house she heard Lizzie and Baker start to cry.

*What just happened? Am I OK?*

She stood up in the darkness, knees wobbling, and felt for the wall. She followed it to the door, opened it. Light from the kitchen windows flooded the room.

Her glasses were knocked askew. She straightened

them with a shaky hand and wondered what she'd done wrong.

The multimeter was still warm. She looked stupidly at it and saw that the needle point of one of the test probes was fused into a ball of slag and charred plastic.

*Holy crap! I shorted it! Tripped the main circuit breaker, too!*

And now she could see that she'd had the multimeter set up incorrectly all along. She'd plugged the test probe into the wrong socket on it, an unfused one that was rated for far less current that had actually passed through it. Which meant that she'd been holding a live circuit in the palm of her hand. Two hundred and twenty volts. Zap.

*I checked it three times,* she remembered.

PJ started shivering.

~

"And that's why I'm not going tonight," she told Ross after he got home. "I've been tied up in knots over this guild meeting all day and now I just can't deal with it anymore. I've got enough to worry about as it is. I'll be so preoccupied that I'll crash on the way there or something."

"Wow," he said. He was still in his suit, holding Lizzie in one arm and Baker in the other.

"I feel like an idiot," she carried on. "I could have blown my hand off! That's what I get for trying to accomplish something. I take a bad situation and make it worse—what am I good for? Some electrical engineer, huh? Why did I even go to college? And now I'm a mess, I can't shower, I was still washing clothes—and I think we're going to have to replace the whole hot water heater. I'm so sorry."

Ross set the kids down and picked up the ruined multimeter from the counter. He frowned. "PJ, what were you thinking? Could this not have waited until I got home?"

It stunned her. "Ross, I didn't want you to have to deal with this!"

"I appreciate that, but it's not like mowing the grass or something. Hand, nothing. You could have been killed!"

She put her fists on her hips. "I am perfectly capable," she stated, "of fixing a hot water heater."

He spread his hands helplessly. "You are?"

~

PJ sat on the back porch and sipped iced tea and nibbled a sandwich. The swing set seemed oddly still, now, with the kids gone. Ross had dressed Baker down about the Talking Gun, but when the snuffling had subsided he sighed and told PJ he was taking the twins to the pizza arcade. He said he was trying to make the best of the hot water situation, but PJ knew better.

*I wish I could be a better wife to him,* she thought. *He deserves so much better.* She mentally added her freak-out to her tally of the times she'd let him down.

*I'll make it all right someday. I swear I will. And I can start by taking care of that hot water heater tomorrow. But I'll have the store put it in instead of trying it myself.*

"Because I need to fast on the home repairs for a while," she said aloud.

And she smiled sadly. Bebe's words, coming unbidden to her lips.

What exactly had Bebe said that one time? When her eyes were bothering her and PJ was trying to coax her outside for some fresh air?

"Oh, I think I'll fast on the exercise today, Cupcake," she'd said. That was it. And Bebe had chuckled, surely recognizing the absurdity in passing vice off as virtue. Though nobody had ever accused Bebe of laziness. Even towards the end there, she'd never rested, never given an inch.

"There's no seam allowance in real life, Cupcake," she'd cough.

It was another of her pet phrases, one that had baffled PJ at first, back when she was a sixth-grader and barely knew which was the needle's eye and which was its point.

"What's a seam allowance, Bebe?" PJ asked. She was hunched over the kitchen table with scissors and template plastic, laboring to cut out a square exactly two inches on a side—which was much harder than it sounded. PJ sat before a heap of failures, each lopsided or jagged-edged.

"When you're quilting you leave yourself a little slack," Bebe explained. "Around the outside. Since you're working on a nine-patch pattern, you make each of your squares a quarter-inch too big, all the way around. That quarter-inch is where you sew them together. Then when you've used up your seam allowance what you have left over is a tic-tac-toe board of nine two-inch squares. And that's your block."

"Oh, I see," said PJ. "The extra gets hidden."

"Right!" Bebe turned back to the bowl and kept talking as she cranked her old hand-mixer. "It's tempting, if you have a little trouble getting the dimensions exactly right, to try to hide the difference in the seam allowance. And you can get away with that for a while—it's an easy shortcut. But it's a bad habit. You get lazy and the quality of your work goes to pot."

PJ held the ruler to the template paper and squinted through her glasses at the line she'd drawn. "Why would anyone do that?" she asked.

"You'll find out," Bebe chuckled as she set the mixer down. She opened the cabinet door and brought out a baking tray. "How many blocks are there in this quilt you're making?"

"Nine."

"And how many pieces of fabric are in each block?"

"Nine more."

"OK, so how many two-and-a-half inch pieces do you have to cut, total?"

"Eighty-one?"

"Eighty-one," said Bebe. "And how many times have you tried to cut a square that size, and not been able to do it?" She started setting little foil cups in the tray.

"Oh," said PJ, suddenly daunted. "I get it now."

"PJ, there are so many ways to hide your mistakes in a quilt," Bebe said. "And nobody'll know they're there except you. But you'll know, won't you?"

PJ put the scissors down. "Bebe, it sounds like you're saying I have to do everything perfectly!"

"No, no, that's not what I'm saying at all." Bebe finished

pouring batter into the cups and wiped her hands on her apron. "There's an old story that Amish women always make one mistake in a quilt, on purpose. Because there's only ever been one perfect person."

She set the tray in the oven. "So saying there's no seam allowance in real life is just a way of reminding you to keep trying your best because you can't always count on hiding what you do wrong. And you should always try to do better. If you're going to be a good quilter, that's what you ought to remember."

~

PJ still had that little lap quilt. It was her first one, that she'd made when she was—how old? In junior high, and certainly before Grandpa had died. Making it had taken her months and had cost her a bathtub's worth of tears. She'd done it entirely by hand, at Bebe's insistence. That was how you learned the fundamentals. But PJ was very fond of it, despite its flaws.

She got up from the Adirondack chair and went into the house and brought the quilt down from the top shelf of her sewing closet. It was twenty-plus years old now. She stroked its fabric, ran her fingers along its wandering seams and uncertain stitches.

It was more than a quilt to her. It was the first hesitant song of a young girl exploring her own voice.

*I wish I could hear Bebe's voice now,* she thought. *What would she say if she were here?*

▶▶▶◆◀◀◀
## Chapter Six

A nd shortly thereafter PJ Hathaway found herself standing at the steel door in Kelly Green Drygoods. Late, of course. Not to mention annoyed by her own wishy-washiness. She was still getting over the afternoon's catastrophe, and the sign on the door seemed less like a hoot and more like a big wet raspberry:

BLOCKHEADS ONLY
EVERYONE WELCOME

*Kelly might as well have added a third line,* she thought. *"ESPECIALLY THOSE NAMED PJ."*

The door was propped open slightly; the room had high ceilings but it had always been stuffy in there. And she could hear the girls talking as they worked.

"Heavens to Murgatroyd," Ellen Sanders was sighing in frustration.

"I've always wondered who Murgatroyd was," said a familiar voice. Missy Rogers?

Ellen's voice brightened. "Well, it's originally a Gilbert and Sullivan reference, from an opera they did back in 1881, called *Ruddigore*

"Ellen, how do you find this stuff out?" asked Missy.

"I mean, you don't look old enough to have been there yourself, but—"

Other women in the room laughed.

"Well, when Isaac Singer and I were inventing the sewing machine," Ellen started.

"No, no, now, you're not getting that one by us," said Missy. "Everyone knows Isaac Singer didn't invent—"

*The Missy and Ellen show,* PJ remembered. *One more thing that will never change.* She swallowed butterflies and pushed the door open.

"Hi, everyone," she called out.

There were six or eight of the girls around the big cutting table at the center of the room. They'd been working on something but now they each sat there, still and silent, eyes on her.

*Uh-oh,* PJ thought.

She'd always figured a good quilting group was like a good quilt; you stood back and took the whole of it in, and then you moved closer and considered its various parts. You might find flaws at both levels, but in general you'd discover interesting individuals celebrating their unity. And the flaws, if any, would be part of the celebration too. Maybe even the focus of it.

*But do they see how flawed I am, right now?*

She was on the verge of bolting when Ellen clapped her hands. "Outstanding! I was just telling everyone I thought we'd be seeing you before too much longer! Did you open it?"

Before PJ could answer, Nadine pounced. "PJ Hathaway! Get in here and let me hug your neck, girl!" And she did so—giving PJ a sturdy, country girl arm-clamping that squeezed her from a size eight to a size six.

"Um," she began, wanting to protest that she could only stay for a few minutes. But all of them—Ellen, Missy, Kelly, Sondra, Naomi, Flo, Nadine, and a young woman PJ didn't recognize—were talking a mile-a-minute and she couldn't jam a word in edgewise. She was the uneasy center of a happy hurricane.

When the storm subsided, Sondra gave her a pincushion and PJ took it gently, being careful of Sondra's gnarled fingers. PJ joined them at the cutting table and they finished pinning together the three layers of a Scotty Dog quilt Sondra said she'd been laboring over for months.

It was pleasant work and conversation; the girls were clearly curious why she'd been gone so long but they were too polite to ask. But not too polite to wonder, she realized, because they kept sneaking looks at her.

PJ focused on the room instead of the people. She'd missed this space—the red-brick walls, the pine floor, the many tables and chairs, the cozy kitchenette, the quilts on the walls.

Someone asked about the twins, so PJ told the story of Baker and the Talking Gun and the near-zizzing she'd endured. It kicked off a long round of recollections about children and their hardware-related shenanigans. A safe subject.

Naomi, who was home-schooling her grandchildren, said she could top the Talking Gun story. "PJ, I was upstairs one afternoon and heard this awful racket—over the noise of my sewing machine, mind you—and I ran down and found my grandson ripping up the sidewalk with a hammer-drill. Kids and tools do not mix! No ma'am, no way."

"I bet Lizzie could handle a scissor," Ellen said. "Where is she? I thought you might bring her when you came back."

"'A scissor?'" Missy repeated. "Why not give her the whole pair?"

"Their dad took them to the pizza place," PJ said. "The one with the mechanical kangaroo."

"That place ought to hand out hearing protection," muttered Kelly.

"What they ought to hand out is Pepto," said Naomi.

And then the new girl spoke up. Crystal Hodges, she'd said her name was. She was young, early twenties, dressed in a headscarf, a tie-dye that crossed PJ's eyes, and an ankle-length khaki skirt.

"I'm sorry to ask like this," Crystal said, "but did you and your husband split the blanket?"

Ellen put down her pincushion; some of the other girls glanced away.

PJ pushed her glasses back up her nose. "I'm sorry?"

"Well," said Crystal, "you just said 'their dad.' That's the same thing my mom does when she talks to me about my dad—she calls him 'your dad' instead of 'my ex-husband' or 'James.' It drives me crazy when she does that—like she's saying he was just a donor or something. As if they were never a couple, you know?"

"Um, no, things are great between us," said PJ. "I'm sorry, I didn't mean to give you—"

Crystal waved a hand. "Forget it, my bad. I'm still getting to know everyone."

"Had a fight with him, though, didn't you?" Ellen jumped in. "I thought so. Bet he didn't want you to come tonight."

"Men," said Missy.

"No!" PJ protested. "That wasn't it! It was—dammit, Ellen! Was that another one of your trick questions?"

"Crystal," interrupted Nadine, "I know this is the first time you've met PJ, but you've heard us talking about her work, right?" She didn't wait for the answer, but glanced back and forth between Ellen and Missy.

PJ's ears burned. *Oh, this is swell. What else have they been talking about? Ross is gonna choke when he hears the girls thought we'd split up.*

And then the thought cut through her: *Or will he?*

Crystal nodded. "I've seen her work. At the Hunter Museum." She turned to PJ. "That memorial quilt you did for your grandmother was the grooviest I've ever seen. I stood in front of it for hours..."

PJ closed her eyes and took a deep breath. "Thank you, really, but I have to get home soon, I'm beat, and I need to show you guys something. I just got a quilt in the mail, and—"

"There was a quilt in there?" Ellen asked. "Nice! Listen, you all, this was the strangest thing. We got this package at the post office that was addressed to Bebe, and—"

"To Bebe, PJ?" asked Flo.

"Yes ma'am," PJ said, a bit surprised. Flo never interrupted anyone, ever. PJ called her "ma'am" because she couldn't imagine addressing her any other way. Florence Geary was the eldest among them; a true

Southern matriarch who'd followed her husband of forty-seven years on preaching tours and mission trips all over the world.

"Why don't you let PJ tell it, then," Flo said gently to Ellen.

"Well, that's true," said Ellen. "I don't know the ending, do I?"

~

They stood around the cutting table together in silence.

An old quilt usually evoked reverence, PJ had observed. Even from people who weren't quilters. To be in the presence of a *made thing* spoke to something in the instinct, something hardwired into the brain stem.

"What do you think, Flo?" asked Kelly, pointing first to one piece and then another and another. "Are these military fabrics?"

Flo stroked her chin and nodded. "They do look familiar. My Walter went through a lot of uniforms when he served—I was forever having to let them out or hem them up for him because they only issued them in two sizes."

"Too large and too—" began Ellen.

"We get it," said Missy.

"I'll buy that, Flo," PJ said. "Maybe Silver was an old buddy of my grandpa's or something. From Korea."

"That could be," Flo nodded. Then she folded her arms and her face grew very thoughtful. Her eyes seemed to turn inward, and she frowned at the floor.

"That's an old cotton bandanna," said Crystal. She covered her mouth with a hand and laughed. "PJ, I shop in vintage clothing stores a lot and I'd swear that one's from an old pair of panties. Kind of naughty, too, for back then."

"Eew," said Nadine, and they all laughed.

"Do you still have some of Walter's things?" Kelly asked Flo. "We could compare them." Kelly moved closer to her. "Flo? Did you hear me?"

Flo shook her head. "I'm sorry."

"I was asking if you still had some of Walter's old uniforms."

"I believe so," said Flo. "What about you, PJ? Did Bebe keep any of your grandfather's things?"

"If she did, I wouldn't know where they are," PJ said. "I don't remember moving them into our house."

Flo still seemed far away. When she spoke again her voice was warm, as usual, but it also carried a subtone of reluctance.

"What do you know about the Korean War, PJ?" she asked. "About what they went through over there?"

"I guess," PJ said slowly, "that those of you who knew my grandpa already know the answer to that."

"The 'Frozen Chosin,' right?" said Ellen.

"The who?" asked Missy.

"The cold," Ellen said.

"Yes," Flo agreed. "The cold."

*The cold,* PJ remembered. *Of course.*

~

"It's finished," she'd said, looking down at the little nine-patch quilt where it lay across her skinny knees. She'd just put the final stitch in the binding and tied the last knot and cut the thread. "At least I think it's finished."

Bebe came and sat beside her on the couch. She ran a hand across the quilt and then squeezed PJ's leg.

"It's finished, PJ," said Bebe. "And it's beautiful. Your first of many. I'm so proud of you."

"You think I should give it to him now?"

"I think you should," Bebe said. "We'll go up together."

Grandpa was sitting alone in his room. The radio played softly and he was staring through the window at where withered leaves skittered through the dead garden, hugging himself and rocking slowly.

"David?" Bebe called. "Are you warm enough, David?"

Grandpa turned and smiled in utter joy, as seeing old friends for the first time in years. "I'm all right," he said. "I was just wondering what happened to the garden."

But PJ knew the truth: Grandpa was never warm enough. You could pile blankets on him until his bed looked like an Indian mound and still he'd tremble with cold.

"I made this for you, Grandpa," she said. She knelt and spread the quilt across his lap.

Grandpa reached down and touched her hair, put his palm on top of her head. "Bless your heart, Cupcake," he said. Then he smoothed the quilt over himself and buried his hands under it.

"Do you like it?" PJ asked.

"Mmmmmm," he sighed.

~

"So maybe somebody made this quilt to keep warm in Korea," PJ thought aloud. "They didn't have much to work with, so they used what they could. Scraps from their clothes. A handkerchief. Whatever they had."

Kelly nodded. "I told you there was a great story in here."

"But panties?" said Crystal.

"And antique Chinese silk?" said Sondra.

"It's not much of a theory, but it's the only one I've got," PJ said.

Nadine was shaking her head. "Ya'll—I agree, it's just a bunch of conjecture. It don't make sense. Why would somebody make a blanket for themselves if they were in the service? The Marine Corps wouldn't send 'em in without tents and sleeping bags. Wouldn't the standard-issue have been better than this thing?"

PJ considered Nadine's question. "My Grandpa David," she finally said, "was a prisoner of war."

No one spoke.

"Conjecture or not," Flo said finally, "when I hear you say that, and I think this quilt might have been all somebody had against those winters, it makes me want to pray irregardless."

"Yes, ma'am," said PJ. "Yes, ma'am, it does."

▶▶▶◆◀◀◀
## Chapter Seven

PJ peeled the twins off each other yet again, and she leaned on the grocery cart while she studied the table of bananas. There were something like four hundred different bunches but none was distinguishable from any other. All she saw was a big yellow blur.

*How do they expect you to choose?* she wondered. She'd never felt this tired in her life.

It was Black Friday in the Week of Whatever Color was Darker than Black. Eight days since she'd ruined the hot water heater, but the installer kept putting her off about the new one. Lizzie had come down with a forty-eight hour virus and had thrown up to the point of dehydration, so they'd been to the doctor twice in three days. Baker was due for the same thing any moment now, and PJ dreaded that she and Ross might get it too. And as an extra-added bonus, the IRS had sent them a letter—something about a missing form—so besides working late, Ross was having to stay up late at home every night trying to sort it out.

And next week he was off to Roanoke for four days.

PJ groaned when her cell phone shattered her daze.

"Yes," she said into the mouthpiece.

"PJ!" exclaimed Ellen. "Where were you last—"

*This I cannot deal with,* PJ thought. She hung up. That

was one more thing—the Blockheads had held their main monthly meeting and she'd skipped it. A scolding from Ellen was the last thing in the world she had energy for.

*How am I supposed to worry about Silver's quilt and what my grandpa went through, when the real war is being fought right here with these kids in front of this banana table? It's the Battle of Chiquita Hill, for crying out loud!*

The phone rang again. And kept ringing. Ellen rang in six more times that morning, until PJ finally turned the phone off.

~

The first time she remembered being stressed out like this was in high school. She'd had a horrible realization, and it had come to a head one Sunday afternoon, when she and Bebe had gone to see Aunt Carol at the public nursing home.

She and Bebe were sewing, and Aunt Carol was pretending to. Mostly, though, Aunt Carol was trying to breathe. Her emphysema had gone hideous and she was what the staff called "between roommates." It meant the stranger who shared Aunt Carol's living space had suffered a nasty late-night heart attack, and if she'd been wheeled out alive it was only because there wasn't a doctor available on short notice to declare her dead.

PJ kept trying not to look at the empty bed. It was still aslant of the wall and there were latex gloves and clear plastic wrappers and glass ampules scattered all over.

"When did that happen?" she asked.

"Fri-Friday," said Aunt Carol.

PJ put down her work. "I can't stand looking at that any more," she said. She got up and stripped the sheets off the bed and dumped them in the doorside hamper, and started collecting the trash."

"Thank you, PJ, that's sweet," Bebe said. "I'm sure the staff is busy."

"Hmmph," said Aunt Carol. "Three-Packs-A-Day and I-Hate-My-Boyfriend are probably watching...watching their soaps."

PJ tidied plastic cups off the nightstand and noticed something. "Did your roommate not have any family?" she asked Aunt Carol. "I don't see any pictures."

"Not that she ever mentioned."

"Poor woman," said Bebe. "Can you imagine that? All alone?"

Aunt Carol shook her head. "I thank God every day for you two. PJ, listen to me. Take care...of your money; don't end up in a place like...this."

"Oh, it's not so bad," said Bebe.

"Elizabeth," Aunt Carol interrupted. "Stop it. There's no...silver lining to look for."

PJ turned away from them to straighten the empty bed. It was on casters and maybe she shoved it too hard, because it thumped the wall, startling Bebe and Aunt Carol. PJ put her hand over her mouth and tried not to cry.

Bebe stood up and came to her. "What is it?"

"I might as well move in today," PJ said.

"What? Why?" said Carol.

PJ turned to Aunt Carol. "Take care of what money?" she asked. "I'm not going to college—they don't give scholarships for quilting, you know—and I'm gonna wind up married to some guy who sacks groceries for a living."

"We may not be able to send you to Harvard, Cupcake," said Bebe, "but there's always a way."

"I should have run track or been a cheerleader," PJ said. She pulled a tissue from the box on Aunt Carol's nightstand and wiped her eyes. "I'm sorry, this isn't the right time for this."

"I didn't realize you were this worried," Bebe said. "You make good grades and I'm sure there are loan programs."

PJ waved a hand. "Forget it."

"No, this is important," said Aunt Carol. "You're right, PJ. Women...women my age got called uppity if they went to...college. Boys wouldn't come near you...who'd want a woman smarter than he was?" She stopped to cough. "Then you grew up and they called you...an old maid. Always seemed stupid...to me."

PJ sat on the edge of Aunt Carol's bed and took her hand. "What am I supposed to do?" PJ asked.

"You can make a living quilting…if you work at it hard enough," said Carol. "See if the Greens'll hire you at the fabric store. Teach classes…Lord knows you're good enough. You'll find something…I know it." She laughed weakly. "You have this talent…stick with it and they'll come to you."

*Maybe it's true,* PJ reflected. She *was* getting recognized already. She'd been in the newspaper a couple of times for her work—how many teenagers won quilting shows, even local ones?

But then again, the whole school knew her as "the quilting geek." It wasn't the kind of attention anyone would crave. The boys, especially the popular ones, confused her. They'd put her down and then she'd catch them watching her with that peculiar hungry look. It was upsetting; if they liked her, they needed to like her for who she was and what she did, and not because her fanny looked good in crummy thrift store jeans.

It made her want to disappear, because the attention from the adults and from the boys made the attention from the girls that much more horrible. There was a stall in the upstairs girl's room where someone had written "QUILTED BY PJ WARNER" above the toilet paper dispenser. Three careless words dismissing years of hard work.

"I don't know," PJ said. "I don't feel like it's getting me anywhere."

Aunt Carol rolled her eyes. "If you have one thing…you can do better than anyone else…you'll never go hungry."

Bebe nodded. "And you'll always have a place you can go when you need sanctuary."

"Right," said Aunt Carol. She chuckled. "You should see…how much we sew around here. There's always someone sewing or…knitting or something. You wake up and you feel a little short of breath…you reach for the needle and thread. We ought to start a factory."

Her laughter trailed off into a fit of coughing.

~

"It's scary when I can't reach you all day," Ross said. He

crunched a fish stick from the plate she'd left for him in the oven. "You know?"

PJ draped the dishtowel over the drainer and leaned against the kitchen counter. "I have eleven missed phone calls from Ellen Sanders. Three from you. And a couple more, I have no idea from who. If this keeps up I'm gonna need my own call center."

"Eleven calls?"

"Apparently Flo brought some of her husband's things to the meeting."

"And you skipped it. Ouch. But what if the plumber tried to call?"

"I gave him your number."

Ross nodded, but his face was stiff. "OK. I've said my piece." He carried his plate to the table and unzipped his laptop case. "Anyway, I called because I had something I wanted you to see."

"Good news?" she asked hopefully. *And what are the chances of that?*

"Yeah, sort of. Come over here and look."

She sat next to him as he typed an address into his web browser. "It's a Korean War Veterans network," he explained.

*Now watch him figure the whole thing out in three minutes,* PJ thought. *Of course I told him what the girls came up with, but I never meant for him to...*

She frowned. "There's no Chiquita Hill in there, is there?" she asked to hide her frustration.

"Hmm?" He shook his head. "Maybe. I don't know; I'm still looking through it. But you know what it does have?"

"What?"

"A POW database. And I found your grandfather in it."

"Show me," she said.

~

NAME: WARNER, DAVID FRANCIS
FROM: CHATTANOOGA TN
STATUS: POW
WAR: KOREAN

UNIT: 3/1 1ST MAR DIV
GRADE: O-3
DOB: 6/16/27
INCIDENT DATE: 11/23/50
CAMP: 5 PYOK-TONG
RELEASE/REPATRIATION DATE: 1954
DOD: 10/14/87
DEC: NC

"That's exactly right," she said. "Camp Five, Pyok-Tong; that's where they released him from."

Ross blew a long whistle. "Twenty-three. What were you and I doing at that age? Drinking beer on the beach? But then I bet they knew all about beer and beaches."

"Mmm," said PJ, remembering what a teetotaler Bebe had been.

"But what's this?" Ross asked. "DEC: NC?"

"That's his Navy Cross, I think."

"Oh, of course. Yeah. You know, when you think about what these guys went through you get a lot less impressed with yourself for having the guts to get up and face your boss on Monday morning."

PJ nodded. "Bebe always said he deserved the Medal of Honor. But they didn't hand out the Navy Cross for getting up in the morning, either." *Or for buying bananas or taking showers in cold water,* she thought.

"Well, do this," she said. "Do a search on the name 'Silver.'"

"That's the bad news I was getting to," he said. "I tried that already."

"Do it again."

NO RESULTS FOUND, said the screen.

"S. Ilver? Sil Ver?"

Ross typed and shrugged. "No results. It's interesting stuff, but it seems like a dead end."

"It's all dead ends," PJ said. "I'm tempted just to forget it."

He fiddled with the keyboard. "There's something you haven't tried."

"What's that?"

"Call your mom."

"No, thanks," PJ said. "And ask her what? Who's Silver? Did you take Grandpa's Marine Corps stuff to San Diego? Do you know who might've mailed a quilt to your dead mother that had a pair of panties sewn into it?"

"Sure. Why not? Your grandpa made it through a prison camp, so—"

PJ breathed deeply. "Ross, you're pushing me."

He stared into her eyes for quite a spell. "More than you push yourself?" Then he picked up her phone and held it out to her.

*He doesn't get it at all,* PJ thought. *When did Ross stop understanding me?*

~

"Do you really think you understand what it's gonna take to do this?" Scott Walsh, the nursing home director, asked PJ. She and Bebe and Walsh were sitting in his office—or vacant bedroom, really, for it was the same sort of beige-on-cinderblock box the residents lived in, only with a desk and a lonely silk ficus tree instead of hospital beds.

He adjusted his tie. "Don't get me wrong, I think it's a great idea. Smart. We're always looking for ways to keep our clients and their families involved with each other. People drop their, quote, loved ones off, and, well…" He held up his hands. "They never come back."

"That's not love," Bebe said.

PJ sensed the vehemence behind Bebe's gentle tone, but she didn't have time to think about it. Walsh was leaning towards her, about to ask her another question. She clutched the file folder in her lap and fought down the sick feeling in her stomach.

"I agree, and I hate it," Walsh said. "What I need to know, PJ, is this. I don't mean any disrespect, now, but you're seventeen and you're a pretty girl. I've seen it before that people come in with some new program, and they run it for a month or two, but then life gets in the way and they stop showing up. And it's always a big letdown for everyone. So how do I know that's not going to happen here? I could see you getting a new boyfriend or whatever, and losing interest."

"Well," said Bebe, "you don't have to worry about PJ losing interest in quilting, that's for sure."

"Mmm," said Walsh. "It's not really about the quilting, it's about the people. PJ, you're asking for a lot of responsibility. More than you realize, I think. With some of our residents, if you get them worked up and then don't follow through, it might be too much. They've already lost so many things. Do you understand what I'm saying?"

"Mr. Walsh," PJ said. "I can do this. Family is the most important thing in the world to me. I'll keep coming for my Aunt Carol, if for no other reason."

"Have you worked with senior citizens before?"

"It depends on what you mean by 'senior citizens,'" she said. "I don't have a lot of friends my age. I started quilting when I was—what, Bebe, in grade school?"

"About that," said Bebe.

"So I've always been around older women. Most of them much older. I think the average quilter is in her fifties."

"You seem pretty mature," he admitted. "What about materials? The home can't buy them, and I doubt many of the residents can. You're most likely going to have to bring them in yourself."

PJ nodded. "The people who own Kelly Green Drygoods—you know the place?"

He shrugged.

"Anyway, they're friends of ours and they said they could help us out with donations. Mr. Walsh, these quilts aren't going to be that expensive to make."

"OK," he said. "I like the sound of that. Show me the pictures."

PJ opened the file folder. "These are some family tree quilts I've seen before. Some of them are a lot more elaborate than what I want to help everyone make; I was thinking a lap-quilt size, or something that could be put in a standard frame."

She waited as Walsh studied the pictures. "They're beautiful," he said. "I like this one—it must have been a big family. It takes up the whole quilt. What is that, an oak?"

"Funny thing about that one," PJ said. "The woman who made it traced her genealogy back to French nobility, and the family crest did have an oak tree on it. Pretty cool, huh?"

"It is." Walsh pinched his lip between his fingers for a while. "How did you get interested in this stuff, PJ? Most girls your age aren't spending their free time taking pictures of quilts and working on program proposals for nursing homes. They're—hmm. What are they doing? Come to think of it, I wouldn't have a clue."

PJ glanced at Bebe—*This is going well!*—and Bebe nodded.

"Mr. Walsh," PJ said, "I don't know what they do either. My family's never had a whole lot of money. We always had to get by, make our own stuff, entertain ourselves, and so on. I guess the women in my family've been quilting since forever. It's kept us close, and it's cheaper than going to the mall and stuff."

She lowered her eyes. "And it's the only thing I really know how to do well. It looks like I'm not going to be able to go to college, or at least not for a while. I'm trying to find a way to turn quilting into a career."

Walsh knit his brows. "Well, I was hoping you wouldn't say something like that. Because we can't afford to pay you for this. You're not the only one that doesn't have any money. What we're asked to do, and what they give us…"

"I sort of saw that one coming," PJ answered. "But like I said, family's everything to me. I've already lost too much of it."

~

Her mother's number gave her the bee-doo-BOOP! announcement that it was no longer in service. Anne had likely moved again; she was forever hopping from apartment to apartment. And of course she hadn't bothered letting PJ know her new number.

PJ looked up at Ross. "The number's been disconnected. And you're hovering."

"Ah. Sorry." He squeezed her shoulder and ducked up the stairs.

PJ sighed and used his laptop to search the web, where she found a current "Anne Warner" listing in the online white pages.

*Let's not hold our breath,* PJ thought as she punched in the new number.

"Hello," came her mother's voice.

"Mom?"

PJ heard her mother giving it her best California smile. "PJ! Oh, how good to hear from you."

*Go ahead,* PJ thought. *Ask me how I got this number.* "Good to hear from you too, Mom," she said instead. "How's everything?"

"Luis and I are leaving for Cozumel tomorrow! How cool is that?"

"Who?"

"Luis. I know I told you about him. We met about four months ago, through this great dating service—you've got to check it out."

"Um, I *am* married, Mom. And no, you haven't told me about Luis."

"Well, I will one of these days. But I can't talk for long, I'm just starting to pack."

"I'll...try to make it quick, then," said PJ. *You haven't even asked about your grandkids,* she thought, *and you're already hustling me off the phone.*

"It's a long story," she continued, "but I need to know if you ever heard Bebe or anyone else mention somebody named 'Silver.'"

There was the slightest missed beat, the barest hesitation, before Anne spoke. "No," she said. "I wouldn't have any knowledge about that. What kind of weird name is 'Silver,' anyway?"

PJ couldn't have spoken to save her life. She knew exactly what had just happened. Her mother had lied to her. Lied!

*Like she's a gangster denying a crime: "No, Senator, I wouldn't have any knowledge about that." She might as well have pled the Fifth.*

"You do know, don't you?" she said. "You've heard that name before! Where, Mom? I need to know!"

"Are you on your cell phone, PJ? You're breaking up."

"I am not breaking up! What do you know about Silver, Mom?"

"Absolutely nothing. PJ, I really have to go."

PJ hesitated. There was no dealing with her mother. No dealing with her at all.

*But you're not getting off that easily,* PJ thought. "Mom, wait! Do you know where Grandpa's old Marine Corps things are? I've checked every place I can think of, and I haven't been able to find them."

"Why would I know that?" Anne said.

"I just thought maybe you'd seen them, or even taken them with you, after Bebe's funeral."

"I couldn't care less about junk like that. Is that why you called me? These are dumb questions, PJ, really dumb. Are you OK? You don't sound well, at all."

PJ rolled her eyes. "I'm fine. Have fun in Cozumel, Mom. With Luis, whoever he is."

"OK, then," Anne said. "See you." Click.

*Not if I see you first,* PJ thought.

"Uh-oh," said Ross. He was halfway back down the stairs, peering at her. "Are you OK?"

"I wish people would quit asking me that," she said. "No, I'm not. Mom knows who Silver is but she won't tell me."

"Interesting."

"You see why I didn't want to call her?" PJ held up her hands. "She's out of her mind! Running off to Mexico with the latest and greatest thing."

Ross hung his head. "I only have one more suggestion, and then I'm gonna shut up about all this."

"What is it?"

"Tomorrow, if you want, I'll keep the kids and you can go over to the mini-storage unit and go through it."

"I thought of that already," PJ said. "Grandpa's stuff wouldn't be in there. I carried every box in there myself, and I would've noticed it."

"Are you sure?"

"Ross, of course I'm sure!"

"PJ, would you just do it? If for no other reason than maybe you can clean the stuff out of there and we can stop paying for the space?"

PJ rubbed her eyes. "All right, all right. If it'll make you happy, I'll do it. But after I do, you have to do something to make me happy, too, OK?"

"What's that?"

"You have to—never mind."

"What? You know I want to help you!"

"You can get off my back," PJ said.

▶▶▶◆◀◀◀
## Chapter Eight

*You really can spot an idiot from outer space,* she thought. *I make a big stink about Grandpa's stuff not being in here, and in here is exactly where I find it.*

PJ wiped her forehead. It was a hot morning to be working in a metal box. She'd been half-heartedly shifting old furniture and crates of books for a couple of hours—and rehearsing the fine talking-to she'd give Ross—when, naturally...

Deep in one corner she'd found three taped-up boxes marked "XMAS" in Bebe's handwriting. PJ remembered storing them here after Bebe's funeral, when they were cleaning out the old house so they could sell it and settle the medical bills. At the time she'd taken the labels on these boxes at face value. Ornaments and wrapping paper and so forth, she'd figured. She'd stacked them and forgotten all about them.

So just now, when she'd opened the first, she'd been flabbergasted to find Grandpa's framed honorable discharge right on top. Ornate script; Eisenhower's signature. And underneath it was a dry-cleaning bag containing his blue dress uniform.

"Well...Merry Christmas to you too, Bebe," she said.

PJ unwrapped her grandpa's uniform and hung it

from the back of an old kitchen chair, stirring the scent of mothballs and old wool. But there was another smell behind those, a spicy masculine odor she associated with childhood explorations of dresser drawers and bathroom cabinets.

Grandpa's cologne. Unreal.

She sat taking it in. A white frame cap. A dark blue dress coat with gold buttons. Sky-blue trousers, emblazoned from beltline to cuff with a crimson stripe.

PJ rubbed her arms, chilled despite the heat. *The blood stripe,* she remembered. *Symbolizing the fallen. The blood stripe is why you can take the Marine out of the uniform, but you can't take the uniform out of the Marine.*

She'd never seen Grandpa wear his uniform, but she'd seen a few black-and-white pictures. Him and a buddy in their service uniforms—jacket and tie; creased slacks; caps emblazoned with the Eagle, Globe, and Anchor emblem— posing in front of what looked like a Japanese shrine. Him in fatigues throwing a football into a crowd of Asian children.

And him in what looked to be this same blue dress uniform, while another Marine wearing two general's stars pinned the Navy Cross to Grandpa's chest. Grandpa at attention, Bebe holding his elbow and looking into his face—which was so very young, but already so very hollow-eyed.

There were three-and-a-half rows of medals pinned to the left breast of Grandpa's dress coat. His Navy Cross hung in the place of honor, at upper left. She also recognized the Purple Heart. She stroked the medals with a finger, thinking about his face in the photo.

"Oh, Grandpa," she said. "What did they do to you?"

~

The women in the nursing home loved working on their family trees, but it was the men who surprised her. Especially Don.

Most days Don kept to himself by the window, sitting in his wheelchair and staring not *through* it but *at* it, with what

PJ took for real hatred. As if the window was barred against him and he'd like to smash the glass.

"My brothers were a pack of thieves and liars," he said when PJ approached him about doing a family tree quilt. "And I've never sewed a lick in my life." He turned back to the window.

But she caught him watching her occasionally—it was that pretty-young-girl thing, maybe—and she gathered her nerve on a rainy Saturday afternoon.

There were a dozen or so residents, mostly women, scattered around the TV room in wheelchairs and on the couches, and all were sewing. A few had family members helping them. And three of their quilts hung completed on the walls.

"You're a military man, aren't you?" she asked. She knew he was, she'd looked that up in his file in Mr. Walsh's office.

"That's right," Don said suspiciously.

"Were you ever overseas?"

"You wouldn't recognize where if I said."

"Try me."

"You ever hear of Tarawa? For instance?"

"You've got me there. Where is it?"

"Not where, what. It's an island in the South Pacific. It's a real—" He eyeballed her. "Excuse me. It's a bad neighborhood."

"My grandfather was in Korea," she said.

"Good for you. Doggie, I guess. G.I."

"No, a Marine."

"Is that right?" A fleeting interest in his eyes. "Well, you know us, then."

"Not so much, I don't."

"Killed over there, was he?"

"No. Practically, but no. He was a POW."

Don shook his head and turned towards the window. But only briefly, and when he turned back the loose crags in his face had tightened. PJ could see a much younger man looking through the mask of pitted skin, broken veins, and rheumy eyes.

"You get to feeling forgotten," this intense youngster said. "That's because there's no way to explain it to anyone

**74**

that hasn't been there. They can't understand you, so they don't try."

"Well, I *have* tried. My grandpa was disabled, had a bunch of brain damage. What he told us didn't make much sense. He died when I was a little girl."

"I'm sorry for your loss," Don said.

PJ tensed for no good reason she could think of. "We never did find out the whole story."

"The story is," he said, "when somebody puts their hand on you or your family, you make them stop."

Then she was relieved to see his face relax. "I'm sorry," he said. "I was a drill instructor for a while. Old habits. But let's drop it. I've been home forty-five years and I still haven't found out the whole story either. Let's talk about whether I can take you to the snack machine and buy you one of those terrible egg-salad sandwiches."

PJ slapped his hand playfully. "Um, I'm not supposed to accept gifts."

"You hear the one about the soldier and the sailor and the Marine and the pretty girl?"

"I heard it. The Marine got close enough, right?"

That afternoon Don started a quilt of his own. PJ suggested he try a twist on the family tree.

"Why not do a tree of one of your units?" she asked. "It could be the chain-of-command instead of the family."

He frowned. "Hmm. I'd have to put the officers at the bottom, then." He grinned. "Yeah, I'd like that."

They sketched out a design and she armed him with fabric and scissors. He cut a few clumsy leaves and branches and she showed him how to start piecing them together.

"Ow!" Don said after a while. He grinned foolishly and put his finger in his mouth. "Do I get a Purple Heart for that?"

"You get a Band-Aid," said PJ. "Use the thimble, Don! That's why I gave you one."

"I don't need a thimble," he said. "The last time I sewed something, I was sewing my buddy's arm back on."

"You're a tough guy," she said.

"*Semper Fi,*" he said. And the glow in his eyes gave her a satisfaction she knew she'd always carry with her.

~

It was strange: PJ knew what Grandpa had done, but not what he'd been through. There was a difference between those two things she knew she'd never fully grasp.

Grandpa had landed in Korea at Inchon in mid-September of 1950. For ten weeks he'd advanced across Korea with the First Marine Division, until, in the bitter cold, they'd reached the Chosin Reservoir.

Towards the end of November, as perhaps a hundred thousand Chinese Communist forces were advancing on the Chosin Reservoir, First Lieutenant David Warner's rifle platoon met with enemy fire while patrolling a brushy, snowbound ridge. They took cover in a narrow ravine for an entire night, pinned down on the frozen earth, trading fire with the CCF soldiers concealed by the boulders and bushes, until it became clear the situation was hopeless and withdrawal was their only option.

It became the twenty-three-year-old lieutenant's finest hour. He took an M-1 and all the magazines his men could spare, and he ordered them back towards the reservoir, to where they'd last seen other Marines while he lay in wait for the enemy.

PJ knew that if asked, he would've said—and Bebe would've agreed proudly—that this was what good folks did.

His men notified higher-ups of the Chinese advance. His action saved others from ambush, for which selflessness the president was pleased to present him with the Navy Cross.

It'd be more than three years before he emerged from the prison camp at Pyok-Tong. Or until his body emerged, at least. Things had been done to him in the camp system. Of these, Bebe had known a few. But they were enumerated in no citation—only in the man himself.

"You have a body, you *are* a soul," Bebe had repeated to PJ at Grandpa's funeral. "But sometimes I think your Grandpa David's soul left him in Korea."

~

PJ shook off the grim reverie and fetched Silver's quilt from its bag. She held it next to Grandpa's uniform and compared them.

*Guess they didn't wear their dress blues where this thing was made,* she thought.

But in the box was another plastic bag, and in it were a couple of pairs of old fatigues. PJ unfolded them and knew she'd found an answer at last.

*No question, it's the same fabric—the same dull green cotton,* she thought. *"Battle Dress Units," or whatever they called cammies before they were actually camouflaged. So what does it mean?*

Suddenly her whole spirit lightened. *If whoever sent this quilt was a friend of Grandpa's from Korea, maybe he finally found out Grandpa was dead. So sending it to Bebe would've been the natural thing for him to do! When he said "I'll be waiting for you," he probably meant them both!*

*And that means I don't have to worry about whether Bebe was cheating on Grandpa while he was away!*

PJ felt genuine happiness then, for the first time in a long while. Energy flooded her. Right away she knew another thing to try. She could return all those phone calls from Ellen; ask her if there was a way to contact the post office in Bluff, Utah. Maybe someone there knew the sender.

Her thoughts raced. *And maybe the sender can tell us more about Grandpa! And maybe it'll be information I can use to patch things up with Mom! Maybe she'd heard something at some point and was suspecting what I was. It'd be great to set her mind at ease.*

Yeah, it was all fitting together.

*And when am I gonna learn to listen to Ross, anyway? It's true what they say: the road of idiocy leads to the palace of wisdom.*

~

Shortly after her eighteenth birthday, Mr. Walsh called PJ into his office.

"I'm sorry about your Aunt Carol," he said. "She was sweet; we really miss her around here."

She folded her hands in her lap. "Thank you, Mr. Walsh. We miss her too."

His face looked pained. "Please. Scott is fine."

"OK."

"How's your program going?" he asked.

"I feel pretty good about it. We've finished twelve quilts already—small ones, but still. They're bugging me to come up with another idea."

"I've been hearing good things too," Walsh said. "But mostly I'm impressed that you're still coming around. I figured you'd stop when your aunt passed."

"I wouldn't do that." PJ smiled. "We haven't gotten you started on your quilt yet."

Walsh laughed politely. "I wish I had time. But look, I have some news for you."

PJ's heart lurched. *He's about to tell me I can't come back. Did I do something wrong? What?*

"We want to offer you a job," he said. "It's only minimum wage, but there's a benefit that might make up for it."

"Um, um...," PJ stuttered.

Walsh laughed softly. "Since you'll be a county employee, you can qualify for a partial-tuition scholarship at Chattanooga State. Enough for a class or two every semester. You need a recommendation letter from your supervisor, but I don't think getting that'll be a problem."

"Wow. This is..." She shook her head, speechless.

"What do you want to major in?" he asked.

She gave up trying to think. "I have no idea," she said. "Something I can earn a good living at."

~

PJ opened the second Christmas box. A badly-painted plaster Santa with "Anne Warner 1960" scribbled on the bottom in a child's hand—a strange reminder that her mother had once been a little girl, herself. Boxes of ornaments, a tangle of lights, half-melted candles.

The third box was larger than the others, and top-heavy. Inside she found a magnificent ivory-hilted sword in a steel sheath.

*No way,* she thought, balancing it in her hands. Grandpa's dress sword, just like the one in the recruiting commercial.

She slid it partway out, admired the engraving on the blade.

*Ross is gonna wet himself when he sees this.*

She set the sword aside, hurrying now, as gleeful as a diver looting a galleon. There was more Christmas stuff wrapped in newspaper. Mice dressed as Santa and his elves, that sort of thing. Old wrapping paper and ribbons. A pine-tree tablecloth.

And at the very bottom of the box, where it had probably lain for decades, an unopened Christmas present.

The label read: "To Silver. Yours forever, Elizabeth."

PJ sat straight down onto the concrete floor. Her lips opened and closed. She couldn't think. She became intensely aware of the heat and she leaned forward and put her head between her knees.

When the moment passed she kneeled before the box and lifted the present out. She knew right away what it held.

The paper was brittle and its once-bright colors were muted. The tape was yellowed and it yielded to her trembling fingers with ease.

But the quilt inside was as beautiful as the day it was made.

PJ stood and shook it out, and what she saw made her catch her breath.

The quilt was a masterpiece of composition. It balanced simplicity and complexity, subtlety and daring, symbolism and clarity, and it radiated a warmth that seemed to brighten the mini-storage unit without adding to the stifling heat.

At the center of the quilt, a pair of life-size yellow-golden hands embraced a crimson heart, and around the hands and the heart was embroidered, in cursive script:

*My Life. My Love. My Heart. My Hero.*

*Bebe's handwriting,* PJ thought numbly.

The heart and hands and words stood in a diamond-shaped field of pale yellow, and that field was bounded by a border, perhaps three inches wide, of triangles that seemed to march together to unite in the border's middle. The triangles were an old-fashioned paisley print in olive green and rusty red and gunmetal blue. It was a pattern PJ recognized, called Flying Geese, which suggested freedom.

This border was likewise diamond-shaped, and from its sides spread four dusty orange rays—each terminating in a star-shaped block of gold and green.

PJ knew this pattern too; it was one that Bebe used frequently. She was too modest to claim it as her invention, but she'd called it a "Chattanooga Star" and PJ had never seen it used anywhere else.

*Very medallion-style,* PJ thought. *And there's hidden meaning everywhere. It's like a love letter that just goes on and on.*

The quilt was edged all around by a series of Log Cabin blocks—long and narrow strips of pale yellow and tan, overlapped around a square of red that was the same red as the heart in the very middle of the quilt, the heart toward which all other elements of this quilt flowed. "The heart is in the home," was the message.

And then PJ's heart sank. For the hands offering the heart could mean one thing and one thing only. Bebe had made this quilt for the man she meant to spend the rest of her life with. And that man had not been David Warner.

It left PJ with a desperate question: when had Bebe made this quilt? If it had been before she'd met Grandpa, PJ could understand it. Maybe she'd had a teenage sweetheart she'd never mentioned. That she *wouldn't* have mentioned, because doing so would've been disrespectful to David. Puppy love. No harm, no foul.

She knew how to check. Bebe had been in the habit of signing her work. PJ flipped up the corners of the quilt until she found a signature and date inked in Bebe's precise script: "Elizabeth Warner, 1953."

PJ slumped backwards to lie on the floor, surrounded by the debris of Bebe's life, feeling lost in the debris of her own. She rolled over onto her stomach and pressed her face to the cool concrete. With one arm she fished around until she'd snagged a corner of the quilt, and she pulled it to her and buried her face in it and wept.

*She cheated on Grandpa while he was a prisoner,* PJ thought. *He put his whole faith in her and she betrayed him. And she betrayed me, too. And I never knew it. Oh, God, what else did Bebe lie about?*

*She told me to tell the truth.*

*She told me to save myself for the right man.*

*She told me to put others before myself, but especially my family.*

*She told me—*

This was no chill. It was real grief scalding her throat. Her sobs echoed off the corrugated walls and she beat the concrete with the desperate futility of a woman pounding a cell door. She cried for losing Bebe and she cried for losing her mother, but most of all she cried for losing herself.

*I was a beautiful young woman. I had a good job and plenty of money. I had a boyfriend to die for. And now I'm a frumpy housewife with a husband who doesn't understand me and two kids that wreck everything they touch and I'm having a meltdown on the floor of a low-rent mini-storage unit in a suburb of Nowhere, Tennessee.*

*And when I need Bebe the most, I find out that Mom was right. Bebe was a hypocrite. I can't even count on her memory.*

*I'm all alone. Even my ghosts have deserted me.*

~

81

"Surprise!" the old men and women in the TV room exclaimed. Bebe stood with her arm around PJ and beamed as everyone sang to her.

There was cake and punch on a table, and a sign PJ had made that said "Happy 60th!" Crepe streamers fluttered between the family tree quilts on the walls, and in the corner stood a rack with a white bedsheet concealing whatever it bore.

There were only three candles on the cake and Bebe blew them out with one puff. "I don't know if I could blow out sixty-one candles," she admitted.

"I blew out eighty-nine last year," said Edna Howard from her wheelchair. Her voice was faint but tough. "My daughter said 'Mamma, we're only puttin' one on there,' but I said to her, 'Joan! You put every last candle on it. I earned 'em and I'm a-gonna blow 'em out.' So I don't want to hear no complainin' from the babies in the room about a measly sixty-one candles." She laughed merrily and they all joined in.

PJ cut and served the cake. She'd made it herself, with artificial sweetener and fake cocoa and low-fat margarine and cholesterol-free eggs. Then she led Bebe to the stand in the corner.

"This is what I've been waiting to see," Bebe said. "I knew you were working on something, but you've gotten pretty good at keeping secrets."

"OK, are you ready?" PJ asked.

"I am! Let's see it!"

PJ whipped off the bedsheet to reveal the quilt.

Bebe clasped her hands. "It's gorgeous, Cupcake!"

And PJ knew it was. She tried to be humble about these things, but there was no denying that the quilt was a work of art by anyone's standards.

It was a dogwood in full bloom, growing out of a rich field of brown to spread its many flowering branches against a background of blue and gold. Each leaf was a man's name, each flower was a woman's, and each name bore at least one date.

Some, like Aunt Carol's, bore two: "1923 – 1993."

PJ pointed to where Bebe's flower and Grandpa's leaf grew together, extending a branch to "Anne Simone

Warner" and "Dewayne Harold Nash," and terminating in "Piper Jo Warner."

Bebe leaned in, squinted, leaned even closer, and squinted again. "Wonderful! And thank you for not filling my date in!" she laughed.

It was a funny thing to say but it gave PJ an unpleasant shudder. *I'll have to keep updating this quilt for the rest of my life,* she thought. A bittersweet prospect; births and deaths would vie for her attention. *And one of these days I'll be sewing Bebe's last day on here.*

*I wonder who'll sew on mine?*

"Did you do all this yourself?" Bebe asked.

"I did," PJ said. "I wanted them to make their own; I just put this one together to show them what they're capable of."

"I wonder how many people would be capable of making something like this," Bebe said, her expression dreamy.

Then someone in the back of the room interrupted the general conversation and cake-munching with a loud hand-clap.

"Excuse me, everyone," said Walsh. He was holding a camera. "I just wanted to say a couple of things. First, thanks to PJ for setting all this up—nice cake! And second, that I'd like to take a few pictures. Seems like you've all done a lot of hard work and we should get your quilts in our newsletter."

He got them lined up, each holding or at least draped with a quilt, and he took several shots. Then he had PJ and Bebe pose, and while they were lining up Bebe said, "You know, Mr. Walsh, you should send these to the newspaper."

Walsh clicked the shutter and the flash popped. "That's not a bad idea," he said as he set up for another shot.

"Scott, I wish you wouldn't," PJ said. "Um, I don't like to call attention to myself."

Walsh lowered the camera. "Come on, don't be so modest. We've got a lot to thank you for. I'll give you copies of the pictures for your college application. Now say cheese, you two."

*Great,* PJ thought, and she put on a big false smile.

"Cheese!" she said.

~

It was mid-afternoon when PJ emerged from the mini-storage unit, her face carefully composed, the sun blinding her. She'd filled a box with the sword and the uniforms and Silver's quilt—*both of them,* she reminded herself—and she set the box in the passenger's seat and slammed the door.

She felt as dry as dust.

As she drove home she felt trembly and she realized she was famished. Why had she let it get so late? She swung the van into the parking lot of a Taco Bell, debated going through the drive-through, and decided she'd rather sit and take her time over her food for once.

*I should probably wash my face, anyway, she thought. Put on some makeup, so Ross won't see me like this.*

She tidied up in the women's room before joining the line that wound through the chrome handrails to the counter. Her thoughts darted aimlessly—Silver's quilt, her mother's Santa figurine, the quilt Bebe had made for Silver, Grandpa's medals. Her heart was a whirl and she couldn't align her head.

"Can I help you, ma'am?" a voice warbled.

She opened her eyes. It was the weedy kid behind the register. "Can I get a burrito with no guacamole, nachos, and a Diet Coke?" she asked.

"Yes, ma'am," he said. But there ensued an extraordinary amount of transaction-voiding and managerial consultation—*What, has nobody ever ordered a gut-bomb with no guac at this place?* she wondered—and shortly the customers in line behind her were grumbling and checking their watches.

At long last Weedy Kid #2 dished her order onto a tray and slid it to her. She took it without comment, found a table in the corner, wiped it clean.

*Warm and cheesy, here I come!* PJ unwrapped the burrito, inhaled its steam, and salivated. *Oh, yeah.* She took a big greedy bite.

"Ugh, urk!" she choked. "Gross!"

She looked down at the burrito in her hand. There was a big blurp of that awful ersatz guacamole, right up the center.

PJ threw the burrito down and put her face in her hands.

▶▶▶◆◀◀◀
## Chapter Nine

When PJ pulled up the driveway she was blocked out of the garage by a big cardboard GE box somebody had reconfigured for deep-space exploration with a magic marker. It rocked back and forth.

*Oh, thank God.*

She stuck her head in the spaceship. "What are you two doing?" she asked the kids.

"Hunting aliens," said Baker. He aimed his ray-gun finger at PJ. "BZZZZZT!"

"We're helping Daddy," Lizzie said.

"Helping Daddy? Helping Daddy do what?"

"Change the hot water."

"Daddy's changing out the hot water heater? By himself?"

"No," Lizzie said. "We're helping."

"Um...OK, well, keep it up," said PJ. But she was furious. After the day she'd had, to come home to this.

*Ross lied to me! He fed me an excuse to get me out of the house so he could fix the water heater himself. Thinks it'll go smoother if I'm not around, I bet. He'll be lucky if I let him sleep in that cardboard box tonight!*

The old hot water heater lay on her side of the garage, still dribbling, and she stormed into the kitchen and set

Bebe's box down. Ross stuck his head out of the utility room. "Hey, gimme a hand for a sec," he said.

She went in chewing her lip. He'd already gotten the new water heater plumbed in and he was screwing wires together with orange wire-nuts.

"Ross—" she said, glaring at him.

He glared back, and it surprised her. "What?" he grumbled.

"What are you doing?"

He flipped his hand at the water heater. "Fixing this thing when I oughtta be enjoying my day off."

"Why? You give me the business about not asking for help and then you wait until I'm gone and you do it without even discussing it with me? And then you're mad because you're having to do it yourself?"

"Oh, here we go," he said. "Look, this isn't one of those Mars and Venus situations, OK? So don't go there—I've been in two fights already today."

She put her hands on her hips. "What does that mean?"

Ross crimped a wire around another connector. "That plumber we called? He waltzed in at about nine-thirty and told me since it was an emergency call on Saturday he was charging double and he wanted it up front."

"We've been waiting on him for a week!"

"Yeah, that's what I said. I told him after all the time he's wasted, he should be paying us. He got all aggressive about it—in front of the kids, mind you—and I told him to shag it out the way he came in." Ross's chest swelled. "I figure he saw our house and decided we could afford it. Sidewalk premium. I should have given him a good close look at that sidewalk."

PJ's jaw dropped, and despite herself she had to giggle. Ross's bartending and his athletic build had given him an easy physical confidence. To picture him seizing a scam artist by the scruff of his neck and bouncing him off the pavement—it was no wonder she was laughing. It was exactly the sort of mental picture she needed.

~

Back in high school PJ'd had a mandatory P.E. class first period, so it was half-dark most mornings when they assembled for calisthenics in the gymnasium.

*I should still be in bed,* PJ thought as she counted pushups. *This is a complete waste of time. When they hand me that diploma I'm never coming back here again. Six weeks and that's it.*

After doing their sets they put up the soccer nets at either end of the gym and Mrs. Chandless split them into teams. Susan Yates—who showed up every morning made-up and dressed to the nines so she could show off for twenty minutes before donning sweats—delivered the obligatory wise-crack about "shirts versus skins."

PJ, who wore her sweats to school like any sensible person with first-period gym, rolled her eyes.

She was only halfway paying attention to the game when the ball bounced her way. PJ trapped it with her thigh and feinted left to throw the defender off, then charged right. She was sprinting up the right line, looking for someone to pass to and wondering if she should take a shot on the goal, when a piano fell on her head.

She woke up on her back. The girls encircled her and Mrs. Chandless was looking down into her face, lips tight. "Try not to move, PJ," she said. "The school nurse is on the way."

PJ leaned up on one elbow. "What happened?"

"Susan slide-tackled you from behind," Mrs. Chandless said. "She knocked you into the bleachers and you hit your head. Here, let me feel back there." She probed under PJ's head and then looked at her hand. "You're not bleeding, that's good, but you've got a goose-egg."

"It hurts," PJ said. "Am I OK?"

"I hope so," said Mrs. Chandless. "Susan, though—she's not going to be. She'll be in detention until she's twenty-five if I have anything to say about it."

The nurse arrived and checked PJ out. She offered her the chance to go home, but PJ, who knew how Bebe would worry, said she'd rather stay.

That afternoon, after final bell, she closed her locker and went back to the gym, intending to thank Mrs. Chandless for looking out for her. Susan had been missing from her classes all day. Word had gone out that she was suspended for a week. Good riddance.

"Mrs. Chandless?" PJ called. Her voice echoed off the hardwood floor and the tile walls. The white lights burned overhead, hurting her eyes.

"Saw your picture in the paper, you little dork," said Susan Yates. "You and that vegetable farm."

PJ whirled. Susan was sitting on the stage at the end of the gym with four of her minions—girls PJ knew by sight but didn't hang out with. Susan hopped down onto the gym floor and walked toward her.

*Oh, man*, PJ thought. *She planned this. Bet she skipped class and followed me around all day.*

"What do you want, Susan?" PJ said.

"I want to go to the prom," Susan said primly. "But I can't now. And it's your fault."

"Why is it my fault?"

One of the other girls—a brunette, named something like Phoebe—cracked her gum and nonchalantly knocked PJ's books out of her hands.

"Hey!" PJ yelled, and when she crouched to pick them up Susan pushed her. PJ's feet went out from under her and she sat down hard.

"You think you're better than everyone else," Susan said. "Don't you? Some kind of...*artiste*?" She changed her voice, trying to imitate PJ's. "'Look at me, everybody, look at how good I am to these freaks!'"

PJ gathered her legs under her and crossed her arms on her knees, feeling sick to her stomach as if she'd been punched already. And her head still ached. "You don't have a clue how stupid you sound, do you?" she said, trying to keep her voice cool.

"They're trash and you're trash," Susan snarled. "If you could make real friends, you wouldn't need to suck up to those old geezers, would you?"

"Susan, don't talk about them like—"

"Shut *uhhhhp*!" drawled Phoebe.

Susan started taking off her earrings. "Here, hold these," she said to another girl. "I'm going to send the macramé geek to the nursing home for real."

Don's voice flashed through PJ's head: *When someone puts their hand on you or your family—*

And she didn't think; she reacted. She launched herself off the floor and exploded on Susan Yates like a white phosphorous shell arcing into the night. She was clumsy about it, but her pure pent-up fury was enough. She was drawing on years and years of it.

Susan tried to defend herself against PJ's pummeling, but when PJ bloodied her nose with a right cross, she dropped her hands and started inching backwards. Then she turned tail and ran, with Phoebe and the other girls close behind.

*Semper Fi, Don,* PJ thought as she watched them run. Then she had to sit back down and catch her breath.

And eventually, she laughed.

~

PJ, still laughing, realized Ross was scowling at her.

"This is somehow funny?" Ross muttered, waving the pliers at the water heater.

"I'm sorry, it's just...well, you're so cute when you're like this. The alpha male defending the tree, or whatever."

"The alpha male," he stated, "is gonna finish installing this water heater and then he's gonna climb Mount Sofa and thump his chest for a while. I haven't even told you what I had to deal with at the hardware store. Why can't you depend on anyone these days?"

PJ sucked her teeth. *Does he think he can't depend on me?* she wondered. *I've gotta do something about that.*

So she took the pliers away from him and pulled him to her, hard.

He hugged her back and rested his chin on top of her head, and her reaction to him, to his animal closeness, surprised her. She went warm all over and weak in the knees.

"You can depend on me," she said in a small voice. "Always. I love you. Thank you for taking care of this."

"Yeah-yeah," he sighed. He let her go and stood back. "Take a look at the wiring and make sure I've got it right

**89**

before I turn the breaker on, would you? I don't necessarily believe everything I read on the web."

"Sure," she said, still smiling. "Then I've got something to show you."

~

When they'd gotten the astronauts fed and packed off for a hibernation period, they sat in the kitchen together.

Ross slid the sword in and out of its sheath, a look of dumb amazement on his face. "Can you imagine the expression on that plumber's face if I'd whipped out with this thing?"

"You're lucky I didn't whip it out on *you*. I'm not what you'd call emotionally stable today."

"Hmm. Well, it's totally understandable. I have about a million questions myself. But mostly I'm just stunned at Bebe."

"Exactly," PJ said. "You remember what I said about opening a package and it not being what you wanted? I feel like I'm only just scratching the surface of it, and it's already put me through the wringer."

"You would have found that Christmas present eventually, though."

"I guess so. But the only other thing I can think of is to call Ellen."

"Yeah," he said. "I don't see what else you can do."

~

"Well, I forgive you for missing the other night's meeting," Ellen said when PJ was finished. "I hate to admit it, but you just blew my mind. This is a side of Bebe I never would have expected."

"That's pretty much where Ross and I are with it," said PJ. "We've been walking around flabbergasted. You should've seen me after I found out, in Taco Bell. I about went post—ah, ballistic."

"When you need to go post-ah-ballistic you don't have to go to Taco Bell," Ellen said. "Seriously. You know where to find me."

"Yeah. I do. Thanks, Ellen."

"Oh, don't thank me. Just bring that little girl of yours to our next meeting, eh? I swear, I don't know how many times I have to repeat myself to people before it sinks in."

"I will," PJ said. "So, is calling Bluff a good idea? I mean, it's just one package and they probably handle truckloads every day."

Ellen snorted. "In Bluff? One truck a week is more like it. It's a small town—beautiful, but they've got sticks in Utah that make the sticks around here look like California redwoods. Tell you what, let me try to conference in somebody from out there."

There was a click and PJ was on hold for a bit until Ellen picked back up. "PJ? Good. I've got Roy Dyer on the line; he's the counter clerk."

"Hi, Roy," said PJ. "Thanks for the time. I'm putting you on speaker, is that OK?"

"No problem," he said. His voice had a deep cowboy twang; she pictured him with a handlebar mustache. "Miz Sanders explained to me—in the nicest way you could imagine—that I'd better take care of you or she'd stake me to an anthill." He chuckled.

"Fire ants," said Ellen. "*Solenopsis invicta.* The kind with the little stingers."

"Um," said PJ, "maybe it won't come to that. Here's the deal: about ten days ago I got a box in the mail with your postmark on it. Eighteen by eighteen, a standard box I think the post office sells. It had a family heirloom in it—a fairly important one—and we're trying to get in touch with whoever sent it to us. We think it was from a guy named Silver. Does that ring any bells?"

"Well," he drawled. "Yes, ma'am, it does."

PJ was sitting forward on her chair and she nearly fell out of it. "You know him?"

"I know *of* him," Roy said. "I see him around town ever' now and again."

"Who...where..." PJ stammered. Ross set the sword on the table and stood beside her, arms folded.

"Whoa, whoa, whoa," Roy said. "Look here, Silver's an all-right fella, but, uh..."

"But what?"

"But he don't come around much. You won't see him for a few weeks and then he'll show up on an old bicycle. Buy groceries, go to church, or whatever. I reckon he's camping somewhere, or lives with a Navajo family or something. He wouldn't be the only one; we got several that does that around here."

"He's homeless, in other words," Ellen cut in. "How would PJ find him?"

"Beats me," Roy said. "I could write down your number and hand it to him next time I see him—if it'll help keep me away from them fire ants, that is—and maybe he'll call you. I don't know, I couldn't promise it; he might be long gone. He looks the sort to drift around."

PJ gnawed a knuckle, thinking furiously. *A dead end again. Or is it?* "What's his name? How old is he?"

"'Silver' is all I know him by. He might be seventy or seventy-five, I suppose. Hard to say, not knowin'."

Ellen laughed. "'Hard to say, not knowin','" she repeated. "You're funny."

"You're frightening," Roy laughed back.

*Enough, you two!* PJ thought. "Roy, have you got something to write with?"

"I do."

~

"I just have to wait," PJ told herself. It was late; she was sitting in a hot—hot!—bubble bath, with candles burning, a glass of wine on the jacuzzi-tub, and her glasses gloriously fogged-up.

*You're forever telling the kids to be patient,* she thought. *Now let's see if you can practice what you preach. Roy'll call, or Silver, even, if there's anything to call about. I hope it's Silver. No, I hope it's not. He'll probably tell me more than I want to know. And even then, I won't know if it's the truth.*

But the water and the perfumed candlelight were leaching the tension out of her bones. She sank lower into the tub, remembering how warm she'd felt when Ross hugged her.

*I need more moments like this,* she thought. *Instead of worrying about stuff I can't control, I need to be worrying about me. And Ross. And Lizzie and Baker.*

*I can start with Ross. He deserves more than a thank-you.*

She smiled. "Hey, Ross?" she called.

"Yeah?" came his voice, faintly.

"Can you help me with something up here?"

"Can it wait a few minutes?"

"I don't know…"

Silence for a moment. "What is it?"

"A cupcake."

"A *what*?"

She kept quiet. *You heard me just fine, didn't you, sport?*

Sure enough, in a moment she heard his feet on the stairs.

~

A while later—not a short while or a long while, but a while that was just right—PJ toweled water off the floor while Ross lazed in the tub.

"I may have to start taking bubble baths more often," he said.

"Some alpha male."

"Ook-ook."

"Oh!" she said. "I forgot to take my pill!"

"Go," he groaned.

"I'll be right back."

She dry-swallowed the pill and put her purse back down on the cedar chest at the foot of their bed.

Then on a whim, she walked down the hall. PJ had hung the family tree quilt among others in the upstairs hallway Ross called "The Louvre." She'd been remembering it that afternoon, and now she stood in front of it, trying to sort through the thoughts nibbling at the back of her brain.

"What are you doing?" Ross called from the tub.

"Looking at the family tree."

"Take your pill," he insisted. "That tree's got enough monkeys in it as it is."

93

"It's not monkeys I'm looking for."

She touched Bebe's flower, remembering how it had taken her months to work up the courage to embroider in Bebe's resting date. Then she slid her fingers on to the flower that represented Anne.

"Born in 1954," PJ said. "September of 1954."

*Bebe made Silver that Christmas quilt in 1953,* she thought. *Nine months later, she had my mom.*

*My mom was born nine months after Bebe was with Silver.*

*Silver is my real grandfather.*

PJ put out her hand, steadied herself on the wall. "Ross!" she yelled.

## ▶▶▶◆◀◀◀
## Chapter Ten

PJ had read once that the person who stayed up all night was blessed; she'd just added another day to her life span.

*A crazy notion if ever I heard one,* she thought. *Every night that I lie awake makes me feel ten years older.*

She lay in the dark entertaining these and other happy thoughts until she realized it was after three, at which point she gave it up and left Ross snoring and went downstairs. She microwaved a glass of milk, feeling overwhelmed and trying not to think too much, and she sipped it at the kitchen table.

Ross's laptop beckoned. She started the Internet browser and checked the surfing history for the Korean War database they'd queried the other day. But the history was completely blank.

*Now why is that?* she wondered. *Ross is on the web all the time. There ought to be a bunch of pages listed here.*

Then it came to her. *If he's deleting the history it means he's looking at stuff he doesn't want me to know about. Porn? I doubt it. No, I bet it's something about me.*

Then she bit her lip. *Stop thinking like your mother. The world doesn't revolve around you, you know.*

PJ sighed and opened a search engine. She keyed in "Korean War POW survivors" and hit return.

~

Four-thirty and she was still reading.

*There is so much stuff out there. How is it I've never researched this before?*

She'd started with histories—the Korean War itself, its individual campaigns, the role played by the Marine Corps. That had led her to the different division histories, including the First Division, which had been her grandpa's.

*My Grandpa David,* she told herself.

The First Division, she found, had been at the thick of the Chinese invasion of the Chosin Reservoir area in November of 1950. About thirty thousand United Nations troops had been overrun by over a hundred thousand CCF soldiers in mustard-yellow uniforms and thin-soled canvas shoes. And the histories credited the Marines with holding them back.

For a while.

PJ read page after page of memoirs, hardly believing them. They slept in the open, in the worst winter storm to hit Korea in a century. Machine gunners would fire periodically to keep their rifles from cold-locking, but when they did so at night the muzzle flashes sometimes revealed masses of crawling Chinese the gunners hadn't even known were sneaking up on them. One man told of being so cold that he didn't realize he'd been set on fire by an illumination shell until his buddies tackled him and started shoveling snow onto his back.

*Twenty year-old kids,* she thought.

She finally found a POW advocacy website called the "Shambo Mambo." What the title signified was beyond her, but it specialized in the First Division and it offered a searchable database of videos and interviews.

Her queries returned what she expected: nothing new.

<u>Contact Us</u>, said a link at the bottom of the page. She clicked it.

There was a picture of a guy in maybe his fifties.

Balding, ponytail, black leather motorcycle vest. Jerry Vicente, by name.

She read his welcome message and his pitch for donations. Her eyes lingered on one paragraph:

> I was a First Division Marine in Vietnam. My uncle, Steven Carlo Vicente, was a First Division Marine in Korea. We've never located his remains. If you know anything about what happened to him and his fire team at Yudam-Ni near Turkey Hill on November, 28th, 1950, please call me day or night. Help Me Bring My Uncle Home!

PJ drew a long breath. She'd never heard of Yudam-Ni, but she knew what *day or night* meant.

~

"This is Jerry." A cigarette voice. Raspy, and a Jersey accent to boot.

"Um, hi," she said. "You don't know me, my name's PJ Hathaway. I saw your site."

"Oh, right, right." She heard the phone rattling on his end and then distant coughing.

"Sorry," he said.

"Did I catch you asleep?" she asked.

His laughter wheezed and crackled from deep in his chest. "Not really, I was just going over some stuff. What can I do you for?"

"I, um, called you because I don't know where else to turn. I don't—I'm not the sort of person who asks for help very easily."

"Mmm-hmm."

"My grandfather," she said, "was a First Division Marine lieutenant, and he was captured near the Chosin in 1950."

"Ah," he said, sounding much more interested. "Well. What's—or what was?—his name?"

"Was. David Francis Warner." She rattled off his service number.

"Hold on a minute," he said. She heard a keyboard

clicking. "Oh, sure," he said. "Yeah, Navy Cross. Strong work; there weren't that many of those given out in Korea. You ever do an SF-180 on him?"

"Did I what?"

"SF-180. It's the form you fill out to get a copy of his service record."

"No," PJ said, feeling stupid. "Never even occurred to me."

"You should do it; there's a guide to how on my site somewhere. Shoot me a copy if you do, I'd like to have it. If you don't mind, that is. What about his debriefing? Was there a transcript?"

"Mr. Vicente, I'm really new at this," she admitted. "I probably haven't done anything you're going to ask me about."

He paused. "OK. I see. What have you done, then?"

"I got a quilt in the mail."

A pause, then: "Give me that again?"

~

"I get a lot of wingnuts calling me up," Jerry said. "Especially at this hour. If you didn't sound so confused I'd say you were shining me on."

"Confused is right," she admitted.

"Let's try something. I've got access to forty or fifty databases and I'll run the word 'Silver' through all of them and see what comes back. It'll take a few weeks, probably—some of 'em are on paper." He chuckled. "You'd think the government would scan this stuff, but, no, they'd rather spend tax money on whether goats can breathe seawater. Trust me; it's true."

PJ smiled. *This guy's OK.* "I can't thank you enough, Jerry."

"Least I can do for a fellow night-owl."

"Is this what keeps you up? The POW/MIA thing? Finding your uncle?"

"Yeah, sometimes. My wife jokes about it. Says, 'Who needs a smoke-detector when you've got an insomniac?'"

"Spoken like somebody who sleeps well."

"Spoken like somebody nagging a smoker. No, I just…

it's…" He exhaled. "You know how all the World War II vets are dying off? It was sixty years ago; hardly any of 'em are left."

"I know."

"Well, the Korean War guys are going too. Ten years from now and we'll all be wondering what happened to them. That's what keeps me up. That, and whether anyone's going to ask what happened to me."

"I think I understand," PJ said.

"Do you? Listen, that quilt is a piece of history. Some of the stains on it are blood, I'd think. You have to find this Silver guy. Absolutely have to. If you have to get on a plane and go out there, do it."

"He's family," she agreed.

"Well, sure, but I'd be saying that if even if he wasn't. Because nobody who did what those guys did ought to be living on the streets. I mean, it's a travesty. Criminal. Did you know there were still reports of Korean War POWs shuffling around in the Soviet Gulags as late as the mid-eighties?"

"How is that possible?"

"I bet you fifty bucks," he said, "that every time you go downtown you see a guy in a camouflage jacket in a wheelchair with his hand out. Claiming to be a vet. So which do you do: stop and make sure he's OK, or chew him out for being a poser?"

PJ looked around at her kitchen, at the stainless steel refrigerator, the big basket of apples and oranges on the island, the shelf with all the boxes of herb tea. She thought about Ross's salary. She thought about the coat closet that she was perpetually vowing to clean out.

"I don't do anything," she confessed.

"Yeah, you do," he said. "You look away and keep walking. And that's why it's possible."

"I'm feeling pretty ashamed of myself," she said quietly.

"We all should." Jerry coughed. "Anyway. Hey, I'm just noticing something, bear with me. What it says here is that your grandfather was reported KIA. And then he was released from Pyok-Tong in December of 1953. Operation Big Switch."

PJ lifted an eyebrow. "That's not the way I've always heard it. Nobody ever told me he was first reported killed in action. Are you sure?"

"That's what it says."

"And released in 1953—my grandmother always said he came home in early 1954."

"Yeah, maybe, but that's two different things. When he got released and when he got repatriated might be weeks apart. Thing is, the Corps would've notified her right after they had him back in their custody. They were pretty good about that."

"I don't think he would've been able to tell them who he was."

"Tags would've said. And even if he didn't have them, they came out of the camps in batches. Somebody would've known him."

"OK," she said. "I still don't see where you're headed, though."

"All right. Picture this. It's Christmas Day and you're about to exchange presents with your new boyfriend or fiancé or whatever. You're sad about your husband—God rest him!—but you've moved on. Then the doorbell rings. It's a sergeant in full dress.

"He tells you," Jerry continued, "that it's a very Merry Christmas indeed! There's wonderful news! Your husband is alive! And he'll be home as soon as they release him from the hospital in Munsan-ni! So what do you do? Go back in and keep opening Christmas presents with your fiancé?"

"I'd...I'd..." PJ trailed off. *I'd climb out the bathroom window and nobody would ever see me again, that's what I'd do.*

"Are you there?" he asked in a moment.

"Was that sort of thing common?"

"No, but it happened. I know of three or four cases."

PJ rested her forehead on the table. "I hope you're not telling me this to help me sleep."

Jerry's laugh was sad and sympathetic. "*Now* I think you're starting to understand what keeps me up."

▶▶◆◀◀
## Chapter Eleven

*Mother's Day is the worst day of the year,* PJ thought.

Ross stood at the white headstone chewing a fingernail. She couldn't see his eyes from where she sat; he was wearing dark glasses against the bright sun. But he was quiet; far too quiet.

*It's always when I'm the most tired that his job calls him out of town. And when he finally gets a few days when he doesn't have to travel, he hardly even speaks to me. I ask what's up and he says not to worry, he's fine. He's giving me a dose of my own medicine, I guess.*

Unlike Ross, she didn't need to read the stone. She knew the words on it as well as she knew the sound of the twins' breathing at night.

DAVID F
WARNER
CPT
US MARINE CORPS
KOREA
JUN 16 1924
APR 17 1987
NAVY CROSS

And on the back:

> ELIZABETH R
> HIS WIFE
> NOV 4 1930
> JAN 16 2000

*His wife. No higher accolade. Once I'd have believed that.*

*But now?*

For a week or two she'd felt a spark of interest in the old quilt, in Bebe and Silver and whatever their story had been, but now she was losing interest in things again. Finding walls, no matter which way she turned.

Jerry hadn't called, nor had the postal clerk from Bluff. Nor had Silver, for that matter. She'd started working through the SF-180 form to get her Grandpa's service record, but she'd been stymied when she realized only Anne, as the next-of-kin, could legally submit it.

So she'd called Anne over and over. And her mother had never answered.

Finally she'd done the only thing she could think of. She'd taken Silver's quilt and the one Bebe had made for him and she'd hung them up in the Louvre. She expected the sadness she felt to fade, in time, but here it was two weeks later and she was still going off on crying jags every day.

Growing cold again.

And growing sleepy, in fact, lulled by the shade under the oak where they'd set up for the afternoon. The breeze stirred the flowers she'd set on the headstones, bees tumbled in the dandelions, and beside her Flo hummed as she sewed.

*I got that part of it right, at least.* When PJ had called Flo to apologize for missing her at the Blockheads meeting, she'd asked what Flo was doing for Mother's Day. Flo had said she was spending it alone, which was too much for PJ to bear.

"You're sharing the day with us," PJ told her flat-out. And

then, as an afterthought, added: "Ma'am." She supposed that what Jerry had said about helping a homeless veteran might extend to a missionary's widow. Flo was a mother, and it was Mother's Day. So there it was.

It was what good folks did.

But between Ross and the kids and the darker stuff she had going on in her head, she wasn't being good company. She was hoping to finish one of the much-belated Broken Sugar Bowl blocks this afternoon so she could leave it on Bebe's grave marker, yet she couldn't keep her mind on her work.

Much less on Flo.

Her gaze wandered. "Lizzie, Baker, don't go too far," she called as the kids ranged away. There were other families at Chattanooga National Cemetery, for the most part moving quietly among the stones, and the last thing PJ wanted was for the kids to be kicking up a ruckus.

To be disturbing the living. Or the dead.

"Do you believe in ghosts?" PJ asked Flo. "I've been thinking about that a lot lately. About where we go when the soul leaves the body."

Flo answered without looking up from her sewing. "You have to be careful you don't stray into deception. If you want to believe something, you'll believe it, even in lies sent to mislead you."

"Sent by whom?" PJ asked. "I seem to have spent a good part of my life believing in lies."

Flo's words reminded her of Grandpa's scar. *God put it there,* she remembered him saying. *Would God lie to me, or just allow me to believe the lies Bebe told me?*

*Whichever it is, it's the same difference. It's like losing Bebe all over again.*

"Momma!" Baker yelled from across the way. "Can I have a pop-pop?"

"No, Baker," she sighed. "No eating while we're in the cemetery. Remember I said this was like going to church?"

Ross came over and sat down on the old quilt they'd spread out. "Where's your husband buried, Mrs. Geary?" he asked.

"In the parish cemetery," Flo said. "We do something

like this every year too, where the congregation gets together for a covered-dish lunch, and then we tend to the graves."

"We've been coming here every Mother's Day for years," he said. "Graveside quilting is PJ's little act of ancestor worship, I guess. Good for the kids, to be reminded of their great-grandparents."

"Right," said PJ, remembering how Bebe had accepted Grandpa's flag from the Marine without so much as a change of expression. *In this very same place,* she thought. *Like I need the reminder.*

Flo picked up smoothly. "When you say 'ancestor worship,' you remind me of the years Mr. Geary and I spent in China."

"How so?" Ross asked.

"Well, they honor the dead very much. In their homes they'll have a shrine to relatives who've passed on. And when we share a meal in a cemetery it's not worship, but they'll set plates of food and wine in their shrines to venerate the ancestral spirits."

"Didn't the Chinese government crack down on that?" Ross asked.

"Oh, yes. But they couldn't stop it. Neither could we; our converts would carry right on with their old beliefs."

"But their beliefs were the same as Christian ones," Ross said. "'Honor your father and mother,' right?"

"It's not quite the same," Flo said. "Confucians think children owe a duty to their parents, true, but it's more because the happiness of the dead depends on the behavior of the living."

"The way it works here," said PJ, "is that the happiness of the living depends on the behavior of the dead. You're not supposed to hold what the parents do wrong against the kids, but the kids'll hold it against themselves anyway."

And suddenly she was crying again, for at least the tenth time that day. Lizzie hid her face in PJ's lap. Ross got up and rubbed PJ's shoulders. Flo leaned forward to gather Baker into her arms. For a while, the only sound was the rustling of the breeze in the oak.

~

"They're calling it 'macular degeneration,'" Bebe had said as she climbed into PJ's beat-up Volkswagen outside the optometrist's office. "I have to go for some more testing, but they're pretty sure about it."

"Oh, my God," PJ said, instantly forgetting the physics mid-term she'd been studying for all afternoon. "What did the doctor say?"

Bebe tsk-tsked. "He said the sight in my left eye's about eighty percent gone. The right one's better, only about forty percent. He thinks they can arrest the progress with medication, but what I've lost I can't get back."

"Bebe!" PJ said. "Why didn't you tell me how bad it was? I just thought you needed a new prescription, that's all!"

"Well, Cupcake," Bebe chuckled. "I'm not licked yet."

PJ took off her glasses and rubbed her eyes. "Um, listen, I'm gonna take you home and then I'm going to the library and do some research on this. I'll skip class for a couple of days and we'll get a handle on it."

"Oh, don't do that. Don't skip school. It's not that big a—"

"No, no," PJ said. "Isaac Newton's been dead a long time; he can wait until we figure out what's going on with you."

~

After they left the cemetery Ross suggested stopping at the Formosa Restaurant.

The place assaulted PJ from every side. Paper lanterns hung too low and their table was trimmed in a garish red. Acrid vapor arose from the jar of hot mustard on their table. Her chopsticks splintered when she snapped them apart. And the stench of fried food roiled her stomach. She salivated uncomfortably, feeling she might be sick at any moment.

"Do you still speak any Chinese, Mrs. Geary?" Ross asked.

"I never knew more than a few phrases," she said. "I was always surprised how many Chinese spoke English."

A blonde kid in a red vest appeared at their table. He welcomed them to the restaurant, told them about the specials, took their drink orders, and said he'd be back when they were ready.

Ross looked at PJ. "Hang on one second," he told the kid. He took out his wallet and thumbed a slip of paper out of it.

"PJ, I, ah, thought it might be fun to see if some-body here could translate the characters off Silver's quilt."

PJ felt as if she was watching herself from another table. "If you want, I guess," she said. Her attention strayed to the other families in the restaurant, happily demolishing their dinners.

Ross handed the paper to the kid. "What do you think? Do you have anyone here who could translate this?

The kid angled his head and studied the paper. "I don't know, let me ask in the kitchen." He took it with him and pushed through the swinging doors.

Ross tapped his chin. "Sorry; I'm not trying to take charge, but you had that flurry of activity at the end of April and then you quit doing anything. I thought this might be a nice surprise."

"I was waiting on…" she began, but she stopped. *What's the use? I obviously can't help myself, so let Ross think he's helping me. Why not?*

The kid came back from the kitchen. "OK. 'An inch of love is an inch of ashes,'" he quoted. "That's what it means."

"An inch of love is an inch of ashes," Ross repeated. "You're sure about that?"

"That's what the cook said."

"But what does it mean?" Ross frowned.

The kid shrugged.

*What do you think it means, Ross?* PJ thought. "What do you kids want to eat?" she said wearily.

"Noodles!" they chorused.

Flo held her menu close to her face and squinted at it.

*If she tells me she's got macular degeneration, I'm gonna jump off a bridge,* PJ thought.

~

After PJ got Bebe home from the optometrist, she went straight to the college library and worked her way through the stacks for hours. That night she and Bebe sat in the living room going over the medical textbooks and journals PJ had checked out.

PJ watched how Bebe held a Xerox copy up close to her right cheek, her head turned towards the lamp in which an oddly bright bulb burned.

*I should have paid more attention. She's probably been noticing the symptoms for a long time, but she'd never complain. She'd just put hundred-watt bulbs in the light fixtures and keep right on sewing as if nothing was different.*

Bebe set the sheaf of papers aside and shrugged. "So now we know. Meanwhile, life goes on."

"What is it, like tunnel vision?" PJ asked.

"More of a big grey spot hanging in front of my face. And the shadows are heavy, too."

"Does it hurt?"

"No, not the least bit."

*Bebe, you're going blind!* PJ wanted to shout. But instead she stood. "I'm gonna make some coffee for us," she said.

While the coffeepot chuffed, she leaned on the counter and covered her eyes with her palm.

*What am I going to do?* she wondered. *There's gotta be something. I won't be helpless. I won't.*

~

"I got it," Ross yelled from downstairs when the phone rang.

*Like I was planning to get up,* PJ thought. It was only seven. The kids were still awake but she'd already been in bed for an hour. And she planned to stay there for a week. At least. Maybe until next Mother's Day.

*An inch of love is an inch of ashes.*

She heard Ross's feet on the stairs. "It's for you," he said, coming in and offering her the handset.

"I'm not home," she said.

"Come on. Sit up."

She twisted around angrily and jammed a pillow against the headboard. "Here," she said, holding her hand out. He handed her the phone, searched her eyes, and went back downstairs.

"Hello," she said.

"PJ Hathaway?" said a voice with a familiar twang.

"That's me."

"This is Roy Dyer, from Bluff."

PJ hiccupped. "Can you excuse me for a minute, Roy?"

"Sure," he said, sounding confused.

PJ hurried to the bathroom. She knelt in front of the toilet and threw up everything she'd ever eaten. The heaves went on and on, until she wheezed for breath against the cramping in her chest. Her throat burned and she would've sobbed if she'd had the air for it.

*Ashes, ashes, we all fall down,* she thought dizzily.

When the spell passed she rinsed her mouth and wet a rag with cool water and went back into the bedroom. She lay back on the bed, spread the rag across her eyes.

"Are you still there, Roy?" she asked.

"I'm here. Are you OK, ma'am?"

PJ was shaking. "I, um, think I ate some bad Chinese food this afternoon."

"Oh, I'm sorry. I wish I couldn't say I'd—"

"What is it?" she interrupted. "Why did you call?"

"I have some news for you," he said.

"Of course you do."

"I'm in the volunteer fire department," he said. "Fire and rescue. We picked up Silver this evening. Some rock climbers found him passed out in a canyon outside town. I just got back from running him up to San Juan Hospital in Monticello."

She sat up. "Is he OK?"

"No, he ain't. He was unconscious and close on to dead. Do you know who he is? Is there anything you can tell them at San Juan? Anything you can do?"

▶▶◆◀◀
## Chapter Twelve

"Well, I'm the triage nurse," the woman on the phone said. "I know about as much as anyone in the ER."

"What can you tell me?" PJ asked. She still tasted acid in her throat.

"What can you tell us?" the nurse said. "You know the position we're in, I think. We're not supposed to give out patient information without a HIPAA release. Now, I understand you say you're a family member, but can't you see why the fact you don't know his name puts me in a tough spot?"

"But I just found out he was a relative."

"I get it, I get it," the nurse said. "Believe me, I sympathize."

"Just tell me this," PJ said. "Is he expected to live?"

"Ma'am—" the nurse began.

"OK, let me ask you another way. Hypothetically, if you picked up a patient in his condition—late seventies, say—what would you expect to happen? In general?"

There was a long silence. "Hello?" PJ said.

"I'm here. In general," the nurse said, speaking slowly, "an elderly man in this condition might make it and might not. Someone who's very dehydrated and has…ah…taken a bad fall, well, we just don't know."

"Taken a bad fall?" PJ asked.

"This is silly," said the nurse. "All right, give me your number."

"Why?"

"I'm gonna call you back on an unrecorded line. Be a minute."

PJ gave her their number and hung up. She waited, heart pounding, until the phone rang again.

"I hate HIPAA," the nurse began immediately. "This gentleman's got trauma consistent with a fall. A couple of cracked ribs, some abrasions. A laceration on his scalp and a concussion. He's unconscious, mild coma. From his sunburn I'd say he was outside unprotected for a day, maybe, after he fell. Dehydrated, of course. But—"

"But what?"

"When we put his chest x-rays up we found two things we weren't expecting. One, pieces of metal. And two, growths on his esophagus and in his lungs."

"Are you telling me has cancer?"

"No," the nurse said. "I haven't told you anything, understand? But I will say this. Unless someone comes forward, indigent John Does like this one wind up in the county cemetery with no headstone."

~

"I'm sorry," Dr. Selvin, the optometrist, had told PJ. "Even with the medication your grandmother's probably going to lose most of her sight."

PJ was sitting in Dr. Selvin's fitting area, surrounded by thousands of pairs of eyeglasses, and though he wore an expression of deep concern she detected a trace of impatience behind his fatalism.

*Any more talk like that and I'm gonna strangle him.*

"I don't think you get it," she said. "Bebe's lost her husband. She's the baby of the family; her sisters are dead. Most of the rest of the family has moved off or passed away. She's estranged from her daughter."

"Your mother," said Dr. Selvin.

"My mother. Look, she doesn't have anything! She lives for quilting and teaching Sunday School. If she goes blind..."

Dr. Selvin was shaking his head. "PJ, you know that if there were something—"

"But there's gotta be something! Transplants, or..." PJ waved her hand around the showroom "...new glasses. I don't know, new drugs! Maybe in Europe!"

"I promise you," he said, "that I read every journal article that comes out about this. The drugs are all we can do right now."

"I can't believe that."

Dr. Selvin sighed. "You want to do something? Put up a lot of bright lights, all over the place. If her bedroom's upstairs, move her to the first floor. Get her one of those wireless pushbutton help alarms; they're at the pharmacy. You can even have a security company put in a special system if you want to go that far. But I'm telling you, if it's possible, we're doing it. All we can do is maintain the status quo. We're powerless."

"Nobody is ever powerless," PJ said. "Especially not Bebe."

He stroked his beard. "Well. Granted that 'if you don't use it, you lose it,' carries some truth. Quilting, you say? If you keep her using her visual acuity—especially with close-in work—it might not delay the deterioration, but it'll at least help make the adjustment easier."

"See?" PJ said. "There's always something you can do."

"Good luck," Dr. Selvin said.

~

"Absolutely not," Ross answered. He stacked the last of the dishes in the cabinet and closed the door and crossed his arms.

"Ross, I have to!"

He shook his head. "No way. There's no way I'm letting you get on a plane."

"Letting me?"

"PJ, all day—all month, is more like it—you've acted like you've lost interest in your own life. Now you're frantic over a complete stranger!"

"I know what I'm doing!" she insisted.

"No you don't! Look at you! You look like you've got black eyes! You get head rushes every time you stand up! You take two-hour baths but your hair looks like you haven't washed it in a week! You won't eat—you're skinny as a flagpole! How're you gonna cope with it when you get out there and they've lost your bags or something?"

She shook her head angrily. *He's exaggerating; I don't look that bad. I know I've been doing better than that.*

"I'm just TIRED, Ross!" she insisted. "I've got a lot going on!"

"Tired people sleep and then they get up and get on with their lives!"

"Why are we even talking about me? This is about Silver! He could be on his deathbed, and if I don't do something, who else is going to?"

Ross rubbed his forehead. "The hospital staff?"

"The hospital staff," she repeated, infuriated by his sarcasm. "Strangers. I'm his biological granddaughter. I owe it to him."

"You don't know that! And what good are you gonna do him even if you go?"

"There's a lot I can do! Even just being there is doing something!"

"He doesn't even know you exist, PJ!"

"But I know he does! Am I supposed to forget about him?"

Ross looked at the floor. "When I encouraged you," he said in a quieter voice, "to check out that quilt, it was because I was happy to see you getting interested in something. Yeah, I've been pushing you, trying to fix your problem. And man, am I sorry. If I'd known this is what it'd lead to, I'd've left that quilt in the trash."

"This is the hot water heater all over again, isn't it? You think I can't handle it?"

"PJ, if you want to paint the living room or wire in some speakers, or God help us, reshingle the roof, be my guest. But if you think you're in any shape to fly out West and rescue some homeless guy who may or may not be related to you, you're delusional. And I'm not standing by and letting it happen."

"Let me tell you something I heard once," she pressed on. "It was a Catholic bishop somewhere. He said, 'The homeless man on the corner raving at you that he's Jesus Christ *is* Jesus Christ, in a disturbing guise.'"

Ross said, "I am completely losing the ability to understand you. Are you having, like, a religious experience now? All that talk about souls and ghosts?"

His face was growing angry and she whipped her glasses off to blur him out. Not seeing him made it easier. "Do you understand what it means when old people start giving their stuff away?" she demanded.

"I'm not stupid, I just wish you could hear yourself!"

"If you're not stupid then you know I'm right! I have to help him, Ross. I have to. Something passed between him and my grandmother once, I don't know what. But if he needs help—and since you clearly think I do—then maybe we can help each other!"

"That's not the kind of help you need!" Then he squeezed his eyes shut and tightened his lips.

PJ chuckled once, in shock. "You think I'm out of my mind."

"I don't think you're out of your mind. I think…"

"What?"

When he raised his head his eyes were slits. "My best friend has checked out on me," he said slowly through clenched teeth. "I don't know where she is. I'm trying to find her."

"I'm right here!"

"I want you to give me five days," he said.

"For what?"

"Just give me five days. You'll see."

"What's happening in five days, Ross?"

"I can't tell you."

"Oh, Lord," she groaned. "Whatever you're planning, forget it. I'm not gonna be here. Silver could be dead in five days."

"*You* could be dead in five days," he said. "I'm not putting you on a plane."

~

"Mother's going blind?" Anne asked. She'd answered the phone on the thirtieth or fortieth ring. It was an old phone number; PJ was surprised she'd answered at all.

*What do I say?* PJ wondered. "Can you get on a plane and come home, Mom?" she asked. "Just for a few days?"

"Hang on for a second, I'll get the calendar." There was a long pause, and then PJ heard paper rustling. "OK," Anne said. "Not for a few weeks, at least."

"Mom, she'd really like to see you. I mean, while she still can."

Anne's tone flattened. "Don't guilt-trip me, OK?"

"I wasn't!" PJ said. "I'm sorry, I didn't mean it that way."

"No, of course not." The sound of more pages being flipped. "But have you thought about bringing her to San Diego?"

PJ considered it. "I don't think we can afford to. These drugs are—"

"Well, that's probably for the best. I wouldn't be able to put you up anyway."

"Where are you living now?"

"It's incredible, PJ. I've got a place right on the beach. Here, listen to this."

PJ heard the phone rattle and then a faint roar of white noise.

"That's the Pacific Ocean," Anne said.

"How is it," PJ asked, "that you've got a beach house and you don't have a spare bedroom?" *Oh, crap,* she realized. *Of course. Mom's living with someone.*

"House?" Anne said. "It's a camper, a pop-up. I'm in a state park."

"What is this, a pay phone?"

"That's right."

"And are you working?"

"Well, it depends on what you—"

"Mom," PJ interrupted. "Pull your camper to Chattanooga."

"But I'll lose my spot! It's first-come, first-served. And I—"

PJ took her glasses off and rubbed her eyes. "Your mother

**114**

is going blind, and you won't come see her because you don't want to give up a beachfront campsite."

"It's a lot more complicated than that! And you said she's got time."

"Mom, please!" PJ said. But she resigned herself, knowing that the rift was too wide, the wedge driven in too deeply. Why had she even bothered calling? She knew the answer to that one: it was what she, as a dutiful daughter, was supposed to do. But dutiful daughters were apparently short supply in the Warner family.

It had been, what, a decade since Grandpa had died? And how many times had Anne called since then? Once a year PJ could expect a birthday card with ten bucks tucked inside. Sometimes a week or two late. And on Bebe's birthday, nothing at all.

*How did it come to this?* PJ wondered. *How do I make Mom care?*

"You know what?" PJ said. "Bebe and I can get along just fine on our own. Lord knows we have up until now."

She hung up.

~

PJ took her suitcase out of the closet and unzipped it across the bed and started throwing clothes into it. Not thinking, not working off a list, just stuffing in whatever came to hand. She could hear Ross on the phone with someone, talking urgently.

*The guys with the paddy wagon, no doubt,* she thought. *But let's say I'm a complete basket case. Isn't it better for Silver to have me than nobody at all?*

Ross came into the room and set the phone on the dresser. "Not on my watch," he said when he saw what she was doing. He leaned across the bed, dug an armful of t-shirts back out of the suitcase, took them to her dresser, and started returning them to the drawers.

PJ pushed past him. She reached for the shirts he'd just unpacked. He seized her wrists, pulled her backwards into his arms, held her tightly.

Claustrophobia took her. "STOP!" she shrieked. She

threw herself from side to side, trying to tear away from him.

"What are you doing?" he said, his rough cheek on hers, his voice directly in her ear. "You don't even have plane tickets!"

From the doorway there came soft crying. It was Lizzie, eyes huge, tears on her cheeks. Ross's arms relaxed. PJ elbowed free.

"It's OK, sweetie, it's OK," she said, kneeling and trying to embrace her daughter.

"Why are you hurting Momma?" Lizzie asked Ross.

"Lizzie, please go back to bed," Ross said. "I'm not hurting Momma, I'm trying to stop her from hurting herself."

"Are you going somewhere, Momma? Where? Can I come?"

*I'm leaving you,* PJ thought. Then guilt crushed her. *No! It's not gonna go that way! I just need a few days! I will never walk out on my kids!*

She pulled Lizzie into her arms. "Lizzie, please. Go to bed. Yes, I'm going somewhere, but I'll come back. I promise you, I will always come back. And don't start thinking it's about you. Never believe that it's about you."

*It doesn't matter what I say,* PJ thought as she soothed her daughter. *She'll believe that anyway. Even when I do the right thing, it's the wrong thing.*

~

"Where are the keys, Ross?" she asked, searching the kitchen counters.

"You know better than that," he said. He was holding Lizzie in his arms; cradling her head on his shoulder with his hand.

"Fine, I'll just call a taxi." PJ took the phone book out of the drawer and was flipping through the yellow pages when there was a knock on the front door.

"Finally," Ross said. He jogged out of the room, taking Lizzie and leaving PJ alone with the phone in her hand and a puzzled look on her face.

**116**

She put down the phone. *I should go out the back way,* she thought.

And then she heard Ross open the door. "Thank you so much for coming over," he said to someone.

"Where is she?" said Ellen Sanders.

~

"PJ, Ross is right," Ellen said. "There's no way for you to establish a relationship. One nurse might have told you a few things, but the hospital won't let you take any action unless you can prove you're the next of kin."

"What am I supposed to do, then? Forget about him? If I don't get out there right now, I'm never going to find out what happened! I'll be dealing with this for the rest of my life!"

"Think, would you?" Ross said. "If you show up at an airport in the middle of the night looking like you look, half-out of your mind, with no ticket, demanding to fly somewhere, they'll taser you and lock you in a holding cell."

Ellen shook her head. "Ross, I know you mean well, but you're not helping."

"*Thank* you!" said PJ. "I could try to explain the situation?"

"Well, let's not get ahead of ourselves," Ellen said. "You have to find a way to work within the hospital's rules."

"Anne knows all about him," Ross said. "What if she goes instead?"

"Now who's delusional?" PJ muttered.

"Ross," said Ellen, "maybe you should go put Lizzie to bed. Boil some water, or something." She stared at him significantly.

Ross looked down at Lizzie. She was still draped over his shoulder, arms dangling, her eyes closed and her hair in her face. "OK, OK," Ross said. "But I'm not done with this yet."

He stabbed the counter with a finger. "Nobody—leaves—this—house." Then he took Lizzie up the stairs.

PJ sank into a chair at the table. The tide of tension ebbed, but it kept sucking at her as it went. "Wow," she said. "This is nuts."

"Hmm," Ellen said. "Any chamomile tea?"

"On the shelf by the paper towels."

Ellen fiddled in the cabinets and found the teakettle. She started filling it with water from the island sink. "Midwives," she said, "will sometimes send the husband to boil water as soon as the baby starts crowning."

She took the kettle to the stove and lit a burner. "But they don't do that because they need boiling water."

"I don't follow," PJ said.

Ellen came to sit down by her. "They send the husband to boil water so he'll have something to do. It gets him out of the way. Gives him the illusion of control." She tapped her temple with an index finger. "Ninety percent of the game's half mental."

"Yogi Berra?"

"Ah, you are thinking!" said Ellen. "Hip-hip-hooray!"

"What happens when the husband comes back with the water?"

"She tells him to boil some more. A good midwife can keep him whizzing back and forth like a yo-yo until the baby's delivered. At which point she has him start cleaning up."

The teakettle sang. Ellen went to it and poured and came back with two cups. "So here's how we're gonna get Ross to boil our water," she said.

~

"Bebe, I don't know," said PJ. "It seems like a tough competition."

"Nonsense," said Bebe. "We can do this."

They stood together in an aisle at Kelly Green Drygoods, reading the flier. It was for a quilting show in a rural county not far from Chattanooga. "THE 1994 POLK COUNTY MINERS HERITAGE FESTIVAL AND QUILT SHOW," it read. It looked to be a decent time; the flier promised food, bluegrass bands, and fireworks.

"I don't know squat about traditional Appalachian styles," PJ said. "And that's what we'd have to enter."

"So you'll learn," Bebe said. "Since when have you ever

turned down a chance to work on your craft, Cupcake?"

"But I've got school and stuff. The deadline's in six weeks. That's right before finals."

"You're a straight-A student. You can manage the time."

PJ straightened her glasses. "I'm not sure. You might wind up doing most of it…"

"If that's how it goes, then that's how it goes," Bebe said. "When we go home we'll get the books out."

"You mean you want to start the design today?"

"We've only got six weeks! And you've got me all excited!"

PJ smiled. *Funny how that works,* she thought.

~

PJ yawned. If she and Ellen didn't wind up this little psyche-ops show in the next few minutes, she was going to pass out face-first onto the table.

*Bonk! And then Ross'll call 911 for real, instead of another one of my friends.*

But then a cold thought came to her. *Like who? Name one other friend who'd come running over like Ellen did. See? You can't.*

She realized both of them were looking at her.

"Once I'm there I'm fine," she said, hoping it would fit into whatever they were talking about. "But to get to Monticello from Grand Junction I have to drive something like four or five hours."

"You'll fall asleep," Ross said. "Like you did in the van this afternoon." He held his hand out, palm down, and flipped it over. "*Pow.*" He fluttered his fingers to mimic the car aflame.

PJ groaned inwardly, remembering how she'd jolted awake outside Flo's apartment, the seatbelt like a tourniquet across her chest, no idea where she was. Flo had said goodbye politely, but…

"I could take a bus," PJ said.

"Come on," Ross said. He toyed with his coffee cup.

"A taxi?" Ellen asked.

"A four-hour taxi ride?" Ross retorted. "She might as

well buy a car." He shook his head. "Pfft. Listen to me: 'She might as well buy a car.' As if."

He took a deep breath. *Here it comes,* PJ thought.

"PJ, I know you want to do this by yourself, but I have to come with you."

She let her mouth fall open. "What about work?"

"Aah. Rick owes me about a million hours. He'll be ticked off, but I can straighten it out." He chuckled softly. "I'll tell him it's a family emergency."

"I don't know," Ellen said. "Have Lizzie and Baker flown before?"

"No. We might be able to find a flight that lays over in Chicago so my parents can pick them up, though."

"Sounds like a hassle," Ellen said.

"This is probably a dumb idea, Ellen," said PJ, "but what if you kept them?"

Ross started nodding slowly. "I hate to ask you to do that, but it would make things a lot simpler."

Ellen chewed her lip. "I guess I could try," she said reluctantly. "It'll give me a chance to show Lizzie how to hold a needle and thread. And does Baker know how to run a vacuum cleaner?"

"You are fully empowered to teach Baker to run a vacuum cleaner," PJ said.

*And to play poker,* she thought.

~

"Bebe?" PJ called as she came through the kitchen door.

She dumped her books on the table and went into the living room. "Bebe, are you here?"

*Her car's out front,* PJ thought. *Not that she'd dare drive anymore.*

She found Bebe in the back yard.

With Anne. They were sitting on the brick patio with a pitcher of iced tea between them on the wrought-iron table. Bebe, as usual for these last couple of weeks, was piecing fabric for the quilt they'd designed for the Appalachian competition.

"Mom!" PJ blurted. "This is a surprise. Where's your—um, what are you driving these days?"

Anne turned and PJ glimpsed her own face at forty. Anne was losing her young-girl looks; her skin was coarsening from the sun, her cheekbones were sharpening, and she was clearly bleaching her hair.

But she was still thin and beach-bunny attractive and her smile still showed all thirty-two of her white and perfect teeth. "Hi," she called, patting the seat beside her. PJ came and sat, and Anne put an arm around her shoulders and hugged her.

"Well," Anne said, "it's quite the saga. My car gave it up about halfway across Arkansas and I had to hitch the rest of the way in. I made it from Little Rock to Nashville in one day, but I had a run-in with—ah, the less said about that, the better. Anyway, I'm here! Now what do you need me to do?"

PJ glanced at Bebe, and Bebe said, "We were talking about the quilting show, Cupcake. I was thinking Anne could help us."

"But I want to *do* something," said Anne. "Not just sit around sewing."

"Uh-oh," PJ said.

"Now, Anne," said Bebe. "Sewing *is* doing."

Anne picked up a piece of fabric and rubbed it between her thumb and fingers. "But can't machines do it faster?"

Bebe smiled gently. "Not if they break down in Little Rock. PJ, show her the pictures you sent off for."

PJ went into the house and came back with a thick notebook. "This contest is supposed to be about traditional Appalachian quiltmaking," she explained, handing the notebook to Anne. "We did a bunch of research and tried to pick out methods that had been handed down from generation to generation in this area."

"Mmm-hmm," Anne murmured a bit vacantly as she turned pages.

"There, that one," said PJ. "One of the curators at the Library of Congress sent me that picture. It's from West Virginia in 1930."

Anne slid the photo out of its plastic envelope and

studied it. "OK, so it's an old lady and her granddaughter sitting by a frame quilting together."

"Well, sure," said PJ. "But look closely."

"Hmm. Grandma's got her hair up in a bun. They're in homemade clothes. The girl needs to see a dentist. I don't understand—what am I supposed to be looking for?"

"There's a ton of information about traditional quiltmaking in that picture," PJ explained. "But here's what it boils down to: everything they're using is scrappy. They're using a sliver of soap to mark the fabric. The fabric they're using is mostly big pieces so there's not a whole lot of waste, and from square to square the colors don't match up. The patterns are cut out of old newspaper. Even the frame they're using—it's different kinds of lumber. I bet it's hand-sawn."

PJ took a deep breath. "Mom, these are people who don't have any money. But look how happy they are, just keeping busy and enjoying each other's company. That's the essence of quilting, right there. Every picture of Appalachian quilting I found shared some of those same elements.

"So we're not using machines or modern products in our quilt for the contest. The fabric's all recycled from old clothes and so forth. Everything we're doing for that show, we're doing the way those two would've. And that's the quilt we're planning to make, too—a simple Churn Dash pattern."

"Churn Dash?"

"Yeah, it looks like the blades in a butter churn. It's rectangles and triangles arranged around a central square."

Anne nodded. "OK," she said. "When in Tennessee, churn butter. So what do you need from me?"

"As far as what we need," PJ said helplessly, "I guess we need whatever it is people need in this situation. We're sort of making this up as we go."

"I could help with the quilt," Anne suggested.

*Oh, no, no, no,* PJ thought. "Sounds good, sure," she said. "But it's gotta be done right. I mean, there's a lot riding on it—first prize is five hundred bucks."

Anne smiled a big patient mom-smile and patted PJ's

hand. "You just tell me what you want and I'll handle it. OK, Cupcake?"

~

Upstairs, Ellen helped PJ pack.

"Get some good sleep tonight and don't worry," Ellen said. She tapped her forehead again. "And remember: half mental."

"I'm the only one who's half mental around here," PJ said. "If this trip doesn't pan out, maybe I shouldn't come back. Baker and Lizzie'll be better off without me."

Ellen paused, a hairbrush in one hand and a can of shaving cream in the other. "Well, now, that's horse-petunia, isn't it?" she said. "But we'll handle that when you get home. And uh—speaking of horse petunias—as long as you're picking up men in Utah, say hello to Roy if you see him. And bring him with you if he's cute."

She frowned as she zipped PJ's toiletries into a bag. "On second thought," she said, "just bathe him and bring him anyway."

▶▶◆◀◀
## Chapter Thirteen

They got the travel arrangements squared away on Monday and left early Tuesday. PJ woke up in Chicago and woke up in Denver and woke up in Grand Junction, Colorado.

"Better?" Ross asked as he unloaded their carry-ons from overhead.

"I don't know. I've got a splitting headache." She was three or four kinds of blown out—exhausted, woozy from the antihistamines she'd secretly taken to knock herself out, a stiff neck from sleeping in the cramped seats, hungry for a real meal—but also, in a strange way, feeling like she'd left her troubles behind in Chattanooga.

*Wrong,* she thought. *You've just traded them for new ones. We spent eighteen hundred bucks on airplane tickets, and that's not the beginning of it. We've still got to rent a car and find a hotel. Buy gas. Eat out.*

"I imagine Ellen has a headache too, right about now," Ross laughed.

~

There was a little boy holding his father's hand at baggage claim. The boy wanted to ride the conveyer but his father wouldn't let him. Finally, the man nodded and released his son's hand. The little boy climbed onto the conveyor and giggled as it bore him along. A businessman standing next to them smiled and said something.

PJ tried not to watch them.

~

As they left Grand Junction PJ aimed the air conditioner vent downwards so it wouldn't blow in her eyes. The air fluttered the wrapper in her lap, little flecks of bun and meat littering her jeans where she'd picked a cheeseburger apart without really tasting it.

*Setting out across the desert with my husband,* she thought. *There's a biblical metaphor in there somewhere, but I'm too zonked to remember it.*

She looked up, suddenly remembering something else. "What was supposed to happen in five days, Ross?"

He glanced at her but didn't answer.

"OK," she said, turning to the window. *When did we start keeping secrets from each other?* she wondered. And she immediately felt guilty and foolish for it, because she knew the answer.

The highlands diminished to sandstone crags which themselves scattered into a wide and wind-scoured plain of gullies and scrub. A lone antelope bucked through the sagebrush. All dry, everywhere dry, with the sun a brown study before them.

PJ tried to take it in. To step from the everywhere-sameness of a Chattanooga strip-mall suburb into the barrenness of the high Utah desert, winking through the glass-and-chrome gateway of an airline terminal—such a displacement should make her feel like an alien, she reflected. But it didn't.

*The two places are so similar. But how? There's nothing here, and there's everything back there. So what is it? The peace and quiet? The distance? The emptiness?*

"This is beautiful," Ross said, as if affected in the same

way. "Look how clear the light is. We could park and just start walking forever."

"Roy told me some climbers found Silver outside town," she said. "I can't imagine what it'd be like to be lost out here."

"You'd sell your soul for water."

She glanced back at the mountains, saw how snow glistened on their peaks even now with summer close at hand. They were already thirty miles across the badlands and there was no end to the shimmering, pebbly heat. Until you reached the Pacific Ocean, she supposed, beyond the westward curve of the earth.

"Grandpa would've liked this," she said.

~

"I like this," said Anne. She was sitting at the kitchen table opposite from PJ, a cup of coffee at her elbow and a mostly-finished Churn Dash block in front of her. Between them was the heap of triangles and squares they'd spent all evening cutting from old clothing and bedsheets.

"It's nice, isn't it?" said PJ. "But I can't believe that's the first block you've ever sewn. I mean, we were—well, I'm sorry to put it this way—but we were raised by the same woman, you know?"

Anne tied a knot. "I was always outdoors a lot more than I was in," she said. "And I had a lot going on at school, too."

"My mother, the cheerleader," PJ said.

"Don't forget the drama club," said Anne, holding her block up to the light. "I was the president. Still am, I guess."

It surprised PJ to hear Anne say something so self-deprecating, and she was trying to think of something lighthearted and clever to say back, when she heard Anne swear under her breath.

"Mom!" she said. "It's a good thing Bebe's asleep. She'd wash your mouth out."

"Look at this thing," Anne said darkly. "It looks like a jigsaw puzzle. How do you keep everything lined up so straight?"

**126**

"Here, let me see it," said PJ. "Yeah, that's what I thought. You put the bias on the edge. Look, do you know what the 'grain' in fabric is?"

"Quinoa?"

"Whosis? Keen-who?"

"Sorry, that's a terrible joke."

PJ tried to ignore it. "Fabric," she said, "is made with a crosswise grain and a lengthwise grain. It's a weave, with threads running left and right and up and down, see? Very strong that way. The trouble is, though, if you cut the fabric into triangles, you're always cutting at least one side on the bias."

"On the bias," Anne repeated.

"The bias is when you're cutting across the horizontal and the vertical threads at the same time," PJ said.

But seeing the blank look on Anne's face, she took a square of fabric and held it up. "Horizontal threads," she said, moving her finger from left to right. "Vertical threads," she said, moving her finger up and down. "And the bias," she said, moving her finger at a forty-five degree angle from corner to corner.

"Why is the bias important?" Anne said.

"When you cut on the bias, you're cutting across the weave in both directions. That makes it easy for the threads to fray. It also makes it easy for the weave to stretch. And when the weave stretches—"

"Oh, I see," said Anne. "That's why my block's so lopsided. With all these triangles in it, I must've been pulling it too hard. Stretching it."

PJ nodded. "Probably."

"So how do I get myself out of this?"

"You don't. You either have to start over, or you have to spend a bunch of time picking all the pieces apart."

"You mean I just wasted all that work?"

"Well, I wouldn't say 'wasted.' It took you a half hour, but look what you learned."

Anne put the block down. "PJ, at the very least you could've said something. You're enjoying this, aren't you?"

"Enjoying it? Mom! Look, quilting isn't easy. Learning how was the most frustrating thing I've ever done. And you'd think Bebe would've tried to make it easier for me, but I swear, it felt like she was throwing up obstacles every time I turned around.

"I made the exact same mistake you just made, Mom, and you know what Bebe told me? She said, 'You behave yourself into trouble, you have to behave yourself out of it.'"

"More of Mother's fortune-cookie advice."

"I don't know. It seemed harsh to me, too."

"So what did you do the first time you realized you had to start over?"

PJ grinned. "I ran outside crying."

"I'm not going to run crying, but this is way too structured," said Anne.

"The structure's what makes it so beautiful."

"Structure's ugly. Think about...I don't know...a factory. All that concrete and smoke. Straight lines, and people coming and going when a whistle blows."

"But what does the factory make?" PJ asked. "Stained glass, maybe? Quilts are beautiful, Mom, but without the math and the precision and the know-how, the art's impossible. It's the fundamentals that make or break you, and I think that's what Bebe was really trying to teach me."

PJ realized Anne was watching her in a strange way. Measuring her, almost, as if Anne had come home to find that PJ was a foreigner, living in a foreign culture and speaking a foreign language.

*Well, no surprise there,* PJ thought.

"Did you set that up deliberately?" Anne asked. "So you could feed me that lecture? And that line about behavior?"

"Um..."

"No, no, never mind," Anne said, waving the question away. "Regardless whether you did or not, if you did, you played it just right. And I think that's how I'd like to remember you."

"I don't understand," said PJ.

"What time is it?" Anne asked.

"Time? It's, uh, eleven-thirty."

"And the quilt's due in two weeks. Tell you what, let

me make another pot of coffee. We might as well stay up all night—we've got a lot of catching up to do."

~

"Do you want to stop for the night?" Ross asked as they passed southwards through the town of Moab. Even now, well after sunset, the main road was jammed with dusty, fat-tired jeeps and hippie vans laden with absurd numbers of mountain bikes.

"Let's go on," she said. "I won't be able to sleep if we stop."

They reached Monticello ninety minutes later, in the dead of night. Ross swung the car into the ER parking lot.

PJ gasped. There was a hearse backed up to the ambulance door.

▶▶▶◆◀◀◀
## Chapter Fourteen

PJ took the concrete steps two at a time and hit the doors at a dead run. The left-hand one was locked— *OW!* she thought, feeling her wrist bend back too far—and she bounced clumsily off the door with her shoulder and opened the other one.

"Where's the ICU?" she called to the security guard in the lobby.

He pointed the way. "Is someone hurt, ma'am?"

"I hope that's all it is," she said as she hurried past him.

He got up and followed her. "Ma'am? Ma'am? If you need help you need to tell me!"

PJ accelerated. The ICU doors ahead of her were bright red.

~

The old man was more bone than flesh. The bed engulfed him, its clean white linen offsetting his sunburned and blotchy skin. Under the oxygen mask, a tube arose from his nostril to a bedside machine. Another snaked from the back of his hand to an IV bag hung from an overhead

130

hook. An old tattoo, faded beyond recognition, marked his forearm where the IV needle pierced him. The smell of antiseptic was strong but not strong enough to fool her into thinking he was clean.

"I thought we were too late," PJ said. "I thought he was gone. Thought I'd never know…"

She squeezed Ross's hand and stood up and went to the side of the bed. Silver, like the old quilt he'd sent, was hard-used. He still had a full head of hair, white though it was, but she could see where they'd shaved it back to expose a caterpillar trail of steel staplery. Perhaps his hair had been reddish, once, and his complexion good.

But no longer. And there was no family resemblance she could find. His face was spotted, his eyebrows bushy, his nose long and thin. His eyes were sunken; whether by nature or from his ordeal, there was no way for her to know. His chin was scrubby with several days' worth of stubble. His teeth were yellow with nicotine. One, in front, was missing. Another was broken off.

Jerry's words came back to her: *You look away and keep walking.*

*I need to call that guy,* she thought. *Tell him what's happened.*

"What do you want to do?" Ross asked. "Go unpack? Get something to eat?"

"I don't know. Yeah, but on the other hand, I hate to leave. If he wakes up…"

"Right. Well, I tell you what. Hang out here and I'll get us checked in. Call me if anything happens."

~

A quiet night in the ICU. There was little movement and the phones beyond the curtain seldom rang. She took out her quilting bag, saw how her hands trembled, and put the bag away again. Presently she stood to stretch her back.

It was then she noticed the shape of Silver's feet under the blanket. One was shorter than the other. She glanced around furtively and decided to sneak a look. Under the blanket and sheet his legs were emaciated and raw, and half his right foot was gone. Cleanly truncated and glossy with old scar tissue. And the left was missing toes. She averted her eyes and quickly covered him back up.

*Did Bebe really love this man once?* she wondered.

Silver breathed on. In time there was a knock behind her. PJ turned, expecting Ross or a nurse, but it was a Vietnamese-looking guy in jeans and a straw cowboy hat.

"How's old Silver?" he asked in a strangely familiar voice.

"Roy?"

He doffed his hat to her. "Atcher service."

PJ blinked. "You're not...what I was expecting." *Stupid, stupid, stupid,* she thought. *So he's Asian, so what?*

He smiled. "My momma always said the same thing."

"Well, Ellen Sanders said hello." *And somebody ought to be waiting to catch her if she ever meets you.*

Roy did a double-take. "She's not here, is she? I was just on the phone with her, for crying out loud!"

PJ laughed at Ellen. Then she laughed again at the puzzled expression on Roy's face.

~

In twenty minutes or so Ross returned and Roy coaxed them to a diner across the street. "Don't worry, they'll call me," he said, patting the nickel-plated cell phone in the little hand-tooled leather holster on his belt.

They sat near the window in a red vinyl booth. From her seat PJ could see the glass double doors of the emergency room. Two nurses paced in the ambulance bay smoking cigarettes. The traffic was sparse, the street quiet.

"Turns out he was living in an alcove above the canyon floor over at Dark Canyon," Roy said. "Had him a cot and a stove and everything. Paperbacks. I wouldn't mind knowing how he got it all humped up there."

"And no ID?" PJ asked.

"Not so much as a Social Security card," he said.

The waiter brought steaming platters. "Three Navajo tacos, one with no guacamole," he said. He set a pink slip of paper on the table and left them.

**132**

PJ stared at her plate. "This isn't a taco," she said, studying the wheel of frybread mounded over with lettuce and cheese and sour cream and red onions, the whole of it drenched in thick green sauce.

"What do you think a taco is?" Roy asked.

"Well, a tortilla shell and ground beef. Warm and cheesy. I don't know if I can eat this."

Roy laughed at her, but not unkindly. "How about you just trust me and give it a whirl. Here," he said, and he dumped his saucer of guacamole over her plate without asking permission.

She tried not to twist her face in disgust and shoved the ridiculously small fork into the haystack of food and lifted it to her mouth. Then she blinked. It was just the right balance of temperature and flavor—rich, piquant, and cheesy. The lettuce was cool and crisp, the onions were sharp without biting, and the shreds of chicken carried hints of chili pepper and citrus. The green sauce made her toes tingle like the first taste of coffee on a winter morning.

*This is phenomenal,* she thought as she chewed. *Even the guac. It's real avocados, real cilantro. I didn't know they still made this stuff. It's like this is the food all the plastic drive-through stuff I've ever eaten was modeled after.*

"How many calories does one of these have?" she asked Roy.

He stroked his chin. "Not more than eighty thousand, I'd say."

She smiled. "Is that all?"

They ate for a while and then Ross wiped his lips. "Dark Canyon," he said.

"Mmm-hmm," Roy mumbled around a mouthful. "Way off the beaten track. Thirty miles from here, most of it four-wheel drive roads."

"You get a lot of rescues?" PJ asked.

"Depends on what you mean by 'rescue.' Kid a while back had a rock fall on him in a slot canyon across the river. Pinned his arm. A few days later he got thirsty enough to amputate with a pocketknife so he could walk back out." Roy shook his head. "We get a fair number

**133**

of body recoveries but hardly any rescues. Silver's real lucky."

Then Roy's phone rang. PJ spun to the window. The nurses had gone inside.

Roy quick-drew his phone, flipped it open. "Yellow," he said. "That's right, they are. Yes, ma'am, I did. Yes, Ellen. OK." He flipped the phone closed and flicked an invisible fleck off his shirtsleeve. "Your kids are fine."

Ross slid PJ a sideways glance that said several funny things at once. "Maybe you'd better go back across the street," he said to PJ.

"I have to finish eating."

"What, the plate?"

"Oh," she said. It was empty, wiped clean. "Yeah. Well, can you bring me another one of those when you come back across?"

"Navajo soul food," chuckled Roy.

~

Anne looked up from the drinks menu. "You look great," she said, studying PJ. "How do you feel?"

PJ glanced around the fern bar and rubbed the gooseflesh on her arms. "Am I supposed to say sexy? My legs are freezing in this skirt. My eyes feel goopy. And that wax thing—when the girl at the salon told me where she wanted to put that stuff…" PJ shuddered. "I'm not ever doing that again."

Anne laughed. "It's not fun being beautiful, is it?"

"Why would you ever put yourself through that?"

"You're good raw material," Anne said. "You're young, you've got a good figure, you're smart—you just need to work it."

"Work it," PJ repeated glumly. "I never thought of being attractive as work. More of a curse. All the pretty girls I know are shallow. Um, present company excepted."

"Take off your glasses," Anne said.

"Excuse me? Why?"

"Because those tortoiseshell frames make you look like a quilter."

"I am a quilter. And I won't be able to see!"

"Well," Anne said in a dry voice. "Sometimes that's a good thing."

"This is—"

"Just take off your glasses." Anne held up her right hand. "You see how swollen my knuckles are? I've sewn more this week than I have in my entire life. Now it's my turn to teach you something. So take your glasses off. And trust me."

PJ took her glasses off and folded them carefully into the case, which barely fit into the microscopic handbag her mother had bought her that afternoon. Everything Anne had picked out for her was microscopic, in fact—the skirt, the top, even the underwear. And thinking of the underwear made PJ shift her hips uncomfortably.

*I feel like I've got a piece of selvage up my butt,* she thought. *Which is freshly waxed, too. Like a new car at the lot. Big Sale, Test Drive It Today!*

"Stop fidgeting," Anne said. "This isn't work, and it isn't a curse, either. It's a game. There are rules. That's the beauty of it."

"What do you mean?"

"You're the one who gets to make the rules up. That's what we call 'power.'"

"I just want to find the right guy, not run the world."

"But you are running the world. I want you to watch me when the waiter comes over. Just watch."

"I need my glasses for that."

"Just watch," Anne repeated, smiling in an annoyingly patronizing way.

~

PJ came into the ICU to find three doctors and a nurse working around Silver's bed.

*Why did I leave?* she thought. *I was over there pigging out, and—*

A nurse turned. Her words were hurried. "He came out of it."

PJ stood on tiptoe to get a better view. Silver was

thrashing and kicking in the bed, groaning incoherent words. His eyes were rolled back. He arched his chest high off the bed, and he twisted to and fro.

The doctor, who looked barely twenty-five, was pinning him by his shoulders. A nurse fumbled with velcro straps.

"Ativan," said the doctor. "In my coat pocket."

The nurse darted to the doctor's side, reached into his pocket, and brought out a syringe. She flicked the cap off with her thumb, bared Silver's shoulder, and sank the needle in.

PJ stepped forward, holding her breath.

Silver's eyelids fluttered.

"Sir? Sir?" said the doctor.

Silver looked around the room. His eyes were wide, panicky. He looked first at the doctor, then at the nurses, until he found PJ.

Something like calmness settled over him.

"Elizabeth," he croaked. "There you are."

He held PJ's eyes with his for what felt an endless time. And then he fell asleep. Or fainted, she wasn't sure which. The light in the old man had flickered out like a faraway searchlight benighted by the vacuum of space.

~

Ross and Roy sat vigil with PJ until midnight. Roy excused himself, pleading work the next morning, and a short while later she woke Ross and told him to go to the hotel.

In the early morning the young doctor pronounced Silver stable and had him wheeled to an ordinary room. The kid—Dr. Myers—seemed competent enough, PJ thought. He was a blonde peach-fuzz Mormon type who seemed genuinely moved by what Silver had gone through.

"What can I do to help?" she asked him.

"Just be here for him when he wakes up. Ring the duty nurse."

"No. I meant when you release him. As far as taking him home."

"We...have a staff oncologist," Dr. Myers said, looking at his feet. "You can consult with her. Judging from what I saw, though..."

PJ swallowed.

*Oh, man, I wish Ross was here to hear this.*

~

The waiter approaching their booth was a tall guy, V-shaped, with good arms and thick brown hair. But it was his eyes PJ liked the most—deep-set and liquid brown, with long lashes and a definite gleam of intelligence. She was curious to see what Anne would do, but she also wanted to slide under the table.

"Welcome to Chili's," he said, smiling. He had nice choppers, too. "Can I get you something to drink before you order?"

Anne flipped her hair back. "I don't know, I'm having trouble deciding. This Singapore thing, what's that?"

"Singapore Sling," he said. "It's basically a bunch of gin and pineapple juice."

Her *eyes* lit up. "Oooh, that sounds good! Do I get a little umbrella in it?"

"I will personally make sure you get a little umbrella in it," he grinned.

*This is like watching a snake hypnotize a bird,* PJ thought.

The waiter turned to her. "And you?"

"I'll have, um, tea," she mumbled.

"Long Island?"

"No, sweet. With lemon."

He lowered his eyebrows, gave her a quizzical look. "You want an umbrella too?"

"Mmm-no."

"If you insist. I'll be right back."

When he was gone PJ leaned across the table. "What is Long Island tea?"

Anne shook her head. "All right. This is going to be tougher than I thought. First of all, men want to be helpful. You have to let them."

"But I knew what I wanted."

"No you didn't. See, you don't know what you want. That's the idea. And since you don't know, he'll want to

**137**

show you. It makes him feel smart. And when he feels smart, he feels confident. And when he feels confident…" Anne grinned like a hungry shark.

"What's with wiggling your neck at him? It looked painful."

"You have to focus him on your best features. I have good hair, so I make sure he notices it. Next time he comes over, you should lightly touch your cleavage. Just a little."

PJ's neck grew hot. "I will not!"

"OK," Anne sighed. "Maybe you better not, anyway. You don't want to tart it up too much the first time around."

"Or the second, or the third, or—"

Anne put a finger to her lips. The waiter was coming back with their drinks.

"A Singapore thing, with umbrella," the V-shaped guy said, setting it down, "and a sweet tea and lemon, without. Are you ladies ready to order now?"

Anne ignored him. She studied the menu, frowning, and he stood waiting patiently.

*What is she doing?* PJ wondered. *It's like he's not even there.*

PJ waited a few more seconds and then spoke up. "I'll have—"

"Uh…yeah," Anne interrupted. "This fried chicken salad—what kind of oil do you use?"

"Peanut, I think?"

"No, that's no good. How about the Caesar? Are those free-range eggs?"

"I'm pretty sure they're not," he said. "Do you want me to ask back in the kitchen?"

Anne's smile was dazzling. "Would you mind?"

"No, of course not." He smiled back. "My pleasure."

When he was gone Anne winked. "See what I mean?"

"I think the phrase is 'completely clueless,'" PJ said. "One minute you don't know what you want, the next you want free-range eggs. You giggle at him, then you're a jerk."

"Ahh! The harder you make it for him, the harder he'll have to work at it. You'll seem mysterious. Alluring. Men like high-maintenance. Plus, it's nice to be chased every once in a while."

PJ covered her eyes with her palm. "It's all crazy."

"Well, crazy is good, too."

"Why is crazy good?"

Anne's smile was very knowing, very earthy, and PJ felt her stomach shrink.

"They'll never admit to it," Anne said, "but men think crazy women are the best ones in bed."

"You're telling me I have to act crazy and sleep with a guy to make him like me?"

"Oh, Lord no," Anne laughed. "What kind of mother would I be if I told you that?"

"I sometimes wonder," PJ admitted.

"Watch and learn," Anne said.

~

At mid-morning PJ awoke in her chair beside Silver's bed and went to the bathroom. Ross called her name and when she came back, Silver was staring at her.

"I thought you were Elizabeth," the old man said. His voice was gravelly and his breath whistled slightly. "But you're not. You're her spitting image, but you're not my Elizabeth."

"Bebe...couldn't be here," PJ gulped. "I'm sorry, I'm so sorry." She sat quickly. "I'm her granddaughter."

Silver looked away. "Bebe, huh," he muttered. He turned to Ross. "And you are..."

"Ross Hathaway, sir." Ross extended his hand.

Silver shook it weakly and looked back to PJ. "And who're you?"

"PJ Hathaway. Um, Piper Jo."

His face was expressionless. "Piper Jo," he said. "Piper Jo. Well, Piper Jo, my name is Joe Piper."

PJ felt the blood draining from her face.

~

*I cannot believe I let Mom put me up to this,* PJ thought. *I shouldn't have let her talk me into that wine, either.*

Their waiter, the V-shaped guy, was behind the bar now, pouring tequila and green sludge into one of several blenders. With her glasses off PJ couldn't make out much of her reflection in the mirror wall behind the bottle-laden shelves, but she didn't mind that. She knew she wouldn't recognize herself anyway. The makeup, the hair, the tight little number she was wearing—nope, it wouldn't be her at all.

She took a deep breath. He looked up at her. She couldn't tell if his expression changed, but he returned his attention to the blender. Then he looked up again.

PJ tossed her head, sending what she hoped was a graceful ripple through her hair. She touched herself between her breasts and let her finger linger there for an instant longer than necessary. Then she poked her tongue into her cheek, put a hand on her hip, and started strutting towards him. Never taking her eyes off his.

*In the movies this is always the part where the girl trips over her own high heels,* PJ thought. *How do you not strut in these stupid things?*

As she neared him she parted her lips slightly. Moistened them with the tip of her tongue. Felt him watching her. Felt every guy there watching her, in fact.

*Monkeys in a zoo. And I'm the fruit.*

She put an elbow on the bar and leaned across it, trying to show him more without showing him too much.

There was a slight smile on his face. "Can I help you?" he asked.

"I don't know, can you?" she purred with what she hoped was a mischievous grin.

To her great surprise he laughed in her face. He shut the blender down and popped the top and poured the icy mix into a glass, still laughing.

"What?" she demanded. "Did I say something?"

"That's quite some act you've got there," he chortled. He turned his back on her, plunged the blender into the sink, and toweled his hands dry. "Do you two have a bet or something?" he asked over his shoulder. "I've been hit on a lot of ways, but tonight has been the absolute pinnacle of it. Do you have, like, a hidden camera crew?"

"I think I made a mistake," PJ said. She didn't wait for

him to answer. She whirled and crossed the room in a heartbeat, banged her way through the saloon doors, and stomped to their table, the CLICK-CLICK-CLICKING of her heels reverberating throughout the restaurant.

"Well?" Anne asked. "What happened?"

"I want to go home," PJ announced. "Right now."

~

A nurse came in. She busied around Silver, took his blood pressure and shone a penlight in his eyes, and said a doctor would come by shortly.

After she left, PJ was stumped for a way to kick-start the conversation. There was so much to ask, so much to say. Finally, she leaned over and unzipped her quilting bag. She hadn't meant to do this yet, but what else was there?

"I brought something for you, Mr. Piper," she said. He watched unmoving as she spread the tattered quilt across the foot of his bed.

"Hoped I'd never see that thing again," he said.

"How long have you been carrying it?" she asked.

"Fifty some-odd years."

"You made it in Korea, didn't you? When you were a prisoner?"

He looked away from her.

PJ studied him. Then she reached into her quilting bag again.

"There's something else," she said, bringing out Bebe's Christmas present. She'd rewrapped it in its original paper, doing her best to hide where she'd torn it open, and she'd affixed Bebe's original label to it. She put it in his lap.

He lay still. "What's that?"

"Read it."

Silver craned his neck, narrowed his eyes. "Where'd you get it from?"

"It was in with some of my grandmother's old things. When you sent your quilt I got curious and dug them out."

He looked away.

"Why don't you open it?" she said. "Here, let me help you."

"I'll do it, I'll do it," he said, and he began struggling with the tape and paper. "Hold this thing up, son," he told Ross when he was finished.

Ross took the quilt and stood at the foot of the bed holding it with arms widespread.

"She made this for you in late 1953," PJ said.

Silver studied it a long time and then lowered his head.

"Do you know what it means?" she asked.

"I know, all right." He lowered his face into his hands and began making muffled sounds.

"Oh, man," Ross said, holding the quilt and looking up at the ceiling and blinking.

~

Silver's energy waned and he seemed to lose interest in them. He lapsed in and out of sleep. When it grew late PJ and Ross decided it'd be kindest to leave him be until the next day.

"I've seen this before," PJ told Ross as they rode the hospital elevator down. "Remember that old guy Don I told you about? At the nursing home? It's like that witch doctor thing—they just give up and if you don't pull them out of it, that's it."

"So what do we do?" Ross asked. "Move to Utah?"

"I don't know," she said.

▶▶◆◀◀
## Chapter Fifteen

The next morning Ross asked one of the hospital's IT guys to hook him up to the wireless network so he could check his e-mail. It took him a half-hour to sort through it all—and PJ watched as his face grew more and more concerned—and then he had to sit out in the hallway making phone calls. It was no big deal, he told her, just a customer fretting over contract details.

"Go home if you need to," she said. "I can deal with Silver and the hospital."

"Stop trying to get rid of me," he laughed. "I can handle it from here. Somebody's gotta talk the guy down off a ledge, that's all."

Ross left her alone in the room with Silver. He was turned on one side, snoring. It struck her as healthy sleep. She took out her quilting bag, thought about working again, and then just sat watching him.

She and Bebe had sat up with Aunt Carol like this. At all hours. And even at the very end, when Aunt Carol was certainly gone no matter what the hospital machinery might say, Bebe would still sing to her and talk to her.

"Carol might not hear me with her ears," Bebe had said. "But she hears me."

PJ contemplated the slackness of Silver's face and the

**143**

high sounds of his breathing. "You have a daughter you've never met," she finally said to him, hoping Bebe had been right. "At least, I think she's yours. She's…well…you'll see."

~

PJ got up early the day after the debacle with her mom at the fern bar, and bid Bebe goodbye while Anne was sleeping it off. PJ sat in class all morning and then realized she'd forgotten to pack a lunch. She threw herself down on a bench outside the student center.

*Watch and learn,* PJ fumed as she unzipped her quilting bag. *Yeah, that's a plan. Act ditzy and throw yourself at a guy and hope you stick.*

She thought about her own father, then, for the first time since she couldn't remember. Dewayne Nash—*Nash,* she thought sarcastically—the man Anne had stuck to and PJ had rolled right off of.

He'd never been there when she bloodied her knee or made up a song. Or on winter mornings when she'd waited at the bus stop, alone and shivering, while her classmates sat in their fathers' cars with the engines running and warm air blowing. When her bike had needed fixing. When other girls' fathers had spoken at career day.

And then she had a flash from a wedding. She wasn't sure which one it was—she and Bebe had attended dozens together. They'd stood as an usher escorted the mother of the bride down the red-carpeted aisle, and then, as the piano swelled into the wedding march, there came the father, his chest heaving with pride, his daughter on his arm. Her shining in her white dress, him shining in his love for her.

*That'll never be me,* PJ thought. *And I shouldn't blame Dewayne for it. He didn't even know I was alive until it was too late. It was her. Her. She had me and gave me up and never looked back.*

She stood up and stuffed her work into her quilting bag. *It's time Mom and I had this out.*

But on her way home she passed the fern bar where they'd eaten the night before. It was on the outskirts of the mall, and she gritted her teeth and swerved into the turn lane.

144

Inside the fern bar, back at the scene of the crime with the potted plants and sports memorabilia all around, she asked the greeter if she could leave a note for a waiter.

"Which one?" the greeter asked. She was wearing a highway billboard's worth of buttons, among them one that featured a one-eyed smiley face and the motto: "MUTANTS FOR NUCLEAR POWER."

"Um," PJ said, identifying with it. "I'm not sure. Tall guy, dark hair, nice eyes."

The greeter smirked and PJ wanted to swat her. "He's at the bar," she said.

PJ went around the corner and through the cheesy saloon doors, dragging her feet the whole way. He was fiddling with a beverage hose down at one end of the bar. She sat at the other end, as far away as she could, and studied her reflection in the mirror and waited.

"Hi there," the V-shaped guy said when he caught sight of her. He came over and put a cardboard coaster down on the bar. "I almost didn't recognize you, with the glasses on. What'll it be? A Singapore thing?"

*Oh, great.* She looked down at her sneakers, feeling sick. *Thanks, Mom.*

~

"Mom's a sore subject," PJ told Silver, who slept on. "We should talk about something else. You know, you have two great-grandkids, Lizzie and Baker. We named Baker after Ross's grandmother, Ruth Baker Hathaway, and we named Lizzie after Bebe—'Elizabeth Belinda,' hence 'Bebe.' But you know that, I guess.

"Ross wasn't too wild about 'Belinda,' but I thought 'Baker' was kind of hokey, too. Don't tell him I said that."

She paused, absently touching her C-section scar through her jeans. "Baker had acid reflux for nine months. I had to hold him upright all the time or he'd start screaming. I guess I got in the habit of not sleeping. I couldn't. There's something about hearing your kid scream that goes in your ears and straight to your adrenal glands.

145

"Ross and I waited for a long time to have the kids. We married pretty young. Mid-twenties. Which wouldn't have been young for your generation, would it? And then I was, um, an electrical engineer for about ten years after Ross and I got married. I guess I was OK at it; I was always good with numbers. I think quilting did that for me, actually."

PJ laughed then, but it was sad laughter. "I miss having a career a lot. It's hard, now, living on one income. I feel guilty when I spend money. But it's more than that. I miss—I don't know—the validation of sitting in meetings and getting treated like what I'm doing matters. When you draw up a plan for a control system for an electric utility, you're doing something. When you mop up breakfast cereal, though…"

She broke off, watching Silver's eyes dart and roll behind their papery lids.

"But Ross is great," she continued. "I've made a lot of mistakes and he's stuck right there with me. He dropped everything to come out here. Worried sick about me, I guess. I feel terrible about that.

"He was the first guy I ever dated. You know what he said to me the first time we went out? 'I only go out with artists,' he said. Like he got it, right away. Why I quilted. He could be a great photographer if he just had time to work at it. I guess that's my fault too."

She sighed. "Like I said, I've made a lot of mistakes. Would you believe I can't even quilt anymore? I just don't have it in me.

"And I don't know where it went. Any of it."

~

PJ bowed her head. The bar was made from some kind of dark wood and it was streaked with watermarks. "I just wanted to apologize for the way my mom and I acted last night," she said to the V-shaped guy. "You were really nice and I'm really sorry."

He laughed. "That's a new one. You came in here to apologize? Man, I wish they were all as easy as you guys."

**146**

PJ put a hand on the bar and stood up. *Easy? Who's he calling easy?*

"I have to go," she said.

He held up his palms. "Whoa, whoa, whoa. Peace. Maybe that was the wrong word."

"What did you mean by it, then?"

"You're really embarrassed, aren't you?"

"Well, yeah. Wouldn't you be?"

He cocked his head to one side. "What was that all about, anyway? That little game you were playing?"

"It's a long story."

"I'm here until eight. Come on, sit down. Do you want a menu?"

"No."

"Let me see if I can guess," he said. "That was your mom. She thinks you need to get out more."

"Something like that," PJ admitted. She pushed her glasses back up her nose.

"Do you think she's right?"

PJ looked up at him.

"Never mind, I'm sorry," he said. "Maybe that was a little too personal. Would you please sit down?"

She did, and her words tumbled out. "Mom has all these ideas about how women should go after men. I think she knows about catching them, but not a whole lot about keeping them. And it's not the way I was raised."

"You lost me," he said. "She's your mom, didn't she raise you?"

"Last night was the first woman-to-woman conversation she and I have ever had. My grandmother raised me. A lot differently, I might add. Mom lives in San Diego. I think that's where she gets it."

PJ's stomach rumbled and he studied her again. He turned around to a computer screen and started punching buttons.

"Is it true what men think about crazy women?" she blurted.

"I don't know. What do you think we think?"

"That..." she blushed. "That crazy women are best in bed."

"Are you serious?" he asked. "I mean…I guess some guys, if a woman doesn't have any self-esteem…but why would anyone want to…" He trailed off, thought about it, and tried again. "Let me put it another way. If I was attracted to crazy women, wouldn't I have asked you for your phone number last night?"

She grinned sheepishly. "I suppose so."

"But did I?" he shrugged. "There you have it. Look, when I said you were 'easy' I didn't mean *that* kind of easy. I meant harmless. Unlike most of the drunks I see. Funny-cute. You were trying so hard."

A waiter set a big plate of nachos on the bar. The V-shaped guy thanked him and hefted it and put it in front of her. "What do you want to drink?" he asked.

"I didn't order that," she said in surprise. It smelled wonderful, and she was starving, but she didn't want to blow seven bucks on nachos when she could eat at home.

"You look hungry. Dig in." When she hesitated he said, "It's on me. What do you want to drink?"

"I don't drink." *Quit blurting!* she scolded herself.

His eyes danced with amusement. "That's a new one too. What's your name, anyway?"

"PJ. PJ Warner."

"PJ. I'm Ross Hathaway." He stuck out his hand. "I don't think you're crazy. But that doesn't mean I think you're…well, it's way too early for any of that, right?"

~

PJ sat bolt upright when she realized Silver's eyes were open and alert. He still lay on his side, but she knew he'd been awake and listening to her for some time.

"'You can't quilt anymore,'" he repeated. "'Your grandmother was that way when I first met her. You know, you've got her hands. Shame not to use 'em."

"I do?"

"It's true. Yours are just like hers. Thin, graceful…" he trailed off into silence.

PJ held her hands up, flexed her fingers, studied them. She spoke around a lump in her throat. "That's—

**148**

extraordinary. I've never heard—I mean—not too many men notice things like that. Is it true?"

"It's true. There was a lot more to her than her...uh."

Then he smiled. It was the first time she'd seen him do that. His mouth was set a little crooked and his teeth were no good, but his embarrassment was so offset by his devil-may-care grin that she found herself utterly charmed.

"My earliest memories of her are when she was maybe fifty," PJ said. "I've seen pictures, but..."

"Pictures aren't the same."

"No."

She got up and went to his bedside. Bebe's Christmas quilt, her gift for him, was twisted and pushed down. She straightened it around him and found the center, where the hands clutched the heart.

"Bebe would have traced her own hands onto this quilt," she said.

Silver sat up.

PJ spread her fingers and placed her hands into the outline of Bebe's hands. They fit perfectly, as if Bebe, over fifty years ago, had somehow reached into the future and traced them there herself.

"See?" the old man said.

"Did you ever see the movie *Cinderella*?" PJ asked.

▶▶▶◆◀◀◀
## Chapter Sixteen

It had been Saturday, Fourth of July weekend, when PJ drove her Volkswagen into Copperhill, Tennessee.

The mountains all around were lush with summer. Tourists milled on the street corners, their children eating pale blue snowcones that dripped on the sidewalk like the hydrangeas strewing petals from brick planters on every side.

An old couple emerged from a shop and stood blinking at the crosswalk in the strong sunshine. PJ waved for them to go ahead. They linked arms and smiled at her as they passed, strolling towards the old iron bridge that spanned the mossy-rocked river at the heart of town.

PJ noticed none of it. Her thoughts were tense and literal. For one thing, she dreaded unveiling this quilt. And for another, Ross Hathaway was sitting in the back seat next to Anne.

*She'll say I told you so forty times before this is over,* PJ thought.

She drove across the tracks and up the hill and parked at the town hall. Everyone climbed out. "Oh, I love bluegrass," Bebe said immediately. Down the way, on one side of the lot, people clustered where several musicians were picking. Banjo and guitar and big bass fiddle, and an old fellow wailing on a harmonica.

"Yeah, let's check it out," Anne said.

"We have to…" PJ started, but Anne was off, weaving through the crowd towards the fun.

Ross lifted his camera. He was a shutterbug, he'd told her during one of their phone conversations, and he'd enjoy taking pictures if she didn't mind him tagging along.

*No, can't say that I mind,* she thought.

Anne worked her way to the stagefront. She kicked her shoes off and hiked up her skirt and started twirling like a hippie, right there in front of everyone. A big grin on her face. As PJ watched, she caught a little boy by the hands and swung him around in a circle. He giggled and people in the crowd clapped.

"She sure knows how to enjoy herself," Ross said, lowering the camera.

Bebe nodded. "I like to see it. Doesn't she seem happy to you right now?"

"I don't know what to think about Mom," PJ confessed. "But we need to go register for the contest."

"Let your mother dance," Bebe said. "She deserves it."

PJ stared. "That's a strange thing to say."

Bebe smiled. "You'll understand when you have a daughter of your own."

"That'll be the day," PJ replied. But then she looked at Ross, and a secret thrill melted the last shards of her nervousness.

The band took a break and PJ collected Anne and they moved on. A sign over the town hall welcomed them to the festival. Ross took Bebe's arm as they climbed the steps. Inside they found three women at a card table taking quilt show entries.

PJ filled out the form and handed it over. "You're number one hundred and forty-eight," said one of the women.

*Big show for a small town,* PJ thought. *Oh, well.*

Inside the assembly hall, quilts hung everywhere. They found their spot and hung the quilt over the rack that had been set up there. PJ pinned up the old pictures and a handout she'd written describing what they'd learned about Appalachian techniques.

Ross came back with three folding chairs over one arm. He set them out around their display. "I'm gonna go wander around, take a few shots," he said.

"OK," said PJ.

He pursed his lips. "Well, then I'll see you in a little while."

As he started away, somebody pushed PJ from behind. Right between the shoulder blades. She turned, and there was Anne, with her back to PJ, studying a quilt across the aisle as if nothing had happened.

Bebe tittered.

*Oh, right, right, right,* thought PJ. "Ross, wait up," she called. She glared at Bebe in mock exasperation, and Bebe tittered again.

Ross smiled when she caught up to him.

They drifted around the show. He bought them cinnamon cupcakes from the high school band boosters and they munched them as they explored.

"Why's that woman over there giving me a dirty look?" he asked.

"Where? Ah—the one in the white gloves. Well, it's like this. You never touch a quilt with your bare hands, and especially not with icing on your fingers."

"The icing on the fingers thing I get," he said. "But if your hands are clean—why not?"

"Because it's like going to an art museum. You wouldn't fondle the Mona Lisa, would you?"

"Uh…"

"OK, OK, bad example. But you get the point, right? Anyway, the women wearing the gloves are there to handle quilts for you if you want to look at the backs."

"I guess that makes sense," he said. "But I had no idea that quilts were so sacred."

"Sacred? I wouldn't say that. They're…well…they're *intimate.* They take so much time to make and they're such special things."

"I'm glad I've got you to show me around," he said. "I'd sneeze in the wrong direction and I'd get myself stomped."

"Take that one there," she said, pointing to a quilt that was now faded with age but had once been bright green with summer.

"That's a fancy one," he said.

PJ laughed. "So it'd surprise you to find out that it's made from feedsacks?"

"Feedsacks? Animal feed?"

"Flour, animal feed, sugar, something like that."

"But look at it—it's beautiful."

"Yeah, visually. But there's a different kind of beauty in it, too. Can you see it?"

He squinted. "I'm not sure. Like I said, it's a good thing you're here to show me what's what."

And it dawned on PJ that here was a unique experience: a grown-up, intelligent, good-looking guy who seemed genuinely interested in her for what she thought and how she felt. It should've made her feel self-conscious, but somehow it relaxed her instead. Which should've confused her, but it didn't.

Was she connecting with him? She'd dated now and then—clumsy boys who'd made a great show of opening doors and picking up the check but tried to grope her on the front porch at the end of the evening. And she could count the intelligent conversations she'd had with them on the fingers of no hands. There had been nothing at stake, so she'd felt no need to worry about how they felt when she pushed them away.

"So...do you like quilting?" she stammered to start them talking again. *He's gonna say that his grandma used to quilt.*

And then his whole demeanor changed. He became curiously shy. "I like quilters," he said.

"Flattery'll get you everywhere."

"No, I'm serious. I've never really been interested in women who didn't practice some kind of art."

"Why's that?"

"It just seems like if the art's there, a whole lot more comes with it. You can make some...character assumptions, I guess."

"People have always assumed I was a geek for this." She indicated their surroundings. "You get told something long enough and you get to believing it."

"But you've won shows," he said.

"Yeah," she said, reluctant to appear immodest.

"Are you gonna win today?"

She grimaced. "I doubt it. You know, I'm glad Mom helped—that's what it's all about, really—but our quilt looks like it was sewn together by Doctor Frankenstein."

He laughed quietly. "I guess quilts are just like women, then. It's not necessarily how they're put together, it's what's in them. Or something like that."

That stopped PJ in her tracks. "What did you just say?" she asked.

He turned. "What?"

Something flowered up in her—and later in life when she felt it again she'd always associate it with the taste of cinnamon and hot days in July—and she knew what was going to happen before it did. He leaned his face to hers and they closed their eyes at the same moment and kissed.

When they came up for air an old woman sitting across the aisle was wiggling her finger at them. "You weren't expecting that, were you?" she teased them.

"Who?" they asked together. Then they looked at each other and laughed.

~

PJ went to the door of Silver's room and asked Ross to come in.

"You have to hear this," she told Ross. "We were talking about the old quilt and I asked him if he knew what the Chinese characters mean."

"An inch of love is an inch of ashes," Ross said. "Is that right?"

Silver eyeballed him. "Who translated it for you?"

"A cook at a Chinese restaurant. I'm still a little skeptical he got it right."

"Oh, it's right." Silver tugged awkwardly at the oxygen tubing that ran from over his ears to the cannula under his nose.

"What's it from?" PJ asked. "A proverb or something? It's too sad for a fortune cookie."

"From an old poem," Silver said.

"Do you know it?"

Silver frowned.

"Please? It'd mean so much if you'd just—"

"There's just no saying no to you, is there?" the old man sighed. "Well."

At first his voice was weak.

~

*The East Wind sighs, the fine rains come.*
*Beyond the pool of waterlilies,*
*the sound of faint thunder.*
*A gold toad gnaws the lock. Open it, burn the incense.*
*A tiger of jade pulls the rope.*
*Draw from the well and flee.*
*Chia's daughter peeped through the screen*
*when Han the Clerk was young.*
*The Goddess of the River left her pillow for*
*the great Prince of Wei.*
*Never let your heart open with the spring flowers.*
*An inch of love is an inch of ashes.*

~

But as he spoke his weakness and unsteadiness fell away, as if these were words he'd said to himself over and over until he'd perfected each one. When he was finished he sat silently, gazing down at his chest. The skin over his heart was translucent and mazed with veins.

"I'm gonna have to write that down and think about it," Ross said.

*It's deep, all right,* PJ thought. "What does it mean to you?" she asked.

"It's about a woman waiting for her lover to come home," Silver replied. "Who never does. And she gets cold."

Ross grunted.

PJ remembered the picture of Bebe staring into David's empty-eyed face as the general pinned the Navy Cross to him. And she thought about this strange old man who'd known her grandparents in a way she never could.

"I think I understand how she felt," PJ said. "Love can

**155**

be the coldest thing there is. I think my grandfather could've understood that, too. He knew a lot about the cold."

~

PJ picked at a curl of paint on the bench for a long time, trying not to look at the other people waiting at the bus station, trying to work up the courage to speak.

"Mom, I wish you could stay," she finally said.

Anne played with her suitcase handle. "I wish I could too, PJ. But I've gotta get back."

"Why? I feel like…well, I feel like we're just getting to know each other. It's not the campsite, is it?"

"It's not the campsite, PJ. It's not you, it's not even Bebe. I just…" She curled her hands into fists and uncurled them slowly. "It's Chattanooga. I don't belong here. I have too many bad memories of this place. It, ah, disturbs my *wa*."

"Your…wha?"

"My balance, my harmony. There's too much negative energy here. I could never explain it all."

"Try me."

"PJ, why do you think I came?"

"To look in on Bebe."

"On one level, maybe. But I also wanted to see you, what you're like. And you're fine! Bebe's done a great job. I could only screw you up if I came back into your life right now."

"That's a cop-out!"

Anne's face grew distant. "Cop-out, huh? PJ, a state trooper at a truck stop in Nashville accused me of being a hooker while I was trying to flag a ride to get here. So don't give me an attitude, OK? I'm doing the best I can."

PJ tried to meet Anne's stare, but couldn't. She looked across the station to where a soldier in his dress uniform slept on a bench. His duffle slumped beside him like a weary old comrade-at-arms.

"I think this is the same bus station Grandpa left for Korea from," PJ said. She smiled slightly. "Probably the same benches, too."

"The difference between David and me," Anne said, "is

that I came back. You have to give me credit for that. But I have a whole other life. I'm so proud of you, but I love that life and I have to get back to it. You don't need me anyway; you have each other."

Desperation rose in PJ. "Mom, please. I feel about ten years old, here. Begging you not to run out on me."

Anne closed her eyes. "I don't want to talk about that. Can we please not talk about that?"

"No, we need to talk about it! I'm a grown woman now! I need to know who you are, because I'll be you someday! Who are you? Why have you avoided us for all these years?"

"The woman you need to put those questions to," said Anne, "is hiding right under your nose."

PJ didn't know what to say to that, so she didn't say anything. Eventually Anne checked her watch and they got up together and went outside to where the bus waited. The diesel fumes stung PJ's nose and the heat from the sun-baked blacktop was murderous.

Anne gave her a brief hug and pecked her on the cheek. When Anne was halfway up the stairs, about to turn down the aisle to her seat, she stopped.

"You look good," she called back at PJ. "Don't say I never gave you anything."

PJ suddenly decided. "Can you hold the bus a minute?" she asked the driver.

"We're on a schedule," he said from his seat.

"Just one second?" she pleaded. "My mom forgot something."

He rolled his eyes. "Go."

PJ took off sprinting through the terminal and out to her car. She rummaged the cardboard box out of her trunk and ran back.

Anne was still waiting in the stairwell, a confused look on her face, and the bus driver was glaring and thumping the steering wheel pointedly.

"What is it, PJ?" Anne asked. "We've gotta roll."

"Don't open this until you get to San Diego," PJ said, reaching up into the stairwell to hand the box to her.

Anne glanced down at it. "It's the quilt we made, isn't it? PJ..." She started shaking her head.

"Can you take your seat already?" grumped the bus driver.

"Chill out," Anne said. "That's my daughter."

"Yeah, and it's my bus." He punched a button on the dash and the door started swinging closed. As it did, Anne tossed the box through the narrowing gap between the door and frame. PJ caught the box as the door thunked to.

Anne looked through the glass, smiled sadly at PJ, and shrugged. The driver popped the air brakes, making PJ flinch away. When she looked back, Anne was gone from the stairwell and the bus was backing up.

PJ watched the bus pull out, holding the quilt and asking a question in her heart that she didn't dare give voice to.

## Part Two: The Changjin Quilting Circle

*Make my hands steady*
*And sure as a rock;*
*When the others go down*
*With a wound or in shock.*

—from "A Hospital Corpsman's Prayer"

▶▶▶◆◀◀◀
## Chapter Seventeen

PJ, why your granddaddy was always so cold is that the Chinese came and got him one night and took him away, and locked him in a cage outdoors so he'd freeze to death.

Now, are you sure you still want to hear this? The story of that old quilt? There is such a thing as more than you bargained for. Trust me, I know it.

Well. If you're bound and determined…

People throw the word "hero" all over, but I'd have to say your granddaddy was an honest-to-God hero from the first day I met him. The story of the quilt is the story of the man—him and a bunch of other good men, that is. And the story of a good woman, too.

Me? I was just the caretaker.

I'd also have to say there's so many stories in that quilt that I could never tell them all. Every piece of that fabric is a story unto itself, and every one of those stories stands for thousands more nobody tells or remembers.

To tell one and not another—why, who should play God like that? Deciding which man's life is worthy of memory and which man's isn't?

I never thought men should play God. I came to that

belief in Korea, when I had to pick which men would live and which would die.

Playing God is a sin, and I carry it with me always. But the truth of it is that you can't stand idle, either. A man does something. Does what he can. I carried that quilt for fifty years, thinking if I kept the stories alive I'd keep the men alive too. Like it was a penance for surviving them.

Because the men who made that quilt were brave men. Or boys, I realize now. But heroes all. And they deserve remembrance.

Your grandfather not the least among them. But my God, sometimes I wish I'd never heard of him.

~

I was a hospital corpsman when I met him. What a corpsman does, is he tries to keep boys from dying on the battlefield.

I was working the aid station at Hagaru-ri during that whole episode at the Choisin Reservoir. I reckon you've heard of that, and if you haven't, you ought to have.

It was oh-dark-thirty, men gutshot and artillery shaking the tents, when word got run back to us that a corpsman had been killed on East Hill and they needed another one. I just stood up and said, "I'll go." Wasn't the first time I'd done that.

I had my medical pouch and my forty-five close by. It was a quarter-mile to what we called the main line of resistance. Bodies all over and stray bullets overhead. Craters and foxholes.

Koreans used their own sewage in the paddies and the mortars would pop and blow it all over you. You wouldn't notice it.

If it was misery below it was absolute chaos up there on top. Nighttime is when the Chinese always attacked, but everything was lit up by the phosphorus flares. Flickering across the snow like silver flame.

Picture bodies in heaps three feet tall. We loaded a dozen wounded—on the fenders and everywhere else we could—and down the hill came some stretcher-bearers saying, hold up, there's more where those came from.

So I went back up with them.

~

East Hill. I got up towards the top and there were some Marines dug into a long trench, trying to lay machine-gun fire to a Chinese mortar.

"You're shot, son," I told one fellow. Had a crease across his face.

"Get off me, Doc," he said. "You bring any goodies up with you?"

I was probably the only medic up there that wasn't called "Doc," but I didn't tell him that. I passed over some grenades and some .45 ACP. You never went to the main line empty-handed. He started clipping the grenades to his vest.

A sergeant crawled down the line. "Up and over at oh-two oh-five," he whispered. About three minutes from then. Boy next to me started loading his grease gun with the rounds I'd given him.

When it was time they started hollering together and climbed the embankment and charged off the other side. One got hit right away. A corporal. He was screaming, "Oh, God, corpsman!"

He had holes all over him and all I could do was just jab—uh, we had these morphine syrettes that looked like a toothpaste tube with a needle on it—and all I could do was jab him with one and start patching him. Keeping as low as I could, trying not to look up as wave after wave of Chinese poured down the hill at me.

That corporal was in a bad way. Shrapnel had laid his thigh open and his femoral artery was cut in two.

~

See, I heard the Chinese had twelve divisions. By the time you added the North Koreans, they outnumbered us eight or ten to one. Us pushing north, them pushing south, everyone meeting in the middle.

Our engineers were bulldozing an airstrip. I say bulldozing, though they were mostly blasting away at the frozen earth. Everybody was low on ammo and food and it turned into a race between the dozers and the Chinese, to see whether they could run us over before we finished the airstrip. We knew, and they knew, that we could hold our own if we could resupply.

And we need to get our wounded out. God, there were hundreds. Mostly ours, a few of theirs. You'd let the blood freeze to stop it from flowing. When it froze it foamed up like strawberry ice cream.

About the time the engineering battalion got the strip finished, the Chinese got desperate and tried to take East Hill back from us.

Why East Hill was so important is that from there you could see the bulldozers working. We'd been fighting back and forth over that hill for a week, it seemed like. They'd push us off, we'd push them off. Nobody could get the upper hand. It would've been the perfect place for them to mortar us.

We had to hold them.

~

I saw them coming. I had time to run, probably. Then the fighting swelled up all around us, rolled over us like a red tide. The Chinese were blowing horns—yeah, I said horns—like Joshua at Jericho. Me crouching there in the shadow with my hand wrist-deep in this fellow's leg. The Chinese soldiers swept past us, pushing the Marines back. Then they had rifles in my face and I couldn't understand a word of what they were saying.

I sat there pinching that corporal's artery. In these very two fingers.

And I want to ask you a question. If I'd run, or fought back, they'd have shot me. When they saw what I was doing for that corporal, when they saw I was a medic, they let me live.

So who was I saving? Him? Or me?

**163**

It didn't matter, in the end. They knocked me down and the kid bled to death, right there.

~

They tied my hands and marched me a mile or so back from the main line, to a farmer's house, and set me out in the snow in what looked like a dog run. The farmer was long gone, of course. They'd done took my medical pouch. Took my pistol and my parka. One changed shoes with me—pulled my boots off and gave me the pair of thin canvas sneakers he had, the ones they all wore. I tried to fight back, but it took them a day or two to get around to untying my hands.

They kept me in that dog run for some number of days. Gave me water now and then. Once a handful of some kind of animal feed from a burlap bag. I curled up as best I could and tried to dig a hole to get down out of the wind.

Through the slatboards I could just make out the Chosin Reservoir itself. A flat plain of ice where nothing moved that wasn't driven to it by the Siberian wind. You ever read that fellow, Dante? About how the depths of hell are frozen rather than fiery?

I had a New Testament in my pocket—we carried them because you never knew what a dying man might ask for. I found the story of Paul and Silas, how they'd been beaten and chained in prison. How they'd been freed by an earthquake.

I prayed for an earthquake but all I had were the four morphine syrettes I'd been carrying in my mouth. We learned the trick of keeping them there to keep them from freezing, and I'd never seen any point in telling the Chinese I had them. They got to be an awful temptation. Go right to sleep and not wake up.

I woke up to somebody kicking me. A Chinese was standing there waving his rifle.

Three of them walked me north however far it was. All night. By dawn we'd come over one ridge and halfway up another to a burnt-out village. The smell of napalm everywhere. Sky the color of chalk. Oxen charred and frozen solid and drifted over with snow.

They shoved me into an ox pen and there were a half-dozen Americans. Marines. Slumped here and there in filthy straw, hugging themselves, trying to keep warm.

One says, "Thank God, a medic." A lieutenant. It was your granddaddy.

▶▶▶◆◀◀◀
## Chapter Eighteen

Lieutenant Warner, the first time I met him, was bloody all over and he had a rag around his head. His left sleeve was cut to ribbons and just absolutely stiff black with blood. He was sitting with his back against the wall and another man was leaned against him and the lieutenant was holding him.

"See what you can do for Leon, here," your grandaddy said.

I knelt and looked Leon over. The boy was shot on the left side, in what you'd call the love handle. I could see red streaks and the wound smelled bad. I had to press on his abdomen and when I did he screamed. But it was soft, which was good. Generally men with hard abdomens got the last rites. It meant they'd already bled to death, inside.

I took one of the syrettes out of my mouth and slid the needle under the skin of his belly. It took a while to work.

"So?" the lieutenant asked me.

"There's not much I can do. I don't think his kidney or intestine got it, but it's infected and the bullet's still in there."

There was this towheaded PFC. He said, "Give him another shot."

"I can't do that."

The PFC got up. About six-foot-four, but maybe only a hundred and sixty pounds. "I said give him another one!"

"I can't do that. You know what it'll do."

He balled his fists.

The lieutenant never budged. "Stand down, Bravo," he said.

"Dammit, Lieutenant Warner!" Bravo yelled. "You just gonna let him suffer?"

The lieutenant's voice got lower. "I said stand down."

"Well what're we gonna do, then?" Bravo yelled again.

~

We tried the best we could to clean up from around Leon. We kicked the manure back and put down the cleanest straw there was.

The lieutenant had the men turn their pockets out. They had a whole bunch of odds and ends. What they'd had on them when they were captured that the Chinese hadn't stolen yet. Toothbrushes and spoons and letters from home. A scoutknife.

The lieutenant pulled me over to a corner. "What do you think, Corpsman?" he said. "Is there a chance he'll make it?"

"Nosir, there's every chance he won't. It's what you'd call a desperate situation. You should let me help the people I can help, instead of this guy. Show me that head wound of yours."

"You worry about him and let me worry about me. Now, look, there's not but three ways I can play this. And only one leads to him living. You understand me? Now you do everything in your power to help this man. It's my responsibility."

I said, "Aye, aye, sir."

I set the men to pounding on the walls and yelling. In a few minutes a Chinese banged the door open. He was all het up and there were others behind him in what you'd call a similar condition.

Another PFC, Fritz, that spoke some Chinese, jabbered back and forth with them until they slammed the door in his face. Fritz shrugged. "They will or they won't," he told us.

The door banged open again and the same Chinese threw my medical pouch into the room. Waved his rifle at us and yelled for a while and left.

I opened my pouch and found my sewing kit and some sulfa packets. Everything else was gone. No surprise there.

"Have you got what you need?" the lieutenant asked.

"It'll have to do," I said.

~

I make it sound easy but it wasn't. I cut Leon open right there on the floor. Your grandfather helped.

We tried to keep it clean. I used the scoutknife for the incision and the spoon handles to probe for the bullet. Nothing vital was hit, thank God. I sprinkled sulfa all over everything and made a drain with a ballpoint pen and sewed everything back together as best I could.

When it was over the lieutenant hunkered down beside me. "Where'd you get the stones to try something like that?" he asked.

I just looked at him. Didn't say a word.

But here's a fact. When I showed up at Camp Pendleton they took my Navy uniforms and issued me a full USMC kit. Besides Marines, a Navy corpsman is the only military man allowed to wear a Marine Corps uniform.

Think about that.

~

"You hold still, Lieutenant," I said.

"I'm fine," he said.

"Now see here," I said. "I've doctored every other man in here. Did you get a good smell of Leon before I put that sulfa in him? That's what your arm's gonna be like if you don't let me tend to it."

"All right, all right," he said.

"Now, here. I got one more syrette left."

"You save that, Doc."

"They call me Silver, sir."

"Silver," he said. "Silver. Seems like I've heard of you.

You're the one that—"

"Probably somebody else." I went to stick him with the syrette.

"You save that," he repeated. "Somebody'll really need it later."

I sat back on my haunches. "You're about to feel what pain really is," I told him.

"Pain," he said, "is what I feel when I look at my men here."

It hurt him pretty good when I started sewing his arm back together, but he never did cry out.

~

We got to know each other right well in that ox pen. We looked forward to Sundays, when your grandfather would keep church. He'd say a little something and we'd sing and pray. Sometimes the Chinese would stick their heads in and watch. I think there might've been a Christian or two among them.

But there were some rough ones, too. Stole our watches, our wallets. Your grandfather's wedding ring. They—

Ahh. I shouldn't dwell on stuff like that. It's past, long past. The ones that did it are dead these many years, or should be.

Finally one morning they mustered us out front. Leon marched out of there under his own power. I'll always be proud of that. He stood in line hunched over, leaning on Bravo, eyes front.

We could see down across the ridge towards the reservoir, where a river came in. I forget what the river was called but Fritz said the reservoir's real name was the Changjin, and Chosin was just what the Japanese had called it during the occupation. There were a lot of things that had changed in Korea during the Japanese occupation. Or rather, a lot of things that hadn't. Korea'd been the spoils of war for somebody or other since God was a boy. The Chinese and the Americans were just Johnny-come-latelys.

Their captain walked down the line looking us over. He was as close to the devil wearing a skin as any man I've ever seen, and that's saying something. Had ice-blue eyes; I'd never seen that in a Chinese before. Mongol blood in him somewhere. Thin mustache and a fur hat.

He looked at the lieutenant where I'd stitched his arm up, and looked at Jim Rollins's leg where he was shot through-and-through, and then he stopped in front of Leon. He said something. Reached out and touched Leon in the belly, delicately, almost like a woman would. The gentle brutality of it.

Leon yelled and doubled over, holding himself. Bravo lunged up and went to swing at Blue-Eyes and the lieutenant grabbed him around his shoulders and pulled him away. A Chinese ran up on Bravo and smashed him across the chest with his rifle butt and then brought it down on his head.

Then Blue-Eyes shot Leon through the forehead like it meant nothing more to him than putting a dog out of its misery.

~

They marched us in a column of Chinese soldiers and vehicles. By night, always by night. Fed us on cracked corn and sorghum seed, in our sweaters and wool pants, no field jackets or parkas, wearing those Chinese sneakers. Every one of those Chinese soldiers wearing a pair of US-government-issue shoe-pacs. Looked like a bunch of duck hunters. They'd pulled them off the dead and pulled them off us.

They got their just desserts for it, though. Those rubber shoe-pacs didn't let any air circulate. So when your feet got sweaty, the moisture was trapped in there and it'd soak the insoles and the insoles would freeze. More than one Chinese had black toes before it was over.

I know I did.

The thing was, you couldn't show it. That very day, a private from Maine, Jackson, started lagging behind. Blue-Eyes ran up the line in his jeep and walked out to Jackson drawing his revolver.

I couldn't take it. Just couldn't stand to see the man shot. I turned and your granddaddy caught me across the

**170**

chest with his good arm. "You stay right here, Silver. That's my job."

He broke away from the line and ran back down the road and got between them. Blue-Eyes put the pistol right between his eyes.

Blue-Eyes stood back and lowered the pistol.

"What do I do, Silver?" your granddaddy yelled.

"Find the knot and rub it out," I yelled back.

He probed Jackson's thigh muscle with his thumbs and dug at it. Then he put his hands above and below the knot and pushed the muscle together. Blue-Eyes was watching with no trace of any human expression whatsoever. A kid watching an anthill.

After a minute Jackson nodded that it was better and the lieutenant told him to stretch his leg. A Chinese shoved him along and I got up and we kept walking. Every now and again Blue-Eyes would drive up behind us and I could feel him watching us.

The lieutenant whispered to me, "If you get yourself shot without my say-so, I'll shoot you myself afterwards. There'll be a lot more of us who need you when we get where we're going."

~

They'd build fires and cook rice. Give us a cupful apiece. It wasn't much.

The fourth night out we turned northwest. Towards the Yalu River and Manchuria, we figured. The reservoir below us was a dim hole in the earth that, for all we knew, had swallowed every American north of the 38th parallel. By then, your grandfather was carrying Jim Rollins piggyback. I walked behind them, ready. I don't know how he did it.

Well, Jim was considerably lighter by then. We all were. I'd long since cinched my belt down past where the buckle had kept it from fading. When the lieutenant started weaving I took Jim from him and walked on up the road.

Then Fritz fell over. Bravo took Jim and I went to Fritz. Blue-Eyes drove up with two of his soldiers. Didn't say a word. Didn't have to.

I told Fritz, "Come on, devil dog, we've got to move along."

Fritz was slurring, that's how bad he was. "Let him do it, just let him do it. I can't take it any more." He looked past me and yelled something in Chinese at the soldiers.

Blue-Eyes climbed out of his jeep and unholstered his pistol.

"Get back in line, Silver!" the lieutenant hollered as he ran up to us.

He drew back and slapped Fritz across the mouth. Grabbed his shirtfront and tried to haul him up. Fritz just hung there. Collapsed when your grandaddy let go.

One of Blue-Eyes's soldiers laughed.

"That chink'll shoot you and leave you in the ditch," your grandaddy told Fritz.

Which Blue-Eyes did.

~

They paraded us through a village. Big news that they'd conquered the American supermen, I guess. Dirt roads and oxcarts and children in filthy rags. A couple of the villagers threw cigarettes to us. One woman ran out into the road and put her hand in the lieutenant's pocket. They shoved her back.

It was rice balls. He gave us one apiece that night. "There were five. I ate mine on the road," he said.

But thinking back, I wonder if maybe there weren't only four to begin with and he saved them for us. That's what kind of man your granddaddy was.

You know, after I got back home in 1953, I sat down in a restaurant and the waiter brought me a whole plate of rice. I slung it through a plate-glass window.

PJ, you tell those nurses not to bring rice in here.

~

The time came when we couldn't see the reservoir any more. We'd left it behind us.

As long as we kept together we were all right. But Jackson went wild and tried to run. The Chinese clubbed him down. He lay there convulsing. I wanted to pick him up but a Chinese pushed me off and a couple of others grabbed me. It left me with nothing to do but what your grandfather told me not to.

I kept saying, "Get up, Jackson, get up!" Fighting my way loose.

Blue-Eyes worked his way up the column in that jeep of his. That jeep, and yea verily I kid you not, was a U.S. Army jeep they'd captured somewhere. Or found.

Blue-Eyes sat there. Said something to his driver. Got out slowly.

I got Jackson behind me. "You're gonna have to kill me," I said. I leaned over and spat right on his boot, not taking my eyes off him.

His jaw muscles worked and I knew I was a dead man.

Blue-Eyes said something to a Chinese that was covering us with his burp gun. That Chinese hupped to attention and came double-timing it over and knelt. Then Blue-Eyes polished his boot toe on that soldier's britches like the sole reason God put him on this earth was to be Blue-Eyes's own personal snotrag.

And there was a strange thing in him—something different than the detachment I was used to. Like there was some kind of regard, some kind of curiosity. Like he was wondering how far he could take me before I broke.

His eyes scared me in a way I hadn't been scared before. And, sure, I was scared. I'm not too proud to admit it. I'd already—uh, filled my drawers up a couple of times. Everybody had! If it wasn't the dysentery from the bad water, it was an eight-two mortar exploding thirty feet from you.

I couldn't look into those eyes anymore. When Blue-Eyes shot Jackson, I had my back turned. And that's something I'm not proud of. But that's how it was.

~

We limped around a long curve and down below us was a village. You could smell the cooking. Only four of us left.

The lieutenant carrying Jim, and Bravo and me waiting our turns.

There must've been a thousand Chinese soldiers down there. Shacks all over. Smoke rolling out of the stovepipes. Wind cutting through the passes above like a sickle.

They put us in with eight other Americans in what looked to be a horse barn out behind a big house. A few of them were GIs from that Task Force Faith that had gotten destroyed north of Pyungnyuri inlet. The rest were Marines. All enlisted.

There was a kid in there, a soldier, that didn't have but a wisp of beard. He said, "They're gonna kill us, aren't they, Lieutenant? Aren't they?" Like he knew the answer already and was just waiting for us to tell him, yes, it's so.

Tired as he was, your granddaddy took charge. He split the men into squads of three and gave them details. Cleanup and scrounging and lookout, that sort of thing. They took to his leadership without questioning it—most of them were broken by then, anyway. The Chinese had been after them.

He ordered me to do what I could for the men. Everybody was beat up; a couple were cut and one had some shrapnel in him. I used up the last of my morphine, doing what I could.

We slept that night huddled up in a stall with as much clean straw as we could find. It helped a little against the cold. The next morning they gave us some horse feed, I believe it was, and the lieutenant divvied it up. That's when Preston told us about the cages.

## ▶▶▶◆◀◀◀
## Chapter Nineteen

"There's wire boxes about three by three and you can't stand up in them," Preston said. He was a staff sergeant, a Marine regular. "You have to sit there at attention and they won't let you sleep."

"What, out in the open?" your grandaddy said.

"That's right, Lieutenant, in the middle of the village, up on a platform. They've took two of us already and nobody's lasted through the night." He frowned. "They made us go out and look at them. Made us bury 'em afterwards."

"Who'd they take?" Bravo asked.

Preston said, "Captain Snell and Second Lieutenant Biggs."

"The officers," I said. I didn't have to ask how the Chinese knew they were officers. They could tell, even without the insignia.

"I'm sorry, sir," an Army corporal named Chersky said. "We've been here five days and they took Snell the night we got here and Biggs a couple days later. They haven't touched the rest of us. Well, when you go out to the latrine they'll try to steal your clothes, but one or two of us been fightin' back."

He pointed to another soldier, Harrison, who was in

175

the corner with his jaw swollen. I'd checked him out
the night before and he was missing some teeth on that
side.

"They like wool pants," Harrison lisped.

"Christ," said the lieutenant.

"When we found out about Captain Snell we gave
Lieutenant Biggs some of our clothes," Preston said. "I wish
I could tell you it helped him."

"They stripped him naked," Chersky said. "To his bare
ass. We lost his stuff and ours too."

Everybody got real quiet.

The lieutenant sat against one wall, a little ways off,
rolling straw between his fingers and staring up into the
rafters.

~

They came for him a day later.

See, they wanted to keep the officers from organizing
the men. And if anybody could've, it would've been the
lieutenant. I'd come to admire him. Greatly. He never
complained, not one time. Kept his distance from us but
listened to us. Good officers did it that way—it was hard
to send a man up the hill when you knew he might be
leaving a wife and children.

He never once asked me how I came to be called
"Silver." I think he might've known, but he also knew I
wanted my privacy.

And he'd carried Jim for days. He'd carried all of us,
really. The way he'd taken personal responsibility for what
happened to Leon. He was a good man and there weren't
that many good men to be had.

And now we figured he had a death sentence. He
fought back, tried to get free, and we all got up and
pressed forward. But there were four of them with rifles.
Big Thompson guns, American-made, most likely ones
our own military had sent to China as aid to Chiang Kai-
Shek and that the communists had captured when they
overthrew him. So here were our own rifles, being aimed
at us.

The last thing the lieutenant said to us before they barred the doors behind him was, "Gung-ho, boys."

Like he was Randolph Scott or somebody.

~

I watched through a gap in the wallboards as they drug him away, and I wondered what was going through his head. He was thinking about his life, I figured. Who wouldn't at such a moment?

I know I sat there and thought about mine. I'd come about as far from Des Moines as a boy could. My daddy had been a roofing contractor working the war boom, and I'd spent years laying black asphalt shingles under a sun that'd cook you. But if you let your head go, you'd fall to your death, about that fast.

That was the main reason I'd joined the Navy. I'd never yet heard of a ship that had shingles on it.

But here I was in weather twenty and thirty degrees below zero. Would've given about anything to be broiling on a rooftop. Even though I knew if I lost my head here I'd've come to the same end as if I fell off a roof. Broken and dead.

So what exactly was a roofer kid from Des Moines supposed to do, anyhow?

What would your granddaddy have had me do?

I thought about sitting there with him, sewing on his arm.

*Gung-ho,* he'd said as they took him away.

~

I got up and said, "Listen up, everybody! Wake up and pay attention! Sergeant Preston—what's the meaning of the words 'gung-ho?'"

"Work together," Preston said.

"Work together," I repeated. "That's right. We got to find a way to do that. Now, I don't think the Chinese ever counted on taking prisoners. They don't know what to do with us. That's how come there's no fuel or food. Some of them think they'd be better off without us, I'm sure. As little effort as they have to put into us, they will. If we want to make it out of here, it's up to us."

I pulled my sweater off. Took off my shirt. Then I started cutting pieces off them. The shirt collar. Patches off the sweater elbows. Cut my long john sleeves off above the wrists.

Bravo said, "You have absolutely gone section eight, Silver."

~

I got the suturing kit out of my pouch. I said, "This is a needle." Threaded it and held it up.

I took my shirtcollar and an elbow patch and sewed them together kind of slowly so they could see. "This is a simple interrupted everting stitch. You use it for straight lacerations."

Then I held up the piece I'd sewn. "This is a square."

I teased a loose thread off the longjohn cuffs and pulled it out and unraveled the cuff into a big ball of cotton. "This is your stuffing," I told them. "I've got six needles, a mile of silk thread, and we can all throw in scraps."

A PFC named Harrison, stocky kid, started nodding his head. "That ain't a bad idea. Make a big thick quilt. And if they steal it, the rest of us haven't lost nothin'."

"That's the game, gentlemen," I said. "Unless somebody has a better one."

~

Everybody threw in. We had to work fast and we were trying not to think about what they might be doing to your granddaddy. But when you get to working with your hands you get to talking. Takes your mind off things.

You asked about that handkerchief. That was Monkey's. He was a big private, forever saying "Join the Army and see the world."

Chersky said, "That's 'Join the Navy,' isn't it?"

I bit some thread off. "It's not the Navy," I said. "Trust me on that."

Monkey nodded. "If the recruiter had told me I'd come halfway around the world to sit in a horse barn in the dead of the winter and sew, I'd have had him put in a home. Thing is, I thought they'd fight this war with buttons."

"How's that?" said Preston. He'd already sewn a piece as big as four hands put together. All those old regular Marines could sew. Not too many tailors in the Corps, you understand.

Bravo laughed. "Yeah, is the Army issuing cards of buttons instead of rifles these days? That'd explain a few things."

"No, buttons as in what a professor pushes to launch a missile," said Monkey. "Is this how you want it to look, Silver?" He held up what he'd pieced together.

"Well. Keep after it."

Harrison said, "Nothin' about the Army makes sense. Why, I got cavalry and there ain't a horse in it. First week we're in boot camp the DI comes over and wants to know who's got a commercial driver's license. I raised my hand and for the next week I was pushin' a wheelbarrow full of sand everywhere we went."

"Join the Army and see the world," said Bravo.

~

I think this piece of shirttail right here was Fuzzy's. I hadn't really noticed him when we came in. He was a soldier and had a big fuzzy beard like he'd been on the lines for a while. He was in a corner, keeping to himself. Rocking back and forth. Humming. Shook, is what he was. Seen one too many things.

It was the weepy kid with the wispy beard that took up the song Fuzzy was humming. Kid had a good tenor. It was a hymn. I'd never heard it, but I remember him singing, and how quiet we were while we listened.

> *Now God be with us, for the night is closing.*
> *The light and darkness are of His disposing,*
> *And 'neath His shadow here to rest we yield us,*
> *For He will shield us.*

*As Thy beloved, soothe the sick and weeping,*
*And bid the prisoner lose his griefs in sleeping.*
*Widows and orphans, we to Thee commend them,*
*Do Thou befriend them.*

Fuzzy kept rocking but he sang the last lines right along with the weepy kid.

*We have no refuge, none on earth to aid us,*
*Save Thee, O Father, who Thine own has made us.*
*But Thy dear presence will not leave them lonely,*
*Who seek Thee only.*

We sang it around a couple of times, and I'll tell you, there was more than one weepy kid in that barn.

~

Oh, the panties. Well, Pirate had them.

We called Pirate "Pirate" because he'd lost an eye in a firefight. Don't know why he hadn't been sent home over it. He'd made himself an eyepatch and I guess if there'd been parrots in Korea he'd have had one of them, too.

Pirate said, "I hate to give these up, but they might as well do somebody some good."

And then Bravo said, "Panties!" like he'd never seen a pair before. Probably he hadn't.

"Flowerdy ones, even," said Harrison. "Betcha that's the only pair north of the 38th. Go on, let's see if they fit you. They oughtta, from the size of 'em."

Pirate's face got red and he handed them over. I ripped the seat out before he could change his mind. Started sewing them up.

Jim said, "Where'd those come from? You have a sweetie at Inchon?"

"I'll have you know I'm a happily married man," said Pirate. "Fourteen months now."

Jim shuddered. "Happily? Come here for a little of that Morning Calm, did you?"

**180**

"She's a terror, all right. Fight all day and get over it all night."

"What did you fight about?" Monkey asked.

"Oh, I wouldn't want to say."

"Come on. I doubt word's gonna get back to her anytime directly."

"Well. Crazy stuff. Which way to scrub a head. I do it the way they taught me in boot camp and she does it the way her mama showed her, and she says her way is better and if I loved her I'd do that her way. And say, come on baby, it's just a head, and off she goes."

Harrison said, "You know, I told my wife how a man cleans a head. When there's a stain in the bowl, I told her, he stands there and aims directly for it, and tries to wash it off. Like target shooting. She was horrified."

"Pirate," I said. "Did you steal those panties from your wife, or did she give them to you?"

He didn't answer that one.

~

There was this PFC everybody called None. When you don't have a middle name the Corps puts "None" on all your paperwork, and that's your name forever after.

"Hey, None," I said. "Unravel these pants cuffs."

"Yes sir, Mr. Silver."

"Thank you, None," I said.

Pirate got this gleam in his eye. "None, None," he sang. "Ain't never had none."

Bravo picked it up. "None, None, won't never get none."

Then it was Monkey. "None, None, don't want none."

We were falling out laughing by then. None just stood there looking around at us. "Well, there ain't none!" he yelled.

I guess if the Chinese were listening, they must have thought we were losing our minds. Maybe we were.

~

We had one side of the quilt done together and were

working on the other. Preston had a padded vest he'd taken off a dead Chinese, and he was picking the seams open so he could rob the cotton out. It was generous of him; that vest was a warm garment.

He said, "All this sewing's got me thinking about somebody. You guys ever hear of Mabel Savageau?"

We hadn't.

"None of you ignoramuses knows her. Well, what about the flag loft at Mare Island? Where they made number three-twenty?"

Monkey said, "Flag loft?"

Preston's eyes got sad. "Poor dogface. Fear not, son, we'll look after you. But you Marines, that's shameful. I mean, come on now. Mabel Savageau saved the Corps from Harry Truman. You'd think one of you woulda heard of her."

I said, "Do tell."

He cleared his throat. "Once upon a time, some Marines raised a flag over Mount Suribachi and some photographer snapped a picture. Ya'll have seen that, right?"

We had.

"That was the second flag they raised. What happened was, the Secretary of the Navy, Forrestal, was on Iwo Jima that day with General Howlin' Mad Smith. They came ashore just as the first flag was going up. Forrestal said, 'That flag means there'll be a Marine Corps for the next five hundred years, Smith.' Of course, four years later, Truman tried to give us all our walking papers.

"Anyway, Forrestal decided he wanted that flag for a souvenir. The battalion commander went ape. Said, 'What's the Secretary of the Navy got to do with it? That flag belongs to battalion!' So a fellow found a replacement in an LST and they pulled the old bait-n-switch. The original got taken for safekeeping and they hoisted a replacement. The Marines you see in that picture, they were just up there laying telephone wire when they got ordered to raise the second flag."

I said, "Lest you forget, sergeant, one was a corpsman."

He looked happy. "Well spoken, swabbie! Anyway, that picture got famous and somebody noticed the flag in it had a serial number on it, three-twenty. They traced it back to the flag loft at Mare Island Naval Shipyard in Vallejo. They had hundreds of women sewing flags around the clock at Mare Island. Mabel Savageau happened to be the woman that made that one."

Bravo held up a half-dozen scraps he'd tatted together. "Well, God bless Mabel whatshername. Wish we had her and a hundred more like her to help us with this thing."

"I'd settle for one," Monkey said.

~

"My little girl wears panties now," said Chersky.

"Uh-hunh," Bravo said. "Hand me that pocketknife."

"You know what she told my mother? She said 'I wear panties and Gramma wears BIG panties!'"

"You gonna hand me that knife?"

"I wrote my wife to send that one to the *Reader's Digest*. And her gramma's talking about getting her a pony."

"That's great, Chersky, but I need that knife sometime this evening, OK?"

Chersky glanced up at him. "You think she'll be safe on a pony?"

~

When we got the quilt mostly done I held it up.

"That's not pretty," Monkey said.

"No, but it's thick," said Pirate. "When you need it it'll be the prettiest thing you ever saw."

"All right," I said. "Now tell me where they keep their stinking cage."

### ▶▶◆◀◀
## Chapter Twenty

They argued with me but in the end I won. I knew it had to be me. I was the corpsman, and if the lieutenant needed medical help—which we all knew he would—I had to be there.

I traded for the darkest clothes any of them had. We pried a slat off the back corner and I peeked out. The moon was a sliver and the shadows were deep in the alleys. Down the hill two men with slung rifles were warming their hands over a fire in a steel oil drum. Puffing clouds of red steam.

I wriggled out. "Low and slow, Silver," Monkey whispered.

"I'll be back," I said.

I crouched in the shadows and took my bearings by the stars. We were a lot further north than I'd thought. The thought came that I had the quilt rolled up under my arm and I could've just struck off south. Could've left the lieutenant and the men to fend for themselves.

But I'd've rather died. I kept to the shadows of the shed and crept past a hitching rail to the back of the main house. Heard voices out front.

There was a ditch that led from the house down the hill and I crawled into it. I wouldn't want to say what was in there, but it was mostly frozen. It led down to a cesspool

**184**

by a frozen rice paddy. I skulked around the bank to where some shacks stood. My heart jackhammered and I tried to keep my breathing quiet. I was tempted to stop and see what was in those shacks.

I marked them in my mind for later. A little way off there was a footpath that skirted the paddies. I guessed there'd be sentries walking it, but I couldn't see any. I ducked low and ran along it until I heard voices, and I flung myself into the dark of some pines and lay still with my arms over my head.

One of them was smoking a cigarette and they were laughing. Their boots crunching the snow. I felt my front soaking through as the ice and snow under me melted, but I held as still as I could. Hoped the quilt wasn't getting wet. Then they were past, and I was up and running past another shack, and then through the shadow of an alley to the main boulevard, if you want to call it that.

I squatted behind a pile of trash and watched the square. There were three soldiers sitting on the steps of the platform smoking cigarettes and there were two cages up on the platform and the lieutenant was in one. Slumped-over and his face gleaming with blood in the moonlight.

I did the only thing I could. I crept back down the hill.

When I got back to the shacks by the paddy I jimmied a door open. I had to feel my way around but I found some heavy sacks. Rice. I slung two of them under my arms. If I had to go back to the men, I wasn't going back empty-handed.

Then I stopped and thought about it, really thought about it. In North Korea, in wintertime, where there was food there was always one other thing.

Fire.

I snuck out and stashed the rice and the quilt under a bush a short way off and came back and searched the shack until I found an oil cookstove. With the thumbscrew and plunger you have to pump to pressurize the tank. There was a steel matchbox with it.

So I lit the stove and piled everything I could find around it. Scraps of sacking and kindling wood and I don't know what all.

Then I took off. I made it back to the alley at the square

about the time the shack lit the whole place up. The guards saw it and threw their cigarettes down and snatched up their rifles and ran off in different directions.

The cage was rusty wire and when I knelt by your granddaddy I could see the streaks of rust on his skin. He was wearing his long johns, that was all, and his lips were blue and swollen. He wasn't good.

I said his name.

"Silver?" he moaned.

"It's me, it's me. I brought you something, Lieutenant."

I unrolled the quilt and stuffed it through the wire. Behind me I heard a bell start clanging.

He couldn't move his arms much so I reached in and doubled the quilt around him. He let out a long sigh like a dying man.

"Open your eyes, Lieutenant. Look at me."

His head lolled and I saw for the first time that his head was reinjured. Big knot and a gash on one side. I pulled his eyelids open and saw his pupils were sized differently—the left one was twice the size of the right. I covered and uncovered it with my hand, but it didn't react to the change.

He clutched the quilt around him. "Did Elizabeth make this?" he asked.

Elizabeth? His wife, I guessed. He'd never mentioned her.

"Yes sir, Lieutenant. Elizabeth sent that for you. Said for you to keep warm so you could come home."

He nodded, or tried to.

I looked all around the square. "I've got to go, Lieutenant. The men are fine. Said for you to hurry."

He didn't say anything. He was already warming up and it was putting him to sleep. Which wasn't necessarily a good thing, with a head wound like that. He could nod off and an artery in his brain could let go.

And maybe that would've been the kindest thing.

~

The men and I ground the rice to powder and mixed the powder with what little water we had and ate for the first

**186**

time in two days. We heard the Chinese running around and shouting all night.

Dawn broke and nothing happened. That was bad; I expected they'd come in swinging their rifles. And I feared for the lieutenant. We sat there all that day and worried.

Finally, in the evening, three of them came in. Two waded through the men towards me while a third covered us with his rifle. They stood me on my feet and marched me out with the boys yelling at them.

It might've been a tad warmer, but not much. They walked me straight up the street to the square. The one on the left was a kid that didn't look any more than fifteen years old. Smoking a cigarette and jabbing me in the kidneys with his rifle barrel like a big man.

They stopped me at the platform steps. Your granddaddy was still in that cage. He was bundled up in the quilt, on the floor, asleep. I didn't know whether to laugh or cry over it.

Then the smoker kid jabbed me again and motioned for me to get my hands up. He stood there with the rifle aimed at my heart and his buddies pulled my sweater over my head.

They left me blinded that way for a minute and one of them punched me in the stomach. I doubled over and started to puke. Then one of them hauled the sweater off me and busted me in the mouth and grabbed my shirtfront and started tearing it off. Buttons spraying all over.

When I was naked from the waist up the smoker kid grinned and pointed to the steps.

I saw that the door to the second cage was open.

Then I heard another voice say something behind us, and the three guards came to attention real fast. I turned, and there was Blue-Eyes.

He said a few words, gave me a long look. Then he disappeared into the shadows.

The three of them started jabbering at me. Pointing to my belt and my pants and my sneakers.

~

I tried to fight them but I couldn't take all three. I doubt I could've taken the young one, by that point. Weak as I was.

They beat me down to the ground and stripped me off bare naked and carried me into that second cage. Chained the door shut. Then one of them said something to the others and they went off. Dinnertime, probably.

I'd been in that cage for about sixty seconds when I knew I was already dying. The wooden floor was cold and while there wasn't much wind I was all broken out in goosebumps already. It was the first time I'd seen myself undressed since—well, Inchon, probably—and I'd say I'd lost twenty pounds. Black toes and my backside shrunk practically flat.

I stood up, started doing jumping jacks. Looking through the wire at the shacks, and past them at the mountains. Trying to keep the blood flowing. I counted my exercises— one-two-three. Silly thing to do, I knew. There was no way I could keep moving all night. Fact was, I was winded already.

But I think it was my counting that woke your granddaddy up.

"Silver?" I heard him say, his voice weak. "Silver?"

"Yessir," I said, trying to keep my teeth from chattering. "You all right, Lieutenant?"

"What day is today?" he asked.

"Uh, George Washington's birthday, maybe. I don't know."

He sounded sleepy, confused. "That's all right. I think Bob Hope was here."

"Of course he was. You need to try to stay awake, Lieutenant. How hard did they hit you?"

"Old Bob left me a Christmas present."

"Lieutenant?" If he was seeing Bob Hope in that cage with him, he was worse than I'd thought. I guessed that they'd fractured his skull this time, where he'd already been injured from when he was captured.

"See?" he said, holding up the quilt we'd made for him.

"No sir," I said. "That was your wife."

"It was? Well, that's just like Elizabeth."

"Yessir," I chattered. "That's a fine woman you got there."

I couldn't exercise anymore. I was shivering and my

fingers were numb. I put my hands in my armpits and squatted on my calves. Tried to huddle myself up as small as possible.

"She is that," he said.

I rolled over onto my side, hoping I could warm up the wood floor, and I drew my knees up my chin. I was shivering harder. Soon, I knew, I'd be getting sleepy. It didn't seem like such a bad way to go.

"What's that, honey?" the lieutenant said.

"I didn't say anything, Lieutenant," I chattered.

"No, I wasn't talking to you," he said. "You want me to—oh, sure. Sure. Hey, Silver. Elizabeth says for me to give you this."

I squirmed around to see. He'd taken the quilt off and he was stuffing it through the cage wire towards my side of the platform.

~

When I look back on it now, I should've made him keep it. But I was just then getting to know the depths of my own cowardice. Pirate was right; that quilt was the prettiest thing I'd ever seen.

"Merry Christmas, Corpsman," he said.

I snaked my arm through the wire and snagged the quilt and pulled it in. Wrapped myself up in it.

"Thank you," I said, trying to stop chattering. "Thank you."

"Don't thank me," your granddaddy said. "Thank Elizabeth. She's the one that sent it to you."

~

I got warmer. But that was truly the longest night of my life. The men had said the guards wouldn't let you sleep in the cages, but I couldn't sleep anyway. I lay there wrapped in that quilt all night listening to your granddaddy breathe. Afraid he'd stop.

Have you ever done that? Sat by the bed and listened while somebody you care about breathes?

**189**

It's the most beautiful sound there is.

~

Dawn broke and he was still alive. I don't know how.
A miracle. If the weather hadn't kept warming that night,
we'd probably both be dead. Not that it was ever warm; it
couldn't've been more than twenty or thirty.

But about mid-morning they unchained us from the
cages and took us to a big house at the other end of the
village.

It was hot in there. Hot. It burned my skin and made my
ears and toes throb.

Blue-Eyes and two other well-dressed Chinese were
sitting at a table by an enormous stove. There was a pot
boiling on it, some kind of reddish stew, and the smell was
beyond anything I'd ever known.

Blue-Eyes stood up when we came in. His face was
still impassive, but his eyes held almost a trace of sadness.
Maybe I imagined it. He put his hand on his pistol and said
something.

One of the Chinese behind him stood up too. "Cap'm
say, enemy trezha."

"Enemy—enemy treasure?" I said. The smell of the stew
was making me lightheaded and I wasn't sure I'd heard him
right. Did he think we were hiding money?

"Give us some of that and I'll tell you where the treasure
is," I said.

The Chinese repeated my words and Blue-Eyes lifted an
eyebrow. He said something else to the second one, who
went to the stove and ladled me out a dish of stew. I wolfed
it down with my fingers while they watched. Rice and greens
and hot peppers and a little chicken. Garlic. My God. Your
granddaddy got a bowl and he was wolfing it, too.

When I finished Blue-Eyes took a cloth from his pocket
and handed it to me. I wiped my fingers and mouth on it and
offered it back to him. He studied me for a while—still trying
to tell me something—before waving his hand at me and
going back to his chair. Then he said the same words again.

"Cap'm say, tek you, enemy trezha."

"Take me to the enemy treasure," I said. "I don't understand."

Blue-Eyes looked very sad. He said something else. But they didn't beat on us or anything. Just marched us back to the shed and pushed us in.

I didn't know what to tell the men about it.

~

And I don't know what to tell you, either. Except that now you know where that quilt came from. Why I carried it. What it means.

For a long time I thought about whether I should sew that cloth Blue-Eyes gave me to the quilt. I didn't know what the characters said and I didn't want to honor a man who'd killed so many of my friends. On the other hand, I didn't think he'd just give away something precious like that. If his mother or his wife had sewn it for him, say. I thought maybe he'd taken it from another soldier. Someone weaker than him.

But I had two years in the camps to consider it. And I finally understood what he was trying to tell me. About enemies and treasure. The Chinese have a saying that you can measure a man by the strength of his foes. I guess that's true.

Your grandmother helped me see that Blue-Eyes's story was a part of ours too. Later, when I found out what the characters on that square of silk meant and read the poem for the first time, I started hoping he made it home to the person who loved him enough to make it for him. I'll never forgive him for what he did to us. And that's a sin, too, I guess.

But what he did to some of us kept the rest of us alive.

▶▶▶◆◀◀◀
## Chapter Twenty-One

Outside, in the camp, we could hear men laughing and yelling. Ringing in the New Year.

"Here's to nineteen and fifty-two, boys," Bravo said. "Our last days in this jerkwater, one way or another."

Bravo toasted Monkey and me with a shot of the rice wine Monkey had brewed. We knocked our wine back and cursed it for mule piss, but it was strong and it got right up on us.

While we drank, the lieutenant was sitting in the corner of the tent, wrapped in that quilt we'd made, drawing in the dirt with his finger. Sometimes he'd look up at the ceiling and move his lips.

I was worried about him. It'd been two years since the Chinese had captured us, and they were treating us better—we were the makings of a fine propaganda tool, in their eyes—but tents and thin blankets and woodstoves were a long way from the French Riviera. And there was never enough food.

We were all thin, but the lieutenant was gaunt, emaciated. The padded clothes the Chinese had finally issued hung on him like he was made of kite sticks. He'd go days without speaking. Run week-long fevers.

"Next year this time we'll be in Times Square," said Monkey, raising his cup.

He had more than the usual conniving look in his eye, I noticed. "That's an odd thing to say," I told him.

He winked. "I hear tell the Chinks're gonna ring in the Chinese New Year in style this time around."

"Exactly when is that?" Bravo asked.

"Early February," said Monkey. "Two new moons from now."

"Ah-so," I said, beginning to catch on.

~

Five weeks passed. When our night finally came and it got good and dark I walked your granddaddy out to the latrine. Took a good look around. It was warmer than in previous years, but still cold enough to keep the prisoners inside. Our part of the camp was quiet. Our tents, a couple of hundred of them, stood in dark rows, their flaps tied closed, smoke rising from the stovepipes. I couldn't even see the parade ground. The only light came from the search lamps on the corners of the perimeter.

A sentry crossed in front of us, walking the wire. He had his earflaps folded down from his fur hat, and his collar turned up.

I watched as he glanced up the hill at the guard's camp. He had envy in his face. Their camp was situated so it overlooked us and the Yalu River, and there was a lot of activity going on in it. The yard lights were on and there was a big cookup happening at their mess tent, it looked like.

The lieutenant was just standing there at the latrine and I had to help him take care of his business. "All right, let's go," I told him when we got done.

~

There were tin cans hanging on the inside wire and Monkey wrapped them in strips of canvas he'd cut from the inside of our tent. Bravo was watching him, his face daubed dark with clay. When Monkey was done Bravo crawled forward and snipped the wire with the pliers he'd found on a work party and had been rat-holing for months.

I watched, ready to hiss them back, but it was clear. They wriggled through the inner wire into the perimeter and went to work on the outer wire.

Monkey turned back and hissed *pst-pst-pst!* In the shadow I took the lieutenant's hand and pulled him along with me. Put my hand on his back and shoved him so he'd know to crawl through the wire. Monkey and Bravo watched, their faces angry.

We sprinted a hundred yards—with me pushing the lieutenant along—and when we reached the brush line we laid out and checked our backtrail.

Monkey hissed, "I thought we'd settled this!"

I stared at him. "We never settled anything," I whispered. "Me and him are a package deal. Always have been. You want to take him back through the wire, go ahead."

Suddenly there was long series of flashes and explosions. We froze. For a split second we were all thinking the same thing: they'd found the cut wire and they were going to shoot us the same way they'd shot the other three teams that had tried to run for it.

Then another round went off, and we saw the gold and green fireworks glittering in the sky.

"Year of the Dragon," Monkey spat.

"Just bring him and let's go!" said Bravo.

~

We followed the Yalu east. Five long and hungry and cold nights later we settled into a culvert above the train tracks outside Hyesanjin.

A train passed by under us, wheels screeching. Boxcars and flatbeds with artillery under tarps. It slowed to a halt and we smelled hot brakes. A Chinese soldier came walking around the bend, checking under the cars.

"Gentlemen, your chauffeur awaits," said Bravo.

"The plan was to stay on foot," Monkey said, watching the soldier by the train. "This is stupid. That's a military transport."

The lieutenant was flat on his back, sleeping. Quilt

wrapped around him like a shroud. Breathing fast and shallow, though we'd been sitting there for a while.

"Monkey, the lieutenant needs to ride," I said. "That train goes to the coast and we can steal a boat. Head out to sea; the Navy owns it out there. You know that."

"If I know those jackass swabbies, they'll blow us out of the water," Monkey muttered.

I lunged for him before I even knew what I was doing and Bravo pushed us apart. The lieutenant looked up in alarm and cried out. Down below, the soldier looked up the hill, and I reached back and put my hand over your granddaddy's mouth.

"Shh—shh!" Monkey whispered. The first soldier and three others had left the train and were starting to pick their way up the hill towards us through the rocks, rifles ready.

Bravo looked at Monkey and me and held up three fingers, then waved one in a circle. Monkey nodded but I stared at Bravo. I didn't like it. But we didn't have time to argue.

As the Chinese worked their way up the hill they passed from sight below us for a moment. The three of us—me, Monkey, and Bravo—darted silently from the culvert and scattered into the rocks nearby. I said a little prayer and made myself as small as I could.

They reappeared and saw the culvert. One of them stuck his head in—which was idiotic, I thought—and he banged his fist on the steel to wake up what he must have taken for a sleeping peasant.

Monkey reared up behind the one nearest him and brought a rock down on the back of his neck so hard I heard the bones snap. The second one spun and Monkey blocked his rifle and bayonet, but that's all I had time to see.

I leaped off the boulder I'd hidden behind and came down with my arms around the neck of a Chinese twice my size. I hadn't known they made them that big, and I'd lost fifty or sixty pounds by then.

He dropped his rifle and got his arms around my neck and shoulder and wrestled me over to the ground. I heard a shot from behind me and the world started to go red as the soldier on me brought pressure on my windpipe.

I scrabbled around with my hands, looking for anything, and I finally hooked my thumb into his eye and pushed in as hard as I could. He screamed and let go, and I lay there gasping for a split second, until I heard the second shot.

Then I was up and running down the trail to where Bravo and two Chinese lay crumpled and Monkey was grappling with another one. Monkey had a long slash across his face and his shirtfront was red. Then something came down on the back of my head.

I had time to remember that the capital of Wyoming is Cheyenne—which tells you how hard I was hit—and I fell to my knees.

I heard another *crack!* and I fell forward, not knowing whether I'd been shot or not.

And in a few seconds there were hands under my arms, boosting me up and hustling me away. Monkey's voice in my ear: "Come on, come on! There's more on the way up!"

I got my feet under me and ran, but my vision was blurry. I wasn't quite sure what we were doing or who we were leaving behind.

~

My head cleared as we ran up a gorge that twisted this way and that. Finally we both collapsed in a thicket. Monkey had snatched a bag from one of the soldiers, a pistol, and a couple of knives. He also had the quilt.

My heart turned to wood when I saw the blood on it. "The lieutenant's dead?" I said, hoping he'd tell me I was wrong. "And Bravo?"

"What do you think?" he asked bitterly. He sat down next to me and wrapped the quilt around our legs and started going though the bags.

"Here," he said, handing me a rice ball. Then he sucked in his breath, real hard.

"Open your shirt," I said.

He did. There was a hole punched between the short ribs on his right side. He tried to smile. "Huh. For once, there's a corpsman when I need one."

I'd've given anything if I could've smiled back at him. But I'd seen the hole bubbling when he spoke.

His smile faded. "What?"

"Your lung's hit."

~

The night came on, and with it the cold. I put Monkey under a tree, bundled up in the quilt, and he said, "Mr. Warner came howling out of that culvert like the devil. Bravo and me didn't have to do nothing. Old Warner scared 'em to death."

He laughed. "Scared 'em to death." And that was the last thing he ever said.

Monkey was a good soldier. Bravo was a good Marine. And your granddaddy—your granddaddy—

▶▶▶◆◀◀◀
## Chapter Twenty-Two

I was warm, and full. Clean. I had on socks and underwear, and a suit that I still felt strange walking down the sidewalk in.

Well, limping down the sidewalk, anyway.

When I found the house I was looking for, I stood on the sidewalk for a while, still not sure if what I was doing was a good idea. The house was cheerful, if run-down—blue with yellow trim, sitting in a neat yard with spring roses peeking in the windows. I climbed the steps and set my suitcase on the porch and knocked on the front door, but nobody answered.

I sat in the porch swing and rocked. It was Sunday afternoon. May. I felt like I should feel something. I don't know how long I sat there.

Presently the door rattled and a young woman came out. "Oh!" she said, when she saw me, and she put her hand to her chest. "You startled me!"

I stood up. "I'm sorry, ma'am." Suddenly I wished I'd had the foresight to pick one of the roses for her, because she was the prettiest girl in the whole world. Fresh face, long chestnut hair. Green eyes and lips like strawberries.

But she was wearing a black dress, of course, and I cursed under my breath.

She cocked her head; I guess she saw I was struggling with something. "Can I help you?" she asked.

"I...you're Mrs. David Warner, right?"

Her face fell. "I am."

"I, ah...served with your husband. In Korea."

"I see."

"He...he saved my life. I wanted to thank you for that. And I...I have..."

She glanced at my suitcase and then looked at the street, looked around the neighborhood.

"Maybe I should just..." I cleared my throat. I was having trouble getting words out. Had been for a while, now.

"How long have you been home?" she asked.

"A few weeks."

"Are you hungry?"

"I've got some money."

"That's not what I asked you. I mean for a home-cooked meal. The lettuce and peas are in and I bake on Sundays."

"You're a baker? Well...maybe I could stay for a few minutes." I tried to smile, but I knew from the formality in her voice that I should've listened to my gut. Coming had been a mistake, all right.

~

She led me to the kitchen, where she tied on an apron and handed me a bowl, and I followed her into the backyard in an awkward silence. A big garden there; peppers and squash blossoms, new rows of corn. Piepans flashing in the sunlight to frighten the birds. But the weeds were getting away from her, and the tomatoes were sprawling.

"Where are you from?" she asked as we searched the pea vines together.

"Des Moines," I said.

"Have you seen your folks since you got back?"

"For a few days, yes ma'am."

"Good," she said. She took a knife from her apron pocket and whisked off a head of lettuce. I stood watching her, immobile as a scarecrow, and I put the bowl down.

She stopped. "What is it?"

"I'm sorry," I said. "To be able to just walk out and pick fresh vegetables, as much as you want—I'm not used to it."

Those green eyes, on me. "Do you want me to call somebody, Mister...uh...now that I think of it, you know my name, but I don't know yours."

"Joe Piper, ma'am."

"Why don't I call my pastor, Mr. Piper? Tonight's church night, but he'll understand. Maybe he can even give you a place to stay."

"I don't think that'll be necessary," I said. "I just wanted to give you my regards and one of your husband's effects, and I'll get going."

"You have something that belonged to my husband?" she asked.

"Yes ma'am."

~

I unrolled the quilt onto the dining room table and told her everything I could.

"Is this his blood?" she asked at last, touching a stain.

I put my palms on the table. "I don't know. Yes ma'am. Maybe."

She wiped an eye. "Would you excuse me for a few minutes? I'd like to be alone."

I stood up. "I'll just get my bag and say—"

"No," she said. "I promised you a dinner. Just—sit in the back and enjoy the sunshine, would you? I bet you enjoy the sunshine."

~

She was right, and I sat on the back porch with my face turned to the sun. In a while I heard the phonograph playing inside—music I didn't recognize at first. In a few minutes I heard her play it again, and I caught it. That song from *Casablanca* that had been everybody's favorite.

I pictured her sitting on the couch by the phonograph, lifting the needle back to the beginning of the song over and over. I wondered what memories the song brought to her, and whether their coming was a kindness. Probably not, I thought, and I felt terrible for inflicting myself on her—for burdening her with the unavoidable question I saw in her eyes when I repeated what she already knew: that her husband had died while other men had lived.

I stood up and walked down to the garden and watched the tomato plants. I'd always helped my mother with her Victory Garden, and I remember how she stirred the tomatoes with her hand on days when the air was still. She'd said she did it because tomatoes thrive best when troubled.

The vines in this garden were growing thick and unruly, escaping their stakes to sprawl in the dirt, and blight was spreading through the lower leaves. I ran my hands through them, lifted them from the ground, and wove the loose ones into those that were tied up.

Then I smelled my hands. Breathed in the rich green perfume, the promise of summer to come.

~

Her voice came from behind me. "Mr. Piper, I didn't mean for you to go to work."

I wiped my forehead on my sleeve and threw the cluster of crabgrass I'd just pulled onto the pile with the rest of the weeds.

"Mrs. Warner," I said, "I know this'll sound strange, but weeding a garden seems about like going to heaven."

Her face fell.

"I'm sorry, I'm sorry," I said. "I keep putting my foot in my mouth, don't I?"

"Well. Let's put some food in there instead. Come on in and wash your hands."

~

In the dining room where I'd unrolled the quilt, she'd spread out salad and fresh bread, a pot roast, jars of pickles and dilly beans. Glasses of iced tea sweating on the cloth.

A wonderful meal, but we ate it without speaking, except for the scraping of forks and knives. Finally I looked at my fork, really looked at it.

"This is your wedding silver, isn't it?"

She nodded. "We had an enormous wedding and my friends—" and I saw her smile for the first time "—worked it out so everybody bought one piece. Nobody had any money."

"Well, I hate to say this, ma'am, but you ought to give me the cheap stuff. I'm a stainer."

"A stainer?"

"Yes'm. There's something about my skin—it's a little acidic—and it tarnishes sterling silver."

"Oh, now I get the nickname," she said, and she smiled slightly.

"Well," I began, and then I thought better of what I was about to say.

"I've never heard of people having that problem," she said.

"Oh, yes, ma'am. When my family would get the nice silverware out, I'd be sitting there eating with the everyday stuff."

"Well, look here," she said. She got up and went to the sideboard, pulled a drawer open and took out a black case. Inside were rows and rows of silver utensils on blue velvet. Most of it tarnished.

"There," she said, handing me a fork. Its handle was dulled in exactly the spots where you'd grip it in your fingers. "We had a going-away dinner for David and...and I started polishing it I but couldn't finish...because I didn't know which one..."

Her shoulders started shaking and she snatched her napkin off the table and covered her face and turned her back to me.

I could've gotten up and gone to her and taken her in my arms. Could've tried to comfort her. But I didn't. I just sat there looking at the fork in my hands, at the proof of David Warner's touch—and seeing in his wife and in his house the proof of its absence.

I'd thought there was nothing more I could do for the

lieutenant, that he'd gone beyond my help on that hillside above the train tracks in the snow. But when he was in the cage I'd told him that Elizabeth had sent him a quilt. And now the lieutenant had sent her one. I was only his messenger.

So if there was one thing I could do for them both, it was stay out from between them. Grief was bad, but there was worse trouble out there.

Still, letting her cry was a hard thing. Hard.

~

A few days later I threw the last of the old shingles and aluminum flashing off the roof of Elizabeth's house, gathered the hammer and prybar and so forth, and climbed down the ladder. It was early afternoon. I was pouring sweat and feeling dizzy with the heat as I walked around the yard collecting the old shingles and stuffing them into the bed of the truck I'd rented.

I heard the front door open and there was Elizabeth, still in black, with a pitcher and glasses.

"Tea?" she asked.

"Sold," I said. "I'll be right there."

She set the glasses on a little iron table and started pouring. I reached down for a piece of the aluminum flashing and that's when it happened.

I wasn't looking directly at it and the edge of it caught the underside of my forearm and sliced it open for six or eight inches. Sharp as any scalpel. I gasped and saw a bright red spurt and clapped my hand over it.

Elizabeth rushed over. "Mr. Piper!"

"Get me a towel," I said. "I nicked an artery."

She ran into the house. I sat down in the grass. The sun began to widen in the air until all I could see was a white light that pulsed in time with the throbbing in my forearm.

Then she was there beside me with towels. "I'm going to the neighbors'," she said.

"No, don't," I said. "I think I might pass out." When I lifted my hand from the wound to take a towel from her, the blood welled up immediately. I wadded the towel and pressed it down hard, and the towel started soaking through.

Her eyes were inches from mine, full of fear. "I don't know what to do," she said. "What do you want me to do?"

"What I need," I told her, "is for you to clamp your hands around my upper arm and dig your thumbs into the side of my bicep. That'll squeeze the artery off."

"Like this?" she said, doing it.

"That's it."

I was feeling dizzier. "Look, it'll be fine. But if I pass out, get a belt and make a tourniquet and go for help, OK?"

We sat that way, her hands around my arm, and in a couple of minutes I felt better. I moved the towel. "I think it's slowing down but I don't want to bleed all over your house," I said.

"I don't care about that."

"I do. Let's just get to the porch and you can go get my first-aid kit out of my suitcase. There's a suturing kit in there."

~

If I'd thought her eyes were wide before, they were twice as wide now. On the porch, with the towel off and the bleeding at a slow ooze, I could see that the edges of the wound were clean.

"Pour that iodine over it," I said. "Get it good." I winced as she obeyed.

"I'm sorry," she said.

"Don't be. This is the stupidest way I've ever been hurt. I want you to open the little green bag and get out the card and the spool of thread. Take a needle off the card—careful, they're curved—and clean it with the iodine and thread it and knot the end.

"I can sew if you need me to," she began. "I haven't done it since I was a little girl, but—"

I laughed. "No, I'm gonna to do it myself."

I kept quiet and I saw realization come over her. She started nodding. When she'd disinfected the needle and threaded it, I took it from her. I worked the needle through the edge and pulled the thread tight to the knot and started working in quick loops—the same old simple interrupted everting stitch I'd been using for years.

"There, cut it," I said when I finished.

"You sew better than my sisters," she said as she snipped the loose end and balled it up to throw away. "Where in the world did you learn that?"

"Here and there," I said. My hands were shaking and I took the tea pitcher in my good hand and drained off about half of it at one pull.

I blew a long sigh. "That's good. Anyway, I trained for corpsman at Beaufort Naval Hospital—that's right by Parris Island—and we showed up one day and there was a Navy MD, a captain, doing needlepoint. So we laughed at him and he got real mad. Yelled at us to knock it off, because sewing was the most important skill a field medic could learn. And you know, he taught us for about six hours and then he made us stitch on each other? Ten stitches on the shoulder."

I pushed my sleeve up higher and there were tiny pinpricks, lighter than the skin around them.

"Well, you can laugh about it, but that was the bravest thing I've ever seen," she said. Her lips were parted and her face was only inches from mine.

I didn't know what to do or say. There were things I could have told her that were braver by far, but why burden her with them? She had this innocence of spirit, and I was afraid to stain her, afraid of tarnishing the first pure and clean thing I'd seen in so long.

When I'd looked at her, I'd seen my blood on the front of her mourning dress.

~

A couple of weeks after I'd cut myself she looked up from her plate—pork chops and applesauce, that night—and said, "I'd have thought you'd've taken those stitches out by now."

I held my arm up, ran my thumb down the inside of my wrist. The cut was still red, but it was healing cleanly. I tugged on a stitch and felt it give, a little.

"I could, I guess. If the cut was over a joint I might wait a while longer, but it's probably OK. What, do you want to help?"

She laughed. "I don't think so. When you get ready for me to let the waist out of those pants, you tell me, but I'm not picking stitiches out of your skin."

"You don't pick them out. You snip the thread and it pulls out. It's easy."

Elizabeth puffed her cheeks out and rolled her eyes as if she was getting sick.

"Fine," I teased her. "But you said you wanted to start sewing again."

This time she rolled her eyes. "All right, you big tough sailor, you. Wait here."

She got up and went upstairs and came back with a tiny little pair of scissors. "Will these do?"

I looked them over. They were dull and a little rusty. "Why not?" I said. I handed them back to her and I unrolled my shirtsleeve and laid my forearm on the table, the inside of my wrist up.

"What do I do?"

"Clip it right next to each one of the knots. There, there, there…"

There were, I don't know, eight or ten stitches. She cut them all, one by one, with the tip of her tongue stuck out. When she was done she glanced up at me.

"Now what?"

"It's pretty easy," I said. I pinched a knot between my thumb and finger. "You do it fast, straight up and out." I jerked up quick and the stitch came free. Sure, it stung a little bit, but I wouldn't say it hurt.

"And you want me to do that?"

"Well, all I'm saying is that if I can do it you can."

So she took a stitch in her fingers and she closed her eyes tight and she pulled the stitch out of my arm. Then she opened one eye and looked down at her fingers. "I got it."

"You did just fine," I said. "Keep going."

She closed her eyes again for the next couple of stitches, but then she just started yanking them out like it was nothing.

Coming up on the last one, though, she tugged at the stitch and it caught and came on out, but not without bleeding a tad.

"Oh," she said. "I'm sorry."

"It's nothing, nothing," I told her. "Happens that way sometimes. Go on, do the last one."

She did, and she stood up. "I'm going for some soap and water," she said. "A tough guy like you, you think you won't get an infection."

"I *am* an infection," I joked.

"Well, then, you need an extra-hard scrubbing."

She came back with a bowl of hot water and a white rag and a bar of soap. She wet the rag and wiped it on the bar of soap and started cleaning my wrist with it.

"There, is that good?" she said when she was finished scrubbing the blood away.

"It's fine," I said. "Nice and clean."

Elizabeth cocked her head to one side. "Nice and clean, you call this? I guess I forgot to look at your hands before you sat down to eat."

"What's wrong with my hands?"

She took my hand in hers and made me spread my fingers out. "Where in my house did you find this much dirt?" she asked.

"That'd be in the cellar," I said. "Replacing that floor joist."

"Show me the other one."

I did, and she shook her head and clucked at me.

"Can I have my hand back now?" I asked.

"Nope." She kept hold of my hand and took the rag in her other and started scrubbing it. When the rag got soiled she rinsed it in the bowl and kept going.

She did my left hand and then my right. I watched, feeling uncomfortable, and presently I said, "If you like sewing, I wish you'd do more of it."

"You like it, and I wish you didn't have to do it at all," she said, and she finally let my hand go. "OK, don't move."

I laughed. "What is it this time?"

She went somewhere else in the house and came back with a jar of Sofskin.

"Hand cream?" I said. "Oh, no."

"Oh, yes," she said as she unscrewed the lid. She scooped up a glob of the stuff and started rubbing it into my hand before I could say no again.

"I should dry this with my hair," she said under her breath as she worked.

"What's that?"

"Nothing."

She started smoothing the lotion into my skin, massaging my fingers, and the feeling of her soft skin, slick with the hand cream, and her strong and graceful fingers stroking mine—it stirred me to my soul.

Elizabeth let my hand go and pulled back. "You're trembling," she said, and her eyes were garden green.

"I...uh...maybe that's enough," I told her.

She lowered those eyes.

"I'm sorry, Mrs. Warner," I said.

~

I rented a room by the week and spent my days working on her yard and on her house. Keeping busy. Every couple of days I'd clear the weeds out of her garden. I replaced some pipes that were leaking in the cellar and I hung a square mile of wallpaper.

Elizabeth had a daytime job at a department store. When she'd come home she'd make dinner. We'd eat and talk about stuff that didn't matter. I never met her friends or her family, didn't go to church with her. Though she invited me.

I'd leave after dinner and go to the rooming house and stare at the ceiling until I could sleep. Sometimes I'd take home a bottle of wine to help the sleep come faster. There was a working girl in the room on the end of the motor court, but I'd always walk past her door without stopping.

What I was doing, I realized, was trying to replace Lieutenant Warner's life with my own. I had the best of intentions, but there's that road we all hear about.

I think we both knew where it was taking us. But there

wasn't any hurry. She never played dance music around me, and I never talked about Korea with her. What she'd done with the quilt, I couldn't say. Put it away with that silver fork, maybe.

~

It was early August. The tomatoes were heavy on the vines, pulling them to the earth. The soil was grey and powdery from drought, but the sky was thick with clouds of a luminous orange-brown color I'd never seen before. The air had been still all day, but now the breeze was freshening and I smelled dust.

I weeded my way through the sweet potatoes and started on the peppers.

"Mr. Piper?" Elizabeth called from the porch.

I spun; she wasn't due home for another couple of hours. I got my shirt from the trellis where I'd hung it and pulled it on.

"Oh, hi there," I said. "What are you doing home?"

"They closed the store because of the weather," she said. "Don't you see the sky?"

"What does that mean, anyway? That color?"

She looked worried. "You've never seen it? It's tornado weather. Now come on in the house. You don't want to be working out here."

The wind stiffened and I felt a cold drop of rain sting my cheek. "What if it hails?" I asked. "Maybe we should get these tomatoes in right now."

Elizabeth studied the sky and frowned. "OK," she said at last. "Give me a minute."

I got the buckets from the toolshed and started picking. The tomatoes were blood-warm in my hand, ripe to bursting.

She came into the garden in a dress that had once been blue but was now faded almost white, and I was so surprised to see her in a color besides black that I stopped working for a moment. Then I bent back to the vines.

The wind built, beginning to whistle, and raindrops struck puffs of dust from the ground. We each filled a bucket and we raced inside and dumped them on the kitchen table and went back out for more.

It was pouring a torrent. The tomatoes were slippery and the dust was churning to mud. There was a silver flash and an instant later a clap of thunder. Elizabeth gave a frightened little scream and for a moment I was frozen, far away, back on a hill in Korea with only a number to distinguish it from any other. But then I heard Elizabeth giggling at her own fright, and it made me want to laugh at my own.

I finished my row and ducked through it to the next so I could help her finish picking the last of hers. And that's when the wind hit us in earnest. There were sheets of rain spinning through the air like steel blades, and I heard the branches cracking in the trees nearby. The sky had gone black with orange streaks.

Elizabeth shrieked at the fury all around her, and I seized her hand in mine and pulled her up the row. I could barely see; my eyes were slits against the driving rain. I got my arm around her waist and pulled her toward the porch. Got the door open, felt it snap back as the wind caught it, cracking wood and making hinges scream. Forced her inside and followed her and pulled the door shut with all my strength.

We stood there in the dark house, the power out, panting and dripping and listening to the howling outside.

"The cellar," she said.

We took to the stairs. Down below it was pitch black. We felt for the corner and sat down with our backs against the wall. Sopping wet, still breathing hard, shoulder-to-shoulder. Our arms were touching and I realized she was covered in gooseflesh. I put one arm around her shoulders and rubbed her skin with my hand.

"Are you all right?" I said.

"There should be some blankets on the shelf over there," she said.

I stood up, whacking my head on something, and felt my way across the shelf. I got the top one and came back and sat down and wrapped it around us. Then I realized which one it was.

"This is the quilt we made," I said, surprised.

"Maybe it'll bring us luck," she said. "That scared me half-to-death." Her voice was trembling. "When I was a little girl a tornado came right by our house. It blew our barn down and killed some of the livestock."

"I'm here, Mrs. Warner, it's OK."

"Will you please stop calling me that?" she asked in a very small voice.

I took a long breath. Tried to make sure.

"Elizabeth," I said.

And I kissed her.

She opened her arms to me and we lay down in the blanket together on the cold floor, half mad with the din of the storm and the slow wet friction and heat of our bodies against each other. Her mouth was warm on mine and her fingers drew electric currents across the skin of my back.

And then I pulled back, horrified by what we were so close to.

"I can't do this," I said. Her hands were knotted behind my neck and I reached to them and gently untangled her fingers.

"I need you to," she said, twining her fingers again and refusing to let me go.

"Elizabeth," I whispered. "I want to be strong for you. All those years—those years in those camps—you were the one I was being strong for. I just didn't know it. I want to get this right. I need to get this right."

"It's right," she said.

"It's not right. Not yet. But I'll make it right, I swear to you."

"You will? You're not just saying that? You're not going to leave me?"

I laughed softly, lying there next to her in the darkness with the storm raging overhead. "It'd be like leaving my own heart."

"Then it's right," she said. "We'll always have each other and it'll always be right. We'll get old together. You'll tend the garden and I'll take up quilting again. Maybe we'll have a daughter or a granddaughter so I can sit in the shade and teach her."

I took another long breath, said a silent prayer to David Warner, and pulled his wife to me.

~

I kept coming around and working on the house during the day, and she kept wearing black. We wanted our plans to be secret so nobody would gossip. Not enough time had passed, and I was the one who'd reported her husband KIA.

But we figured we could decently elope on New Year's Day.

And when she snuck over to my rooming house at night, to get away from prying eyes, she'd wear every color of the rainbow.

~

I hung the last string of lights on the little tree and stood back from it. It sat cheerful and sparkly beside the fireplace, where we'd lit the Yule log and she'd hung a couple of old knitted socks.

"Feliz Navidad," I said.

Elizabeth clapped. "And Happy New Year!" she exclaimed.

"It will be that, won't it?" I laughed and sat down in the easy chair. I hooked a cupcake off the coffee table and looked at my swelling stomach and put it back.

"I'll be as fat as Santa if you keep making these," I said.

"You're a long way from fat," she said. She came over and sat in my lap and nuzzled my ear.

"Is this going to be one of those 'Here's what I want from Santa' scenes?" I asked.

She slapped my face gently. "What more could I ask for?" she said. She looked into my eyes and once again I found myself falling into her. That green, that green.

I reached up and buried my fingers in her hair, but she leaned away and smiled mysteriously and stood up from my lap. "I have something for you."

"Well, where is it?" I teased.

She went upstairs and came back with a package. "Right here," she said, showing it to me.

"Can I open it now?" I said.

"No, no, you have to wait."

"I don't know if I can."

"You have to. This is very special. Something I made myself."

"Ah. Well, if that's the case, you better put it under the tree. But I don't know if I'm going to be able to sleep tonight."

She winked at me. "You better not."

That one really made me laugh, and for the hundredth time I dropped my hand to my pocket to check that the little jeweler's case was still there. Something I'd bought a while back. All along we'd assumed we were getting married, but I had yet to go down on one knee. It was evening, dark already, and I was starting to think that I wouldn't be able to wait until morning. If I was lucky I'd be able to hold out until midnight, so I could honestly say I'd proposed to her on Christmas Day.

When the knock came on the door I thought it was a neighbor and I gave Elizabeth a quick look.

She shrugged. "Carolers or something. Don't worry, it's Christmas Eve and everybody knows how nice you've been to me this year."

"They're going to be surprised in a week when you turn up missing," I said.

"We haven't established that I'm *going* missing," she said. "You still have to—"

The knock sounded again and she went into the front hallway and opened the front door. I stood up to listen.

"Ma'am?" a man said in a clipped voice. "I'm First Sergeant Brighton."

*This can't be happening,* I thought. *How did they find me all the way out here?*

"What can I do for you, First Sergeant?" I heard her say. "Would you like to come in?"

I stepped into the hallway, revealing myself. "I think he's here for me," I said.

He was in dress blues, standing on the porch, and when

he saw me his face, already in shadow from the front porch light, grew darker, as if a job he'd been looking forward to had just been spoiled for him.

Then his face blanked out and he straightened even more and saluted Elizabeth.

"Ma'am," he said. "it's my privilege to report to you that your husband, Captain David Warner, is alive and in the custody of the United States."

"Captain?" I said.

Elizabeth swayed and I thought she might fall. "David's alive?" she gasped.

He moved forward smoothly and gave her his arm. I said, "In here." We took her into the living room and sat her on the couch beside the Christmas tree.

"Where's my husband?" she said. I felt her words cut me to my marrow.

The first sergeant removed his white frame cap. "He is currently a patient in Tokyo, where he's being treated for injuries sustained while a prisoner of war. You'll be contacted by telegram upon his discharge and he'll be flown home by first available transport."

"He's a captain now?" I repeated stupidly.

"Your husband has been promoted to captain and decorated with the Navy Cross for his actions on or about twenty-eight November, nineteen-fifty," he said to Elizabeth, ignoring me. He took out a business card, offered it to her, and when he realized she was too shocked to lift her hand for it, he placed it on the coffee table next to the plate of cupcakes.

"If you have any questions," he continued, "you can contact me directly. I am available at any hour."

He stood for a moment, waiting on her. "Ma'am? If you don't have any questions now, I'd like to wish you goodnight and Merry Christmas."

Elizabeth was pale. Her mouth was halfway open. The Marine put his cold eyes on me and spun smartly and left as abruptly as he'd come in.

I followed him outside. He was still deliberately ignoring me, heading straight for his car.

"I thought he was dead," I called after him.

He turned and came back up the sidewalk to stand eye-to-eye with me. "I don't know who you are, buddy," he growled, "but that's a war hero's wife, and I oughtta break your neck for messing with her."

"I thought he was dead," I insisted.

He leaned and spat, then spoke through clenched teeth. "Sure you did."

I knew what was coming. He popped me in the jaw and the force of it carried me halfway around and I was already going down when he punched me in the kidney and chopped the back of my neck, one-two. I dropped like a sack of sand.

Then he was standing over me, fists balled. "Break your homewrecking neck," he muttered.

I waited for it. But he let me off with a few kicks in the ribs instead. A shame. He could've snapped my head clean off, for all I cared.

~

After he left me I lay there for a while until I got some breath back. I crawled around the house and into the back yard. It was very cold and the moon was low in the sky. I lay down where we'd grown our garden, in a walkway strewn with dead leaves, between where the skeletons of the tomato vines still clung to the trellises I'd built.

I looked up to where the stars wavered, wondering why this had all happened. Wondering what I should do.

She never even came out of the house. After a while, I heard her playing that song from *Casablanca* again, except I recognized it now. It was "It Had To Be You."

And now I finally understood what it meant.

I lay there until the moon set, and then I stole into the cellar through the outside door. I found the old quilt on the shelf where we'd decided to keep it. Out of sight and out of mind, so we could start a new life together.

I wrapped the quilt around my shoulders against the cold, and limped away into the night.

And I never saw your grandmother again until you walked into the room.

## Part Three: Silver's Quilt

*Lord, I'm no hero.*
*My job is to heal.*
*And I want you to know*
*Just how helpless I feel.*

—from "A Hospital Corpsman's Prayer"

### ▶▶▶◆◀◀◀
## Chapter Twenty-Three

PJ crossed and uncrossed her legs, trying to get comfortable. Her chair was molded from hard plastic, like the look on the face of the financial services representative who sat across from them in the hospital's business office. The woman's demeanor was at once sympathetic and uncaring.

*Sorry for your trouble,* PJ thought. *Now pay up.*

Ross was fidgeting, too. "OK," he said to the rep. "But it seems like you're trying to have it both ways. Either we're related to Mr. Piper and you can release him to us, or we're unrelated and we don't have any responsibility for seeing that his bills get paid. Which is it?"

"All I'm saying," the woman sighed, "is that we need your contact information."

"Our social security numbers aren't contact information," Ross said. "They're credit information. And you're not getting anything like that from us until some sort of kinship is established. By the hospital, I might add."

This made PJ cross and uncross her legs again.

"But you're the ones maintaining that he's..." the woman began.

The back-and-forth went on until PJ lost patience and stood up. "I have to get back to Silver's room," she said.

"I'm coming with you," said Ross. "Thanks for your time, ma'am," he said to the rep. He offered his hand and they shook neutrally, but he walked out with a dark expression.

Outside, in the hallway, he stopped short and pulled PJ into a corner.

"Seventeen thousand dollars?" he said.

She folded her arms across her chest. "It doesn't make sense to me either. Why are they coming after us so hard? You hit the nail on the head, right there, about them trying to have it both ways."

"It blows my mind," Ross said. "Last I checked, we had freedom of movement in this country. What'll they do if he decides to leave without paying? Have a doctor commit him? We don't have debtor's prisons anymore, either. No, I think it's just a hard shakedown. They've got nothing to lose by trying it."

"That's not what I meant," PJ continued. "I mean, why *us*? He's a vet, so go to the VA. That ought to be the first thing they think of. The VA's great—I should know."

She stopped and studied Ross's face. "Why are you frowning like that?"

~

PJ heard the tinkling of glass from upstairs.

"PJ?" Bebe called.

But PJ was already moving, dropping her calculator and pencil and pushing her chair back so hard that it slid halfway across the kitchen.

She found Bebe standing in the hallway outside her bedroom, body rigid, arms extended. Shards of glass and ice were scattered around her in a pool of water on the hardwood floor.

*She's barefoot!* "Don't move, Bebe," PJ called.

"I won't. I'm so sorry."

PJ knelt and started gingerly lifting bits of broken glass into her cupped palm. "Is it getting darker again?" she asked as she worked.

"Some," Bebe said. "Were you working?"

"I think they call it 'competing,'" PJ said. "I swear, I bring more work home now than when I was in college."

"And then you have to take care of me on top of it."

PJ closed her eyes. *Nice bedside manner, Nurse Ratchet,* she chided herself. "Bebe, no, don't think of it like that," she said. "Hang on, I'm not quite done." She went into the bathroom for the trash can and came back with it.

"Well," Bebe said. "I feel like the only reason you're working so hard is because you're worried about the bills."

"It's not that at all," PJ said, finding more glass by the wall. "For once, I get to take care of you. It's only fair."

"Still…" Bebe trailed off.

"What?"

"You're gone so much," Bebe said. "It gets lonely. And I haven't learned my way around the house so well. I keep bumping into things, losing things."

PJ paused, a handful of ice dripping through her fingers.

*I feel like I'm splitting down the middle.*

~

"What is it, Ross?" PJ asked.

Ross looked away from her and down the hospital hallway. He toed the blue stripe on the floor that supposedly showed the way to the elevators.

"I know why Silver can't go to the VA," he said, still not meeting her eyes. "Man, I can't believe I'm telling you this."

"Excuse me?" PJ said. Ross's lips were tight and his eyes were slitted. He turned his back on her and gripped the handrail tightly in both hands.

What *was* all this? Ross never acted this way, like he was trying to hide in plain sight. It wasn't the caught-you-in-the-cookie-jar show she sometimes got from Baker, but much worse. Ross was acutely uncomfortable, like he was deeply ashamed of something. But his face also said he was angry at her, and she didn't get that at all.

"The reason he can't go to the VA is because he got

a dishonorable discharge from the Navy," Ross said. "He deserted in 1953."

"Dishonorable…" PJ closed her mouth and opened it again. "How do you know that?"

"Jerry Vicente," Ross muttered. "He called a couple of weeks ago. You were locked in the bathroom and I decided not to bug you with it."

"You did *what?* I don't believe you!"

"It's true. He e-mailed me a bunch of stuff he'd scanned. Silver really was a POW, but when he got back he caused a bunch of trouble and the Navy DD'd him."

"But he was a hero! He kept all those men alive!"

"PJ, the evidence isn't—"

"There's a ton of evidence! The quilt! My name! And he knows things about my grandfather and my grandmother that nobody—"

"Maybe he does," Ross interrupted. "I'm not saying he's lying, he's just not telling the whole story. He's telling us what he wants us to know."

A horrible feeling sank into her and she put her fists on her hips. "And you didn't tell me any of this! You didn't tell me anything! You let me go on worrying about it, let me get all worked up, and you didn't say a word."

"Look, I was worried too," he said. You were—"

He started moving closer to her and reaching for her hands, and she recoiled.

"I was what?" she demanded. "Helpless? Too fragile to hear it? You're saying you lied to me and it's my fault? You heartless—heartless—and you even knew I was named after him, didn't you? *Didn't you?*"

She didn't wait on his reply. She bit her words back and strode away down the many-doored hallway, following the blue line to wherever it was leading her.

*This is what I get for asking for help,* she thought.

~

Silver was asleep and she sat in one of the abysmal chairs waiting on Ross to come back for another round.

There was a knock behind her and Roy came ambling in, wearing a straw cowboy hat, a faded red workshirt, and run-down black boots.

"Hey!" he called cheerily. And then "Whoa!" when he saw her face. "What is it? The old man OK?"

"Silver's fine," she said, waving at him. "I'm just trying to get myself sorted out. He...um...told us his story and it was pretty horrible. War stories."

"I wondered whether he might've been a vet," Roy said. "My daddy used to tell stories that'd curl your hair. Said that was how his had got that way."

"Your dad was a vet? Vietnam?"

"Vietnam," Roy agreed. "He was a soldier over there in the mid-sixties."

"I see," PJ said, beginning to understand Roy a little better. "So how does a cowboy wind up working for the post office?" she asked.

"Well, that's Daddy again. Said, 'Hard to beat a government pension, son.' Vietnam wasn't enough to chase him out of the Army." Roy chuckled. "For that matter, the *Army* wasn't enough to chase him out of the Army. He was a tough old boy."

"Is he still living?"

"No ma'am, Daddy passed about five years ago."

"I'm sorry," she said. "What about your mom?"

"Went back to Can Tho after the old man passed," Roy said. "Living with her sister's family. She was a farmgirl—having trouble getting by. I guess that's how she and daddy met—but daddy was a good Mormon kid and he came and got me and her after the war."

Roy gave her a smile that was friendly but also knowing. *He must've given that little speech a thousand times,* PJ realized. *He knows people think he's an oddball. And he enjoys it. No wonder Ellen likes him.*

"Roy," PJ mused, liking him herself, "will you tell me the truth about something?"

"I'll do m'best."

"Do I seem helpless to you? Like I have trouble getting by?"

"Oh, no ma'am. Miss Ellen says you're the most capable

woman in the world, and you make most folks look dim—
that is, when you're firing on all eight cylinders—"

He clapped his hand over his mouth and smiled. "If you
tell her I said that, she'll skin me alive." Then he cleared his
throat. "Ma'am?"

*Dim,* PJ was thinking. "I'm sorry, I was just
remembering something," she said, looking up at him.

~

"It's all dim," Bebe said to the specialist, Dr. Adams.
She was in his chair, surrounded by robotic-looking ocular
equipment, but all Dr. Adams was using was a flashlight.
He was shining it in Bebe's eyes, back and forth, back and
forth.

"I think we've gotten to the point," PJ explained to him,
"that we need some in-home care. But they said we needed
to come to Nashville and get your sign-off."

Dr. Adams flicked off the flashlight. "I'll sign the
paperwork today," he said to PJ. "You're probably past due
for it."

"Past due?" Bebe asked.

"Mrs. Warner," Dr. Adams said gravely, "I'm sorry. I
know this is going to sound blunt, but your eyesight's almost
completely gone."

~

Ross came back to Silver's room bearing a Navajo taco
as if it were a box of fine chocolates.

"That's very sweet," PJ told him, understanding right
away that the real truce was still to come—however much
negotiation it might require.

"I'll see how many of these I can get them to make to
take home," he said.

"Yeah," she replied. "About that. Look, I need a big
favor from you guys. Roy, would it put you out to take Ross
down to that canyon where Silver was found? I was thinking
you could have another look around there to see what you
might find. Anything. ID, pictures of my grandmother, a

diary, anything. And anything that looks like it might be personally important to him."

"Why don't you just ask him what he wants from there when he wakes up?" Ross said.

She rolled her eyes. "Ross, now who's trying to have it both ways? Either you believe what he says, or you don't."

Roy glanced back and forth between them. "Er, I think I just heard my name on the PA."

PJ held up a hand. "No, no. Ross has been talking about getting away to see the desert anyway, and as long as we're out here he might as well do it. What do you think, Roy, are you OK with that?"

"Well, I'm obviously not workin'," he said.

"What about you, Ross?"

Ross leaned against the wall, scratching one shoulder. "Yeah, I guess so. But what're you gonna do while we're gone?"

"I have to call somebody," she said. "Somebody who owes me a few answers."

~

"Mom?"

"PJ?"

"How was Cozumel?"

"I think I need to go back to Cozumel to rest up from being in Cozumel," Anne said. "We had the best time."

"I'm glad. Look, we need to talk."

"Are you OK? You sound uptight. You should go where we were, it's—"

"Mom, I'm sorry, but this is really important. Listen, I'm in a hospital in Utah with a man I think is your real father."

The line went very quiet. "Hello?" PJ said.

"This," Anne said in a voice that was flat and detached, "is not a conversation I care to have." And she hung up.

PJ stared at her cell phone. *Well, that figures,* she thought. *Leave it to Mom to duck out at a critical moment.*

But then PJ's anger surged, and she thumbed the redial button. The phone rang and rang and rang, until someone finally picked up.

"Hello?" said a man with a Latino accent—Luis, probably.

"Can I speak with Anne, please? It's urgent."

"One minute, please," he said. PJ heard conversation in the background—*are they speaking Spanish to each other?*—and then she heard the phone being handed off.

"What is it, PJ?"

PJ closed her eyes. "Mom? If you hang up on me you're gonna regret it the rest of your life, OK? I know you're not very interested in us, but I'm telling you now that you might as well forget we ever lived if you don't hear me out."

She waited silently, afraid of having pushed her mother too far and at the same time proud of herself for doing it.

"Why can't you leave this alone?" Anne asked. "I've been trying to forget this for twenty years!"

It was a strange confession, but PJ understood it immediately. *I was right all along! I knew it! She's been hiding this from me all that time!*

"Mom," she said, "if you wanted to forget it, why'd you put it on my birth certificate? Why'd you name me after Joe Piper if you didn't want to be reminded of him?"

Anne laughed without a single iota of humor. "You're a smart cookie, you know that? Or cupcake, or whatever Mother called you."

"Why, Mom? Why did you do it?"

Anne's voice grew even more bitter. "OK, PJ, OK. You think you really want to know this, eh? Well, you've had kids, maybe you can relate. You're flat on your back with your legs up in stirrups and ten people are poking at you down there. There's this thing in you trying to tear its way out. You've been pushing for fourteen hours and you're screaming in agony because you fell for that stupid natural childbirth scheme. And they're telling you it's way too late for an epidural."

"Then," she continued, "there's a gush of blood and fluid and all kinds of nastiness, and a baby comes out, bright blue. It's been breathing its own body waste and they have to take it away immediately and rush it to a special, I don't know, incubator. You don't get to hold your baby at all. They don't even tell you whether it's a boy or a girl because they've forgotten all about you. Your own mother deserts you—your only company is some goody two-shoes nurse who's shoving bandages up inside you like you're a stuffed animal."

"Mom," said PJ, "this is a little too—"

"No, you have to listen to this," Anne said. "And then you get your turn. Finally, when you think you've been drained of every possible bit of your life and energy and voice and everything else, and the painkillers are making the whole universe spin around you, your mother comes back to check on you.

"'It's a little girl and she's beautiful,' your mother says. 'She has a full head of hair already.' And you lie there and try to remember what those words mean. And then she asks what you want to name it. Name her."

"So, why, then?" PJ said through the iciness that was creeping over her. "Why Piper Jo? Did you know Silver was your father, even back then?"

"No!" Anne shouted. "It was your holier-than-thou grandmother's idea! I was too far gone to think and she suggested it! 'What about Piper Jo? It's a name that's very important to this family,' she said. My God, I didn't find out who Joe Piper was until ten years later, when Daddy died!"

"When—" PJ said, and she stopped short, her mind rewinding time. "When Bebe slapped you, after the funeral, and you cursed her and left."

"Yeah," Anne said. "Yeah. I found you asleep in the bathroom—you were the most beautiful thing I'd ever seen, just then, all limp and peaceful, and I was starting to wonder if I should move back to Chattanooga and try being your mom one more time—and I carried you up to bed. Mother was in the kitchen washing dishes and I started helping her. She started crying and I hugged her, and she started crying even harder. Like, hysterically. She scared me. I asked her what it was and she told me."

"She told you about Silver."

"All about him. Said she'd cheated on Daddy while he was a POW and I was probably somebody else's daughter and she'd had to hide that part of herself away from the whole world for most of her life. She said she'd…"

Anne gulped and PJ realized she was crying. Then she heard Luis's voice in the background again.

"No, estóy bien," Anne said. "Váyate, querida. PJ, I hate this. I hate this. Why are you making me relive this when I obviously don't want to?"

"Because I need to know," said PJ. "I need to understand what makes a woman reject her family. Her own daughter."

"Rejection? You think I rejected you? OK, how about this? They finally get you cleaned up and stabilized and they bring you to me. I'm in my own room, now—cleaned up, some, feeling a little bit human again—and they tell me it's time to learn to breast-feed. 'Finally,' I think, 'I get to bond with my daughter.'

"You're on my chest and I take my breast and start rubbing your lips with my nipple, as gently as I possibly can. Just like the nurse is telling me to do. And you look up at me and you start howling. I try again, and you get worse. You're screaming, breaking my eardrums. I couldn't understand it, and I started crying.

"The nurse comes over and takes you away from me. 'Don't worry,' she says. 'Sometimes a baby won't take the breast. We'll get her some formula. It'll be fine. It doesn't mean anything.' And she took you and left me alone in that room. And that was the first time I met you."

Anne laughed sourly. "So who rejected who, PJ?"

~

"I want, like, six kids," Ross said.

"Six!" PJ said, looking up from her piecework.

"I don't know," he said, shrugging. "You grow up an only child, and you're supposed to start a big family, right?"

"But I'm an only child, and six kids…"

Bebe smiled. "Six would be fun. You'd never be bored. Ross, could you fill my glass back up?"

"Yes ma'am," he said, getting up from the easy chair that had once been David Warner's exclusive domain, and taking Bebe's glass into the kitchen.

Bebe leaned forward and felt for PJ's knee. PJ looked

226

into her eyes—a faded green now, and sightless, but still lit by a love of life that PJ knew would never fade.

"PJ," Bebe said, "you're the luckiest girl in the world."

"Six kids?" PJ repeated. "As in, six more than zero? I mean, we've only been dating for three years, and now he wants six kids?"

Bebe smiled. "Three years is a long courtship."

Ross returned with Bebe's fresh glass of lemonade. He took Bebe's hand and put the glass into it. She patted his hand in return. "Thank you, Ross."

"OK," PJ said, "if we could *please* return our attention to this quilt. I did some checking around and I was surprised to find out how much quilting is being done by the blind. So I had this idea—'Blind Woman's Bluff,' we could call it, and—"

▶▶▶◆◀◀◀
## Chapter Twenty-Four

The Navajo taco Ross had brought her as a peace offering was every bit as scrumptious as the first and second ones she'd had. PJ sat in Silver's room listening to the machines bleep and chasing bits of guacamole around the box with her fork.

*Real guacamole is the secret of life,* she thought. *Maybe I'll make Ross a quilt that's an avocado half on one side and a lime slice on the other. Call it "The Palace of Wisdom."*

Silver tossed in his sleep.

*Well, O Wise One,* she chided herself. *Where do we go from here?*

*It's seems simple, but it's not. We can leave Silver here by himself—not an option, really—or I can send Ross back and stay here, or we can take Silver home. I don't want to stay out here any longer than I have to, and taking Silver home is a big commitment. So what's the answer?*

*I just don't see any other choice but to take him with us.*

*And that's a big deal. Explaining him to the kids, setting up a room for him, hooking him up with doctors—not to mention dropping the bomb on everyone who thought they knew who Bebe really was. And Mom'll go through the roof.*

*But what do I care what Mom thinks? If Mom had her way I'd kick him out of the car at the Dark Canyon trailhead and never think about him again.*

PJ smiled, remembering the phone call.

*The number one confirmation that Silver is family was Mom's consternation. That was the first genuine emotion I've seen from her since I can't remember when.*

*No, I can handle Mom and the kids and Bebe's old friends. The problem is Ross. Somehow, I have to convince Ross that taking Silver home is OK.*

PJ took her sketchpad out of her quilting bag and started doodling avocados. The shadows moved across the room. Eventually Silver stirred again, and his eyelids fluttered open.

She set her pad aside. "Morning," she said, although it was four in the afternoon.

"Morning yourself," he croaked. "Reach me the water?"

There was a plastic pitcher on the swing-out dining tray, and she poured him a cup.

"I, um, sent Ross and—you remember Roy, right? The Vietnamese cowboy from the post office? Anyway, I sent them to Dark Canyon to get your stuff. We're gonna get you out of here today or tomorrow."

"Thank God," he said. "But don't bother with my gear. I'm just going back down to the canyon anyway."

"Um, no," she said. "We want you to come home with us."

He lowered his eyebrows and squinted. "Now why would I do that?"

"Silver, if you want to die—and I'm not saying it's not your right—Ross and I want to get to know you before you do. We just found each other! Don't ask us to abandon you."

He sat brooding. "I never thought, when I sent that quilt back east, that this would happen," he finally said.

"Well, be glad it did. You've got a home now. Family."

"I already have a home."

"A cave in a canyon wall isn't a home."

"Sure it is. People've been living in that cave

for thousands of years. There's paintings in there—petroglyphs—of whole tribes of 'em. Families holding hands. And stars, and the sun, and animals—everything in life. And when I look out, I can see the sunset."

"In Chattanooga," she said, "there's a little boy and a little girl who've never seen you. Real, not paintings. There's a back yard where you can plant tomatoes. I can take you to the Hunter Museum and show you the last quilt Bebe and I ever made together. And if you want to," she added delicately, "there's a cancer center."

"A cancer center," he repeated. "You want to cart me across the country and lock me up in a cancer center. Which one of these quacks told you I had cancer? Lord, I hate doctors."

PJ grew puzzled. "But…you were a medic. Doctors save people's lives."

"Some doctors do. Others are trying to kill you."

"I don't understand," she said. Then she was afraid that maybe she did. Some of the websites she'd read about the Korean POW camps had mentioned experiments being performed on prisoners. "Did they…do things to you in the camps? Medical things?"

"Oh, no. No, this was our own people. At Balboa, when I got home"

"Where?"

"The Navy hospital at San Diego."

"Silver, why would our own doctors try to kill you?"

He shook his head impatiently. "I got back to Pendleton a free man. Got my back pay and everything. Told them I wanted out of the Navy. They were all very polite and eager to please. Then some orders came down for me to report for a mental evaluation. Fine, you do what you're told."

Silver's voice grew louder and hoarser and the spots on his face stood angry red against his sunburn.

"So I show up at Balboa and start answering questions, and the next thing I know a panel of doctors are signing papers on me and I'm being walked to a padded cell by armed guards."

PJ wrapped her arms around herself, barely aware that she was doing it. "They locked you back up?"

"They locked me back up!" the old man raged. "All that time in the prison camps, and they locked me back up!"

~

"Jerry? Hi, it's PJ Hathaway."

"Hey, there," he said in a voice that was, if anything, raspier than last time they'd talked. "You look that stuff I sent you over yet?"

She laughed briefly. "That's a bit of a sore subject. But I won't bore you with it."

"Uh...OK. To what do I owe the honor?"

"Well, there's some pretty good news. We found Silver and he's got the most incredible story." PJ related it to him; it took a few minutes.

"As near as I can figure," she finished, "my Grandpa David was recaptured after the escape attempt and they put him back in the camps. Silver had already reported him dead, though, and it was so close to the end of the war that the mix-up didn't get sorted out until the prisoners were already being released."

"That would explain some of the inconsistencies I see in the records," Jerry told her. "The name Joe Piper was on some of the earlier KIA lists, too, but then he shows up on a POW list about halfway through the war. And then he escapes, of course. But he doesn't show up in any interviews I found."

"You'd think more men would remember him, since he was a medic," PJ said in frustration. "We're sort of—or at least Ross is—sort of dubious about the whole story, especially in light of his discharge," she finished.

"Yeah. I could see somebody having that reaction."

"It's not fair. It's not *right.*"

"No, it's not," Jerry agreed. "But a UOTHC is a bad ticket. Anything he might've done before he got it is more or less wiped out."

"A what?"

"I sent you this," he said, sounding puzzled. "UOTHC. It's his discharge classification."

"Ross told me Silver was dishonorably discharged."

"Well, your husband's mixing that up. Silver wasn't DD'd, he was given what's called a 'discharge under other than honorable conditions.' It means he was booted by the Navy, but they didn't want to go to the trouble of court-martialing him."

"What's the difference? Ross says he's still ineligible for VA benefits."

"He's right about that," Jerry said. "There's no way Mr. Piper can qualify for any benefits with a UOTHC. Not any benefits whatsoever. No disability, no pension, no military funeral. It's a casting out."

PJ tried to keep her voice even, but it was very hard. "Jerry, they railroaded him. He escaped from a prison camp and the first thing the Navy does is lock him up. So he escaped all over again. What else was he supposed to do? I know exactly why they didn't court-martial him—can you imagine how embarrassed the Navy would've been if the press had gotten hold of the story?"

"You're preaching at the choir," Jerry said. "They were trying to help him, but I don't say they were right to take his freedom away. The military's come a long way on treating post-traumatic stress disorder since then. I can't blame him for breaking out. Wouldn't dare after what he went through. Did he tell you how he did it?"

"No, he got so upset when I started asking him about it that I decided to keep it for later."

Jerry whistled. "I would love to talk to this guy. But the only idea I have for you right now is that you might want to appeal his discharge. You'll have to show an appeals board that there was a grave injustice in the way he was treated."

"I can certainly do that," PJ said. "If there's one thing I know, it's that Silver deserves better than this."

"Hey," Jerry said. "Why do they call him that, anyway?"

"I think it's because he's a stainer," she said.

"It's not the horse?"

~

"We want to hold you for observation for a little while

more," Dr. Singh told Silver. "These x-rays of your lungs, you know."

He seemed like a kind man, PJ decided—his voice lilted gently, his glasses were round, his beard flowed to his chest, and he was wearing an elaborately-wrapped turban—but if his words frightened her, she could well imagine how they sounded to Silver.

"I feel fine," Silver insisted. "Right as rain. I could get up from this bed and walk out right now, I think."

PJ raised a finger. "Is there any reason why you couldn't release him today, since we can call an ambulance if there's a problem?"

Dr. Singh studied his clipboard. "Oh yes, plenty of reasons."

"Tell me the truth," she said. "This is about money, isn't it? He's homeless and you don't want to release him because you think he's going to disappear."

Dr. Singh's bushy black eyebrows threatened to disappear up into his turban. "Ma'am, no! He's a free man. But his cancer's advanced, and it's best to be careful! He's a long-term admissions candidate, because—"

*That settles it,* PJ thought. "Can I talk to Mr. Piper alone, please?" she asked Dr. Singh.

"Of course," he said, looking back and forth between them.

When he'd stepped out of the room, she crossed her arms and tried to stare Silver down.

"What?" he muttered.

"You heard the man," PJ said. "Do you want to spend the rest of your life in here? Or are you going to listen to me?"

~

It was Valentine's Day, three-thirty in the afternoon, and PJ was sitting in a grey conference room listening to a grey man in a grey suit mumble about loop flows overheating a power transformer in some switchyard somewhere. Lunch debris was growing stale on the table and the breathing of ten people had deoxygenated the air to pretty much the minimum required to sustain human life, if not human consciousness.

*Hallelujah!* PJ thought when her pager went off. She unclipped it from her belt and checked the screen and stifled a gasp.

Her home phone number, followed by 911.

She came to immediately and fully awake. *It's the hospice nurse!*

~

"Don't go back to the hospital, Ross," PJ said on her cell phone.

"Where are you?" Ross demanded. She could hear highway noise in the background, and country music.

"I'm at the hotel, sitting on the bed," she said. "You need to get over here. We're all packed."

"We?" he asked.

"I dressed Silver and wheeled him out to the car. He's right here."

"Please tell me you didn't send me off on a wild-goose chase so you could sneak him out of the hospital."

"Ross, it's not a prison in there. People come and go. I dressed him in some of your clothes and now he's here, OK? He's just fine."

"PJ," he said, "take him to the car and drive to the hospital and wheel him back in again. Right now."

"I'm not gonna do that," she said. "The doctor said he was all right, but they were talking about long-term care. It was Silver's decision, not mine."

"Then fine, give him some money and tell him we'll drive him back down to the desert."

"I think you know—" she began.

Silver started trying to get up from the bed. "What is this?" he said.

"Hold on, Ross," PJ said. "Silver, sit down."

"You-don't-know-if-he's-related," Ross said deliberately.

She gripped the phone in frustration. "OK, Ross, let me lay it out for you. Say I get a paternity test. DNA."

"That's a great idea." The relief in his voice galled her.

"And say it turns up negative. What then? Do I tell Silver not to let the door hit him in the butt on the way out? Ross, like it or not, we're responsible for him."

"What color is the sky in your world?" Ross asked.

"Nobody's responsible for me except me," Silver said at the same time.

*These two are worse than the twins,* PJ thought.

"Silver, will you please sit down?" she said. "And Ross—"

~

"No, I will not sit down!" PJ shouted. "I want to know where that nurse was when my grandmother was lying in the bathtub for an hour with her hip broken!"

Her voice rang the walls in the doctor's office and Ross put his hand on her arm.

"So do we," the doctor said in a dull and placating tone that only served to increase PJ's anger. "I've already suspended her and there'll be an investigation, I promise you. Meanwhile, let's get your grandmother back up on her feet."

He went into a short description of Bebe's X-rays, which PJ caught very little of. Something about surgery and weeks of bed rest followed by physical therapy. The recovery to be complicated, of course, by Bebe's high blood pressure and poor eyesight.

At some point she felt Ross tugging her arm gently, and she allowed him to lead her out of the office.

"All I want to do is find an attorney," she said as they walked down the hallway. "I want to own that hospice service so I can fire every last person who works there."

"We will," Ross said. "But PJ—are you hungry? I know this great little place…"

PJ looked at her watch. "Oh, Ross, I'm so sorry. It's Valentine's Day! I completely forgot!" For weeks he'd been teasing her with how he'd snagged reservations at a restaurant on the brow of Lookout Mountain overlooking the city.

"No worries," he said. "Let's just go down and get a couple of burgers from the cafeteria, and then we'll look in on Bebe, OK?"

She reached for his hand, wove her fingers into his. "This isn't what you had in mind at all, is it?"

He squeezed her hand. "You keep me on my toes, I'll give you that."

~

"Silver," PJ said as they waited for Ross and Roy, "what happened after you and Bebe? Fifty years is a long time."

He nodded. "Fell back into my old ways. Longest part of it, I ran a roofing business. Laying shingles under the sun wasn't so bad the second time around. Warm, y'know. Worked out of a house trailer, all over the country. Built base housing, did a bunch of work up in Detroit. Phoenix. Few years here, few years there. Following the war boom, like my old man did."

"Were there any other women?"

A touch of the devil-may-care smile returned to his face, and he shrugged.

"Did you ever get married?"

"Yeah," he said. "I got married."

"Where is she?"

Silver shrugged again. "We weren't very good for each other."

PJ stroked the cheap hotel bedspread—the stitching was unraveled in places and the fabric, once burgundy, was faded to drabness.

"Why's that?" she asked. "Didn't you love her?"

"I loved," he said, "sitting in a bar after a hot day in the sun, with a beer and a shot, and my crew all around. There was this tough girl in Reno, a codes inspector, and we struck some sparks off each other on the job site. She liked to drink with the boys as much as I did. Every so often I'd come home and catch her with somebody else. About as often as—" he wrinkled his mouth "—she'd catch me."

"Did you have kids together?"

"No, no kids," Silver said.

"Hmm," she said, wondering whether she should bring up Anne.

"What?"

"Well...it's the first time I've thought about whether I had aunts out there I didn't know about. Uncles."

"Well now you know," he said. "Know what it's like for me, seeing you. They say how a father falls in love with his daughter right there in the delivery room, and I never understood it until now. And you're no baby, either. Not even my daughter. Listen, what you said about a paternity test—it could be that's the right thing to do."

PJ shook her head. She'd been heartbroken when she first opened Silver's package and found only a filthy quilt. And how selfish that heartbreak had been. So now, what if she opened the man himself, so to speak, and found only heartbreak again? She knew it'd be a mistake beyond any she'd ever made. People weren't packages. After all, what if Ross had looked inside her and moved on?

*Who's to say he isn't doing that right now?* she wondered.

"I want you to come to Chattanooga and live with us," she said. "In my heart, I know you're family, and that's the only place where it matters. Bebe would have agreed with that."

"I said no, honey. I'm too old to start over."

"What does that mean, anyway? 'Too old to start over?' You talk like you're already dead, like getting to know us is too much trouble."

"As far as trouble," he said. "You ask your husband whether I'm trouble or not."

"You let me worry about Ross. If you want to get on his good side, tell him you'll reshingle the roof. I don't think it's so much about you, it's just that he's...he's a lot more analytical about this kind of thing."

"He should be; I don't blame him. Old lions and young lions, y'ever hear that one? You're asking me to go across the country to be a guest under another man's roof, and, PJ, let me tell you, that's not far removed from being locked up in a hospital. Especially when the man in question doesn't want you for his houseguest."

"It's not that he doesn't want you," she said. "It's more about me than it is about you. He doesn't—man, this is hard to talk about. He doesn't trust me very much right now."

"Well, maybe you should listen to him. It wouldn't be the first time I'd caused trouble to a woman in your family."

"If you think you troubled Bebe, you need to take a closer look at that quilt she made you. You were everything in the world to her."

"She was all I ever needed," Silver said. "I don't need anybody else."

"How can you sit there and say that?" she asked in wonder.

His smile, when it came, was sad. The ragged old quilt was in his lap and he ran his hands across it. "I've got my family, right here," he said. He touched his temple. "And right here."

PJ reached out and put her palm on his chest. "But what about here?"

~

"He said he'll come home with us," PJ said simply.

The bartender came with a beer and Ross lifted it out of his hand before he could set it on the bar.

"Don't run off," Ross told him, and then, as PJ watched, Ross quaffed half the bottle. He was still in the jeans and t-shirt he'd worn to Dark Canyon, sweaty and dusty and scratched and sunburned, and as PJ watched he killed the rest of the beer off and handed the bottle straight back to the bartender and waved a circle in the air with his finger.

"PJ," Ross said, "it's not that I don't like Silver, it's that— my God, do you have any idea of the impact this'll have on our lives? On our finances? On the kids?"

"I'm not saying it's forever," she said. "Jerry told me— yeah, I called him—that there might be a chance we could get his discharge reversed. So I was thinking he could stay with us while we start that process, and when the reverse came through, he'd qualify for VA and his pension and all that. And he could get his own place."

She lowered her eyes. "But Ross, forget all that. And forget that he might be my grandfather. How can you ask me to walk away from family? And how can you ask me to walk away from the man Bebe loved?"

The bartender returned with another beer, and Ross chugged a quarter of it before swiveling on the stool to rest a hand on PJ's knee.

"PJ, regardless whether he's family, it's obviously not forever. You need to look up 'mesothilioma' on the web," he said.

She couldn't meet his eyes. "I know what it is. Silver was a roofer. I imagine he handled asbestos every day."

"Then you know how malignant it can be. He doesn't have time for an appeals process. He doesn't have time for much of anything."

"Ross, that's just one more reason to bring him home! He has so little time to get to know us!"

"Listen, I know that I'm beaten on this," Ross said. "If I don't let you do it, you're never going to forgive me. No, no—let me finish. He can come home with us, and live with us, and it's all good. But I want something from you."

She sat forward. "I'll do anything you want."

"You will, huh? OK, what I want is for you to start seeing a counselor. You say you're just tired, but I think there's more to it. Every day we're moving further and further apart, and you're...you're just not yourself. Not the woman I fell in love with."

"Um...a counselor, like a shrink?"

"I'll go with you," he added. "We're in this together, but it has to happen and it has to happen now."

*And here it is,* she thought. Somewhere in a corner of herself she'd known this was inevitable, that he'd start digging her out of the bunkers where she'd entrenched herself, shining lights where she didn't want them, lobbing grenades into dark rooms where...

*Ridiculous. This isn't a war. What Silver went through, that was a war. And now Ross comes after me like I'm some sort of shell-shocked victim. Can't he see that this is just what women go through? And can't he see I don't have time for this? People are counting on me. And there's no way I'm debating my mental health in the bar of some crummy hotel a thousand miles from home.*

"All right, I'll look into it," she said.

"You'll go," he insisted. "I want your word on this."

~

"Ross, what are you doing?" PJ laughed when she came back into Bebe's hospital room. She'd come directly from the office, still in her pantsuit and trenchcoat, and she had her dinner in a little cooler.

"It's called 'quilting,'" Ross said. "It's an ancient and honorable craft, dating to…uh…the Shroud of Turin, I think, and—"

PJ and Bebe were both giggling at him now.

"It's my fault, I encouraged him," Bebe said. She felt for the fabric and took it from him. "Oh, I don't know, Ross," she said, running her hands across his stitchwork. "I know it's called 'Blind Woman's Bluff,' but not because we want it to look like a blind woman sewed it."

That one set PJ off again, and she sat down and let the laughter have its way with her. She snorted once, and Ross looked at her in mock horror, which set her off a third time, and so on and so forth.

"Well," she said when she could speak again, "I didn't expect to see you tonight. I only brought dinner for one."

"Ah," he said. "I can fix that too. I came by to see if Bebe'd let me check you out this evening because that place on Lookout Mountain had a cancellation and they called me. So you get your Valentine's dinner on February twenty-third. How about that?"

"It beats cold spaghetti," she said. "Bebe, do you want us to bring you a dessert or anything?"

"What? And waste this nice hospital food?"

*Amazing,* PJ thought, *how her eyes can still twinkle.*

~

PJ stretched. They'd been driving for what seemed like days.

"What I didn't know," she finished telling Silver across the backseat, "was that Ross had come to the hospital that day to apologize to Bebe for not being totally honest with her."

At the wheel, Ross nodded. "And she goes, 'Young

man, you can't talk your way out of a problem you behaved yourself into.'"

"Did she ever tell you that one?" asked PJ. "It was one of her favorites."

"I thank the good Lord she never did," said Silver. "But what kind of behavior was she talking about?"

"His intentions towards me," PJ said. "But I'm getting to that."

"She gave me this look," Ross said, "like I was a puppy that had just wet the rug and needed a good paddling. And that I couldn't be expected to know any better, but I was just too cute to cut loose."

"Now, I *do* know that one," said Silver. "She came home one time and I'd painted the front steps purple."

"Her favorite color," PJ mused.

"Not for the front steps," said Silver.

"If we're going to get into mistakes we made with our significant others," Ross said, "it's a good thing we're only halfway across Kansas."

PJ twisted her engagement ring on her finger. It was a stunner, everyone had told her, and she knew they were right. A little over a karat, flawless, on a band of gold that had tiny platinum stitches worked into a lovers' knot around it.

"You get it right more often than not," she said, understanding that an uneasy truce was better than no truce at all.

"Take it and run, son," said Silver. "Take it and run."

"I believe I will," Ross said.

~

Below PJ and Ross the lights of Chattanooga glittered around the long lazy bend of the Tennessee River like the cinnamon sparkles in the ribbon of caramel syrup that garnished PJ's plate.

She mopped it all up with her last bite of chocolate cake. *That was the most incredible meal I've ever had,* she thought.

Ross was watching the view. "I can see forever from up here," he said. He turned back to her and took a sip of his wine. His suit was shadow-dark and his face was burnished soft gold in the candlelight.

"Can we do this all over again?" she asked. "Come in again and order again and eat again?"

"Valentine's Day comes but once a year," he smiled. "Every February twenty-third, like clockwork."

PJ smiled back, enjoying his mischief. "OK, well, can we at least get to the box?"

She'd been curious throughout dinner, ever since he'd gotten out of the car with a red-wrapped package the size of a phone book. Too big to be a ring and too small to be a sewing machine. But he'd told her to wait, the devil.

"See for yourself," he said, and he reached under his chair for it and offered it to her. "For once, I made you something. Uh, and I asked Bebe's permission to give it to you."

"What? Why?"

Ross shrugged. "Just my raising, I guess."

PJ tore the paper off and there was a black leather photo album inside. She opened it, and the first picture was Ross standing behind the bar where she'd first met him, holding a plate of nachos, grinning.

"What is this?" she asked.

"Keep going, you'll see."

She turned the page. The next three photos were from Copperhill, from what PJ thought of now as their first date. There was Anne, dancing with the little boy while the bluegrass band played. Bebe and PJ and Anne, in front of the quilt they'd made together. And a red cupcake with a big bite out of it.

"This is funny," she said.

Then there was a scene from a hike she and Ross had taken together in the Smokies. On top of a mountain, like they were now. On top of the world.

A blues concert at the plaza downtown with some of Ross's coworkers. A minor league baseball game—PJ being hugged by a red furry monster-mascot that was obviously a skinny kid in an ill-fitting costume. The duck that had once laid an egg on her car. Ross working on her car. Ross working on Bebe's car. PJ and Bebe and Ross, wrapped in a quilt together in front of a Christmas tree.

The trip to Ross's parents' house in Chicago, when she'd first met them—the Sears Tower, the lake, a pizza five inches thick. The four of them standing together on the Miracle Mile, arms around each others' shoulders after the weekend they'd enjoyed.

PJ flipped the pages faster and faster now; there were so many of them. Good times, three years' worth, since day one and arranged in chronological order. As she neared the end of the album she found herself hoping there were still plenty of blank pages, or even whole albums waiting to be filled with pictures they had yet to take.

"This is great, Ross," she said, and she wiped an eye with a fingertip.

He smiled.

PJ turned another page and there was Bebe in her hospital bed, smiling, the beginnings of the "Blind Woman's Bluff" quilt spread across her lap, but her eyes sadly misdirected, aimed elsewhere than the camera lens.

She turned the page again. It was a picture of the front door of the restaurant, the very one they were in now. Iron filigree and rich brown walnut.

"When did you take this?" she asked.

"A few..." and he cleared his throat. "A few days ago."

Another page, and there was a picture of this very table. On this same terrace, candlelit and set for two, and the city lights spreading towards the horizon.

She fingered the final page in the album for a long moment before turning it.

And there she found a picture of Ross, at tableside. Down on one knee, with a velvet box in his hand. Which was open and had something shining from within.

When she looked up, not believing it, the picture had become reality. Ross knelt there, the ring blazing in his hand with a light that outshone any table candle or neon skyline.

"I find that I love a nice cupcake," he said.

▶▶▶◆◀◀◀
## Chapter Twenty-Five

"PJ!" Ellen exclaimed, hands on her hips and exasperation in her face. "I send you out there to collect one man, and you come back with a different one."

The Blockheads came unglued with laughter and PJ rolled her eyes. "You're starting to repeat yourself, Ellen. That's the same line you used on me when we got home."

Missy looked around the sewing table and said, "Well, since he's an extra, you won't mind if I—"

"No, no," said Sondra. "He needs somebody closer to his own age—me, say—and—"

"He's my grandpa, not yours!" Lizzie said, swelling with the righteous suspicion only a four-year-old can muster, and evoking more laughter from the girls.

Silver waved his hands for their attention. "Ladies, ladies," he said from his wheelchair. "If I'd've known I'd be causing a riot, I'd've—"

"What?" PJ interrupted. "Stayed in Utah?"

"No! I'd've come to Chattanooga a lot sooner!"

And everybody fell out all over again.

*It's good to be home,* PJ thought. And she found herself seeing Silver as the girls saw him—as a weatherbeaten old man, true, but one with a good head of hair and strong cheekbones and a sly light in his eyes that was an open invitation to fun.

*Now,* she thought. *If I can just keep them focused on him and his quilt.*

~

"So you see how it is," she finished. "It went a whole lot deeper than I thought."

"I knew, the day I saw that old quilt, it was an incredible story," Kelly said.

"It's like an Alfonso Arau movie," Crystal said.

"Exactly," said Ellen.

"Who the heck?" said Missy.

"'*Like Water for Chocolate,*'" Crystal and Ellen said together.

"You too, Ellen?" Missy said, "Sometimes I don't know whether to smack my forehead or smack you."

"And that's really how it went down?" Crystal continued.

"That's...the truth," PJ said. *Mostly. Maybe I left out a few minor details, about fights with my husband and bouts of sleeplessness and maxing out the credit card to pay for the trip and sneaking a cancer patient out of a hospital and promising to see a counselor when I'd rather be gonging myself over the head with a big steel spoon...*

"Why do you look so sad, Mr. Piper?" asked Flo. As usual, she'd been watching and listening while everyone else gabbled.

"Well," he answered, "two weeks ago I was the only person for twenty miles around. And I hate to think that me turning up after all these years is somehow making Bebe look bad, like she had a skeleton in her closet."

"It's pretty complicated," PJ said. "We're just trying to focus on, well, being here now, rather than digging up old dirt."

Crystal frowned. "But old dirt is kind of the point, isn't it?"

"How do you mean?" PJ asked uneasily, remembering how, weeks ago, Crystal had asked if PJ and Ross were on the brink of divorce.

"Mr. Piper," Crystal said, "what does it feel like to know that you're about to die with that kind of secret hanging over you? It sucked, what the Navy did to you! They should've been ticker-taping you in Times Square, not putting a black mark in, you know, your 'permanent record.'"

"Sheeew!" said Nadine. "You don't beat around the bush, do you?"

Silver surprised PJ by chuckling. "How old are you, sweetheart?" he asked Crystal.

"Twenty-one."

"Old enough to buy beer now," he said, and his voice was at once affectionate and playful and sad.

"I, uh, like Scotch, but that's right."

"Scotch?" he repeated. "A woman your age drinking Scotch." He shook his head. "Well, I spent my twenty-first birthday locked in a little metal box, about so-by-so. I'd been in there three or four days, and from way off I thought I heard some men singing. Thought I was finally losing it. And I realized what they were singing was 'Happy Birthday, dear Silver, happy birthday to you,' over and over again."

"Happy birth-day, dear Siiilll-verrrr," Lizzie sang. But if anyone else in the room was even breathing, PJ couldn't hear it.

Silver bit his lip. "Or was it my twentieth? I don't remember. Sweetheart, I couldn't care less what the United States Navy thinks about me. Those boys were my family, and they sang to me."

PJ glanced around the circle at the other women. They were quiet, their faces thoughtful. "Silver," she said, "don't you see how much people want to hear about what you went through?"

He closed his eyes. "Now, do you have to start with that?" he asked. "What if everybody you talked to felt that way? Said they felt like they couldn't be honest with you because what you'd been through was so much worse than what they'd been through? Couldn't even have an everyday conversation with you, because the elephant was always in the room? 'War hero, war hero, war hero.' You'd feel like a carnival freak, that's what you'd feel like.

"I'm no story for people to write down," he insisted. "I've done things—killed people. Broke my word. Left a man for dead and stole his wife. Ran out on her when it got tough. Despaired. PJ, if it wasn't for Elizabeth's face looking out of yours, I'd be gone right now."

The girls were all silent. Flo sat toying with the gold cross she always wore.

"But you can make it good, Silver!" said PJ. "It's never too late to make good!"

"I am beyond any making good," he said.

The flatness of his voice made her sit back in her chair and fold her arms across her stomach.

*What do I do now?* she wondered.

Then her eye fell on the quilt Bebe had made for him. She began to smile.

~

"Are you comfortable?" PJ asked.

"I'm sewing, aren't I?" Bebe said.

PJ smiled. "I can adjust the bed up if you want," she said. It was weird, having a hospital bed in their living room, but PJ understood full well that stair climbing, for Bebe, was a thing of the past.

*At least she's still interested in quilting,* PJ thought. *But I swear, it's like she knows she's at the end of the road. And she's fine with it. How does she do it?*

And the thought she'd been thrusting away for weeks crowded in yet again: *And what am I going to do when she's gone?*

"The bed's fine," said Bebe. She turned her head sideways and squinted at the square she was sewing—just a tiny corner of vision left to her, she admitted, and that cloudy and shadowed.

She took a few stitches and then held the square up. "How does that look?"

PJ took it and studied it. It was a stylized eye in greens and whites, on a sky-blue background. The pupil was a tiny sun—amazing that a blind woman had sewn this!—and it glowed deep yellow and gold.

"If I'm ever ten percent the quilter you are," PJ said, "then I'll be just fine."

Bebe clucked. "I wish you'd seen my great-grandmother Rachael at work. I was just a little girl, but I knew I was watching something special. She was selling her quilts back before the turn of the century."

"You mean in the eighteen-hundreds," PJ said.

"That's right. She made a commemorative quilt for the dedication of Vanderbilt University, did you know that?"

"You've never told me," said PJ. "Really?"

"That's the story."

"Do you know what happened to it?"

"Oh, no. I'm sure it's hanging in a museum somewhere." Bebe sighed. "I like to think it is, anyway."

"Bebe," PJ said thoughtfully, "where did she learn quilting? Great, however-many, Grandma Rachael?"

"I don't know," Bebe said. "That's a good question. If I ever knew that story, I've forgotten it."

PJ felt very sad then, diminished by the loss of what would have been a wonderful bit of family lore to be treasured and kept for the next generation—*all six of them, if Ross gets his way,* she thought.

She reached for Bebe's hand, took it in both of hers, and held it to her cheek.

"I promise you, Bebe," she said, "that I will never let you be forgotten."

"It's nice to think that I'll live through this quilt. Quilting's my refuge, now, like it never was before."

"It must've been a comfort while you were taking care of Grandpa."

"It was," Bebe said. "I hadn't quilted for a long time, and then your Grandpa David went missing, and someone told me I should start up again." She seemed to be on the verge of saying something else, but she lapsed into silence instead.

PJ squeezed her hand. "I'm glad they did."

"Me too, Cupcake," said Bebe, squeezing back. "Me, too."

"I can't imagine what our lives would be like without it," PJ said.

~

*She was trying to tell me about Silver,* PJ realized. *And she couldn't. How many times did I miss a connection that might have led to complete honesty between us? I can't believe I was so self-centered back then. It's like I wasn't even listening. If I could do it all over...*

PJ stuck out her tongue at herself, and tried yet again to concentrate on the notepad on her sewing desk.

She'd already crossed out several possible titles for her new project: SILVER'S QUILT, FREE JOE PIPER, REMEMBER THE FORGOTTEN, et cetera.

"Momma?" said Baker, coming in. He was wearing a red bandanna and his cowboy boots.

"Baker, for like the nine millionth time, please, if I'm in my sewing room it means I'm trying to work. Can you just go watch *Cinderella* again?"

"That's a girlie movie," he said. "I want Clint Eastwood this time."

"It's not a girlie—um, never mind that," she said. "But we're not watching any war movies in this house. I tell you what, if you'll just—"

"There he is!" called Silver, sticking his head through the doorway. From his wheelchair he leveled a finger at Baker and shot him out of the saddle. "Bang! Run away, buck-a-roo!"

Baker hollered a big *yee-ha!* and wheeled his imaginary horse around and spurred it down the hall.

"I'll keep him out of your hair," Silver said. "Sorry about that."

"No problem," she said. "I appreciate you watching them."

"They're fun. While I've got you, I took care of that creaky tread on the stairs."

"How'd you do that?" she asked.

"Construction adhesive."

She winced. "Was Baker watching?"

"I put the fear of God in the boy about playing with

construction adhesive," Silver said. He looked back down the hallway. "Look out!" he yelled at someone out of her view, probably a pygmy cowboy holing up for a bushwhacking. Then Silver flicked his wrist and made the *whi-pow!* sound of a whip cracking, and went rolling after Baker as fast as he could manage it.

PJ tried to concentrate through the noise of Baker ambushing him. But after ten minutes she found herself doodling the same quilt block over and over. A jagged pattern called "The Fool's Puzzle."

She threw her pencil onto the desk and heaved a mighty sigh.

*Holy cow, I can't get a single word down. Is this what writers go through? Where do I even start?*

*The customer,* she thought. *Start with the customer.*

She wrote in block letters across the center of the page:

JOSEPH MONTGOMERY "SILVER" PIPER
STORY QUILT
1) WHO BENEFITS FROM THIS PROJECT?
2) WHY DO THEY NEED IT?
3) HOW WILL THIS PROJECT MEET THOSE NEEDS?

*OK, that's the high-level stuff. Now, some specifics. Who benefits from this project? Well, it's mainly Silver. And Silver's family, meaning us. Baker and Lizzie. Ross. I guess you could include other Korean War vets, POWs, and people like that, too. Their families.*

She wrote all of those people down under the first question. "Now why does Silver need this?" she asked herself aloud.

And that one stumped her. He didn't, according to him. Wasn't this the main problem she was wrestling with? Not so much the dirt, as Crystal had put it, but the fact that Silver didn't care whether or not he was dirty?

*This is impossible,* she thought. *But I have to do it. Remember what else Crystal said?*

"What does it feel like to know that you're about to die with that kind of secret hanging over you?" she'd asked Silver.

*I wish I could've asked Bebe that question. My God, she must have suffered just like he did. Like he still does. She carried her secret for her whole life, knowing what people would've thought of her if it ever came out. And the one time she tried, it cost her her only daughter.*

*What's it like to be ashamed of the love of your life? How lonely was it? How many times did she hide her tears from her friends and family and even from her husband?*

*And did Grandpa David even know? Did she ever confide in him?*

*No,* PJ decided. *She couldn't have. He wouldn't have understood, anyway. And Aunt Carol and Aunt Margaret would've been horrified. No, Bebe only ever told one person, Anne, and look what happened.*

*So she died thinking she was right to keep her life's tragedy unresolved. And she had to keep up appearances, so she shut her family out of her inner self, and never let them come near her. She shut them out and locked them out until the day she died.*

*But what am I thinking—"them?" It was us. Bebe shut us out. Bebe locked us out. Anne. And me.*

The wall thumped behind her, rattling the family pictures hanging on it, and she heard Baker giggling and Silver neighing like a horse. PJ scowled at the interruption and stood up and closed the door on them.

Then she looked at the knob in her hand.

*What am I doing?*

In her mind she heard a door crashing on its hinges. She heard hydraulics hissing closed with a finality no amount of time or heartache could appeal to. Felt herself clutching a cardboard box. Remembered Anne's words: "Who rejected who?"

*What in God's name am I doing?*

The world shifted under her feet and she gripped the doorknob tighter to steady herself. She heard herself slamming a trash can lid down over a quilt that was no less sacred than the bones of a saint. Felt a live wire thrumming under her fingertips. Heard herself hanging up on Anne. Saw herself walking out of the house leaving her kids crying in Ellen's arms, with Ross following after her, his eyes anxious.

*And you, of all people, called Ross heartless. Who's the heartless one, here?*

PJ stared down at the doorknob. She put her other hand on it and pulled the door back open, as if fighting a great weight—

—to find Lizzie standing there. "What are you working on, Momma?" Lizzie asked, twirling a strand of her cornstraw hair.

"I don't know," PJ said. Her throat was dry.

"Can I help?" Lizzie asked.

~

PJ was asleep. Deeply, blissfully asleep, like a baby with a bellyful of warm milk. No antihistamines to knock her out, no hours on the treadmill to exhaust her. A natural, healing sleep, its gentle fingers stroking the dark plaque from the haggard wrinkles in her brain.

She was flying, swooping towards a dream horizon that shimmered like a highway mirage.

*I can see it. I can see everything. It's all so—*

Then there was a bang somewhere and Ross was up in her face—"PJ! PJ! PJ!"—and he was shaking her shoulder. The bedroom lights scorched her eyes. The kids were crying and there was a terrible noise coming from down the hallway, and for a second she imagined herself on a battlefield.

A rush of adrenaline cleared her mind. It was a great gasping sound that she heard. A man desperate for air, choking for it, screaming for it.

She was up and sprinting down the hallway, Ross inches behind her, talking into his cell phone.

Silver thrashed on the floor of the guest room like she'd first seen him thrashing in the emergency room. He'd knocked the nightstand over, shattered the lamp.

His face was ashen and his lips were going blue. But his eyes were open, bright with the terror of a man conscious of his own agony.

PJ knelt to him, took him by the shoulders. "Silver, we're here."

Silver's pupils grew wider and the heaving of his chest grew deeper.

*Airway, breathing, circulation,* PJ thought, trying to remember the first-aid training she'd gotten from the nursing home. His mouth gaped open and she could see his tongue. No plate by his bedside; he hadn't been eating anything.

He just couldn't breathe. And it didn't matter why.

"4212 Ridgetrace," she heard Ross say behind her. Giving the EMTs their address.

She wrestled Silver away from the bed, got him clear of the nightstand and lamp he'd knocked over. Knelt over him and inhaled.

"I'm gonna breathe for you," she said, looking into his eyes. He nodded slightly, his eyes bulging. Then she bent, put her lips to his, and forced her life into his own.

▶▶▶◆◀◀◀

## Chapter Twenty-Six

"Here we are again," PJ said to Silver. "I hate this."

"Here" was Erlanger Hospital, downtown. Somber wallpaper, the smell of disinfectant rising from floor tile. Machine-bed. Plastic tubes, bags of saline. And a regulator on the wall pumping oxygen into Joe Piper at fifteen liters per minute.

He reached for her hand.

"Silver," she said—knowing the time wasn't right to be springing things on him but wondering how many more chances she had—"there's somebody I keep meaning to tell you about. A guy named Jerry Vicente. He helped me figure out who you were, after you mailed that quilt. Jerry runs a POW-assistance network, and he wants to fly down from New Jersey and talk to you."

"Jerry's a good guy," said Ross. He and Lizzie and Baker were sitting in the corner on folding chairs. "He lost an uncle in Korea, at Turkey Hill."

PJ looked at Ross. "Did he ever tell you what that means?"

Behind the oxygen mask, Silver smiled. "They served a big Thanksgiving dinner in 1950. The men threw turkey bones all over. Then the Chinese came down…" and he left off, his breathing labored.

"Happy Thanksgiving," PJ muttered.

"Is it Thanksgiving?" asked Baker.

Lizzie rolled her eyes. "It's not even Dependant's Day, stupid."

"That's enough, that's enough," Ross rumbled. "Dependant's Day is April fifteenth, anyway."

PJ didn't laugh. She studied Silver—his stubbled face, his thin frame, the effort of his breathing—and her resolve grew. *It's Aunt Carol all over again. I have to quit stalling. I have to get things off my chest while there's time.*

"Silver, I think it's important for you to talk to Jerry, tell him what you went through. Jerry's network has an attorney, and Jerry thinks he can help you get your discharge upgraded—maybe even get you some of the recognition you deserve.

"I've had this idea," she went on, "to pay for the attorney by making a quilt for you. A memorial quilt, like the AIDS Memorial Quilt or the quilts that have been made to benefit the Susan G. Komen Breast Cancer Foundation. I heard about one called 'The Quilt that Raised the Roof' that a group made to raise money for their church after a tornado demolished it. They raised around thirty thousand dollars, publicizing the quilt and selling squares on it. That's the kind of thing I want to do."

"When did you think of this?" Ross asked.

"When I was asleep the other night." She opened her bag, took out her notepad and found the right page, and held it up to show them. "I haven't colored it yet, but this is the pattern I want to use."

It was a simple drawing of a square quilt. "I got the inspiration from the quilt Bebe made for you, Silver," she explained. "You see at the bottom, that pair of open hands? Instead of Bebe's, I want to outline yours."

"That's a lot more hearts than just Bebe's," Silver said. Into the hands there cascaded a whole blizzard of valentines, each perfectly drawn.

"Those are what I'll sell," said PJ. "I think that gentle spiral pattern is nice—it's very organic—and it gives me a lot of room. As I sell more hearts, all I have to do is make the quilt taller. And I have some other ideas for details that'll play into this theme. It's all these people sharing their hearts with Silver."

"Selling hearts," Ross said. "What? I'm just thinking out loud."

"I know what you want to say, Ross," PJ said. "Why would anyone buy one? I was thinking I'd pitch them to the veterans' groups. The American Legion, the VFW, and so forth. Korea's called 'The Forgotten War,' but there are a lot of people who remember it—people who were there, people whose family members were there, people who lost family members—and I'll let them sign their hearts, or write a message on them, or whatever. That is, if you're OK with it, Silver."

He lay there on the white hospital sheets, the hollows of his eyes dark and tired looking in the stark flourescence. "It sounds like a beautiful quilt," he said. "I guess I might've said, sure, if it were years ago. But…" and he stopped to catch his breath. "But all I wanted to do when I went down into the desert was watch a few more sunsets. I wasn't looking for another battle. Can't you hear me, PJ?"

"Silver," she pleaded, "think about what it'll mean! If we get your discharge reversed you'll be eligible for VA benefits! We can pay for a decent cancer clinic!"

"I told you I don't want a cancer clinic," he said. "I want peace!"

"Listen…" she said, still afraid this was her last chance. "Listen. You said—didn't you?—that you carried that old quilt to keep the stories alive. But those stories are dying, Silver, like you're dying! Monkey, and Bravo, and…and that poor kid None? Come on! You're their…their last chance! And what about us? When Lizzie and Baker tell your story someday, how do you want it to end?"

"Ma'am?" said a voice behind her. PJ turned to see that a nurse had stuck her head into the room. "Can I ask you to keep it down?" the nurse said.

"Was I shouting?" PJ asked in surprise.

The nurse nodded and put her finger to her mouth as if shushing a child, and withdrew her head.

Silver coughed. "PJ, I'll talk to this Jerry fellow, if you want. Tell him what I know. Maybe it'll help him find his uncle. But this discharge thing, I laid that to rest a long time ago. And I just don't see the need for it. And I'm sorry if that hurts you. I don't want to hurt you."

"But you are," she said.

"Why does it hurt you to hear that, PJ?" Ross asked. "Why can't you just respect it?"

*Because you keep telling Cinderella to do stuff,* she thought.

PJ took Silver's hand again. "Please?"

"I can't," he said. "I just can't."

~

"Rise and shine, Cupcake!" PJ said as she threw the living room curtains back.

Bebe blinked at the sunlight. She said the difference between light and darkness was all she could see, these days—which seemed a curious distinction, to PJ. Not the light, or the darkness, but the difference. As if there were some waypoint between the two, a place Bebe was coming to understand and even feel comfortable with. Sunset, perhaps.

"I smell bacon," Bebe said.

PJ placed the tray across her grandmother's lap. "Bacon *and* sausage," she chuckled. "Eggs and cheese. Grits and butter. Grapefruit juice. Coffee."

"Now, I seem to remember that I'm not supposed to have any of what you just said," Bebe said.

"Woman does not live on pills alone," said PJ. "Hunger'll get you before high blood pressure does."

*And you must be hungry, you must be. You eat more medicine than food, and the food you eat wouldn't keep a mouse alive.*

Bebe nibbled at a slice of bacon. "What's today?"

"Sunday morning. I thought we'd have breakfast and then catch the late service at church."

"Church," Bebe repeated.

"Sure, you haven't been in a month," PJ said. "Your Sunday school kids want to see you."

"I'd love to see them, too, but..."

PJ frowned at herself. *Idiot. Of course she can't see them.*

She pulled her chair close to the bed and took the napkin and dabbed at the corner of Bebe's mouth. "What's it going to take to get you out of this bed today?" she asked.

Bebe turned her face away.

PJ closed her eyes and rubbed them until she saw spots. Little stars, and suns.

*Little suns in my eyes,* she thought. *Like on Blind Woman's Bluff.*

She raised her head. "Bebe? We can go to church, and then I need to go to the fabric store." *Assuming I can get Kelly to open it, that is.* "Do you feel like coming?"

~

Mommy-time at the YMCA again, and again PJ was neglecting her workout.

She parked the van in front of Kelly Green Shaw's and pushed the door open—*Arghh! That bell!*—with her notepad under her arm.

Kelly was at her desk, in the back. New catalogs were piled a foot deep all around her, glossy and enticing, but she was glaring at her computer as if she'd like to feed it into a log chipper.

"I thought you'd be done with your tax return by now," PJ said.

"No, this is the quarterly estimate," Kelly said. "It's twice as much fun as the annual. Not only do I have to pay taxes on what I know I made, but I also have to pay taxes on what I might not ever make at all. And then I have to file the state sales taxes, too. And the county. And the city!" She smiled brightly. "So…unless you've got a margarita in your handbag…"

"Um, not so much. But I have a quilt idea I wanted to ask you about."

"PJ," Kelly sighed, "can't you see that I'm trying to run a fabric store here? I don't have time for quilting." But a corner of her mouth was turned up and PJ knew she was grateful for the interruption.

PJ explained.

Kelly studied PJ's sketches. "So Silver's gonna play along? I'm surprised, after what he said the other night."

"It can be so hard to move older people outside the boxes they've built around themselves," PJ said. "I'm still working on him."

"Good on you for trying," Kelly said. "What about your box?"

"My box?"

"Yeah, your approach," Kelly said. "Follow your heart and forget the practicalities. It's always been the strangest thing to me, knowing your quilting style, that you'd take up engineering. If you're gonna do this, you need to think like an engineer, not an artist. Get organized and stay that way. Inspiration's all well and good, but—"

"You think this is a bad idea?"

"No, I think it's great! You just have to work on the hows and whens and wheres and whos before you get started on the quilt. And if you're gonna be handling money, trust me, that's a whole other can of worms. You'll have to keep records like nobody's business."

"Right," PJ said.

"One hint on that," said Kelly. "You might be able to get cut-rate fabric, or even free—did I just say that?—if you'll check around with some of the manufacturers. It's a good-for-you, good-for-me thing. If you get some publicity, they like to see their name in it."

"Good to know," PJ said. "Publicity. It's been a while since I tried to attract any attention."

Kelly put the sketches down. "Since when has getting publicity for your quilts ever been your problem? Go back and look at the walls in the Blockheads room. Half those articles are about your work."

"Point taken," PJ said, "and appreciated."

"And," Kelly continued, "hit the blogs and websites. Five years ago you wouldn't have had those avenues."

"OK," PJ said. "I'll get started on that too."

Kelly lifted an eyebrow. "You know, I get the weirdest feeling that I'm having this conversation with somebody who's pretending to be PJ Hathaway. Are you sure you've thought through this? It's a huge amount of work! Say you get fifty bucks a heart. What does a lawyer charge? Three, four hundred dollars an hour? You're gonna have to sell a couple of hundred hearts, at least, and at four-by-four each, you're talking about a massive quilt."

"I can handle it," PJ said. "I can do it. You asked about my box—I'll be honest, I feel like I've got something to prove, here."

"Prove?" asked Kelly. "What have you got to prove?"

PJ dropped her eyes. "Do you remember, several years ago, when I called you on a Sunday and asked you if you could open the store so I could bring Bebe over?"

"Sure I remember. My one day off. I thought you were out of your mind."

PJ nodded. "You said as much. Kelly, you and I have had our differences, but that was one of the kindest things anyone ever did for Bebe. Her hip wasn't knitting, she wasn't eating, her blood pressure was through the roof—and I remember—I remember she couldn't even see the fabric. But I pushed her around and she kept taking cloth in her hands and feeling it and smelling it. And it was like I could see the life coming back into her."

"You know," Kelly said, resting her chin in her palm, "last year, and I'll deny this if you tell anybody, I sent a pickup truck worth of stuff over to the battered women's shelter in East Ridge. That place where they can live with their kids? It's a good program. Most of the women didn't have jobs and they needed something to keep them busy, so I got some of them started making clothing. I sent over a bunch of kids' patterns, but I also sent over some patterns for evening dresses."

"Evening dresses," PJ said.

"I figured a woman that's put up with being beaten on by her husband, she doesn't have much self-esteem left. So making herself a nice dress might help her get it back. Just a little bit."

Kelly looked down at one of the catalogs on her desk and smoothed a crease on the cover.

"Yeah," said PJ. "I know. That's the reason I miss working at the nursing home. I had to quit when I got that—well, 'real' seems like the wrong word—but that 'real' job. I missed those old folks. Helping them find something to hang their lives on, and put themselves back together. I got to thinking I could do that a little closer to home, this time. Set Silver's life right."

She sighed. "And set mine right, too. I'm working on a quilt, and I'm working on me."

"OK," Kelly said. "Now I think we're getting somewhere. You know, we've all been worried about you."

"You've been worried about me? You, personally?"

Kelly smiled. "Well, you're so good for business!"

~

"So you're the infamous Joe Piper," Jerry Vicente said when PJ ushered him into the living room.

His hair was a little greyer than in the picture on his website, and of course his ponytail hadn't shown up there, but he was still wearing the black leather vest. And now PJ could see that the vest's entire back was emblazoned with the POW/MIA logo—the black-and-white silhouette of a man, head bowed, against a guard tower and barbed wire.

He offered his hand and Silver raised his and Jerry shook it manfully, a second or two longer than was necessary.

"It's an honor, sir," Jerry continued, setting his briefcase down beside the coffee table. "And you must be Ross. Thanks for having me into your home."

"You're welcome," Ross said, sticking his hand out. Jerry shook it briefly and PJ, watching, realized that while Jerry might respect Ross, he esteemed Silver.

"Well, I don't know why you'd want to go to all the trouble," Silver said.

"Yeah," Jerry agreed. "You know how it is; I'm trying to track some people down. I just need a few minutes."

*Huh?* PJ thought. *After flying down all the way down here from Newark?*

"I'll tell you whatever I know," Silver said.

"You ever hear of a Steven Carlo Vicente?" Jerry asked.

"What outfit?"

"First Battalion, Seventh Marines. Baker Company. He went MIA south of Yudam-Ni."

"No," Silver said. "There were a few boys from the Seventh in the camp with us, but I don't remember that name."

"It's OK," Jerry said. "What about Raul Sandovar?"

"No, I don't think so."

"Constantine F. Smallwood?"

"No, I know I'd remember that one," Silver laughed.

"Yeah," said Jerry. "How about an Army private, name of Luke Vandergriff? They put him up for the Medal of Honor, later on, but he didn't get it. Political thing."

*How many of these names does he know?* PJ wondered. *For that matter, how many of them are there?*

"I didn't mingle with too many hero types," Silver said.

"Mmm," Jerry nodded. "Well, that's about all the questions I had."

*What?* PJ thought.

"I'm sorry I couldn't help you more," said Silver.

"It's all right," said Jerry. "There is one thing, though."

"Sure," Silver said.

"What about all those Silver Stars you got? How come you didn't mention those to PJ?"

Nobody spoke. PJ glanced at Ross and Ross raised both eyebrows at her and shrugged slightly. "Wait a minute," she said. "Silver. *Silver.* So that's how you got the nickname. And not because you were a stainer?"

The old man lowered his eyes and pinched the bridge of his nose. "Now, don't go—"

"How many was it, Jerry?" PJ asked.

"At least three, that I can find."

PJ stared at Silver. "And here you've been downplaying what you did this whole time. When were you going to tell me this? When did you think I'd be ready to hear the whole story?"

"I told you everything that mattered," Silver said.

"Everything you wanted us to know," said Ross.

PJ ignored his comment. "Silver, would you please tell me the truth about this?"

"Yeah," Jerry nodded. "What about it, Silver? If you didn't want anyone to know what you'd done, why go letting people call you 'Silver' in the first place? You need to come clean, here."

"You come clean with me," Silver said. "Who sold you that swampland, Slick?"

Jerry leaned back in his chair and smoothed his ponytail. "Slick," he chuckled. "Well, nobody sold it to me. I read it."

"Read it," said Silver.

"In *Life* magazine," Jerry said. "Look here."

He opened his briefcase and took out an old issue and held it up—November 13th, 1950, with a football player in an old-school helmet on the cover. Jerry opened the magazine to a page he'd marked with a yellow sticky and passed it to PJ.

It was a black-and-white photo of a crowd of men encircling two others. Everyone wore fatigues and mismatched winter coats and hats, and the ones on the outside of the crowd stood on tiptoe to see in.

At their center, a stocky, grim-faced man was pinning a Silver Star to a young, rangy-looking kid. The kid had his eyes fixed into the distance.

The caption read:

> *First Division Marines look on as Colonel Lewis "Chesty" Puller awards Joseph M. Piper, Hospital Corpsman Second Class, his third Silver Star since arriving in Korea.*

PJ looked from the picture of the kid to Silver and back again. There was no mistaking who it was, despite the fifty years that had passed.

"And they're hounding you for hospital bills," she said in disgust. She passed the magazine to Ross.

Jerry cleared his throat. "To answer your question, Silver, it's public record. It just takes a while to dig up. I didn't know myself until a couple of days ago."

"I didn't deserve them."

"Oh, Silver Stars were a dime-a-dozen," Jerry agreed sarcastically. "General Almond came out of his helicopter east of the Chosin one time pinning Silver Stars on people he picked at random. Trying to 'raise morale.' The men thought he was crazy."

"I heard that story," Silver said. "Almond wasn't crazy, he was a bona fide lunatic."

"But there was another man I heard of, a BAR man, who charged a mortar nest at Toktong Pass and got hurt pretty bad. Got the Silver Star later on, himself. Wouldn't say he got it for nothing, either. He was a POW like you. Maybe you knew him."

"He have a name?"

"Charles Foster. Lost an eye in that fight. 'Pirate,' I think they called him."

Silver's face lit up. "Sure, I knew Pirate. The panty thief. Only, it wasn't just a mortar nest—when he knocked over that first mortar they opened up on from a gun emplacement and he took that out too, with grenades. Then he got—but how is old Pirate, anyway?"

"He's been dead," Jerry said, "since 1977. But his family lives in Macon, Georgia, and I know they'd love to hear the straight dope on their grandfather."

"Well, they won't hear it from me."

Jerry leaned forward in his chair. "But Mr. Piper, as near as I can tell, you're one of the last living survivors of that camp. So, what, is a man with three Silver Stars afraid to tell everyone about what happened?"

"Afraid?" Silver said.

"Yeah, afraid," Jerry said. "I think I know what David Warner would say about that."

Silver's expression grew sullen. "What would David Warner say?"

"He'd say that if it's true that the Korean War's a forgotten war, it's the fault of people who want to forget it. The truth's a duty on those who know. Even if it's the truth about yourself."

"Slick," Silver said, "you don't have the first idea."

"I know what the records say."

"Records," Silver spat.

"They say you were a coward, a deserter, who wouldn't let people help him when he needed it most. And by your own admission you ran off on your best friend and then took advantage of his bereaved wife."

"By God," Silver said, "if I could get up from this wheelchair—"

"Aahh," said Jerry, waving a hand dismissively. "But you can't, can you? Maybe you should get back to the psyche ward and stay there this time, instead of busting out like you did—"

"OK, that's it," PJ said. "Jerry, thanks for coming, but I won't sit here and let you abuse Silver like that."

Ross began to get up.

Jerry sat back and casually crossed his legs. He speared Silver with his gaze. "So you let a woman do your fighting for you?"

Suddenly PJ saw his game, and she almost laughed in disbelief. *For once, I understand a genius.*

Silver sat without speaking for a moment, and then he reached into his pocket for a handkerchief.

*Maybe Jerry took it too far,* PJ thought. *I wouldn't have made Silver cry for...*

But no. Silver shook the handkerchief out by the corner—a square of white in his scarred, wrinkled hand—and he waved it in surrender.

▶▶▶◆◀◀◀
## Chapter Twenty-Seven

"Listen," Ross said from behind the wheel. "It's been three weeks since you said you'd see a counselor, and you haven't."

PJ turned around to look at the kids in the backseat. "Do we have to talk about this right now?"

"I don't want to debate it," he said. "I just want to know what your plans are. You promised me you'd go, and you haven't."

He was wearing dark sunglasses and she couldn't quite gauge his eyes. "Well," she said, reaching for her notepad, "let me read you my schedule for this week. At six this evening I have to wash and press forty or so thousand yards of fabric. Then—"

"Never mind, never mind," he said, and his hands tightened on the wheel.

~

PJ, at work, sat in her cubicle and took pen in hand.

Dear Mom,

I keep calling you but I can't get you on the phone. Maybe your schedule's keeping you too busy for your family.

She crumpled the sheet of paper, threw it in the trash, and started over.

Dear Mom,

I keep calling you but I can't get you on the phone.

I need to let you know a couple of things. First, Bebe's taken a turn for the worse again. She never really got over breaking her hip, and now she's starting to retain a lot of fluid. Her ankles are swollen and her face is puffy. The doctors are saying it's because her kidneys are wearing out—related to the high blood pressure, they think. The diuretics they're giving her are keeping her up at night, and it's not easy for her to get from her bed to the bathroom.

PJ frowned harder and thought about trashing this draft too, but decided to battle on instead.

She's hardly even quilting. She was doing some great work, despite her vision, but now all she does is sit and listen to the radio—old dance music.

I tried to ask her doctors what it all means, how much time she has left, but the only one who'd give me any real information was an intern, and he said she probably wouldn't make it much past the New Year.

The steady grimacing was making her face hurt, now.

So Ross and I have decided to move the wedding up. We're getting married on September 27th, at the church, at 1:30. Bebe says five months is a short engagement, but then again, she said three years was a long courtship.

I'll send you an invitation and I'll keep calling. I know I'm always telling you it's important and you need to come to Chattanooga, but it really is important.

I got in touch with Dewayne, Mom. I told him I wanted my father to escort me down the aisle and give me away on my wedding day. And he told me, "I couldn't do that to my real daughters, PJ."

Those were his exact words. "Real daughters." So what does that make me, then? A counterfeit?

"Ow," PJ said. She dropped her pen and massaged the sudden cramp that had seized her hand. When the spasm passed, she continued.

I really need you, Mom. I want you to walk me down the aisle and give me to Ross. I feel like I need your blessing in this because I'm scared to death. Ross is a good man and I've never really understood why he picked me out of the crowd. When I ask him that, he tells me he loves me because I don't know how wonderful I am.

And that's what scares me.

"No, no, no, no," PJ chanted. She tore the letter into shreds, tore the shreds into confetti, scooped it up and carried it all to the toilet, and flushed it.

~

"I'm sorry, I know it's a great cause but we never give away ad space," the woman on the phone said. "I get a dozen calls a week from people like you—good people!—who want us to—"

"Thanks very much," PJ said quickly. "Bye, now."

*No, no, no, no,* she thought. *Cell phones aren't the same. Time was, when you had a real phone with a dial, you could hang up like you meant it. Boom! Now it's just pressing a button, and it's nowhere near as therapeutic.*

She twirled her pencil between her fingers and opened her notepad to the SALES page. Eleven hearts, she'd sold. Eight to the Blockheads, three to Ross's coworkers. Which meant there were five hundred and fifty dollars in the bank account she'd opened—more than enough for supplies!—but only a sneeze-worth of attorney time.

PJ sighed and thumbed through the pages until she found ATTORNEY NOTES.

~

"Some fifty years have passed," Charles Lowell, Attorney-at-Law, had told them in a voice as precise as the tailoring of his suit. He was a thin man, sixtyish, and PJ recognized the Harvard stickpin in his tie. But he wore another pin in his lapel, one she'd never seen. A sword, arrow, and laurel.

Jerry sat in the office with them. He'd stayed in Chattanooga overnight after interviewing Silver, and they'd driven to Atlanta together for this meeting. Now he shifted in his chair. "Times change, though," he said. "Post-traumatic stress disorder's a recognized disability these days. Does that help us, or hurt us?"

"It helps and it hurts," said Lowell. "True, veterans have recently won PTSD cases, but time forces the military to rely on the records rather than on medical experts and other such forms of tangible evidence. Whereas normally you could go to the Navy's Discharge Review Board and you'd get a reasonably swift answer—usually no, but you'd get it—in a situation like Mr. Piper's, since more than fifteen years have passed, the appeal has to go to the Board for Correction of Naval Records."

"What do we have to show them?" PJ asked.

"Many things," Lowell said. He swiveled his chair and reached to the credenza behind him for a black binder.

PJ saw that the emblem on the binder was the same as the emblem on his lapel pin. But she could read the words on the binder: "Judge Advocate General's Corps of the United States Army."

*No wonder this guy gets four hundred an hour,* she thought. *A Harvard lawyer and a military lawyer?*

Lowell raised a finger. "To get a hearing—to even get one—" and he started reading aloud, "the board relies on a presumption of regularity to support the official actions of public officers, and, in the absence of substantial evidence to the contrary, will presume that they have properly discharged their official duties. Applicants have the burden of overcoming this presumption."

"Substantial evidence," PJ said. "Define that."

"A dozen witnesses. Widespread contradiction in official records. Forensic reports from experts, and I do mean experts."

Lowell closed the binder and replaced it on the shelf. "Before you start the process you need to decide if you can meet that standard. And I'll caution you. From what you say, it's clear what happened to Mr. Piper isn't fair. But the BCNR isn't about fairness, or even justice. It's about accuracy."

"'The Board for Correction of Naval Records,'" PJ said. "They sound like librarians. Clerks. I can't believe they have so much power. They can literally make or break people, can't they?"

Jerry smiled. "You've never served. Who do you think writes history?"

"I may not have served," she said, "but I've been a few rounds with the VA in my time. Mr. Lowell, what's your track record on discharge appeals?"

"Two in eleven," Lowell said.

"Those aren't very good odds."

Jerry rubbed his cheek. "Chuck, what's the best track record you know of?"

"Two in eleven," Lowell repeated.

~

So even if this quilt raises a hundred grand, PJ thought, my odds are two in eleven. I might as well go to Vegas and put it all on red.

She flipped the notebook open to the CONTACTS page and dialed another number.

"Hi," she said. "My name is PJ Hathaway. Can you connect me to your advertising department?"

She crossed her fingers. Come on, red.

~

"Oh, a letter from Anne?" Bebe said. "What a coincidence, I was just thinking of her. Would you read it to me, Cupcake?"

"Sure." PJ opened the letter and a hundred-dollar bill fluttered to the floor. "She sent some money, Bebe—I wonder if something's wrong?"

Bebe laughed. "What does the letter say?"

"Hmm. She wrote it a week ago."

Dear PJ,

Your letter surprised me.

"You wrote her?" interrupted Bebe.

"I did," said PJ. "And wrote her, and wrote her, and wrote her, until I had a draft of the letter I didn't feel like throwing away."

"Oh."

PJ continued reading aloud.

I'm sorry Mother's not well. I wish there were more I could do.

But your question about what to do about your wedding— well, I've never been married. I'll be happy to walk you down the aisle, if I can make it.

But for sure I can give you some advice about Ross. First of all, you need to cut him off before the wedding. No...

PJ felt her face reddening. "Um, Bebe, this gets kind of personal. I think I'd rather keep it private."

"You can trust me," Bebe said. "What could be so private that..."

"Let me just scan it," said PJ.

...sex of any kind for a whole month. He'll be so happy when it's finally your wedding day that he'll make you the happiest woman in the world on your wedding night.

And if you really want to wow him, take this cash to a

decent tattoo parlor and get some work done. Something
small, where only he can see it. Not his name, because you
don't want to have to cover it later, but maybe a private joke
between the two of you. Believe me, he'll worship you
for it.

There's an old saying: "A whore in the bedroom and a chef
in the kitchen." If you have any money left over, take a
cooking class.

I hope that helps,

Love,

Anne

"No," said PJ. "That's pretty much all I feel like I can
read to you."

"Can you give me the gist of it?"

"She…um…wants me to buy Ross a piece of artwork
for a wedding gift."

"That's a wonderful idea! Ross loves art!"

"Mmm…yeah."

~

"I have never been as under the gun as I am right
now," PJ admitted to Silver. It was Saturday and she'd been
sewing all morning, until hunger had finally forced her to
stop.

Silver didn't answer, but stared across the backyard,
at where the kids were swinging. He took a long sip of his
coffee.

"I'm sorry, I'm sorry," PJ said. She put her hand on
his arm. "I really didn't mean to—after the things you've—
ahhh, there I go again."

"You sound like me, when I first met your grandmother,"
Silver said. "I talked like a halfwit."

"I feel like a halfwit," PJ laughed. "I guess that makes us
halfwits together. Say something smart, Silver."

"The capital of Alabama is Montgomery," he said. "I

used to know all the state capitals by heart. Now, you say something smart."

"Um...in a right triangle, the area of the square whose side is the hypotenuse is equal to the sum of the areas of the squares whose sides are the two legs."

"*What?*"

"It's the Pythagorean theorem. Basic trigonometry."

"You engineers," he said with grumpy good humor.

*Sounds like Kelly Green Shaw,* PJ thought, but instead she said, "Well, it was quilting that got me started in engineering. Knowing how to work with triangles is key in quilting, and trig is the science of triangles. When I went to college I had to declare a major, and since quilting had set me up pretty well in math, I said, sure, sign me up for engineering. I was thinking more about the paycheck than the actual work itself. It took me about three days to fall out of love with engineering."

"Funny," he said. "It's hard for me to imagine you doing anything you don't love."

PJ felt the smile die on her face. She reached for her glasses, took them off, and twirled them in circles.

"Did I say something?" he asked.

"Silver, I—wow. You come out with these little things and I wind up staying up all night realizing what they mean."

He watched her.

"I've had to do plenty I didn't love," PJ continued. "Not to the degree you have, but there's been stuff..." and she shook her head. "Leaving my career. Having kids."

"Burying your grandmother," Silver said.

"Yeah, that." She folded her hands in her lap. "Finishing the last quilt she started. You know, I have yet to show you that one."

"Go get it," he said. "I'd love to see it."

"Well, I can't. It's hanging in the Hunter Museum, downtown."

"A quilt you and Bebe made is in a museum?"

PJ bit her tongue. "I told you about that, Silver. Remember?"

"Oh, right, right, right," he said. "So you did."

"We can always run down there, though."

Silver's eyes grew warm and his gap-toothed smile said all she needed to hear.

~

The tattoo artist had a tooth knocked out.

But PJ had expected a big gorilla biker type, and this artist was a woman. And what a woman—a bodacious redhead in a red silk dress, whose arms were festooned from shoulder to fingertip with pinup girls, fiery dice, and verses from the Book of Revelations.

"Nice to meet you," she grinned. "My name's Frank."

"Frank," PJ repeated. "Hi, Frank. Is that short for something?"

"Frankincense," Frank said with a completely straight face. "Is that a drawing you want to show me?"

PJ offered the paper she held and Frank leaned across the glass, studying it. She had tattoos on the back of her neck, too.

*Now here we have a woman who's entirely comfortable in her own skin,* PJ thought. *And why not? She made it herself.*

"That's nice," Frank finally said. "You draw it?"

"I did. It's…um…a wedding gift."

"Ah-hah. Can I make a suggestion, then?"

"You're the expert."

"Tell me what you think of this," Frank said. She took a red pencil from a cup and quickly added something to PJ's sketch. "I think this makes it a lot more naughty, but at the same time nice. Like you're a bad little good girl."

"A cupcake's not naughty enough already?"

Frank cocked her head. "It's OK. But putting the cherry on top gives it personality. What do you think, do you want to go on back and do it?"

"Oh, Lord no! I'm nowhere near ready for this! I mean, don't you have a portfolio I can look through or something?"

Frank leaned one elbow on the counter and studied PJ from head to toe. "What is it, the needle?"

PJ laughed. "I'm not afraid of needles. It's just the permanency of it."

"Says the chick who's getting married."

"Well, there is that."

Frank slid her a photo album of tattoo snapshots—body parts freshly embellished with every pattern and color out there—and PJ pretended to look through it while she sorted her thoughts for the umpteenth time.

*Mom was right from the very beginning about how to attract Ross—in sort of a left-handed way, but she was right.*

*And Bebe was right, Ross does like art.*

*And it'll be a huge surprise.*

*And, Lord, am I tired of being a geek.*

*And if it's made with a needle, it can't be that bad. Can it?*

"OK," PJ said. "I guess we can do it."

"Great! Now, I need you to sign a couple of releases, and my studio rate's sixty an hour. We're looking at maybe ninety minutes."

"Can you do it for seventy-five flat?" PJ asked. "I was hoping to have some extra cash to sign up for a cooking class."

▶▶▶◆◀◀◀
## Chapter Twenty-Eight

Saturday afternoon, and the weekend shopping traffic was ridiculous. PJ drove and Silver rode shotgun, watching the strip-malls and suburbs roll by on their way to the Hunter Museum.

"What's *that?*" he asked.

PJ looked past him, through the window. "Oh, it's a new subdivision going in."

"No, there must be three hundred houses!"

"I don't know. Why, you looking to get back into the trades?"

"Not in there! I'd never be able to find my way out! Every one of those places is exactly like the others. You'd have to paint your door red to find your way home."

"If the homeowners' association would even let you do that," PJ said dryly.

"Do what?"

"Paint your door red."

Silver snorted. "God's mercy on the fool who tries to tell me I can't paint my own front door the color I want to. Are they really doing that now?"

"They're really doing that now."

"I don't know how people live like that."

PJ punched the gas to get around a gravel truck, and the van grudgingly sped up.

"Well," she said, "you get so many people crammed in together and they have to make up rules to get through life. I do it. Everybody does."

"You call that life? It's a substitute for something else. Like that plastic siding that's supposed to look like brick."

"Equal instead of cane sugar," PJ countered.

"Air-freshener instead of flowers."

"Factory-made quilts instead of your grandmother's."

Silver nodded. "There you go."

PJ thought about it. "Taco Bell instead of Navajo tacos."

Silver thumped his fist into his palm. "That's exactly right! Real food, a real house, a real view out your window. Doing what you want, when you want to!"

"Feeling like you feel," PJ said. "Not like the TV or some quack tells you you should."

"Preach on, preach on," Silver agreed.

"You know what?" PJ asked. "If it'd been me instead of you? I would've broken out of that mental hospital too."

~

"I always stand here and watch the river before I go in," PJ said.

"It's nice, all right," said Silver.

The Hunter Museum was a white-columned brick mansion perched on a bluff a hundred feet above the Tennessee River, and from the balcony where they stood they could see all of downtown Chattanooga beyond the old pedestrian bridge that spanned the river. The afternoon sun played on the water, and families loitered on the bridge leaning over the rail and taking pictures.

"Well," PJ said presently, "I guess we've stalled long enough. You want to see Bebe's quilt?"

"I do."

PJ took the handles of his wheelchair and pushed him back inside. They took the elevator down a couple of floors, and the doors slid open to reveal a long white-walled gallery. Folk art hung all about them—baskets and woodcarvings, tapestries, an ancient hammer dulcimer. And at the end of the hallway, in a niche ten feet across, hung Bebe's quilt.

The quilt was a wall of eyes, large and small, each with a green iris and a golden pupil, in an irregular checkerboard pattern that was hardly a pattern at all. They followed you wherever you moved; there was no hiding from their scrutiny, and though they penetrated you to your soul, they understood you perfectly, and hence forgave you for what they saw.

And they even loved you for it.

"They're Bebe's eyes," PJ said simply. "She could see more clearly than anyone I ever knew, even after she lost her sight."

She stood in silence under the quilt, behind Silver, with her hands on his shoulders. He reached up to pat her hand, and she wrapped her arms around his neck and lowered her face to his shoulder.

They stood that way for a long time. Finally, PJ stood up and sniffled and went to the little brass plaque that hung beside the quilt. She blew on it and buffed it with her sleeve.

"BLIND WOMAN'S BLUFF," she read. "PJ Hathaway and Elizabeth Warner. 2004."

She gazed at it, and then added, "I wish I'd thought to tell them to put Ross's name on here."

~

The September of the wedding was a ten-minute month. PJ had to deal with florists and caterers and the minister and the organist and dozens of other professional nuptialators—all of them pleasant and easy to deal with, and all of them with their hands out.

At T minus sixty hours she was working through the logistics with Ross at his apartment when he stopped her.

"You need a glass of wine," he said. "Purely medicinal."

"What I need is a back rub."

He smiled. "Back rubs lead to other things."

*Yeah,* PJ thought. *And if you could see what I just had engraved onto my tush—*

"Back rubs," she stated, "only lead to sleep." She

closed her notebook and pushed it across the table. "I'm done. This thing's either gonna happen or it's not."

"It's gonna happen. If we have to elope and find a judge, it's gonna happen. And I'm still totally up for that." But he was kidding, she could tell.

"No, no. Your parents are coming in tomorrow. At…" and she pulled her notebook back to her and opened it. "… at seven-thirty. In the morning. What is it now, midnight?"

Ross came around behind her and started rubbing her neck.

"Mmm…" she said, closing her eyes and rolling her head around.

"What about your mom?" he asked. "You hear from her?"

PJ opened her eyes. "No. How does this grab you? I'll wait at the front of the church, and your dad can walk you down the aisle and give you to me?"

"It's not what you'd call traditional."

"No," said PJ. "Well, maybe she'll show up at the last minute."

~

Silver rolled himself closer to the quilt. He reached to the sunlit eye at the very center of it and caressed it with his fingertips.

*It's OK, he doesn't know any better than to touch it,* she thought. But then she realized: *And who has more right to touch this quilt than he does? If he wants to pull it off the wall and curl up in it and take a nap, anybody who tries to stop him'll have to fight their way through me.*

"Um, that's the very first square she sewed," PJ said. "She did the center in 1999, and I did the perimeter in 2004. With an organic pattern like this, you start from the inside and work your way out."

"Work your way out," Silver repeated quietly.

"What?" PJ asked.

Silver looked up at the quilt of eyes. "You sound like…"

~

He was an ordinary guy, an old Army doc. I'd seen a million of them. Standing there with a clipboard and a stethoscope in the hospital tent staring at me like I was some kind of weird animal the guys had brought back from the front to mess with his mind.

Well, I was. Animals like me only grew in prison camps. When I'd walked down the last hill into our own lines—wrapped in that old quilt, blood all over it and me both, screaming the Marine Hymn at the top of my lungs to keep the sentries from shooting me—the men there had handled me real gentle. Whispered and moved slow, like I might go off.

"Shrapnel wounds here, here, and here," the doctor said. "Where'd you pick 'em up?"

"Shaving for Sunday School," I said.

"Right." He knelt in front of the cot and took my right foot in his hand. "Who took these toes off for you?"

"I did."

He gave me that handling-a-wild-beast look again. "Done a few amputations, have you?"

"Some. Several."

"Um-hmm. You've got some frostbite on the stumps, and we may have to take some more tissue off. We'll see, but we have to do something soon.

"And as far as that shrapnel, we can go in after it when you get to the hospital ship, or you can just let it work it's way out. Working its way out is probably better—for the shrapnel, and for you too."

"What do you mean, doc?"

"Well," he said, "given that you weigh a hundred and ten pounds right now, I don't even want to put you on a transport until you come up to a hundred and thirty or forty. Your heart could stop, and then where would you be?"

"Korea," I said. "I'd be in Korea. Can you just send me home?"

"You need to sleep," he said. "And eat. I'll have some food sent in. When you want more, just tell somebody. And see you get hot water. Soap, and—and somebody to shave you."

"I can shave myself."

"I'll send somebody to shave you," he repeated. He got up from his stool and gathered my rags and the old quilt up, stuffed them under his arm, and made like he was leaving.

"Hold up there, Doc. I need that quilt back."

He wrinkled his nose. "This thing? This thing's headed to the burn barrel. It's got lice in it."

I pushed myself up. "That *thing* saved—aw, come on, Doc. It's like an old friend to me."

"I'll spray it with some DDT and send it back to you," he said.

"If it goes, I go," I said, baring my teeth.

He muttered someting about lunatics, but he separated the quilt out and tossed it to me.

~

"I'd like to hear a doctor tell me to gain weight," PJ said.

"Spend a year or two vacationing in North Korea," said Silver. "Then you can gain all you want."

"Do you think there are still POWs over there?" she asked. "Jerry was telling me there were still Americans in the Soviet prison system, back before the Berin Wall came down."

"I've heard stories like that, but I don't know. Seems like if there are, a whole bunch of politicians oughtta be locked up along with 'em."

"Yeah," she said.

"You never abandon your own. Never." He stared fiercely at her.

*That's why I couldn't leave you in Utah,* she thought. But the memory of Baker and Lizzie crying in Ellen's arms rose up in her, and she couldn't make the words come out.

~

I gained some weight back. Lost a little, too—they re-stumped my foot.

When I got sent back to San Diego I was the only living

man in the cargo compartment of the plane. Every other person in there was packed into a coffin, and got buried shortly after the plane landed.

Me, they stripped and locked into a cell with padding sewn to the walls, at Balboa.

I knew that hospital pretty well; I'd been assigned to it for six weeks or so while I was at Pendleton waiting to be assigned to a Marine unit bound for Korea. And now I was locked up in it.

And it was cold in there. Made the stump of my foot throb.

I sat and stared at the padding. The stitches holding it together. I knew why I was in there, or at least I thought I did. I was in there because nobody could understand me.

And I couldn't understand them.

They were trying to help, I knew that. There was this one, a head shrinker, who spent hours and hours telling me, yes, he knew I thought I was OK, but there were reports of brainwashing in the camps. And wasn't it reasonable to admit that the ordeal I'd suffered meant that there might be some merit in a short hospital stay? Just for observation? Just to make sure I was all right?

"There's nothing wrong with me!" I said. "I just need left alone!"

"I know you think that," he said. "You've taught yourself to believe that what you feel, the way you behave, is normal. But it's not. It's a learned response to the stress you've been under, a way of blocking the memories out. There was too much pressure in the pipe, so you welded the pipe shut."

"You sure we shouldn't trade places? You sit in a cell and I'll come around to talk to you?"

He smiled. "And your situation's also physical. The state of your body has a direct effect on the state of your mind. Look what happened to your body, and tell me your mind came through unscathed."

"OK," I said. "You can tie me up with mumbo-jumbo all you want. You got me. I want to shoot my father and marry my mother. But could you at least get me some clothes instead of these pajamas? A book to read? My things? The door key?"

"You have to work your way out of here, like we're doing now," he said. "But as long as we're on the subject of your things, you've had several violent episodes now, over the quilt you say you made in the prison camp."

"Orderlies come in and strip you naked and take everything you own, and you're not supposed to fight back?"

He waved his hand at me. "I understand. It's how you were trained. But why do you talk to it?"

"Talk to it? I don't talk to it."

"You talk to it," he said. "When you first got to Pendleton the guys in your barracks said you sat and talked to the quilt for hours. You called it different names— Monkey and Fuzzy, None, Blue-Eyes, and Lieutenant. You were all the time calling it Lieutenant."

Now his smile was sad. "Are you telling me you don't remember that?"

~

Bebe's eyes gazed down on them from the museum wall.

"Did you?" PJ asked.

Silver chewed his lip, staring up at the quilt. "It was still pretty real," he finally said. "I might've."

"Might've remembered talking to it?"

"No, might've actually done it. You—ah. I hate to get this deep into it, it'll give you bad dreams."

"Go ahead, I know all about bad dreams."

"If you ever find yourself in any kind of solitary, you'll start talking to yourself—even having arguments, fighting with yourself. You'll get mad and not speak to yourself, even. It's crazy. It helps to have some kind of mascot—a bug, a rock, even. That way, it's not you."

"But it sounds like you were talking to dead men," she said.

"You do that too, when you've been alone too much. They even start showing up on you. Half the time, you're telling them to go away."

"And the other half?"

"You're begging 'em to take you with 'em."

~

One night I finally got some of the padding peeled back, and what I saw behind it made me laugh.

The contractors who'd put the hospital cells together had used shiplapped wallboard, one-inch pine, but it must've been green. Wartime construction by the lowest bidder, the same ignorant practice that had sent Navy inspectors all over the Pacific Ocean counting rivets in hulls, to keep the fleet from sinking out from under the sailors.

The walls of the cell would've been strong when they were built, but now the boards had shrunk and gaps had opened up. I could just barely get my fingers between them.

It took me a few nights to work the first board loose, but after I got it, it made a good prybar. It took me an hour or so to open a hole in the front wall, next to the steel door, that was big enough for me to crawl through.

I crept down the hallway. When I got to the doctor's office I pushed the door open and looked around in the dim light. I took a white coat off a hook and kept looking. There was a closet, and in it I found a few sea bags, including mine. When I opened it, I found the new fatigues I'd been wearing when I'd reported to the hospital, and I found the old quilt.

So I got dressed quickly, except for shoes, and I folded the quilt and stuffed it into the front of my pants. Then I buttoned the coat over it and looked at myself in the mirror. Hey, Fatso.

Well, I was out. But I was still in. That was OK, though. I knew my way around Balboa—knew the dispensary, the VD ward, even the operating theaters.

And I'd been to the morgue once or twice.

~

T minus eighteen hours until the wedding.

"If I don't show up tomorrow, check the morgue," PJ said to Ross's mother, April, at the rehearsal dinner. "I never really believed Mom would stand me up."

"I want you to know, PJ, that you can always think of me as your mother," April said. She had Ross's eyes, and they lit up warmly when she smiled.

"I'd rather not," PJ said. "Oh, no, no, no!" she blurted as the warmth faded from April's eyes. "I mean—my mom and I don't get along that well."

~

The morgue was in the basement of the hospital. It took me a long time to get down the stairs, with my foot the way it was, but I'd had years to practice moving silently through the dark.

It was colder in the morgue than it had been in my cell; I could hear the compressors running. I flicked the cigarette lighter I'd taken from the doctor's desk, and I jumped back. There was a dead man on the table right beside me, his chest sawn apart and his eyes halfway open. They had his heart in a jar somewhere. I put my fingers on his eyelids and pushed them closed.

One wall of the room was a bunch of stainless steel doors. Each with a number. Bodies behind some of them, or all of them, I figured.

The last time I'd seen little doors like that was outside a punishment cell the Chinese were about to shove me into. The icebox, we called it. A little ironwalled cubbyhole set into a concrete wall, about the size of a coffin. They'd put you in there for days.

I started opening the doors and pulling the drawers out, one-by-one. Some were empty, and I closed them back. Several of them, though, had bodies on the trays inside, some naked, some in thick plastic bags. When I'd finally slid the drawers all out, and I had my own cadre of the dead, I started reading the tags on their toes.

Most of them were dissection cadavers, in various stages of being practiced on. But there was one in a body bag who was due for shipment the next day.

Perfect.

I unzipped him and rolled a cart over and got him out of the bag and onto the cart. At first I tried to keep the cigarette lighter burning, but I couldn't move him with one hand. Rigor mortis. So I let the lighter go out, and I realized it made it easier if I couldn't see what I was doing.

I carted him over to another drawer and pushed it closed. Then I closed all the other ones.

Then I rolled my pants legs up to my thighs, and tied the dead man's tag to my one big toe. I got up on the tray, wiggled my way half into the body bag with my head to the inside. I zipped the body bag up to my shoulders, and slid the drawer closed. From inside, I zipped the bag the rest of the way.

And then I went to sleep. Twenty-four hours in a cold metal box? I could do that standing on my head.

~

PJ held a hand to her mouth. "Silver—" she said in a shocked voice.

"That's how I did it," he finished. "I waited in there for a long time, expecting to get caught, but they never did catch on. The hardest part was keeping rigid when they hoisted me out of that drawer. But, see, they used civilian undertakers to drive the bodies off the base. We called it the meat wagon. Those boys were so scared when I came out of the bag that they crashed the hearse."

"My God. My God."

Silver stared up at the eyes. "And you know what eats at me? That dead man whose place I took, I don't even remember his name."

~

"It's T minus twenty minutes," PJ babbled to Bebe, "and Pastor Ingram is going to tell the congregation, dearly beloved, we're gathered here in front of God and everyone—except for Anne Warner!—to unite this couple in holy matrimony."

Bebe turned her head at the sound of PJ's voice. "Don't start crying, Cupcake, you'll spoil your makeup, and you look so pretty."

PJ sat in front of the mirror, looking at herself. *I could've made this dress myself,* she thought. *And done a better job of it.*

"I don't feel pretty, and how would you know?"

"I don't need eyes to see how pretty you are," Bebe said. "Nobody does. I'm sorry Anne isn't here, but think about everyone who is!"

"But…" PJ sniffled, "but what are they going to say when I come down the aisle alone?"

"They'll say, look how brave she is!"

"I hate being brave. I want to be valued."

Bebe smiled, and said, "PJ, the point of the whole day is what you and Ross are worth to each other."

PJ sniffled again, and stood up. "I know that. Well, come on. I'd hate to be late to my own wedding."

She went around Bebe's wheelchair and started pushing her out of the changing room.

~

"I pushed her out of the room and through the church foyer, and there were all these people watching me," PJ told Silver. "People I'd known for years, but I was so strung out that they all looked like strangers."

"And then…"

~

She stood in the foyer with her hands on the grips of Bebe's wheelchair, waiting for an usher to come and take Bebe from her and wheel her into the sanctuary.

Bebe said, "I'll be right down front, Cupcake. You'll do fine."

The usher came up. One of Ross's fraternity brothers, stuffed into his tux. "OK," he said to Bebe cheerfully, "you ready for the parade?"

PJ gripped Bebe's hand. "Don't leave me alone," she begged.

"You're not alone," Bebe said. "You'll never be alone. You hold your chin up and show everybody in there what you're made of. Be who you are, you hear?"

"I guess so," PJ said miserably.

"OK, then," Bebe smiled. "Let's go, son."

"Yes, ma'am," he said.

~

The rest of the procession had gone down the aisle, now, and the congregation was silent. Standing and waiting. Some of them had already turned to look at her, and she saw their lips moving.

PJ tried to hold her chin up, like Bebe had told her, but she'd never felt more lonely. She clutched her flowers and looked down the aisle, trying to see Ross's face, but he was so far away—miles, it seemed.

The organist hit the first strains of the "Wedding March," and PJ startled up onto her toes before catching her balance.

*Great,* she thought. *I'll never get used to high heels. Watch me strut down the aisle, everybody.*

She couldn't move. The organist played on and now everyone was staring back at her.

*I have to start walking.*

But she couldn't.

People began leaning together and looking at each other and whispering.

*Oh, God.*

She searched the front of the sanctuary for Ross. He was smiling at her as if she was doing fine, and he beckoned to her: *Come on!*

*OK, OK,* she thought. *You can do this, PJ.*

She took a baby step. Then another.

"Cold feet," she heard someone whisper.

But her feet weren't cold—they were on fire. The carpeting quivered, like she was walking on a bed of jello, and she grew confused and stopped again.

*I am two steps down the aisle,* she thought.

The music rolled on and on, and she thought she heard the organist coming back to the beginning.

*Not like this. Not like this. You're letting everybody down. You're letting Ross down.*

*Be who you are. That's all you have to do.*

She took a deep breath, looked down at her white shoes, and forced herself to take a step. Then another. And another.

Walking grew easier. And when she looked down the aisle to where Ross waited, she saw that he was coming up the aisle towards her.

He met her halfway. He took her hand and put it in the crook of his elbow and put his other hand on it.

"You OK?" he whispered to her as they walked together.

"These stupid heels got stuck in the carpet," she whispered back.

"Yeah," he said. "I couldn't get my star carted—I mean, my car started—this morning, either."

Somehow they made it to the front together.

~

"I can see Elizabeth," Silver said. "How proud she must have been."

PJ crouched beside his wheelchair, watching him watch the quilt of eyes. "There wasn't a dry eye in the church," she said.

"I would've given anything to be there," he said. "I can't believe Anne missed it."

"It took me a long time to come to this, but I'm glad she wasn't. Bebe was there for me my whole life, and she's the one who deserved to be there."

"I wish I'd had more time with her," said Silver. "If only I'd had more time."

"Yeah," PJ said. "I feel that way too."

"But PJ, you still don't understand it!"

His face was clouding with anger, and PJ grew confused.

"For her to have been my wife would've meant your grandfather was dead! I would've been changing places with a dead man just like I changed places with a dead man to

**289**

get out of that ward! Just like I knew I was when she used to sneak over to my rooming house at night, to keep the neighbors from talking. And I knew it was wrong!"

Silver bunched a fist and struck himself in the thigh. "It was wrong! And I knew it! And you know what's worse?"

PJ knelt in front of Silver. "It wasn't wrong, Silver! It was love!"

"And what's worse," he went on, "is that I'd do it all over again! "The only thing…" and his voice trembled and broke. When he went on, it was through tears. "The only person who could ever heal me of that guilt is Elizabeth. Like she healed me fifty years ago."

"But Silver," she said, "you're a healer too! You know, I remember the first time I saw the scar on my Grandpa David's arm. I was, like, five, and I thought God had put it there. I don't know why, to punish him, maybe. And it was you, his best friend, helping him. There's no medal they could give him that could mean more than the scar you put there. I know it!"

"The Chinese put that scar there," he said. "Don't act like you know what it means, having somebody scar you like that."

"But I know exactly what it's like to have somebody put a scar on you!" she insisted.

~

"Your kids," her OB/GYN, Dr. Dawson, said, tapping his Palm Pilot, "are going to be born on April first."

"April Fool's Day?" said PJ. "Why?"

"March thirtieth work better for you? April second? It doesn't matter, within a day or two."

"It's kind of hard to decide what to do when I'm wearing a paper bag. Can I get dressed now?"

"Oh, I'm sorry."

He stepped outside and it gave her a moment to put her clothes on and collect her thoughts.

When he returned she said, "Um…April second is three months from now. Doesn't that mean they'll be a month premature?"

"It does," the doctor said, "but we can handle that. The problem is, with your pelvic structure, you're not going to be delivering twins naturally. We're going to have to do a cesarean section." He smiled. "It's a good problem to have, usually—you're nice and thin. You work out a lot?"

"There's a fitness center at my office," she said. "I run and do yoga."

"Well, I hate tell you, but your fitness center days are over."

"Why do you say that?"

The doctor's face grew sympathetic. "You need to go to bed for a while."

"A while? Three whole months?"

He tapped his Palm Pilot again. "You sure you don't want to deliver on March thirtieth instead of April second?"

~

"I have this big red frown on my belly," PJ said. "My C-section scar. And I hate it. I've been rubbing it with vitamin E for years, but it just gets bigger. You pay for your love, I guess."

Silver sat facing the quilt of eyes and said, "You know, I've seen horses born, but never a baby. I wish…"

PJ waited, but he didn't finish. "You wish…" she prompted him.

"No," he said. "Every time I ask you about your mother, you change the subject."

She looked away from him, hurt by the reproach. "But I don't like thinking about her. It's so painful; I've done without her for so long."

"You don't have to tell me happy stories," he said. "I want to know her for who she is. If she made bad choices, well, so be it. Lord knows I made bad choices too!"

PJ sat down on the floor by Silver's wheelchair and leaned her back against the wall.

"What can I tell you?" she asked. "I don't know who she is. I don't know what she does, where she lives, who she goes out with. We hardly talk."

"All right," he said. "I'll tell you something about her, then. First of all, if she's your mother she can't be that bad. And second, if she's Elizabeth's daughter then she can't be that bad either."

"It's not that simple—"

"PJ, you'll get to be my age one of these days, and you'll wish you'd played things differently with her. You'll wish you'd reconciled. I guarantee you that.

He pointed at her. "And I'll tell you something else. You'll wish you had told me about her, too. Surely, surely, there's one thing you're happy she did for you."

"The best thing my mother ever did for me," PJ said grimly, "was that she abandoned me a month after I was born."

~

"No, I don't want a general," she told the nurse above the beeping of the fetal monitors. "I don't want to sedate my babies."

Ross, standing by her at the head of the bed, smiled and laid his palm across her forehead.

"They get it, Cupcake," he said.

The anesthesiologist hovered into view above her. "OK. We're going to sit you up for the epidural—it's quick—and in twenty minutes or so we'll be ready to start the c-section. Sir?" he said to Ross. "This is considered surgery, and I need to ask you to step out of the room."

Ross patted her cheek. "Be strong, Cupcake. I'll be right back." And he was gone.

A pair of nurses helped her sit up—her belly was roughly the size and shape of her Volkswagen—and they bared her back.

"Am I gonna feel the needle?" she said.

The anesthesiologist smiled. "I'll slide the needle in during a contraction. You won't notice it. But you need to sit as still as you can, OK?"

"OK," she said doubtfully.

And then the contraction was on her, and she was huffing rhythmically, and it went on and on. When it was over she looked up and the nurses were smiling as reassuringly as the anesthesiologist had.

Twenty minutes later—and she'd lost count of the contractions—a cool clean numbness began to radiate out from her spine and slide down her lower back.

When Ross came back she was half-asleep on her left side, and she was only half aware of his touch on her arm.

She awoke to a bustling in the room and suddenly strong hands were rolling her onto her back. PJ looked up dazedly to see Dr. Dawson, in scrubs, standing beside the bed.

"You look mah-velous," he said, giving her the thumbs-up.

Her right leg itched, but when she tried to move it she found that she couldn't. She tried her left one, and it was paralyzed too.

"Dr. Dawson!" she shrieked.

He left off whatever he was doing and looked up over her belly at her. "You all right?"

"I can't move my legs!"

"It's just the epidural," he said. "You'll get your legs back."

"What if I don't? *What if I don't?*"

Dawson's eyes flicked to Ross and Ross put his hand on her forehead.

"Shh," he whispered. "Try to calm down. You remember your breathing exercises? Come on, breathe with me."

He started counting, and she tried to breathe in time.

"Now," Dr. Dawson said a minute later. "PJ, we're going to put a screen up across you."

"OK," she said helplessly.

A pair of nurses spread a blue drape across PJ's chest, cutting off her view of the rest of the world. There was only the field of blue and the ceiling tile and Ross looking down into her face. He leaned and kissed her once on each cheek.

Her body jiggled a bit—"Scrubbing you," said Dr. Dawson—and then she waited.

"OK," he said. "Looks very good."

PJ looked up and saw Ross's eyes widen. He was watching the procedure over the screen.

"What is it?" she asked.

"They're making the incision," he said.

"I can't feel a thing."

"You may feel a little pressure," Dr. Dawson said. "Retract? Nice, nice."

Ross sucked in his breath and PJ saw his face go pale.

"What's happening to me? Ross, tell me!"

He reached for her hand but he couldn't take his eyes away from what was happening to her beyond the drape.

"You're OK," he said in a weak voice, and PJ saw that he was tottering on the stool.

"Mr. Hathaway!" a nurse said very sharply.

"Everybody copacetic up there?" Dr. Dawson's voice.

"Yeah," Ross said, straightening. "I was just a little light-headed for a second."

"Steady up," Dawson said.

PJ heard wheels screeching. "What's that?"

"They're...they're moving things," said Ross. He leaned forward. "Oh, wow. I can see—"

"Am I OK, Ross? Are the twins OK? What's happening, Ross? What's wrong with me?"

He blinked hard and deliberately looked away from what was going on behind the screen.

"I promise you, you're completely fine," he said.

She felt a strong pressure build in her midsection, and she gasped. "You don't know that, Ross. How can you know that?"

Dr. Dawson said, "Now, we're going to lower the screen a bit so you can see the actual delivery. Don't worry about anything else you might see down here, just focus on the babies, you understand?"

"I think so," PJ panted.

"Here we go!"

At once the screen dipped and PJ lifted her head and looked down to see Dr. Dawson lifting a wet blood-streaked baby away from a gaping hole in what looked like a sheet of thick crinkled flesh-colored rubber. The baby—*Hi, Baker,* she thought, seeing his tiny penis—writhed and worked his lips, eyes closed. The cord dangled away and Dr. Dawson clamped it and cut it and whipped Baker into a birthing blanket so fast that she almost missed it.

And then he reached into the hole again—*into me!* thought PJ—up to his forearms, it seemed, and up he came with another baby, tiny as the first, but with a crease between her legs and silken hair.

"Hi, Lizzie," PJ said faintly.

Abruptly the screen came up in front of her eyes again, and there was only the field of blue and Ross's face.

His face was wet, and he leaned to her and dampened her

face with his kisses and his tears. "Thank you, thank you," he was saying. "They're perfect. You did so good, so good. Do you feel OK?"

"I feel...I feel..." But if there was a feeling there, she couldn't give it a name. She started shaking, trembling spasmodically, and she was powerless to stop it. "Ross," she pleaded, "help me. I'm so cold."

~

The eyes on the quilt on the wall were warm green, but PJ was remembering how she'd shaded them in a subtle way so that some appeared happy and others appeared sad. She was shooting for the overall effect of balance, even wisdom, but she wasn't sure she'd achieved it, or even how she'd know if she had.

Silver interrupted her thoughts. "But you haven't finished telling me about this quilt," he said. "2004 was the same year Lizzie and Baker were born, wasn't it?"

"Well, I was on bed rest. Going stir crazy. And when Bebe passed, all she'd done was the inside square. I put it away for a few years, and then when I finally got over missing my job and got bored with soap operas, I decided to finish it. She couldn't be there with me when I was pregnant, and I guess I was looking for the next best thing."

"Why's it here?" he asked. "Seems like quite the feat, getting your work into a place like this."

"It's not that impressive," she said. "An assistant curator told my friend Kelly they were opening this gallery, and could she keep her eyes open for anything special? Traditional, you know? Folk-artsy.

"Kelly had submitted one of her own quilts, and a couple of the Blockheads sent theirs, and I sent this one in. Even though I knew it wasn't what they'd asked for."

"You broke the rules," Silver said.

"Yeah, I broke the rules. That's me. 'Follow your heart and forget the practicalities.' And when they picked this quilt, Kelly was so ticked off. We didn't speak for a month."

▶▶▶◆◀◀◀
## Chapter Twenty-Nine

"You want to take out a *what*?" Ross asked. He was still in his suit, fresh off the plane, standing in the doorway with his leather laptop case and his garment bag slung over his shoulder.

"A home equity line of credit," said PJ. "It's a—"

"I know what it is. The answer's no."

"Ross, we have seventy thousand dollars in equity in our house. We can tap into that, use it for Silver's—"

"PJ, do you not watch the news? Do you not realize how many people are getting foreclosed on out there because they can't meet their house payments? The answer is no! En Oh!"

"Don't talk to me like I'm a child, Ross!"

He set the bags down. "Come outside," he hissed, jerking his chin back towards the front door.

She followed him through the door and Ross closed it behind them and they stood on the front porch together. He looked around the neighborhood before turning on her, his face inches from hers.

"I have had it with this," he said quietly through clenched teeth.

"Maybe it was a dumb idea," she said, putting her hands up.

"It was more than a dumb idea. It was a crazy idea. Crazy, as in out-of-your-mind looney tunes."

"Ross—"

"No," he interrupted. "I didn't complain about it when you paid that lawyer that retainer."

"You grilled me about it for two hours!" she said.

"I wasn't grilling you, I was trying to walk you through it rationally so you'd see—"

"You were pissed off!" she said, her voice rising. "And since when do I have to clear what I spend with you?"

He pointed his finger. "Since you went off the deep end in May! I thought you were bad before, but you're ten times worse now, and you're trying to take the rest of us down with you!"

PJ looked up. They were standing under the window of the guestroom, where Silver slept.

Ross looked up to see where she was looking. "Let him hear. You're forcing stuff on him that he doesn't want to go through, and you're lying to me, and you've got Lizzie and Baker tiptoeing around the house, and it! Ends! NOW!"

"Then why did you bring me out on the front porch if you don't care if Silver hears this?" She turned away from him and cupped her hands around her mouth. "MY HUSBAND THINKS I'M LOSING MY MIND!" she yelled to the neighborhood at large.

"Oh, stop it," he muttered, screwing his eyes shut. "Just stop it."

"You stop it! You bring me out here and tell me I'm crazy and call me a liar?"

"You are a liar! You told me you'd see a counselor, and you were just doing it to—how did you put it?—get me off your back?"

"OK, let's talk about liars, then. The only reason you tried to talk me out of going to Utah in the first place was to cover up for yourself for not telling me what Jerry had found!"

"We settled that already!"

"Settled it? That means you get off the hook, but I have to stay on?"

"You're not on a hook! Seeing a counselor is—"

"So if I go see a counselor, will you let me—"

"No deals," he said, shaking his head. "No deals. Until you get some help, you don't take a step around here without talking to me about it first."

PJ narrowed her eyes. "Ross, come here, I want to tell you something."

"What?"

"No, no, lean closer. I need to whisper it."

He did so, suspicion in his eyes.

She put her lips to his ear. "THERE IS NOTHING WRONG WITH ME!" she shouted directly into his brain.

~

"I have seldom read," said Charles Lowell, Attorney-at-Law, "an affidavit so compelling as Mr. Piper's. I have high hopes."

PJ sighed. "It's beyond—yeah. But I was calling to tell you that we may have to drop the case."

"Mr. Piper has changed his mind?"

"No. I'm afraid we're about out of money."

"Ah," said Lowell.

"Is there anything we can do to work this out? Can you take the case on contingency, maybe?"

"Mrs. Hathaway," he began.

~

PJ parked in a pay lot between office buildings—*ten bucks,* she thought bitterly, *or about ninety seconds of Charles Lowell, Attorney-at-Law's precious time*—and she got out and slid the side door open and pulled the card table and a folding chair and her bag out.

She set up the table at the edge of Miller Park and she hung up her sign so the pedestrians on their way to lunch would have to read it as they passed.

HAVE A HEART FOR A HERO!

She'd written a summary of Silver's story, made copies

of his affidavit, and printed the quilt design on glossy paper. She spread these all out in the card table.

And then she sat and waited.

And waited, and waited, and waited. It was noon, prime-time, a beautiful sunny day, but her mood was dark. As she watched the business-types scurry by on their lunch hours, her resentment grew and grew.

*Why am I sitting here begging for money from these yuppies,* she wondered, *when it ought to be obvious to anyone who thinks about it for five seconds that nothing's more important than taking care of the people who went to war for their way of life? I mean, look at that guy over there.*

Across from her table, in the grass by the fountain, an older man slouched on a milk crate. His eyes were closed above his woolly, unkempt beard, his once white t-shirt was filthy and stretched out of shape around the neck, and his fly was unzipped. But he wore a pair of black leather boots that shone as if he'd just polished them, and his baseball cap said "AIRBORNE."

"PJ?" said a female voice. "PJ Warner?"

PJ turned to see a woman standing at her table. A brunette in an expensive-looking grey pantsuit who seemed vaguely familiar.

"It's Phoebe Carlysle. We went to high school together?"

"Phoebe?" said PJ. "Wow! The last time I saw you was…" *in the gym, when you and Susan Yates were threatening to beat my lights out* "…at high school graduation, right?"

"I guess so," Phoebe gushed. "How are you? What've you been doing with yourself?"

"Well," PJ said, forcing a smile. "Kids and a house. A perfect husband. I'm as happy as I can possibly be. What about you?"

"Oh, I left Chattanooga for a few years," Phoebe said. She wiped lipstick from the corner of her mouth with a fingernail that PJ saw was exquisitely manicured. "Got married, and divorced, I'm afraid. I'm a financial adviser, now."

She looked down at PJ's table. "What's all this?"

PJ gave her the short version and delivered the sales pitch.

"Fifty bucks for a heart on a quilt?" Phoebe said when she was finished.

"It's not so much for a heart on a quilt..." PJ began, until she realized that an impenetrable shield of polite, patient boredom was settling over Phoebe's face.

*Is this the way she looks at her clients?*

"Phoebe," she said, "let me ask you a question. Do you see that guy, over there, on the milk crate?"

Phoebe looked. "The homeless guy. Sure."

PJ dug deep, trying to get it just right. "You see him every day when you come out here, don't you?"

"He looks familiar. But they all look the same."

"Would you say he's a vet?"

Phoebe squinted. "He's wearing an Airborne hat."

"So he at least wants people to think he's a vet, and maybe he really is. The question is, when you see a guy like that, do you stop and make sure he's OK? Or do you chew him out for being a poser? For faking being in the service to get a handout?"

"I don't do either one," Phoebe said slowly.

"You walk on by, don't you?" said PJ.

Phoebe nodded, her eyes growing reflective.

"I'm not asking you for fifty bucks for a quilt," PJ said. "I'm asking you for fifty bucks to help a veteran get the recognition he deserves. He's my grandfather, and I wish you could talk to him yourself; you'd want to write him a check for fifty thousand."

Phoebe unbuttoned her purse. "Let's keep it to fifty," she said.

*Wonder upon wonders,* thought PJ. *Maybe people can change after all.*

~

PJ sat at the card table with her face in her hands.

*Sure people can change. Look how well I've done!*

Phoebe had been the high point of PJ's day. PJ had been sitting for four hours but she'd only sold three hearts.

She stood up and brushed her hair back from her eyes, and walked across the street and folded the bills she'd collected and tucked them into the sleeping vet's pocket.

*Sweet dreams, Airborne,* she thought.

Back in the van, she wove through the streets of downtown Chattanooga, reluctant to admit defeat and go home, but with no other destination in mind.

She headed north across the new bridge—*the Veterans Memorial Bridge, ironically enough, although I bet the money to build it all went to civilian contractors*—and she was already rehearsing the conversation she'd have to have with Ross. Then, as she wound up the hill through North Chattanooga, she looked to her left at the houses dotting the hills.

*I haven't stopped at our old place in years,* she thought. *Not since...*

Not since she and Ross had locked the door to it for the last time. After they'd moved all the stuff out, and after they'd done one more walkthough so they could give the keys to the realtor.

*Wonder how it's holding up?*

She turned left into the maze of side streets. A few more turns, and she was there.

The little house that had once been David and Bebe's sat on a level lot, which was rare in this hilly part of town. And the new owners were apparently in the process of painting it, for half the house was now a flat green she detested. But they'd put up a cedar fence around the backyard, which was OK, she guessed, and there were flowers in the planters.

As she surveyed the front of the house for more changes, a million memories crowded her mind's eye. Skipping in the grass. Swinging on the porch swing. The front door she'd passed through uncountable times. Hanging Christmas lights. Drawing chalk pictures on the sidewalk.

And inside the house—well, she could sit here for the rest of her life, longing for the times that had once been but were no longer. Maybe the owners, whoever they were, would let her take a peek inside. For old time's sake.

She got out and started across the yard, and almost

immediately she heard the barking of a dog from behind the front door.

*Bebe loved dogs, but she'd never have let one in the house,* PJ thought.

So she stopped on the stoop, the iron handrail familiar in her hand. The concrete steps were worn smooth and slightly concave in the center, from the passing feet of a hundred years.

And then PJ knelt to the trim at the base of the posts that supported the porch roof. The old paint was off-white and peeling back. She dug at it with her fingernail to see what was underneath.

*Purple,* she thought, *just like Silver said when we were driving him home. Fifty years ago, he painted this porch purple. And now it's passed out of our family.*

The thought was too much for her, and rather than sit down and cry on the steps that were at once too familiar and too alien, she retreated to the van and drove away, trying not to look back.

~

*Coffee,* she thought. *Find a coffeeshop. I have to get myself calmed down before I face Ross.*

She drove down from her childhood home to the river again, and crossed into downtown Chattanooga by the Tennessee Aquarium, where the sidewalk shops and cafes nestled by the water. There was a coffeeshop she liked across from her old office, a laid-back place, that looked like it had been there since the Civil War.

It reminded her of how much the city had changed. Downtown had been such an eyesore when she was ten years old—a warren of dingy bars and what Bebe called "dirty bookstores," dark corners where people lurked in the shadows doing God only knew what, and run-down motels.

And now it was beautiful, completely transformed, family-friendly. She wondered what the secret of such a renewal was. Envied the city for changing for the better, in fact.

*Unlike me. So how do I tell Silver and Ross and Baker and Lizzie and the girls that I'm a complete failure? How do I tell them I've run out of ideas for raising money, and we're gonna have to drop Silver's discharge appeal? That we won't be able to vindicate him?*

*I can't do that. I'd die if I did that.*

She shook her head and abruptly turned left. *Enough of this driving around,* she thought. *I might as well go home and get it over with.*

Missionary Ridge loomed ahead—the tunnel through it was a shortcut to her house—and she plunged the van into the arch of darkness. She absentmindedly honked the horn for good luck.

*Blockhead,* she thought, when she realized what she'd done.

~

The shortcut hadn't helped one bit, for the traffic was twisted and PJ had to inch along in a cloud of acrid exhaust. As she approached the main highway, she happened to look left and there, in a strip mall between a Chinese restaurant and a used sporting good store, sat a military recruiting office.

She hauled the wheel over almost before she knew what she was doing—turning left from the right-hand lane through a cacophony of honking to zoom across the lot and park in front of the office. In the windows there hung posters of soldiers in blurry digitized camouflage, fighter jets flying in formation, a destroyer throwing a long wake, and a Marine with sword brandished in salute.

Inside, a young Marine sat at a reception desk. "Can I help you, ma'am?"

"Do you have someone I can speak with?" she asked.

The Marine took her name. "Have a seat and I'll get Staff Sergeant Watkins," he said.

PJ sat and studied the waiting room. There were fliers and copies of service magazines on the end tables. Across from her hung a framed print of a grey-haired man leaning with palm pressed against a glossy black wall—*the Vietnam Memorial,* PJ realized—his head bowed in grief.

And from within the midnight stone a patrol of much

younger men gazed back at him, their eyes fierce and timeless, one of them pressing his gossamer palm to the palm of the grieving man as if to comfort him from beyond the grave.

*Bet Silver would empathize with that guy,* she thought.

"Mrs. Hathaway?" a man said. She looked up to see a Marine in a tan shirt and blue slacks—*they call them blouses and trousers,* she remembered—coming into the waiting room. He was lean, medium-height, with close-cropped hair and a strong jaw.

"Hi," she said, extending her hand.

"Good afternoon," he said, shaking her hand firmly and looking straight into her eyes.

She wanted to shrink away. *I must look terrible, for him to be treating me this nicely.*

"I'm Staff Sergeant Watkins, Mrs. Hathaway. I'm sorry, but I'm working with a potential recruit right now. Could we set up an appointment?"

"How long do you think you'll be?"

"It's hard to say, ma'am."

"I can wait for a while." *Where else am I going to go?*

"Your call, ma'am. Could I offer you a soda? Coffee?"

"I'd kill for a cup of coffee."

He smiled. "You don't have to. Come back to the kitchen and make yourself comfortable."

Sitting in the little breakroom, coffee in hand, she could hear him drilling his prospect on something.

"No, no," he was saying. "Let's try it another way. You have a squad of sixteen soldiers—weird squad, but it's the Army. They're ranked four by four, standing shoulder to shoulder and chest to back. They're each three feet wide and three feet thick."

*Big guys,* PJ thought. *But why soldiers instead of Marines?*

"So how many feet across is the formation?" Watkins asked.

"Twelve feet?" said a hesitant teenaged voice.

"And what's the area of the formation?"

"A hundred and forty-four feet?"

"A hundred and forty-four *square* feet, but you did the math right. Now, these are soldiers, so they're standing too close together. When one of the center ones steps on an M thirty-five with, say, an eight foot blast radius, how many soldiers are in it?"

"I don't know what an M thirty-five is."

"You might want to look it up, it's a Belgian antipersonnel mine that turns up in Iraq every so often," Watkins said. "Now, I repeat, how many soldiers are in the blast radius?"

*Come on, kid, it's basic trig,* PJ thought.

"Uh, half of them?" the kid said.

"Negative, negative. You're guessing when you oughtta be thinking. Look, like I said, the area of a circle—"

PJ stood up and went to the breakroom door. "Sergeant?" she said.

Watkins and his pupil looked up from the desk in surprise. The kid was gangly, with a crew-cut and a black t-shirt that said NINTENDO across the front.

"It's 'Staff Sergeant,'" Watkins said mildly. "Yes, ma'am?"

*Great work,* PJ thought. *He gives you coffee and you butcher his rank. Who needs tutoring, here?*

"Um...Staff Sergeant, I'm sorry to butt in, but there's a real easy way to remember the area of a circle. Circles are square pies."

"Oh, I see," he said. "Right."

"I don't get it," said the kid.

"To find the area of a circle," PJ said, "square the radius and multiply by pi. Circle-square-pie."

"Pi's about three point fourteen," the kid said. "I remember that."

"So?" asked Watkins.

"So..." the kid said slowly. "It's eight times eight...times three point fourteen." He scribbled on the paper in front of him. "About two hundred and one square feet. So all the soldiers are in the blast radius!"

"That's correct! All of them! And the real lesson is?"

"Circles are square pies!" the kid answered, flushed with pride.

"No, no, no!" Watkins growled. "Think! The lesson is, don't bunch up your squad!"

~

"Thank you for wanting to help," he said to PJ after the kid had left. "I hope it isn't wasted. There's a term we use: 'brain child.'"

"I feel like a brain child myself," she said sheepishly. "Sorry for interrupting. And for pulling off a couple of your stripes like that."

"Well, it's good you get to see the kind of raw material we work with. You know, he can take out every level in every video game on the market, but he can't pass a simple evaluation exam." Watkins shook his head. "And did you see the t-shirt? I see Nintendo logos in my nightmares, and he wears one in here. I wish he had more pride."

PJ nodded. "Are you saying you don't think he's Marine material?"

Watkins shrugged and looked towards the windows. "He might just surprise us all, ma'am, if he'll take the chance I'm trying to give him."

He turned back to her. "Anyway, what can I do for you today?"

She put on her best smile. "I always heard," she said, "that when you're desperate, you call the Marines."

He bowed slightly, and, once again, she started her story.

#### ▶▶▶◆◀◀◀
### Chapter Thirty

"Corporal who?" PJ asked. *Oh, man, I was almost asleep.*

Ross's voice was muffled by the bathroom door, but she could hear that it was sharp with impatience. "Malone! Can you come on and take this?"

PJ sat up in the tub. *Somebody from the recruiting office,* she thought. "OK, I'll be right out."

She toweled quickly and wrapped the towel around her and unlocked the bathroom door. Ross was already gone; he'd left the phone on the bed for her.

"Hello?"

"Good afternoon, Mrs. Hathaway, Corporal Jason Malone, United States Marine Coah." He sounded young, and there was no mistaking his Boston accent.

"Hi, Corporal. What's going on?"

"Ma'am, I got a call from a Staff Sahgent Watkins in Chattanooger, Tennessee, and I wanted to ask you a few questions. Do you have a moment?"

*Chattanooger?* "Sure, but why?"

"I'm a correspondent for *Marines.* Have you heahd of us?"

"Of course I've heard of the Marines," she said.

"No, ma'am, I mean the magazine. *Marines* is the official publication of the United States Marine Coah."

"Oh, oh, oh," she said. "I think I saw your magazine at the recruiting office."

"Excellent. Mrs. Hathaway, I'd like to do a shoaht feecha for our website on whatchouah trying to accomplish with your memorial quilt, if you'd agree, and I'd also like to write up a story proposal for my editah for possible inclusion in the magazine itself."

"Really?"

"Yes, ma'am, really. I'd be especially interested in interviewing Joseph Pipah, if you know how to reach him."

"I know how to reach him," she said.

~

They did the interview by phone, and Ross got his first professional photo credit when the pictures and story went up on the *Marines* website.

The afternoon the story appeared, PJ was grilling hot dogs in the back yard when her cell phone rang. She hung up the tongs with a grin.

*Come on, now…big money, big money, big money—*

"Is this PJ Hathaway?" a man asked.

"Speaking."

"I'm Randy Whittle, from the Chattanooga Times Free Press. A Marine recruiter emailed me a link to…

*Well, what do you know?* thought PJ. *Marines to the rescue. Semper Fi, Staff Sergeant Watkins.*

~

"My grandfather always talked about the Chosin Few," the woman on the phone said. "Every Christmas, he'd gather us under the tree and tell us how blessed we were to be together, living in a free country."

"We had the same little ritual," said PJ, "except that it was always on Memorial Day. My grandmother and I would go down to a monument the American Legion had set up…

They talked for twenty minutes, and the woman bought two hearts.

~

"Thirty-one?" Silver said. They were all at the dining room table and he was stirring the peas on his plate with his knife.

"Can you believe it?" PJ said. "I've been on the phone for hours. Everybody has a story they want to tell."

"And that's on the strength of two articles," Ross said. "Not bad."

"I know," she said. "And I emailed the links to something like fifty papers and radio stations and websites. I really hope this takes off."

"Eat your peas, Mr. Silver," Baker said.

Silver smiled, started to say something, and that's when PJ's phone rang again. It was plugged into the charger, on Ross's end of the china cabinet, its battery completely whipped.

"Eat, I'll catch it," he said as he scooped up the phone. "Mmm—hmm. Yes. I'm her husband." He waited, and then his face changed. "Really? *Really?* No way."

"What, what?" PJ said.

He held the phone up. "This woman says she's the news director for the Atlanta NPR affiliate. W-something."

"Cool," said PJ, but her stomach started doing a tap-dance.

~

"Why are you crying?" Ross asked a few nights later. "I thought you'd be happy. He tapped the bedside lamp and dim light flooded the room.

PJ wiped her eyes and nose, tried to smile. "I am happy."

"This is happy?" He reached her a tissue. "Look at me, I'm ecstatic. I'm sleeping with a celebrity."

She half-laughed, half-sobbed, and honked her nose with the tissue.

"I don't know what I'm going to do," she said. "I cut the

phone off for a while today because I was getting too many calls, and when I picked it back up my voice mail was full."

"It's a good problem to have, right?"

"No!" she said. "I'm exhausted! I can't even field the phone calls, so how am I supposed to actually make the quilt?"

"Ah, boy."

"It's just too much to keep track of! I have to write these people's addresses down and send them a form to write their memorial statements on—which I haven't even designed yet—and then I have to put the squares together, and, oh, I haven't even told you about this, I've gotten three invitations to speak at quilting guild meetings. Ross, I don't even know where to start!"

"Not to add to your misery, but you haven't even worked out an accounting system for all this, have you? I mean, these are pledges, right?"

"Right. I've been giving out our address, but I may never see a single check. I should've gotten set up with Visa or somebody."

"Giving out our home address?" he asked.

His tone was neutral but it bothered her. "Don't be so critical, OK? I'm doing the best I can, here."

"I know, I don't mean it that way," he said quickly. "Do you—would it be helpful if I took a few days off? Gave you a hand?"

"I don't know."

"Seriously, there's a lot I could do. Do you want me to see if I can get one of our bookkeepers at work to give us some advice? Can I go to the bank and set up an account? See what it takes to set up a nonprofit?"

"It's OK," she insisted. "I'll handle it. I figure it'll die down by this weekend, anyway."

"What if it doesn't? Look, I don't mind helping you."

"I need to do this myself, Ross."

"All right," he said. "But try to stay positive, would you? Look, you try everything you can think of and nothing works. Then, when you're about to give it up, you get a wild hair and actually ask somebody for a hand. A week later, your quilt's all over the place. And you've sold…how many hearts?"

"Six hundred and forty-one."

"Six hundred and forty-one," he said, and then he whistled. "Man, I'm in the wrong business. That's thirty-two thousand dollars."

"And fifty."

"Right. Enough to keep Lowell working for a while."

"And pay off some of Silver's medical bills."

"Jeez, then why are you beating yourself up? It's an awesome outcome, and if you hit a few speed bumps, so what? You never could've seen this coming. And if you feel like you need help, all you have to do is ask me for it."

She lay back in his shadow, feeling the ache in her lower back from sitting hunched over the phone at her desk all day.

"Ross," she said, "could you just rub my back?"

He smiled. "I can do that." But from his tone, she realized he'd mistaken her intention.

*There you go again, making promises to your husband that you don't intend to keep.*

She pulled her t-shirt off and flipped over quickly as he took the bottle of oil out of his nightstand, and she watched while she rubbed oil on his hands. He poured a dollop into her lower back—she jumped, it was cold!—and then his warm hands were kneading her sore muscles.

"OK?" he asked.

"Mmm-hmm," she murmured. But it wasn't.

*Six hundred hearts—I'm gonna have to redesign the whole quilt. I said if I sold a bunch I could just make it taller, but that many hearts'll make it as tall as the Empire State Building. I have to widen it.*

Ross pressed his thumbs deeply into her back and she flinched.

"Sorry," he said. He started working up and down on either side of her spine with the balls of his thumbs, taking long strokes.

*And that means I have to update all the design work. More time lost.*

She sighed heavily.

"Too hard?" Ross asked.

"No, it's fine," she told him. *Plus, I've got to get more*

311

*fabric. I was thinking fifty or sixty hearts, tops. So I need ten times as much. Dammit!*

"I feel like I'm kneading plywood," Ross said. "You need to relax."

"How am I supposed to do that, Ross?" she asked.

"Just try, OK?" He started stroking her shoulders lightly with his fingertips.

*Not to mention that I'll need ten times as much time. And I'm not going to find extra time on the shelves at Kelly Green's, that's for sure.*

Ross was saying something.

"What's that?" she said.

"I said, you're still not relaxing."

"So sue me, OK?" she said. "I'm trying…"

She felt his weight moving away from her on the bed. She rolled onto her hip to see him disappearing into the bathroom.

She got up and pulled her t-shirt on and tied her robe around herself.

"Where are you going?" he asked, coming back in with soap dripping soap from his hands. "You need to get some sleep!"

"I'm gonna go get some work done," she said. "That quilt is just about the only thing I have control of in this entire world."

"Trying to control everything," he said, "is what's keeping you from controlling anything. You need to get help."

"Ross, I'll go see a counselor when I'm good and ready, OK?"

"I wasn't talking about a counselor!"

~

"I'd feel so much better if I had something to keep my hands busy," Bebe said. "I was thinking, could you go to Kelly Green's and get me a few things that feel good? Smooth cotton and flannel and silk—anything with an interesting texture? And don't worry about matching the colors."

PJ could hardly speak. She looked around the dialysis

clinic, at the hurrying nurses, the patients slumped in the green vinyl chairs, the hard chrome of the machines, the miles of tubing, the filtration units spinning like coin-up washers.

She was trying not to look at the shunt embedded under Bebe's right collarbone. For two hours every day the clinicians plugged Bebe into a machine that sucked her blood out and cleansed it and injected it back into her. PJ didn't want to think about that. Because the dialysis would soon be happening every other day. And soon after that, every day.

And what would happen after that? And how would it happen?

"How about some corduroy, too?" she asked, trying to focus on Bebe's face instead of her own fears.

"Pinwale corduroy, and, oh, how about some Ultrasuede?"

PJ chuckled despite herself. "This is gonna be a weird quilt."

"But it'll feel wonderful," Bebe said. "Did you ever wake up in the night, when it was really dark, and feel the quilts on the bed? Just feel them? Trying to figure out what you got right and what you got wrong, by touch, when you don't have your vision to help you see it?"

"No, but I will now."

"Seems like it'd be a good way to teach a child how to sew," Bebe said. "Give them different fabrics and have them sew blindfolded."

PJ nodded. "Use the Force."

"The what?"

"It's from *Star Wars*, remember? The old man's teaching the kid how to...um, defend himself, with his laser sword thingy, and he pulls the kid's helmet down over his eyes so the kid can't see what's coming."

Then PJ sucked her teeth, thinking, and Bebe looked at her. "What is it, Cupcake?"

"Bebe, I should've thought of this myself. I hate the thought of you lying in your room all day when I'm at work with nothing to do but listen to the TV. It's the first time in your life you've not been able to keep busy, isn't it?"

"No, there've been times—like when your Grandpa David was gone to war—when all I felt like doing was sitting around. Worrying, feeling sorry for myself. And those are the times I'd have to force myself to get up and get working. That's when I learned that work's almost as good as prayer, Cupcake."

PJ patted Bebe's knee. "I'll go the fabric shop right now, so you can get to work. And I'll pray, too."

#### ▶▶◆◀◀
## Chapter Thirty-One

The girls—there looked to be twenty of them, a bunch for a Blockheads night—were sitting around working on this and that, and they put down their work and stood up and clapped as PJ pushed Silver and led Lizzie into the back room. Actually stood up and clapped for her, and PJ was so surprised by it that her breath *whooshed* out of her as if she'd been rabbit-punched.

"Um...be seated, my people," she said when she could speak. "We're just ordinary folks, same as you." *Not entirely true,* she thought. But then she and Silver said the same word at the same instant.

"*Roy?*"

There, amongst the Blockheads and suspiciously close to Ellen, stood Roy Dyer in all of his Saigon honky-tonk glory—belt buckle blazing, pearl buttons winking, boot-toes pointing.

"Be seated, my people," he said, smiling enormously. "I'm just ordinary folks too."

PJ crossed her arms in pretended consternation. "Ellen, this is gonna take some explaining."

"What's to explain?" said Missy. "He's got a pulse and four limbs."

"Five," said Ellen, and there was much laughter. Then

she leaned forward and said something to Roy, some-
thing with the tonality and cadence of Vietnamese, and
Roy looked over his shoulder at her and blushed.
And then he said something back to Ellen, and
Ellen—Ellen Sanders the Imperturbable—blushed in
return.

"What's the deal?" PJ asked.

"You remember that idiot labeling machine that
Bert and I got all tangled up in?" Ellen said. "Roy here
knows how to fix it. So he's putting in for a transfer to
Chattanooga, and I'm putting in for a transfer to Bluff,
and we're hoping one of them comes through."

"Don't you get it?" Missy asked. "She finally thinks
she's found a man who's smarter than she is. But the fact
that he's with her—"

"Wait a minute," PJ said. "What if both your transfers
go through?"

Roy and Ellen looked at each other.

"Oh, the Post Office would never—" she said.

"They couldn't move fast enough to get out of their
own way—" he said.

Missy covered her eyes with her palm.

Then Crystal came in. "What's shaking? There's a car
full of—"

"No, no!" PJ interrupted. "That's a surprise!"

"Well?" said Kelly. "Do tell."

And again everyone was watching PJ, listening to her,
judging her. She tried not to squirm. "Um…you know
me, most of you..I've never been good at asking for help.
But this benefit quilt for Silver has gotten away from me,
gotten too big for one person."

"Of course we'll help," said Flo. "What do you need
from us, PJ?"

PJ explained the quilt again—some of them knew the
story, but not the specifics. She told how she'd despaired
of ever selling a square, and then how she'd despaired that
she'd ever stop selling squares.

"Anyway, it's finally time for the fun part," she
finished. "The sewing. I brought enough material to do all
the hearts, so let's see how many we can get through.

Um...and on that subject, none of you know this, and Kelly doesn't want me to tell you, but she donated the fabric."

There was another round of applause. Kelly looked furious, and PJ couldn't help smiling.

"And I have one more surprise. Lizzie, run to the front windows and wave, would you?"

Lizzie obeyed, and PJ watched as the girls buzzed questions at each other until Lizzie trotted back.

"Blockheads," PJ said, "OK, from the Halls of Montezuma..."

And Staff Sergeant Watkins led a half-dozen Marines into the room.

Each of them was carrying a Bernina 930 sewing machine—a 1980s workhorse that PJ knew for a fact was heavier than a school bus—and carrying it as if it weighed less than the empty air. And the biggest Marine, a PFC, had one under each arm.

They stood at the front of the room holding the Berninas, breathing easily in their tan-over-blue dress uniforms.

"Roy," Ellen whispered, "we might have to rethink the engagement."

"Good evening, everyone," said Watkins. "I'm Staff Sergeant Watkins, and these Marines and I have volunteered to help you tonight. When Mrs. Hathaway first contacted me, and I got to meet Mr. Piper, I knew I had a duty to help this man tell his story."

Then he smiled. "Little did I know that it might involve quilting, but when Mrs. Hathaway mentioned a room full of ladies, well—as you can see, I brought a few good men."

~

"Put 'em over here, guys," said Kelly, indicating a table. "Where'd you get these monsters from?"

"The reserve headquarters, ma'am," the big PFC said, following her with his two Berninas.

"You do your own sewing?" Kelly asked. "Really?"

The question made Silver laugh, and PJ, watching him, warmed up just a little.

~

Ellen, Silver, Missy, Roy, and a corporal named Guzmán were wielding scissors around a table on which a pile of hearts grew steadily.

"You've got a lot of war on your chest, son," Silver said to Guzmán.

Guzmán looked down at his ribbons. "Yes, sir. Afghanistan and Iraqi Freedom."

"It get as hot over there as I heard?"

"A hundred and ten, a hundred and twenty. A lot different than the Chosin, I imagine, sir?"

"I'd say not," Silver said. "The summers in Korea got hot enough to bake your head inside your helmet."

"Steel, right?" said Ellen.

"They were steel."

"We got Kevlar, ma'am," Guzmán said, "but the MOPPs, the chemical warfare suits, get I don't know how hot inside. I was drinking six, eight gallons a day."

"I had a mop like that once," said Missy. "And I've got some war on my chest, too."

"Excuse me, ma'am?" said Guzmán, scanning her blouse.

"Sure," said Missy. "I nursed four kids."

PJ, listening from the counter, almost spilled the coffee she was pouring.

~

Kelly held up a heart and a piece of background fabric. "PJ, do you want these at ninety-degree angles, like this?"

"No, use your imagination," PJ said. "I wanted them to look like they were floating down into the hands like snowflakes. Orient them however you want."

Kelly looked skeptical, but she only nodded and went back to pinning. Around her, Flo and Crystal and the big PFC, Lakeshore, went on with their pinning too.

"You know, Private," said Flo, "my husband wrote me

once that the men around him—men who knew they'd be coming under enemy fire—seemed more worried about what their women were doing back home than anything else."

"How do you mean, ma'am? asked Lakeshore.

"Whether their wives were being faithful," Flo said. "It struck me as very sweet and very sad, all at the same time."

"It does come up a lot, ma'am," said Lakeshore. "Whether Jody's got your girl."

Crystal poured more pins out of a paper cup. "Jody meaning whoever. 'Course, these days it could be Josephine, too."

"Times change," Kelly said.

"But people don't," said Flo. "You know, I remember among the wives, we were terrified our husbands wouldn't come home. But we were almost as terrified that they were being unfaithful to us. You'd think, 'Lord, I don't want to know. Just bring him home safely.' And then you'd think, 'But if I find out anything, I'll kill him myself.'"

"Faith," said Crystal. "Sounds like you were as worried about keeping faith as you were about keeping your head stuck to your shoulders. Is that how it is?"

"I don't know a lot about faith, ma'am," Lakeshore replied. "I went to boot camp an atheist. Came out a Protestant, though. It was either, go to chapel or get extra duty. They got several of us that way. Told us God was the drill instructor *everybody* answered to."

~

PJ was showing Watkins how to use a Bernina to appliqué a heart onto the background fabric.

"So I step on this foot switch," he said, "and then—"

She raised her chin and looked down her nose at him. "Negative, negative," she interrupted, unable to hide her smile. "The feet are on the machine, the pedal is on the floor, *Staff* Sergeant Watkins."

He hung his head. "Now who's a brain child?" he said, smiling back at her.

PJ hoarsened her voice into the stereotypical drill

instructor's rasp. *"This is my sewing machine! There are many others like it, but this one is mine!"*

~

"Could you tell us an old breed story, sir?" another corporal named Simons asked Silver.

Silver frowned. "Like what?"

"I don't know, sir. Ever meet anybody famous? Chesty Puller, maybe?"

"Saw him from about a hundred yards off," said Silver.

PJ shook her head. *And then he came up and pinned a medal on you and shook your hand while a photographer shot it for Life magazine.*

"What did he seem like?" asked Simons.

"Busy. Hollering at people."

"That's a good story," Simons said.

"Tell him the one about the pink lady," PJ suggested.

"Pink lady?" asked Simons.

Silver chuckled. "That's right. Corporal, after we took Inchon, we were bivouacked for a while waiting on a boat—one of those amphibious LSTs—so we could run back around Korea and land at Wonsan, on the east.

"There were these drums of torpedo fuel, in a warehouse the Navy had commandeered, at the harbor. Pink Lady, they called it. What it was, was pure grain alcohol with a bad-tasting chemical added in. But it wasn't too hard to distill that stuff back out, if you knew what you were doing."

"I see," Simons said. "Good hooch?"

"Horrible hooch," Silver said. "Set your tailfeathers on fire. The Shore Patrol was standing sentry on it around the clock, but there were still drunk Marines all over Inchon. Nobody figured it out until some bright second lieutenant noticed a manhole cover inside the garage bay where they'd stacked the barrels. Son, they were crawling in through the storm drains!"

"Croton oil," said Ellen. "It's the bad-tasting stuff the Navy used. These days dermatologists use it for chemical peels."

"If you say so," Silver said, eyeing her skeptically. "Anyhow, I was in a craps game along the docks one night, and up comes this SP, his baton thicker than his neck, and he says, 'Sailor! I better not find out ya'll've been crawling through sewers, or so help me God you'll spend the rest of the war scraping paint!"

"Said that to combat Marines?" asked Simons.

"He was a crazy man," Silver said. "I jumped up and sounded off, said, 'Sir! I thank you for your concern, sir! A certain Master Chief Petty Officer's mamasan distilled that for us! A vile harlot, sir! And when I get done scraping paint I'll write that chief's wife a long letter thanking you for being the fine upstanding young man that saved us and her husband from that mamasan's foul clutches! Sir!"

Simons nodded. "And what did he say?"

"Carry on, sailor! Carry on, Marines!"

The amount of laughter surprised PJ. When she looked around the room she realized work had stopped. Everyone had been hanging on Silver's story.

*Now this is more like it,* PJ thought. *He's had this coming for a long time.*

~

"Did you believe in the mission, sir?" Lakeshore asked Silver.

"Believe in the mission, son?"

"I mean, did you think it was right for you to be in Korea?"

"Oh, I see. You were in Iraq?"

"Yessir."

"Had a lot of barracks time?"

"At Al Asad, yessir."

"Well," Silver said, "I guess about all I can say is, in Korea we didn't have much time for that kind of thinking, or at least not at first. Too busy. Later on when we were prisoners we talked about it some, though. I'll tell you this, the Chinese told us we didn't belong there. In their lectures."

"Those were, like, indoctrination lectures?" asked Lakeshore.

Silver studied the scissors in his hand. "That's right. I never heard the word brainwashing until I got home. They tried all kinds of ways to trick us into believing things about ourselves that weren't true. All kinds of ways."

"Such as? If you don't mind my asking?" Lakeshore's face was very serious, very interested, and PJ, at Silver's side, realized the room had grown quiet again.

"I remember," Silver said, "that one time they made us read leaflets. Propaganda cartoons. A dead soldier face-down and under that a fat banker smoking a cigar and counting money. It said, 'You risk your life, big business rakes in the dough.'"

"But these days," he continued, "when you turn on the radio you hear our own people saying that same thing. I don't know how to feel about that. I surely don't."

"Sir," Lakeshore said. "I wish I could tell you we do."

~

Around the room the finished work was piling up. PJ found herself thinking about Silver's pink lady story.

*Those guys really took care of each other back then,* she thought. *And the girls are taking care of me, now, aren't they? I guess it's a good thing.*

*I guess.*

~

Lizzie was fast asleep in her booster seat, and when PJ turned to look at Silver, she expected to see him sleeping too.

He was staring out the windshield instead, his eyes searching back and forth as if he were dreaming or watching a scene play out on the glass a few inches from his face.

"We got a lot of work done tonight," she said.

He seemed to come back to himself. "Did we?"

"Yeah, we did. It was a big help. Huge."

"I'm happy for you," he said. "Your friends are nice. Really made me feel welcome."

He fell silent again and they rode that way for a few more minutes.

"You have fun trading war stories?"

"Hmm?"

"You know. Going over old times with those Marines."

Silver coughed onto the back of his hand. "It brought a few things back." Soon he coughed again.

PJ reached behind her for the box of tissues. "Here you go. You know, I think Roy was a little intimidated. He's the only guy there—and he weighs about a buck-twenty, I think—and in come these warrior Alpha-male types."

Silver was coughing harder, into the tissue. He nodded, got out a strained "Mmm-hmm," and went on coughing.

PJ turned. "Are you OK?"

And that's when she saw the smear of blood on his face.

▶▶▶◆◀◀◀
## Chapter Thirty-Two

"Come on, come on, come on!"

PJ had missed the line she was sewing…again. She lifted the presser foot and cut the thread and yanked the square of fabric out of the machine, and threw it on the pile of others to be redone.

Then she stopped and took a long, deliberate breath.

*Trying to work too fast*, she thought.

But then another side of her said, *Not working fast enough! Maybe they got the bleeding stopped and sent him home, but get real! When you start coughing blood all over the dashboard, how much time do you have left?*

So she bent to her work.

PJ loved this machine, and considered it her most treasured possession. It was a Singer Featherweight, black with gold detailing, and it bore an emblem that said "A Century of Sewing Service 1851–1951." A special machine among special machines, a limited edition to commemorate Singer's hundredth anniversary.

And Bebe had bought it brand new, fifty-seven years ago.

You didn't work with this Featherweight, you communed with it, and communing with it was like communing with all the people who had sewn before you—their heads bowed, their hands carefully positioned, their lips sometimes

324

moving and sometimes still, their minds washed clean of distraction—the same as you did, now.

She finished a block and put it on the done pile and started another one. Eight-thirty, now, at the beginning of another long night. The supper dish that Ross had brought up to her was untouched, but the coffee was long gone. But going down for another cup would interrupt her rhythm, something she was loath to do.

*Reach, feed, step-on-the-pedal. Reach, feed, step-on-the-pedal—*

—and someone knocked at the door. "Mommy?" Lizzie's voice.

The knob turned and Lizzie came into the room as PJ finished another seam.

"What is it, sweetie?" PJ asked without looking up.

"Mommy, look!" Lizzie demanded.

"What?"

"Look!"

PJ took a deep breath and looked. Lizzie was holding out a storebought doll, the horrible one with too much makeup and the gold lamé suit with the big mirrored buttons.

"Baker tore the dress," Lizzie said. "Playing bayonet."

"You probably shouldn't tell me that story," said PJ. "Here, let me see."

She inspected the doll's dress. Sure enough, it was torn along a seam. *Doesn't anyone make nice doll clothing anymore? I could sew something better than this in ten minutes with my elbows broken.*

"Can you fix it?" asked Lizzie, all big-eyed.

"Lizzie, please, I really don't have time. Can you put another dress on her?"

"But it's Tuesday, and that's tea party night."

"Just—Lizzie, take the dress off and leave it with me, and I'll try to get to it."

"Momma!" And PJ saw that Lizzie had tears in her eyes.

"All right, all right," PJ groaned.

Lizzie fumbled with the doll's dress and PJ took it from her and stripped the dress off in one smooth motion. She cleared the piece she'd been working on, found the ripped seam, and went to zip it through the machine.

But she missed the line again—*too fast, too fast!*—and she watched in horror as her own traitorous fingers slid sideways and carried one of the big mirrored buttons right under the needle.

The needle snapped with high *zing!* and PJ winced, expecting to catch it in the face. But where it went was worse. It shot past the needle plate and into the bobbin case, and there was an immediate grinding noise.

PJ jerked her foot off the pedal so fast and hard that she slammed her knee into the underside of her sewing desk, and she yelped in pain as her lower leg went numb.

She yanked out the bobbin case and looked inside. She couldn't see anything wrong, but when she replaced it and turned the handwheel to test the machine, she heard the grinding noise again.

*I broke the machine! I broke Bebe's Featherweight!*

"No, no, no, no!" she yelled, already sobbing with rage, pounding her fists on the desk, the sick pain blooming in her knee. Then she heard a soft noise from Lizzie and she turned to see Lizzie holding her now-naked doll up, an oddly mature and authoritarian look on her face.

"You ruined Momma's machine!" Lizzie scolded the doll. "She was busy working on a quilt for Mr. Silver and you broke it! It's your fault, you're always getting in the way! Pestering! Interrupting! Why can't you go to your room and watch Cinderella and be quiet? Why can't you be a good little girl?"

PJ's heart stutter-stepped.

*Where did she learn that? Who taught her to talk to her doll like that?*

But she knew. Of course she knew.

*Is that what I sound like to my daughter?*

~

PJ was still sitting over the mess she'd made, not crying now, just trying to collect her wits and decide how to keep moving on, when she heard Silver's wheels in the hallway.

"Everything all right?" he asked from the door. His voice was muffled by the oxygen mask he was wearing all the time, now.

She didn't turn around. She took a couple of shaky breaths and tried to wipe her face and nose with her hands—tried to hide her fear and grief and shame from this man who'd endured so much more than she could ever fathom.

He was wearing the Christmas quilt around his shoulders—MY LIFE MY LOVE MY HEART MY HERO. He wore it all the time, now, everywhere, like a young child wrapped in a security blanket, like an old patriot wrapped in a flag.

"I had a little setback," she told him. "I think I'm gonna have to replace some parts in Bebe's old machine."

"Don't you have another one you can use? Seems like I saw three or four around here."

"Oh, they're not the same. This Featherweight—it's like having Bebe in the room with me when I'm working. I've used it on just about every quilt I've ever made, and I think she probably did, too."

"Hmm. Want me to open it up? Have a look?"

"No, the bobbin case is ruined. I'm gonna have to scrounge for parts. Thanks, though, you're sweet."

Silver squinted at the machine. "You know, I do remember that thing. I remember her running up some clothes for a scarecrow on it, for that one garden we kept together. Raggedy pants and a shirt."

"She would've made that quilt you're wearing on it, too. I'm surprised you never found her out."

"She did keep disappearing on me, that's true. Spent a lot of time hiding in that little sewing room of hers. Same as you do."

"Ouch," PJ said.

He raised a hand. "Now, now."

"Ah, it's OK. You're right. This is my little sanctuary— my little battery charger." PJ stretched her arms, arched her back, and felt her spine crackle. "I feel like I've been sitting here ever since we brought you home from the ER the other night."

"You have," said Silver. "Why don't you come downstairs? Ross has the baseball game on."

"No, you're right, I should probably get one of the other machines out. Thanks for checking on me, though."

"PJ," he said, "you can't sit up here sewing for the rest of your life."

"When I finished Blind Woman's Bluff, I sewed for two weeks straight. Ross said I was running on the hamster wheel."

"After Elizabeth died," Silver said.

"That's right."

"Now, PJ, be honest with me. Were you up here sewing, or were you mourning your grandmother?"

She cocked her head. "Why?"

"Because if you're mourning me, you can stop it right now."

PJ ran a finger along the gold filigree on the Featherweight. "Maybe I was mourning her," she said. "Maybe I still am. I wish you'd been there when she—"

~

It was a Sunday afternoon when Pastor Ingram made his shaky way into Bebe's room. "Well, I brought communion," he said, holding up the silver case. "But I see she's asleep again."

"She's been in and out of it all day," said PJ. She was gripping Ross's hand tightly, but Ross let go and stood up and offered his chair to Pastor Ingram.

"Thank you, son," the pastor said, sitting down. He put a thin arm around PJ's shoulders and, in a voice that had lost none of its gentle resonance, began to sing to himself.

PJ didn't recognize the tune, though. A hymn that hovered over the edge of familiarity. She closed her eyes and rocked her head back in forth in time with his singing for a while, and when she opened them again she realized Bebe had opened hers too.

She leaned forward and took Bebe's hand. "Hey, there," she said.

Bebe's lips moved soundlessly. *Cupcake.*

"I'm here. Ross is here, and Pastor Ingram came by. It's Sunday afternoon."

*We missed church?*

PJ nodded.

*Oh.*

"Do you want to take communion, Bebe?"

Bebe nodded.

PJ turned to Pastor Ingram. He stood up beside the bed and opened the case on the arm of it. A thimble-sized cup, a tiny silver plate, a vial of wine, and a small wooden box of unleavened bread.

"Could we pray together?" Pastor Ingram said. He took Bebe's hand and offered his other to PJ, who took it and offered hers to Ross.

They all closed their eyes.

"Lord, we're with your servant Elizabeth Warner today, and we want to ask you to be mindful of her as she prepares for the journey home. Help Elizabeth understand that yours is the power to conquer death, and just as surely as your son rose from the grave on the third day, Elizabeth will be reunited with her loved ones in your light, on the day when all things are made new.

"And, Lord, we ask your blessings on this wine and bread. Let those who partake be washed pure in spirit, blemishless in your sight. In Christ's name we ask this, amen."

"Amen," Ross echoed.

*Amen,* Bebe mouthed.

PJ squeezed the men's hands and released them.

Pastor Ingram opened the little box and placed a wafer of bread on the plate. "This is my body," he said, and he broke off a crumb and placed it on Bebe's lips.

She nodded, and he passed the plate to PJ. She broke the wafer in half and put in her mouth. Ross did the same.

The pastor poured wine into the cup. "This is my blood," he said, and he touched the cup to Bebe's lips, wetting them.

PJ took the cup from him, sipped it, and gave it to Ross.

"There," Pastor Ingram said as he took the cup back from Ross. And then he added the same sentence PJ had heard him add after every communion she'd ever heard him offer:

"We have witnessed a miracle," the old man said.

Bebe smiled faintly. "Yes, we have," she whispered. Her chest rose, and fell, and rose again.

PJ waited for it to fall. And waited.

"Bebe?" she said, still waiting. "*Bebe!*"

~

"She was still smiling when she died," PJ said.

Silver bowed his head and gathered the quilt more closely around his shoulders.

"Anyway," PJ said, wiping her eyes and standing up, "I need to get something to drink. Care for anything?"

"Some of that iced tea," Silver said.

PJ went downstairs and poured two glasses, but on impulse she went into the TV room, to where Ross sat on the couch watching the Braves game, and she put her arms around Ross's neck and kissed him on the cheek.

"I love you," she said.

"You too," he replied. "What was that for?"

"For you."

"Cool. Check it out, it's the seventeenth inning."

"No way," she said. "People are still at the park?"

"Still hanging in there."

"Well, so am I," she said. She unwound her arms from around his neck and fetched the glasses from the kitchen and went back upstairs.

"Ah," Silver said when she came in. He pulled at the oxygen mask and she set her glass down and removed it for him.

"That canned air dries me out," he said, sipping noisily. "Thanks. And thanks for telling me that. About Elizabeth."

"It's comforting that…um, well, she went straight to heaven, right? How can you not, if you die right after taking communion?"

"Leave it to her," Silver said. "She'll be up there sewing baby blankets with the Virgin Mary."

PJ tried to smile. "That's funny."

Silver set his glass down and cleared his throat. "And I'll be shoveling coal."

"Don't say that. You know, it says somewhere in the Bible, I think, that the size of your reward is directly related to the amount you've suffered. You're a shoo-in."

"Everybody I've *ever* known is a shoo-in," said Silver. He winced, put his hand to his chest, and coughed slightly.

PJ was instantly on alert. "Silver?"

"Sorry, I swallowed the wrong way. What was I saying?"

"About shoo-ins."

"Oh, right. That was it, most people are shoo-ins."

"OK," PJ said. "I really hope you're right about that, because most days I'm not doing a very good job down here."

"Hmm," Silver said.

PJ gave herself a mental kick. *There you go again.*

"Um...well," she said, "I told you pretty much my most important memory of Bebe. What's yours?"

"Most important memory? That's a good question." He exhaled through pursed lips, then smiled slyly. "I wouldn't want to say."

"Is it something naughty?"

"Not really. Sort of."

PJ grinned. "Come on, now, you've got me all worked up."

"Well. Your grandmother...she was..."

"Joe Piper, are you blushing?"

"...was such a good kisser."

"Oh, gross!" PJ said. Then she closed her mouth and thought about it. "You know," she said at last, "that's the sweetest thing I think I've ever heard anyone say. I think there was a time—not long ago—hearing that would've really made me angry. Like somebody tracking dirt on white carpet. But when you think about it, what a great way to be remembered."

"It's a great memory," Silver said. "One time she said..."

He put his hand to his chest again, and his face grew pained.

PJ watched him. "Silver?"

He coughed with difficulty, and PJ saw a dot of pink froth at the corner of his mouth.

"I'm gonna go get help," she said. "You stay right here, OK?"

Silver shook his head and gasped. "No, I'm alright, I don't need any help. Listen to me, I was telling you…"

He coughed again, onto the back of his hand, and she saw bright blood.

"Just stay right there," she said, backing out of the sewing room.

She heard him calling her as she sprinted to the stairs. "PJ, listen to me!" he called. But she didn't turn back; she took the stairs at a running leap and stuck her head into the TV room.

"Ross, get an ambulance!" she yelled, and she was back up the stairs in a heartbeat.

She doubled the corner and she could see through the sewing room doorway that something wasn't right. He was half out of his wheelchair, sprawled across the sewing desk, his head turned away from her, very still, and blood pooled around Bebe's sewing machine.

"Silver?" she said, coming to him and putting her hand on his back. He didn't answer, or move.

PJ knelt and looked into Silver's face. There was more blood on his lips and his tongue protruded and his eyes were rolled high in their sockets.

She stood up and almost immediately felt her legs give way beneath her. PJ fell, and fell, and fell. And falling, she saw that Silver was clutching a handful of the hearts she'd sewn for him.

## ▶▶▶◆◀◀◀
## Chapter Thirty-Three

People came and went from her bedroom. Baker and Lizzie. Ellen and Roy once, and Missy, and even Flo. They said things to her. PJ hid under the quilts—hid from the people who came, hid from the things they said.

*How many days since they took Silver, now? Three? Four? A week?*

*My whole life?*

Ross had taken to sleeping on the couch but he'd bring her hot food and take the cold food away. Sometimes he'd sit on the bed and plead with her for hours.

"You're still getting calls about Silver's quilt," he'd say.

"PJ, your mom's on the phone."

"PJ, you need to let me change the sheets."

And once: "PJ, the house is on fire."

But the house wasn't on fire. She knew that, as assuredly as she knew the world was embedded in ice, devoid of so much as a single degree of heat.

So she stayed in bed, burying herself under the quilts the way she'd once buried her Grandpa David under them. She'd close her eyes tightly and trace the patterns on the quilts, blind, trying to remember where and who she was when she'd sewn each stitch.

Among the quilts on the bed was the old one Silver and

the men had made in the camp. The one Bebe had made for Silver for Christmas. PJ had raided the Louvre for the Family Tree, and she'd taken Grandpa David's little Nine-Patch down from the top shelf of her sewing closet. They were all there, all of her quilts, her whole life, her triumphs and failures piling onto her in a weight she sometimes hoped might be enough to smother her.

When the weight felt like it wasn't enough, and sometimes when it felt like it was too much, she'd reach for the cardboard box on the nightstand. What the box held was as heavy as sand, as grey as stone, and though it was the product of a searing flame, it was now as cold as PJ knew her heart would always be.

*An inch of love is an inch of ashes.*

And she'd think, *Silver, what were you trying to tell me? Why did I have to go for help? Why couldn't I listen to you tell me about Bebe? What secret did you share with her, that you carried for so long?*

But Silver's voice never came. Sometimes, in its place, she heard the voice of the triage nurse from the hospital in Monticello.

*"Unless someone comes forward, indigent John Does like this one wind up in the county cemetery with no headstone."*

PJ knew she'd failed at many things. She'd failed as a granddaughter, a daughter, a wife, a mother. She'd failed as a quilter. And now she'd failed as a healer, too. She'd failed to heal Silver, and she'd failed to heal herself.

And that was the worst of it all, the realization that since she'd failed, Silver would forever be disgraced. Forever, in the eyes of history, a deserter cast out under "other than honorable conditions."

No honor guard would stand over him. No flag would drape him. No bugle would blow for him. No headstone would bear witness to his service.

And it was her fault.

In this shame, simple and terrible, PJ passed her days.

~

It was early afternoon and there was activity in the house. Cars outside, the doorbell ringing, distant voices. And then a strange quietude, totally atypical for that time of day. Not a sound from anywhere. At the very least she ought to be able to hear the kids. Something was going on.

She got up and went to the bedroom door and locked it. She thought about pulling the curtains back and looking outside to see who might've come over, but she really didn't want to know. It was probably Ross having a buddy or two over to catch the game. It was the weekend, wasn't it? They'd be down in the basement in front of the big-screen, so she could go back to bed and forget about the outside world.

Presently the doorknob rattled.

*Go away,* PJ thought. She rolled over, turning her back to the door.

The knob fell still for a moment and then she heard scraping at the lock. And then she heard the door swing open.

"Cupcake," said a voice. "It's time to get up, Cupcake."

*I must be hallucinating,* PJ thought. *Or dead. That's Bebe's voice.*

She pulled the quilts over her head. *Please, go away.*

"This is ridiculous," her grandmother said. "Stop acting like a two year-old."

"Leave me alone, Bebe," PJ moaned. "I don't need your help."

"What?"

PJ felt the quilts being stripped away from her. Suddenly she was naked in the cold air, and the lights glared into her eyes, and she curled into a fetal position and hid her eyes with her hands.

"PJ, look at me!" said Bebe. "It's time to get dressed!"

PJ opened her eyes angrily—

—to see Anne standing there.

"Mom?"

"Here," said Anne. She was holding out clothes. Underwear and jeans and a t-shirt. And PJ's glasses. "Put these on and go in the bathroom and wash your face and brush your teeth."

"I don't—"

"Do it right now," Anne said in a no-sass-from-you-young-lady tone.

PJ got up slowly, not taking her eyes off Anne. She slid into her clothes and then she stooped to the pile of quilts where Anne had tossed them onto the floor. She sorted out Silver's old quilt and wrapped it around her shoulders.

"What do you need that for?" Anne asked. "It's the middle of summer."

"I'm freezing," PJ said.

~

Anne stopped her in the kitchen, poured her a cup of coffee and dosed it with sugar and cream and put it in her hand.

PJ sipped it and hugged the old quilt tighter. "Where is everybody?"

"Sit down and drink your coffee and don't ask questions," Anne said. She went to the cabinet and took out a box of cereal and poured PJ a bowl. Then she stopped at the refrigerator door and reached into her pants pocket, and took out a pack of cigarettes and lit one.

"Mom? You can't smoke in here—"

Anne took an unsteady drag on the cigarette, glared at PJ for an instant, and opened the refrigerator door and looked inside.

"The milk's ten days out of date," she said in a moment. She frowned, picked up the cereal bowl, and put it and a spoon in front of PJ. "You're going to have to eat this dry."

"My God, the kitchen's a wreck. What's going on?"

"Eat your cereal!"

PJ put a spoonful in her mouth. Sickly-sweet stuff, bright yellow. It was good, and she crunched the spoonful and took more.

Anne looked at her watch. She took a final hit on her cigarette and smushed it into an ash tray PJ hadn't noticed—that was full of butts, in fact—and said, "OK, let's top your coffee off."

"I'm not doing anything," PJ said, "until you tell me what this is all about."

Anne held out the coffee pot. "You'll find out in about thirty seconds."

~

"Open the door," Anne said. "The answers are in the basement."

"What answers?" PJ said, standing at the door.

"Open the door and go downstairs and you'll see," said Anne.

*This is crazy,* PJ thought. But she put her hand on the door and pushed it open.

As she made her way down the stairs, she realized the basement was full of people. They hushed when they saw her.

~

Half a world and half a century away, First Lieutenant David Warner lay on his belly atop a sharp and stony ridgeline, scanning the maze of canyons that spread below him. Nothing moved. He glassed the brush with his binoculars, strained his ears, sniffed the air, and even tried to *feel* for the enemy. But if the Chinese were there, they gave no sign.

His breath made puffs of white. "This is giving me the creeps, Gunny," he whispered to the man beside him. "It's too quiet down there."

"Where are the refugees?" the gunnery sergeant whispered back.

"Exactly. They've been pouring through here for two weeks and now they've vanished? No." Warner frowned. "Tell you what. Pick three and start 'em down. Use that sneaky one, Halwell."

The gunnery sergeant laughed quietly. "You got it." And he crept away as Warner lifted his binoculars to his eyes again.

~

"Oh, my God," PJ said. "What is this? Ross, is this—have you—"

She spun and started back up the stairs, and there was Anne, blocking her way, hands up. "PJ, hang on, this'll just take a minute."

"Mom—"

"Will you just trust me? Will you just for once in your life trust me?"

"Trust you?" PJ sputtered. "Trust *you?*"

"PJ," Ross called, standing. "Come on, OK? Just—"

PJ barely heard him. There, on the enormous three-sided couch that Ross called the "conversation pit," sat several people—Ellen and Roy holding hands with Missy beside them; Kelly Green Shaw with a notebook in her lap; PJ's OB/GYN, Doctor Dawson; and a sportscoat-clad man that she'd never met.

"Doctor Dawson? What are you doing here?"

Dawson looked at the man in the sportscoat.

Sportscoat stood up. "PJ, my name is Ted West. Think of me as a moderator, for a conversation your friends and family want to have with you today. Why don't you come join us?"

Ross sat down and scooched sideways to make room for her, but she stood her ground. "Ross? Do you want to tell me what's going on?"

"I'll explain everything," Ted said.

"Sit down, PJ," Anne said, coming up behind her and resting her hands on PJ's shoulders.

PJ shied away. "Get your hands off me!" she yelled.

~

The men the gunnery sergeant chose, with Halwell at point, melted over the ridgeline and down the first ravine. Warner had never even heard them creeping up behind him.

*Low and slow, boys,* he thought.

They advanced fifty feet, seventy-five. The wind whistled in Warner's face, the strong Siberian bayonet wind, and though fresh water leaked from his eyes and trickled down his cheeks to join the ice in his beard, he neither blinked nor shielded his eyes. He watched his men, their every step.

Halwell held up at a stunted pine and looked back up at the ridge. He spoke in hand signs. *Ahead, ahead, ahead.* Then he shrugged.

Warner frowned again. He signaled the gunnery sergeant to rejoin him.

~

PJ moved away from Anne and glowered at Ross. "Well?" she demanded. "Are you gonna say anything? Are you at least gonna tell me where Lizzie and Baker are?"

"Lizzie and Baker are at Flo's," Ross said. "They're fine."

"In other words, you got them out of the house so they wouldn't see what you're doing to me. Nice." She pressed her fists into her eyes. "I don't believe this is happening. I want everybody out of here, right now."

"If that's what you want, it's OK," said Ted. "Give us a chance to say what we came to say, and we'll leave. It's that simple."

She glanced up, crossed her arms. Then, for the first time, she noticed the Marine in dress blues sitting in a chair in the corner. Hispanic-looking, his expression unreadable. Wearing silver colonel's eagles and four rows of ribbons. He met her eyes and nodded to her.

PJ gestured at him. "Who in God's name is *that?*"

"Don't worry about him," said Anne.

"PJ," Ted said, "listen to me. What everybody here wants to say, is, they all love you very much. Do you understand how much love there is in the room today, how lucky you are to have these people?"

"If luck means getting ambushed in your basement—being embarrassed to death—then sure, I'm a very lucky woman. My life is totally complete. I wouldn't change a thing."

Ted steepled his hands under his chin. "Good, then this'll be quick. Would anyone like to start?"

PJ tugged at the old quilt. "Start what?"

~

"Get the BAR up here to reinforce those three," Warner whispered. "And then I want you to lead four more down. Spread them out two on each side, and you stay back about twenty feet. See if you can figure out what Halwell sees."

The gunnery sergeant nodded. "That'll leave you a little thin back here, if anyone comes up from behind us."

"Yeah, I know. But I think if they hit us they'll hit us from the north. If we're already surrounded, there's nothing we can do about it anyway."

"What about occupying this ridge for a few hours?"

"Gunny, I guess that might work if we had good radio— we could spot for battalion—but..." and Warner shook his head.

"If wishes were horses," whispered the gunnery sergeant, "I'd eat one."

"Right. I guess the best we can hope for is to confirm they're here and get the word back."

"Happy Thanksgiving, Lieutenant."

"Happy Thanksgiving, Gunny. Now get down that hill."

~

"Dear PJ," Ellen read.

"Where are you? I'd address this letter to you, but I don't know where to send it. It's like you've gone somewhere else and shut the door behind you and the rest of us aren't allowed to come in. I don't know where that place is, or why you like it so much, but I don't think it's a place where there's very much laughter.

"I love you because you make me laugh. And I hate you a little, because you're such a better quilter than I am. But mostly I love you. And it's hard to be around you right now, because you've stopped laughing."

"Of all the melodramatic—" PJ cut in.

"Let her finish, let her finish," Ted said. "You'll get your turn."

**340**

"I want to hear you laughing again, which is why I'm here today. I want to ask you to get help for what you're going through. I love you, PJ, and I want you to come back to us. I know that's not easy for you to hear, but you need to hear it. You need to get help."

Ellen looked up from the letter, at PJ first, and then at Ted.

"Do you understand what Ellen means, PJ?" he asked.

"As I was saying," PJ said, "of all the melodramatic—"

~

The gunnery sergeant peered through the brush and turned back and waved at Warner.

*Four, ahead, civilian,* his hand signals said.

Warner nodded. Refugees, or at least people trying to pass as refugees.

It complicated things; the orders were to handle refugees gently, but sometimes the old man you thought was a refugee was really a young man in a robe, bowed over, with a half-dozen grenades wired together. So it paid to be careful.

Warner turned to the BAR corporal beside him. "I'm going down. Gather them here, string them out along the ridge twenty feet apart, and for God's sake, keep your eyes open. If it happens, it's gonna happen fast."

~

"You didn't see this coming, and you're angry," Ted said. "It's completely understandable. We'll stop whenever you want us to. All you have to do, is tell these people who love you that you're willing to get help for your depression."

PJ, still standing, looked around the room. "Depression?"

Ted's patience infuriated her. "PJ, sadness is a perfectly natural part of life," he said. "You go down and down and it seems like you can't swim back up. Tell me, now, do you think what you're going through is temporary? That if you could just get caught up on things, or if you keep pushing on, everything'll work out and nobody'll be the wiser?"

"That's how life is!" she said.

"OK, OK," he said. "How about this? Do you feel guilty when things don't go your way? Like somehow everything that goes on around you is your fault? Like you're responsible for it, even if you can't control it?"

"What are we really talking about, here?" she asked. "Have none of you ever had a bad day? Overworked yourselves, or been worried about something?"

"Four years of bad days?" Ross said.

"Don't talk to me about bad days, Ross, not after betraying me into your little freak show, here. I wish the planet would just *swallow* me right now! Ritual humiliation is the last thing I need, the very last thing."

"What's the first thing you need?" Ted asked.

"I don't know. Your absence?"

Ted nodded. "Go on."

"Did it not occur to any of you that maybe I need a vacation? Just a few days to catch up on sleep?"

"PJ," said Dr. Dawson, "there's every chance that your insomnia is caused by a chemical imbalance. And we can correct that with drug therapy, but a human being is a lot more than just chemicals bumping into each other. We need to work on you, in a structured program—"

"Did all of you guys write letters?" PJ interrupted. "All of you?"

Some nodded and some said yes.

"Keep reading," she said. "I want to hear every word of this."

~

Warner inched through the snow, trying to keep the muzzle of his rifle clear, with the gunnery sergeant trailing him. Down the ravine, maybe twenty-five feet away, he could see the four civilians seated under a pine tree, their backs to him. A man and a woman, a boy and a girl.

He felt the gunnery sergeant tugging at his boot. Warner turned to see him mouthing words.

*Wire. Wire. Wire.*

Warner nodded. He lay watching the civilians and it came to him that the littlest one, a girl of no more than four or five, was naked from the waist up. But there were no wounds on her that he could see, and she lacked that peculiar frozen rigidity he'd seen so often in the dead.

But why did she hold so still? She wasn't even shivering.

~

Kelly read a short letter praising PJ's skill as a quilter and encouraging her, for the sake of her art, to get treatment.

Roy read a song he'd written, called "Cowboy Up," that thanked her for ridin' out west to rescue a feller in trouble, and that said she orta whistle up a posse of her own.

But it was Missy who drew the first blood.

"PJ, I know it's tough having kids," she read. "'War on your chest,' right? There were times I wanted to give up, asked God to take the cup away.

"My sister told me I had the baby blues. I guess I was lucky, mine went away. I don't think yours have. You need to find out why. And you need help to do that. This isn't something you can do on your own."

"I don't need help," PJ said. "I don't need help. I don't need help."

~

*That radio would've been a huge help,* Warner thought.

He put his lips to the gunnery sergeant's ear. "This is all we need to see. They're here, close by. There's probably a half-dozen set-ups like this, trapped, and when one goes they'll know they've got us. We gotta double-time it back up that ridge if we want to get out of here. Make it happen, and I'll keep watch."

The gunnery sergeant nodded and began crawling backwards, back towards the fire team.

~

"Dear PJ," Ross read. His lips tightened and she realized he was struggling to keep his face composed.

"First off, I love you so much and I'm so lonely for you. This spring I got more afraid than I'd ever been in my life. I had planned something like what we're doing today back then, to help you, but you were going to Utah one way or another, with me or without me, and I had to come along. And when I saw you with Silver, when I saw how determined you were to help him, I thought maybe the best thing to do was let you lift yourself out of what you're going through."

He looked up at her. "I was wrong."

Then he returned his eyes to his letter. "I want you to know that I don't blame you for any of this. You gave us two beautiful children and you're my best friend. But like I said once, my best friend has checked out on me, and I want her back."

"PJ," he said, "please. Let us get you the help you need."

PJ turned to Ted. "What kind of help are they talking about?"

"There's a place called Pinetree Grove, in north Georgia, that has a good program for women who are suffering from postpartum depression," Ted said. "It involves a hospital stay—"

"*What?*" she cried.

"—and regular follow-ups. Treatment with antidepressants, possibly hormones. Whatever's appropriate."

"Postpartum? Are you telling me this is all in my ovaries? In my glands? That what I'm going through isn't real?"

"No, no, no," he said. "Look, fear is always real. It doesn't matter what it's fear of—of being shot in the head, or fear of falling, or even fear of flying spaghetti monsters. It's all real, and it needs to be addressed as such."

"My problems are not mental or chemical," she stated. "I lose my grandmother. My grandfather dies just when I'm getting acquainted with him. I have to make a quilt the size of a garage door because the Navy screwed him over fifty years ago. My mom won't speak to me. My father wishes he'd never heard of me. My kids—" and she stopped

344

herself, reconsidering. "My kids are beautiful, but they're high-energy."

"And my husband—Ross, when I need you to be here for me you're either on a road trip, or…or plotting some meeting, some stupid intervention, to pull me back off an edge I'm not even standing on. I can't believe you even considered this! Aren't you the one who said we should talk our problems out instead of numbing them with drugs?"

"It's easy to believe that," Ross said weakly, "when it's not happening to someone you love."

"Whose gonna take care of the kids, Ross? Not to mention cleaning up around here! Keeping everybody fed? You'll get a maid? A nanny? A chef?"

"I'm sorry," he said. "I've made a lot of mistakes, PJ. I'm sorry. And I'll do whatever I have to do. Change jobs, start staying home more. I'll even come along with you if that's what I need to do. Whatever it takes. But the most important thing is that you recognize that you need help. And ask for it. Please?"

PJ shook her head. "And I guess you're going to finish Silver's quilt and coordinate his discharge appeal, too. Come on, Ross. I don't have room in my life for any more problems! There's nobody else who can handle this stuff except me!"

Ellen's expression was stubborn. "I swear, that's the most selfish thing I've ever heard you say," she interjected. "Look what happened when you asked us to help you with Silver's quilt! It was great! And we'll finish it with you, if you'll just climb down off your high horse. There's a whole roomful of Blockheads who feel like I do about you, and there ought to be one or two of us you can trust with a needle."

"The answer is no," PJ said. "En Oh. Now, who's next? Mom? What about you?"

▶▶◆◀◀
## Chapter Thirty-Four

*B*urp gun, Warner thought. *Now it starts.*

He'd crawled to the Korean family, as carefully as he'd ever moved in his life, to see what kind of snare the Chinese had set. And the gunnery sergeant had called it right; thin wires led from the strangled bodies of the children away into the bushes, stretched as tautly as the nerves of a man staring down the barrel of a gun.

And now the Chinese were shooting over his head, at his men, and the hills echoed with that distinctive ripping B-RRR-PPP! their automatics made.

He turned, keeping low, and began crawling back to where the gunnery sergeant waited—expecting to be lifted and smashed and smeared across the rocks and earth and brush at any instant.

~

"Dear PJ," Anne read.

"I'm writing this, not to ask you to ask for help, but to ask you to help me."

"That sounds about right," PJ said.

Anne sighed. "I ran out on you when you were a little girl, because I was dealing with my own problems, and I never stopped to think that maybe your needs were more important than mine."

"So what are you doing here now?" PJ interrupted. "Did Ross shame you into coming back?"

Ted said, "PJ, let her read her letter."

"You wrote me once," Anne continued, "that you were scared to death about getting married, and you needed my help. And now I need yours. I know I've mentioned Luis to you, but he was good enough to come today."

The Marine in the corner stood up and nodded at PJ again. He had wide shoulders and rich brown skin and his close-cropped hair was salt-and-pepper.

"Luis...uh, Luis and I are thinking about getting married," Anne kept reading. "And I'm the one who's holding it up. Because I look at you, PJ, and I think, what do I know about men?"

"What's that supposed to mean?" PJ asked. "You wrote the book."

"You did your first time out, what I've been trying to do my whole life," Anne read. "Ross is the perfect man for you. And now I've found my perfect man, and I don't know what to do. And I need your help. He wants me to marry him this fall, and I keep putting him off, because I know I'm not ready. And I think you're the only one who can help me get ready."

"Been in any combat, Luis?" PJ asked.

~

Warner and the gunnery sergeant lay a few feet apart, firing at muzzle flashes as the light faded and the night came on. The whole fire team was pinned down. They were only a couple of dozen yards from the ridgeline, but to cross that open space was to die in the sights of the Chinese gunners.

There was sporadic fire from the BAR above them at the ridgeline, but Warner doubted whether it was doing much good. The brush below them was just too thick, and there were too many Chinese.

*No surrender,* Warner thought.

~

"Mrs. Hathaway," Luis said, a bit of Old Mexico still gracing his speech, "what Anne says is true. Your mother and I love each other and we want to get married. But your mother thought, and I agree, that it was important to…repair our own houses, let's say, before we unite them. I have children I don't see very often, and I'm working on that. So I'll ask for your patience."

"Um…sure," PJ stammered, her anger momentarily cooled by his courtesy and courtliness.

But only momentarily.

"Well, Mom," she said, "you finally found yourself a Marine. No disrespect, Colonel. But too bad it couldn't've been Grandpa David, or even Silver. I mean, he was just a Navy puke, but—"

"STOP IT!" Anne yelled. "I feel bad enough already!"

"You should feel bad! You didn't care about your father, you robbed me of mine, and now you're gonna get married to some guy I don't even know?"

"Robbed you?" Anne said. "Didn't care? Bebe robbed me of my father! Do you think I didn't care about that? Of course I cared, that's why I had to leave! Every time I said your name, it reminded me of her lies!"

PJ said, "What about yours?" She started ticking them off on her fingers. "You missed my wedding. You weren't there when Bebe died. You breezed in late to her funeral. You fought with us over the money from the sale of her house. You acted like you were the one who gave birth to Lizzie and Baker, not me. You never even bothered to come meet Silver, when he might have been your real father. And now, when my husband wants to commit me, you're on the first plane East so you won't miss the show."

"PJ," said Ross, "you need to stop and think—"

"Letting her get this out is important," Ted said. "Go on, PJ."

348

Anne looked at Ted helplessly, and PJ laid into her again.

~

The night wore on. Warner thought it might never end.

He'd been hopeful they could sneak away under cover of darkness, but every few minutes the Chinese would fire illumination flares over the ridgeline. One of his men had been hit and was crying, which was bad, and another of his men had been hit and was silent, which was worse.

*I have thirty rounds left,* he thought. *For thirty thousand Chinamen, or a hundred and thirty thousand.*

When the morning came, Warner felt the sunrise like a hammer-blow across his whole body.

He inched his way to the gunnery sergeant. The man's eyes were red with sleeplessness but he smiled. "Hotcha-hotcha, Lieutenant. Man could burn himself out here."

"Hotcha-hotcha yourself," whispered Warner. "You ready to make a run for it?"

"Say the word."

"I'm gonna crawl back down there. There's a ditch just the other side of that family they slaughtered. I'm gonna hide there and see if I can set those booby traps off from a safe distance. Then I'm gonna jump up and see if I can bag a few of these Chinese."

"You're out of your mind," said the gunnery sergeant.

~

From the shelter of the old quilt, PJ grilled her mother. "What's in this for you, anyway, Mom? Don't tell me you came all the way out here because you love me?"

"Of course I love you," Anne said. "How can you say that?"

"Because you're nothing but the worst kind of self-absorbed baby boomer!" PJ yelled. "You talk about peace and love all the time, but the only thing you care about is your own self-gratification!"

She was in the groove of it now—she'd forgotten what it

felt like to let her fury fly, like this—and she felt the delicious coldness welling up in her from her very soul.

"You know, when Grandpa David died you called Bebe a hypocrite, but have you ever looked in a mirror? No, I take that back—you probably stare into mirrors for hours, admiring the high state of your own perfection. You disgust me. Look what you put me through, what you're putting my family through. Look at Lizzie and Baker! They wouldn't even be having to watch me go through this if you'd been around to take care of me when I was their age. I'm turning into a monster right in front of their eyes!"

She leveled a finger at Anne. "And I'm not going to do it!"

Anne was weeping now. "I deserve it, I know," she sobbed through her hands.

"IT'S NOT! ABOUT! YOU!" PJ screamed.

The others in the room sat frozen.

Then Ted spoke, in a voice as calm and reasonable as two plus two. "Who's it about, PJ? Because if it isn't about them…"

"It's about me," she finished, and she felt something break in her when she admitted it.

"That's absolutely right, PJ," Ted said. "Very good. Nobody in this room is here for themselves. We're all here for you. Every one of us. So are you saying you want our help? Are you saying you'll go get treatment?"

~

It was tough, creeping forward under all this weight. The rifle and the extra cartridges of ammo, and the grenades. But Warner found strength flowing from somewhere.

He lay in the ditch, panting. He could hear the Chinese, now, coming closer.

The thread felt loose in his hand. He'd woven it around the hilt of his Ka-Bar, once upon a time when his life made sense, never imagining that something so simple as a thread could become so important to him. He'd unwoven it when he reached the tripwires, wrapped it around and around them, and kept moving forward.

And now he was here, and it was time.

*They should be ready,* he thought. *As soon as I blow these things, they should take off.*

He jerked the thread and he felt a clicking vibration come through it. The slam he'd been expecting finally came, as gouts of bark and splintered wood and frozen dirt-clods erupted in chaos. He felt himself lifted from the ditch and dashed to the earth elsewhere, ears ringing, stunned.

Then he saw them, feet away. The wide eyes of Chinese soldiers.

The Chinese pointed, screamed words he couldn't hear above the roaring still going on in his head. He leaped to his feet, surprised to find himself still holding his rifle. And he screamed back at the Chinese and fired into their ranks without mercy.

*Send help, boys,* he prayed to the Marines that he knew were even now scaling the ridge to safety. *Send help.*

Something pierced him somewhere, a hot wire flaying every nerve in his arm. The pain was colossal. It came a second time, in his side this time, transfixing him where he stood, spilling warmth down his hip and down his thighs and into his boots.

Then the pain ebbed. Only the warmth remained. He screamed, and fired.

And Lieutenant David Warner, believing himself near death, saw the face of his wife.

*This is what good folks do, Elizabeth,* he thought. And as he felt the first of the rifle butts come down on his skull, he was smiling.

~

"I will never," PJ said, "leave my kids like my mom left me."

"Let's talk about the kids," Ross said. "Let's talk about what they need."

PJ felt her knees shaking, whether from anger or fear she couldn't tell. "How would you know what they need? You're hardly ever home!"

"But that's what they need," he said. "I mean—PJ, you and I are supposed to be a unit. A team."

"And you think I've been letting the team down, is that it?"

"No," he said, and the humility in his face and tone surprised her. "If anything, I'm the one who's been doing that."

"What are you telling me?"

Ross glanced at Ted. "I...the words..."

"Just say what you feel," Ted said.

Ross looked back to PJ and took a deep breath. "Lizzie and Baker will never be the most important things in my life. No, don't look at me like that. It's you, PJ, you're the most important thing to me. And we have to put each other first—individually—so we can put them first together. Does that make sense? If we don't have a strong marriage, then what do they have? Nothing, that's what. A house full of plastic junk and a hundred channels of garbage on the TV."

"How does doing this to me," PJ said, waving a hand at the room, "make our marriage stronger? How does forcing me to leave you and the kids make our marriage stronger?"

Ross stood up and came to her. He searched her face—she saw now, how red his eyes were—and he took her face in his hands, so gently, and looked into her eyes.

"Don't you see," he said, his face an inch from hers, "that you've already left us?"

She tried to resist, tried to pull back, but he reached to her shoulders and unwrapped the old quilt from her shoulders and dropped it behind her on the floor.

And the coldness, the God-awful coldness that was as much a part of PJ as her own heartbeat, built and swelled and warred against Ross's warmth until it throttled her whole world to black.

"Do you really think I left you, Ross?" PJ finally asked, to break its hold on her. "Did I really leave you?"

She buried her face in his chest. His breath was warm in her hair and he clung to her as she clung to him.

"Then I'll go get help," she whispered. "If you promise to be here when I come back."

## Epilogue: Heroes Reaching Up

*Lord, bless my friends,*
*If that's part of your plan.*
*And go with us tonight,*
*when we go out again.*

—from "A Hospital Corpsman's Prayer"

A pair of police motorcycles led the hearse through the gates of Chattanooga National Cemetery, and following the hearse came first the limousines and then the cars and trucks. Headlights lit, windshield wipers battling the winter drizzle.

The procession circled the hill at the center of the cemetery, the hill that was encircled by monuments to men and women killed on foreign soil, the hill that overlooked Chattanooga and was crowned by an American flag flying at half-staff.

PJ looked through the window across the fields of white headstones. *So many. Bebe and Grandpa David and so many.*

Her limousine followed the road around the hill towards a steel-colored lake. On its shore, the concrete dome of the committal shelter stood sentry over the funeral bier. The wind troubled the lake and lashed sheets of rain between the columns of the dome, but the bier stood dry at the center of it.

The limousine stopped at the walkway to the shelter. A white-gloved hand opened the limo door and PJ looked up into the stony face of a Marine. She glanced at the other passengers—Ross, Lizzie, Baker, Anne, and Luis, and she nodded at them all and smiled warmly and climbed out as the Marine saluted them.

As Luis exited, he returned the salute. Anne took his arm, and PJ took Ross's hand. The men held umbrellas over the women and children as they walked to the side of the bier where the chairs waited.

Other people began trickling in. People PJ recognized, people she didn't. The Blockheads and Ross's coworkers. Jerry Vicente and Charles Lowell. Other friends, other neighbors. A line of old men in the blue garrison caps of the American Legion, and another line of old men in the red garrison caps of the Marine Corps League.

They stood around the bier and the dome together, waiting in silence.

And now there was a measured heel-clicking, and three Marines came slowly down the walkway, the first bearing the urn, the second bearing a folded flag.

The first Marine placed the urn on the bier and came

slowly into a salute, and the second and third spread the flag over the urn, their every movement as fluid and as deliberate as PJ remembered from Grandpa David's service, years ago. They too saluted, and then withdrew.

"Is Mr. Silver under that flag?" Baker whispered.

"No," said PJ. "It's just something he left us to remember him by."

The rain was stopping. Beside the walkway, between the dome and the hearse, PJ saw Ellen saying something to Roy and Missy and Kelly and Crystal. The five of them walked quickly up the walkway and across the drive to where cars were parked.

Luis stood and crossed the space under the dome to a pulpit that had been set up. He carried his field cap under his arm and, as PJ had asked him to do, he wore Grandpa David's Mameluke sword on his left hip.

"Ladies and gentleman," he began.

"We're here in this place today to say farewell to Pharmacist's Mate Second Class Joseph Montgomery Piper. But as I look out across these hallowed grounds, and I see the markers over other warriors and healers, it puts me in mind of the hallowed grounds of Arlington National Cemetery, where the remains of many of our country's heroes are interred."

"And the quilt that you see being set up now is named 'Heart for a Hero.'"

PJ looked up and saw Ellen and the others draping the huge quilt across the display stand. Seven hundred and more hearts strong, each a story now captured and never to be forgotten. And all of them drifting down to settle into the hands of a man who'd lived and died a healer.

"A special woman," Luis continued, "my daughter-in-law, dreamed of using that quilt to battle an injustice that was done to Joseph Piper some fifty-five years ago. And she made that dream a reality, despite her own battles—battles she fought and won."

*I did win, didn't I?* PJ thought. She looked up into Ross's face and smiled. He smiled back, and she knew that as long as they were together, she'd never be cold.

*No, I didn't win. It was us. We did.*

"But," Luis said, "the injustice done to Pharmacist's Mate Second Class Piper puts me again in mind of the hallowed grounds of Arlington National Cemetery, and an injustice that was perpetrated there on the morning of eleven September, two thousand one. For Arlington National Cemetery is the last place American Airlines Flight Seventy-Seven flew over before crashing into the Pentagon."

Luis's knuckles whitened on the sides of the pulpit, and his voice grew deeper. "I like to think of our fallen heroes, reaching up, trying to hold that aircraft back."

~

The first volley of shots sounded, and PJ's memories began to run together. For a moment she felt herself a little girl again, with Bebe at her side.

*The flag covering Grandpa David's casket. Fire!*

The bier and Silver's urn. Fire!

"Silver would be so proud," PJ whispered.

The bugle. Taps. Men and women, arms around each other. Old men squinting at the sky. Boys shuffling their feet. Women dabbing their eyes.

Anne with her chin high, keeping time with a finger.

Then the three Marines returned to the bier, and two of them lifted the flag.

In silence they folded it lengthwise, stripes over stars, doubled it to reveal the stars again, and rolled it end-over-end into a tight triangle of white-on-blue.

The third Marine, Staff Sergeant Watkins, bore it reverently to Anne.

"On behalf of the President of the United States," he said, "the Commandant of the Marine Corps, and a grateful nation, please accept this flag as a symbol of our appreciation for your loved one's service to Country and Corps."

Anne accepted the flag from him. She hugged it to her chest, and leaned close and put her forehead to PJ's and held it there.

▶▶▶◆◀◀◀

# About the Authors

## Ed Ditto

"When I was in grade school I used to hide under my mom's quilting frame and write short stories," says Ed Ditto. "I knew first-hand that quilters are interesting characters—there were stories being told around that frame that were too good for anyone to make up."

Though an MBA from the University of Tennessee took Ed into the corporate world, he kept hiding out and writing. At last count he'd written over a hundred newspaper and magazine articles, dozens of short stories, and three novels. In 2005 he fled the city and the office for the mountains of Appalachia, where he lives with his wife and daughter and spends his days whitewater kayaking, working in his woodshop, and savoring the peace. While he now writes in the upstairs room of his shop, he remembers his mom's quilting frame very fondly.

## Laura D. Patrick

Laura D. Patrick's mother was an avid seamstress, but as a child, Laura steered clear of the mechanized needle—choosing, instead, the quiet world of needlework. Throughout college she was a lineman fueling aircraft, worked as a Space Camp counselor, and was a researcher at NASA. Following her graduation with a degree in physics, she worked in the air and missile defense program. Laura didn't start quilting, however, until her late twenties, when she started taking handwork on business trips.

Life changed in 2001 when Laura resigned to care for her children full-time, and then gained recognition for spearheading a project known as "The Quilt That Raised the Roof" which raised money to repair tornado damage to her church. At two stories tall and 200 square feet, "The Quilt That Raised the Roof" is now a permanent fixture at Huntsville's Trinity United Methodist Church.

Laura has been married to the love of her life, Brian, since 1993; they have two children. Her co-conspirator and co-author is Ed Ditto. Visit with Laura at www.thegeekyquilter.com.